IT TAKES A TOWN

AOIFE CLIFFORD

ultimo press

Published in 2024 by Ultimo Press,
an imprint of Hardie Grant Publishing

Ultimo Press
Gadigal Country
7, 45 Jones Street
Ultimo, NSW 2007
ultimopress.com.au

   ultimopress

 A catalogue record for this
book is available from the
National Library of Australia

It Takes a Town
ISBN 978 1 76115 273 3 (paperback)

Cover design Design by Committee
Cover images Woman police officer by Anabela88 / Shutterstock; Silhouette of woman by
Zlata_Titmouse / Shutterstock; Stairs by Vitezslav Koneval / Dreamstime.com; Caravan by David
Makings / Dreamstime.com; Man with dog by Harperruki / VectorStock; Woman on back cover by
PanicAttack / Shutterstock
Text design Simon Paterson, Bookhouse
Typesetting Bookhouse, Sydney | 11.25/18.25 pt Simoncini Garamond
Copyeditor Ali Lavau
Proofreader Pamela Dunne

10 9 8 7 6 5 4 3 2 1

Printed in Australia by Opus Group Pty Ltd, an Accredited ISO AS/NZS 14001 Environmental
Management System printer.

 The paper this book is printed on is certified against the
Forest Stewardship Council® Standards.
Griffin Press – a member of the Opus Group – holds
chain of custody certification SCS-COC-001185. FSC®
promotes environmentally responsible, socially beneficial
and economically viable management of the world's forests.

Ultimo Press acknowledges the Traditional Owners of the Country on which we work,
the Gadigal People of the Eora Nation and the Wurundjeri People of the Kulin Nation,
and recognises their continuing connection to the land, waters and culture. We pay our
respects to their Elders past and present.

To my book club – Jackie, Elizabeth, Marg, Wayde, Elissa, Liz, Andrew, Camilla W, Yen, Lucy, Camilla W (not a typo), Chris, Anne – five very bright and shiny stars.

And in memory of Lorraine Smith – a treasured book customer and great reader.

To beguile the time,
Look like the time – bear
Welcome in your eye,
Your hand, your tongue. Look
Like the innocent flower,
But be the serpent under't.

William Shakespeare, *Macbeth*, Act 1, Scene 5

There was no time for Frankie Birnam to eat the dinner. She had been frantic backstage, helping the junior performers change out of costumes and making sure they were collected by parents. It had been her idea that students made up the first act, ensuring families bought tickets to the gala. It also guaranteed that the parents, and their wallets, stayed after the meal to bid enthusiastically on auction items as they waited to see the star of the show.

Frankie had found inventive ways to fit in more people when they were overwhelmed with bookings. The main ballroom was bursting, with overflow tables crammed onto the balcony. Dolly, the unofficial business manager for the Palais, observed tartly they should have charged more per head and insisted that leaflets advertising Walton's Academy's dance classes and the next jazz night be left on all seats, even though others worried it was tacky.

The Palais, a crumbling old two-storey Masonic lodge, had at different times been a dance hall, a function centre and was now *Walton's Academy of Dance – Home of Baby Vee*, as the painted sign out the front proclaimed. It was at its best tonight, with the pockmarked wooden floor covered by tables draped in white sheets. Frankie's husband, Joe, had balanced precariously on a ladder for most of that day hanging thousands of fairy lights overhead.

Frankie gazed at the room. The hairdressers of Welcome had been fully booked for the week. Outfits had appeared from the back of wardrobes, good shoes were checked for marks and worn-out heels. Weathered farmers were squeezed into musty suits that usually only appeared at weddings.

They shared tables with local councillors, doctors and used car salesmen. Nurses from the hospital clinked glasses with Constable Billy Wicks, who had been deputised to represent the police station. His wife was too busy getting in the ear of Ruhan Singh, who ran the pharmacy in the shopping centre, to notice her plate was being cleared. Frankie's table mostly comprised fellow teachers from St Brigid's. Even Assistant Principal Ivan Roland – 'Ivan the Terrible' – had been shamed into buying a ticket.

An assortment of middle-aged men had bussed in that morning from out of town. They had arrived at the Palais dressed in black tie and wearing wigs in the Baby Vee hairstyle (golden curls in bunches) and ordered bottles of sparkling wine. Frankie's best friend, Mer, who had served some of the men at the supermarket that afternoon, discovered they were part of the official fan club.

Many local businesses had been prepared to make a cash donation or provide something to be auctioned, though Janet Ross had made a fuss backstage because the local MP, who was a wealthy property developer, had not contributed a cent. Frankie pointed out that his mother had sponsored a banquet dinner for four at the Wok N Roll and that his stepdaughter was one of tonight's volunteer waiters, but Janet still worried over it. To distract her, Frankie suggested she make a cup of tea for the main attraction.

Frankie felt like she couldn't breathe with excitement – though perhaps it was her new shapewear, bought especially for the occasion, which had somehow rolled itself up to her navel. Beth hadn't let anyone watch the rehearsals, not even when Frankie begged. She hadn't seen Vanessa perform since the free tickets to Carols by Candlelight years earlier, given in part as payment for the assignments and essays that Frankie had ghostwritten for her during high school.

Tonight would be something special.

As the lights dimmed, Frankie took her seat between Joe and her dad, Des. Her untouched yellow curry had been claimed by her father, never one to waste food. Only he seemed nonplussed by the excitement. She had insisted he come along tonight, buying the extra ticket so he couldn't argue.

A spotlight wobbled across the velvet curtain as conversation hushed. There was a trill on the piano keys and the pianist, St Brigid's music teacher, then launched into the theme tune of *Shining Stars*, the TV variety show that Vanessa had joined when she was eight, staying on until her early teens. As the youngest member of the cast (and also because there was another performer with the same name), she had been dubbed 'Baby Vee'. Frankie, who had watched the show every Saturday night growing up, knew that Vanessa had spent years trying to escape that childhood persona, wanting to be considered a serious actress, but apparently she had been persuaded to embrace it, if only for one evening.

There was a smattering of uncertain applause in the ballroom, an atmosphere of nervous anticipation, and all of a sudden Vanessa Walton was there, arms raised as if greeting an old friend. She wore a gold sequinned dress, with artificial feathers at the hem and wrists that caught the light like a glass of champagne as she spun around on the spot. As the music changed to an advertising jingle, Vanessa moved across the stage doing the dance steps she had done as a seven-year-old for a commercial for Sugar Snap Biscuits: The Tasty Treat – the first time she had appeared on television. Frankie could remember begging her own mother to buy the biscuits just to have the thrill of seeing her friend on the packet.

The crowd roared in response.

Lifting her hand to her mouth, Vanessa flung crimson lipstick–covered kisses left and right.

Two of the taller superfans, faces flushed, wigs askew, jumped to their feet, pulling out phones to start recording. This forced the people behind them to stand up in order to see properly, which somehow swelled into a general ovation, and Vanessa stood there beaming, loving the adulation back on the stage where her career had begun all those years before.

She was not a classically beautiful woman, her mouth being excessively large, cheekbones high and haughty, nose sharp and eyes too knowing. She had a long torso with shorter legs that required the assistance of skyscraper heels to pull off the impression of an elongated dancer's body, but Vanessa Walton had the sort of charisma that had caught the nation's eye and managed to hold its faithless gaze for most of the following forty years.

A single hand outstretched brought the room to silence, and people resumed their seats as Vanessa began to sing. It was a crowd-pleasing cover she had sung on *Shining Stars*, which had proved so popular they had released it as a single. Frankie received it as a Christmas present, playing the song over and over until her Walkman chewed up the tape. Vanessa's voice was lower now, the high notes rearranged into something more manageable.

The song ended, but before the crowd could applaud she was on to the next one. That was the plan Vanessa had devised: sing four songs, transfix the audience, then have a break for the proper auction before a triumphant return to the stage to close the night and farewell the fans.

'Dazzle the dollars out of them,' Frankie had said with a smile.

The woman on stage bore little resemblance to the scarf-wearing drama teacher Frankie saw most days. The one who was constantly rubbing her hands with sanitiser and complaining about draughts, teenagers and the assistant principal. There was something bright and hard about her that wasn't just a result of the stage lights, the costume diamond jewellery around her neck or the extraordinary emerald glinting on her finger; rather, there was a luminescence that came from within. A mixture of relief and astonishment almost overwhelmed Frankie, bringing her to the brink of tired tears after an exhausting week of preparations.

The superfans down the front were sobbing openly. Even Frankie's husband, Joe, no fan of musical theatre, gazed in open-mouthed wonder.

At the end of the song thunderous applause echoed around the room.

'Welcome,' Vanessa purred into the microphone, 'to my favourite place in the world.'

The crowd laughed at the wordplay over the town's name, as if they'd never heard that before.

'Tonight we're here to raise money for a cause close to my heart.' She extended her hand and the spotlight moved towards the front table. Her cousin, Beth, rose and shyly bobbed her bald head before sitting again. It had been Vanessa's idea to transform St Brigid's annual gala into a cancer fundraiser.

Vanessa nodded towards the piano and this time it was a big band musical number that had been popular back when a night at the Palais would have been a very glamorous affair.

It started off low and quiet, with Vanessa moving towards the audience, laughing at the end of the first verse, holding the crowd in the palm of her hand, but gradually her voice became louder, gestures more dramatic, and she strutted across the stage during the chorus, demanding attention. It didn't matter that there wasn't a brass section or dancing back-up singers, elaborate props or complicated lighting. Vanessa alone was more than enough.

As her voice began to build and soar, moving towards the climactic high note of the song, Frankie could feel the entire audience draw breath, as if trying to give her enough oxygen to do it, and when she hit it triumphantly, the place erupted.

Vanessa Walton was no longer singing on a rickety stage in a middle-sized country town; she was a star, a giant supernova, and everyone in that room was spinning helplessly in her orbit.

CHAPTER 1

It was raining on the tarmac when they took off. Iron clouds were still sulking over the mountains and the helicopter lurched and bucked, buffeted by the wind, while the pilot pressed buttons and talked. It was equal parts smart attitude and chewing gum.

Sergeant Carole Duffy closed her eyes. She had no confidence in his assurances that the remnants of yesterday's weather event would settle down soon. Storm warnings were still being issued by text and there had been social media posts, mostly about thunderstorm asthma and rising flood levels.

'All right there, Duff?' came the voice of the pilot through her headset. 'Not feeling sick, are we?'

Carole thought about telling him to focus on flying this million-dollar tin can, but instead gave him a thumbs-up, which was exactly how she didn't feel. It had been a scramble this morning once she had word from higher up that she needed to leave for Welcome immediately to help out with the emergency response to possible flooding, packing an overnight bag and finding someone to look after the cat short-term. It was a transfer at level rather than a promotion, and Carole had planned a few days off to take a leisurely drive to her new position, but instead found herself on a police helicopter with a politician, his adviser and a pilot from the aviation unit acting like a cut-price Maverick from *Top Gun*.

Day one in her new job was already a natural disaster.

The politician sitting directly in front of her glanced over his shoulder, as if worried that the contents of her stomach were about to become acquainted with his fancy suit and shiny tan riding boots, which would have been a possibility if she hadn't dosed herself up on travel sickness tablets. Made your mouth feel chalky and dry but better than the alternative.

She smiled at him, remembering how she had put his party at the bottom of the ballot in the last election because their talent pool was little more than a puddle.

Barton Langridge, the local member for Welcome, had the sort of face you instantly wanted to punch, even if you knew nothing about him and his statements about 'crazy lefties', 'Marxist teachers' and 'taking Australian jobs'.

Technically, he was almost handsome, but somehow there was an uncanny valley effect, the way his mouth was trying to smile as if he'd read the instruction manual on how to do it but hadn't got up to the part that explained the eyes were supposed to be involved. Of course, she would charge anyone who aimed a right hook at him, but something in his demeanour suggested there would be television footage in the future with his face and the word 'embattled' on the chyron underneath.

He had repeated her name several times when they were introduced in a way intended to make her feel important, while shaking her hand with both of his in a way that made Carole want to count her fingers afterwards.

No doubt he planned to spend his day seeking out photo ops with people who would have to stop doing useful things in order to tell him what needed to be done and how the government could help, which he would then ignore. Then he'd be photographed looking grim and serious, staring at the flood as though he were Moses about to part the Red Sea. He'd already bragged to the pilot that he'd been instrumental in approving the new fleet of Bell 429s, as if the money had come directly out of his pocket. Thank goodness for the tablets; it was enough to make you throw up.

What Langridge hadn't noticed was that the female adviser next to him, Yvette Something-or-other, was the sort of pale green that Carole had previously only seen on institutional walls or the faces of novice cops attending their first serious road accident. She pulled a couple of barley sugars out of her pocket, leant forward and tapped the woman on the shoulder, gesturing for her to take one. Carole could see beads of perspiration on the woman's brow as she ducked her head in thanks.

Far below them was the tangled ribbon of a river, brown and swollen, cutting its way through the green patchwork of fields. Bullets of rain hammered the window next to her. There was always more money in mud than dust but lately the spring rain had been coming down too hard, too quickly. Crooked rain as much good to you as a crooked nail. Carole decided to play Wordle as a distraction.

She used SLATE as her opening word, as in clean slate, which was what she hoped the town of Welcome might be. Watching the squares turn, she saw a couple become yellow, so not too bad. T and an E but in the wrong spots. Staring at the back of the politician's head, all she could think of was IMBECILE which was too long and had no T, so then tried CRONY, which gave her an N.

The turbulence increased so she clicked off the screen, word unsolved. She stared out of the window, waiting for Welcome to make an appearance. The town would be a change, possibly a permanent one. It had been an awful year. Her relationship hadn't ended acrimoniously, but it had ended all the same. With his daughter, Lexie, they had been a family. Then they became two acquaintances sitting on a couch. He had barely reacted when she told him about the transfer.

So now Carole was an ex-stepmother, which wasn't really a relationship that got you a nice greeting card.

'And here she is,' the pilot whooped in Carole's ear.

Welcome stretched out below them. It was midday and grey enough for streetlights to still be on, but as they flew over the town entire blocks were dark. At least the business area looked unaffected. It meant supermarkets would be open and people could still go to work, get food, while they cleaned up.

The chocolate-milk river had spilt into parkland, some streets and a few houses. Boats were moving about in it. As long as they didn't get more rain, it wasn't going to be that bad.

The pilot started to talk technical to air control, and within minutes they were on the ground. Carole retrieved her suitcase from the back of the helicopter once the blades stopped spinning. The relieved adviser, Yvette, was already there, pulling a battered Akubra and long brown oilskin coat from a bag and handing them to her boss.

Curious, Carole watched as the politician, hat firmly on head and coat flapping in the breeze, marched across the tarmac. Was it a stockbroker or a stockman? It was genuinely hard to tell.

'You got a clown suit as well?' she asked the assistant, who looked much cheerier outside the helicopter.

'I can do high-vis with a bonus hard hat,' Yvette replied with a laugh. 'Cosplay for the socials so people forget that he's actually a property developer.'

Property developer was Carole's least favourite type of criminal. She should have thrown up on his boots.

Flipping the camera in her phone to become a mirror, she inspected her hair, which was pulled back into a serviceable old-school bun at the nape of her neck, then pushed an extra bobby pin in for good luck. A quick smile to check there was nothing stuck in her teeth.

'Leaves me to carry all the baggage.' Yvette pointed to the bags, including a square leather briefcase with the initials B.M.L. stamped on it in gold lettering. 'You know he was here in town only yesterday,' she grumbled. 'Drove down to the city last night so he could make a grand entrance by helicopter this morning.'

Apocalypse Now had a lot to answer for in Carole's opinion.

The politician stopped in front of a group of people wielding cameras and microphones. Local media, Carole deduced, which hardly made her Sherlock Holmes.

There was no sign of the police officer who was supposed to be meeting her. Not a good start. Some might call it inept. INEPT! She quickly clicked on the screen of her phone and typed it in. All five squares turned. Bingo. The day was looking up.

As she walked past the media huddle, Langridge turned and gestured impatiently for her to join him, clearly wanting her uniform as a backdrop. She knew how this game was played, making sure to position herself behind him, keeping her face set to poker as he blathered on about the devastating scenes he had witnessed from the helicopter and how the government was standing shoulder to shoulder with those affected.

A young journalist, early twenties, in a raincoat, gumboots and a no-nonsense attitude, cut him off before he could really switch on the Winston Churchill oratory, and asked Carole for a comment.

It was more of a plea. Please don't drive through floodwaters. Keep kids away from the river. It was the advice police always delivered in such circumstances, but idiots would ignore it.

Langridge seemed annoyed to have the spotlight removed from him for a second and butted in with platitudes about his electoral office being open and staff on hand to render assistance.

Noticing that a police car had pulled into the car park, Carole excused herself, picked up her suitcase and walked over to meet it.

'Sorry I'm late,' said the driver, who introduced himself as Constable Billy Wicks, sticking a hand out for her to shake while he launched into a full report about the levies holding for now, streets that were flooded (a couple), how many trees were down (quite a few), and where the electricity was out (over a quarter of the town). But it looked as if the main bridge would remain above water, which was a good thing because the low-lying bridge had been closed as a precaution.

Carole made a mental assessment of him as he talked. Six foot two, balding, pudgy around the middle, pasty if you were being unkind, which she tried hard not to be because he had probably worked through the night with only a thermos of coffee and a lunchbox for sustenance. A bit old for a constable, suggesting a lack of ambition.

There was a faint sheen of sweat on his face, a look of clamminess. Either he was coming down with something or he had just seen a dead body. Please let it be the latter, she begged silently, because she really didn't want gastro going around the station in her first week.

'Is everything all right, officer?' she ventured, when he paused for breath. 'No fatalities?'

It could be a farmer worried about stock trying to cross the river, young hoons deciding to surf the storm water, a missing toddler, or someone bored to death by Barton Langridge's answers at a press conference – she wasn't fussy, because there was no way she was getting in a car with someone who looked that sick. Had the last two years taught people nothing? Keep your bloody germs to yourself. She had a mask in her handbag and some Glen 20 as well, and she wasn't afraid to use either. Alternatively, she could commandeer this vehicle and let him walk back to the town. He'd know the way at least.

'Not from the flood,' he said, and if anything turned even paler.

'There *is* a body!' Carole said, relieved.

Confused, Billy looked over his shoulder, as if to confirm that the smile really was meant for him.

'Suspicious then?' she asked brightly. It would make her first day a long one.

He shook his head. 'They don't think so.'

Carole was starting to get impatient. There was a police station to visit and she wouldn't say no to a warm cup of tea. What ever happened to country hospitality?

'But she was sort of famous,' he added.

She didn't want to imagine what on earth counted as famous in a place like this. First-prize ribbon for a sponge cake at the Welcome Show?

'And the Langridges own the house she was found in.'

Carole looked back towards the group she had just left. The journalists had disappeared and Barton Langridge was now walking back to the small terminal. His adviser, carrying all the bags, staggered behind him.

'That Langridge?' she asked.

'Technically his mother, Lonnie,' said Billy.

Now that was interesting.

'Get in the car,' said Carole, 'and you can tell me all about it.'

———

The body lay at the bottom of the stairs in a geometric-patterned dressing-gown, kimono-shaped. A red silk nightie, slippery as water, had bunched up under her middle, exposing her legs. She could have been sunbathing, lying on her back, arms outstretched. One leg bent, her heel was up near her thigh, as though she were a ballet dancer. There was a wound on the side of her head, which had already congealed and dried in her cropped hair. She had been there long enough that muscles had frozen, starting with those on her famous face.

Vanessa Walton was not just the most famous person in Welcome. If it was a slow enough news day, there was a chance she might be the most famous corpse in the nation. Carole had even seen her on stage, years ago, before she headed off to the US, as a sexy, scheming young Lady Macbeth.

There was a collapsed vein in her left arm, the skin creased like a crumpled paper bag. Vanessa must have been a junkie at some point, a fact she had managed to conceal from the tabloids. Good on her, Carole thought.

She stood at the top of the stairs where the techies had set up lights. Taking photos, they laughed about Billy who had almost fainted after finding the body. He had to sit out in the garden for a spell, and no one was letting him forget it. Billy briefly introduced those present, then retreated outside to the front of the house. Carole hadn't taken in any of the names. Someone had told her once that the average person could only retain seven pieces of information at a time, so she wasn't going to waste one of them on this lot, all kitted up in identical white protective gear, and certainly not when she already had to remember Barton Langridge, Billy Wicks and now Vanessa Walton.

'What do you know her from?' she asked the man, possibly Steve, but it also could be Mike – or that might be the man who was crouched down taking measurements.

'Baby Vee, of course!' he replied. 'My sister was obsessed with *Shining Stars*. Her and my mum were at that shopping centre appearance where kids got injured in a crush because too many people turned up. She watched that bloody show every Saturday night and I always had to miss the start of the footy.'

'I saw her at the gala a few months back,' interrupted a woman at the bottom of the stairs. 'She was amazing.'

'Didn't she go to LA to become a star?' asked another technician. 'Pretty tragic really.'

'Anything suspicious?' Carole asked.

'No sign of forced entry,' said Steve/Mike. 'Half a bottle of champers on the table, packet of sleeping tablets in the bathroom. Best guess at this stage, she woke up groggy, forgot there was a bucket on the stairs to catch a leak from the rain, tripped over it, fell, hit her head. Coroner will let us know for sure, but I don't think Homicide will be bothered about this one.'

Carole turned away from the stairs and took a look around the living room. It was nice. Stylish rather than quaint. There were shiny German appliances in the kitchen and the place was clean and tidy, except for a few scraps of paper on the floor under the table.

The house was on the small side but Billy had explained that it was originally the servants' cottage for Langridge House next door, one of the grandest estates in town. Hidden behind trees with a tall hedge out the front, high fences along the sides, Carole would have to take his word for it. Apparently, Lonnie Langridge, who had rented this house to Vanessa Walton on some grace-and-favour arrangement, lived there alone, if you didn't count the housekeeper who came every second day and left meals in the fridge to be reheated. Nice for some.

Carole returned her attention to the stairs.

There was a black plastic bucket lying on its side a few steps from the top, a puddle of water next to it. Carole reached over and flicked the light switch to get a better look. Nothing happened. She frowned at this. A feeling, shiver-like, went up her spine, but the thought, whatever it was, disappeared before she could catch the shape of it.

'Electricity's out for half the block due to that gum tree out the front,' said Steve/Mike. 'SES can't do anything about it until we've finished here.'

'How much longer will you be?' asked Carole.

'Not long. Got jobs banking up already.'

Carole had seen enough. This wasn't her problem.

—

She found Billy next to the fallen branch at the front of the house. It was the size of a tree, complete with smaller branches and a full canopy of leaves. The electricity cable was wrapped around it like Christmas tinsel. It was from a giant snow gum in Lonnie Langridge's garden and had fallen on the fence between the two properties. Some palings had snapped like matchsticks and the rest had a dangerous lean to them. There was police tape all around it to keep bystanders away.

Carole stared at the ragged raw hole on the weathered grey bark of the gum's trunk. It felt wrong, like seeing a bone sticking up through flesh. 'It must have been quite a storm.'

'Oh, yes!' A short barrel-shaped woman suddenly appeared on the other side of the branch. She was wearing a large overcoat with a checked collar and an extraordinary broad-brimmed purple hat that sat pancake-like on her head, as if a giant had come along and pressed down on both the hat and owner at the same time. 'The wind howled all night like a toddler having a tantrum.'

'This is Janet Ross,' said Billy. 'She lives across the way.'

Two enormous pale blue eyes turned to stare at Carole. A beak-like nose sat in an otherwise round chipmunk face. Feathery strands of blondish hair fuzzed at the ends. Carole felt as though she were being assessed by a curious owl.

'You're Billy's new boss.' The woman's face changed when she talked, became more pointed. It was the teeth. They were sharp and rodent-like and gave the impression of someone constantly nibbling.

'Mrs Ross was there when I found . . .' Billy pointed back towards the house, beginning to get choked up.

'It was quite a shock,' said Janet, but the glint in her expression seemed to counter this. 'You know, Ruhan saw her out on the street last night around 10 pm, just walking along under an umbrella in the rain.'

'Welcome's answer to Meryl Streep,' said Billy mournfully.

'I don't think Meryl Streep makes ends meet with a part-time job teaching drama at the local girls' school,' answered Janet. 'Billy, have you let Miss Helen know?'

Billy nodded. 'Angie's there now. She's much better at that sort of thing.'

'Nice to have met you, Janet,' said Carole, not meaning a word of it. 'Constable, we need to head to the station.'

'You'll be wanting to be introduced to the rest of your team,' said Janet, nodding. 'And the superintendent, of course. Not the most welcoming of people, I think you'll find. Don't take it personally. He's a bit like a guard dog who growls at everyone walking past. Just his nature.'

'I'll keep that in mind.' Carole began to move towards the car. 'Time to go.'

Janet didn't get the hint, following along behind them as if she were planning to hop in the car as well. 'Forensics think it was an accident then?' There was a tinge of disapproval – or was it disappointment?

'That's up to the coroner to decide, but it's not looking suspicious,' said Carole firmly. Might as well nip any gossip in the bud.

Janet raised her eyebrows. They were thin, almost non-existent, and yet somehow managed to convey disagreement.

That's all Carole needed: a neighbour who'd watched one too many crime series on the telly on a Saturday night. She braced herself for some cockamamie conspiracy theory, but all Janet said was, 'I'm sure we'll catch up soon, sergeant. Welcome to our town.'

CHAPTER 2

Frankie Birnam woke up abruptly on the morning of Vanessa Walton's funeral because the side gate slipped free of its bolt and began banging. Wrapping her dressing-gown around her, she padded out to the kitchen and switched on the light.

Sixteen-year-old Danny, her eldest son, was sitting on the couch in faded flannelette pyjamas. Two small Cavalier King Charles Spaniels, Fred and Ginger, coats white with patches of fox-like red, huddled beside him, eyes dark and mournful. It was 6 am.

All of them were usually unconscious at this time.

'Couldn't sleep?' Frankie asked.

There was a half-shrug, something muttered about checking on the dogs.

In the last few weeks, their relationship had regressed to direct questions and occasional mumbled answers. Joe's current mantra was this too would pass, but so early in the morning the comfort of that was threadbare.

'The gate woke me,' she told the kettle as she switched it on.

Outside the window the sun was struggling to break through the clouds.

Another bang from the gate. The neighbours must be cursing them. 'I'd better close that.'

Danny stood up, causing the dogs to whimper softly in protest. 'I'll do it.'

Opening the back door, Danny slipped outside barefoot. The wind bustled in, impatient and pushing, grabbing at Frankie's dark curls, flinging them in her eyes. She heard the screech of metal as the old bolt was pushed into place and then Danny returned and disappeared into the lair of his bedroom.

Later that morning, Joe handed over Frankie's black high heels, now freshly polished. 'Have to look your best for all those celebrities.'

The town had been buzzing with rumours about famous actors and public figures turning up for Vanessa's funeral.

When Danny grabbed his pair of newly polished school shoes, he gave his dad a hug and then turned and did the same to his mother, so hard he almost squeezed the breath out of her.

'What was that about?' Frankie asked Joe in surprise after Danny had vanished again.

'Let's enjoy it while it lasts,' her husband answered. 'We'll see you at the cathedral.'

'Come on, Ollie – car now,' Frankie called, checking her phone. She leant in to give her husband a kiss, lingered on his lips. Joe had rearranged urgent work to accompany her to Vanessa's funeral for moral support. Danny had asked to come along as well. Anything to get out of school, she suspected.

She drove carefully down the street. The clean-up from last week's storm was continuing, with the occasional vibrating roar of chainsaws still echoing around the town.

Ollie was ten and in his own world most of the time but was happy there. He got out at the top of the hill, a block from his school, to check on the tawnies. There were two babies, tufts of wool, feathered horns and large button eyes, sheltering with the parents. He had become quite obsessed with them, worried about them surviving the recent storm. Ollie remembered his violin but forgot to say goodbye.

'Thanks for the lift, Mum,' Frankie said to the rear-view mirror as she indicated and then swung the car back in the opposite direction. She waited for the traffic to clear before taking a right turn and heading out past the railway tracks. Trees were down near the soccer oval and the river was still churning, the colour of milky tea.

She rang her father to see if he was coming into town for the funeral but also to reassure herself that he wasn't halfway up a tree, pulling out broken branches single-handed. Frankie had caught him on the roof cleaning gutters before the storm. At the time she had joked about putting him in a nursing home if she caught him doing that again, which might be why he claimed to be having a quiet cuppa in his kitchen, methodically working his way through yesterday's paper, though she was certain he was outside.

Des wheezed into the phone and then coughed hard enough that it sounded like his ribs were rattling. Frankie hoped that the coming summer would wind the clock back to the more robust version of him. He was getting too old to be running the farm by himself, but when she tried to talk to him about it, he said he'd sooner get the shotgun and take a long walk to the furthest field. She hadn't mentioned it again, instead organising for Nate Rivett, the neighbour's son, to come and help him a couple of days a week, but now Nate was in jail and Des was out there all alone.

Her father had decided not to come into town for the funeral, he told her, which surprised Frankie. Usually Des put a lot of store by doing the right thing and showing proper respect to friends and neighbours, but apparently there were too many jobs to do around the property that couldn't wait. The last time they had both been at the cathedral for a funeral it had been Frankie's mother's, almost two years before. Part of her couldn't blame her dad for being unable to face it. She was dreading it herself.

'I'll try to come out to see you on the weekend,' she said.

'Only if you're not busy.'

'Love you,' said Frankie, and then she ended the call before Des was forced to reply. This was a new thing for them, a sentiment that she had rarely expressed to her mother and now regretted the omission deeply. It was never too late to change, but that didn't mean it wasn't a bit awkward.

She drove the rest of the way to school.

—

Martha Reynolds stood beside the coffee machine in the staffroom, mug in hand. It was Martha's favourite position, all the better to trap the unwary in conversation. She was the kind of person who talked incessantly about her air fryer. They regularly had retirement morning teas for her but then she would turn up again, backfilling another teacher's position. The Nellie Melba of teachers.

'At least it was quick and she didn't suffer,' Martha said as Frankie moved towards the hot-water urn.

'Vanessa was forty-eight,' Frankie said, horrified. 'She died in pain and alone.' The words snipped through the general conversational hum of the staffroom and everyone stopped talking and stared. Martha blinked at Frankie's outburst, her mouth slack.

Frankie's and Vanessa's birthdays were a week apart, and they were both former students of St B's. Frankie had insisted on a joint birthday celebration to welcome Vanessa as a staff member. Patrick, the music teacher, had brought in a marked-down sponge cake from the supermarket. Everyone had gathered around to sing 'Happy Birthday', which Vanessa had pronounced lovely before cutting herself a slice of cake thin enough to see through. When Martha asked nosily if this was a 'special' birthday (Wikipedia being silent as to her actual birthdate), Vanessa shaved time off, so it turned out that Frankie was the older of the two of them by three years. Vanessa had given her a quick wink when she saw Frankie's look of surprise.

Martha opened her mouth to protest but was interrupted by Assistant Principal Ivan Roland, his clipboard of checklists and chores tucked under his armpit. He cleared his throat, a sign he was about to launch into a lecture about the length of uniform dresses, student mobile phone usage or vaping in the toilets. Two weeks before she died, Vanessa had publicly accused him of going through her office after hours. There had been an ongoing dispute between them over invoices to do with the gala.

Everyone suspected that Ivan did go through his colleagues' waste-paper bins at the end of the day and read discarded documents in the recycling room, but no one had been game to challenge him before.

His denials were not convincing.

Here was someone who enjoyed petty bureaucracy and hated children. Frankie had no idea why he had ever become a teacher and right now she could barely stand to look at him.

'Not this morning, Ivan.' The words were out of her mouth before she could stop them.

Ivan's face became dangerously smooth, but before he could retaliate, Martha interrupted to say crossly that she hadn't meant to upset anyone. Martha never meant to do anything.

Deciding escape was her best option, Frankie said she would round up students to get on the bus to the cathedral. Ivan, who couldn't resist an opportunity to hear the sound of his own voice, reminded everyone that students must be wearing their blazers. He always emphasised the word 'students' as though he really wanted to say 'rodents' or 'cockroaches'. It made Frankie's skin crawl almost as much as when he said to the girls, 'Ladies, and I use the term loosely,' and smile thinly as if it were amusing.

'Students not in full uniform will not leave the school,' Roland reiterated, when no one reacted to his first interjection.

Patrick made a face behind his back, which normally Frankie would have laughed at, but she didn't have it in her today. Instead, she headed for the staff toilets.

It had been a horrible week since Vanessa's body had been found. Eighteen months ago, they had run into each other at the super-market, the first time they had caught up in years. Frankie almost hadn't recognised Vanessa, her hair completely different, dyed jet black and shaped in an angular jaw-length bob with a heavy fringe that sat above her shapely eyebrows, like a 1920s flapper. COVID had cancelled all theatre for the present. 'So I've come back here.' Vanessa hadn't said the words 'to this dump' but Frankie heard them all the same. 'And Beth needs me now.'

Beth Fettling had put up a big picture of Vanessa outside Walton's Academy of Dance. The business had been doing well, even with competition from the Fun & Fitness Centre on the highway and Dance Daze, based at the Anglican Hall, but then it was hit with a double whammy of COVID and Beth being diagnosed with cancer.

Frankie had suggested Vanessa give a talk to some of the drama students at St B's and Vanessa agreed. Next thing Frankie knew, Vanessa had walked into Principal Juliette Pittman's office to introduce herself and came out with a newly invented part-time role to run the school's hitherto non-existent drama department.

Frankie had thought it was a wonderful idea, something exciting for the students but also for herself. Being a friend to the glamorous Vanessa Walton was just the pick-me-up anyone would want.

She fiddled with her hair at the mirror over the sink, trying to keep her curls under control with two combs pulling them off her face. Hunting through her bag, she found her lipstick.

The last time she had seen Vanessa was after final bell on the afternoon of the day she died. Frankie could picture her standing in the doorway of her office. She had been wearing a white silk shirt with oversized black dots, flared trousers and a pair of ballet flats, the type of outfit that looked chic on Vanessa but would be ridiculous on Frankie. Vanessa said that she needed to discuss a delicate matter. There was a piece of paper in her hand which Frankie suspected might be yet another invoice for the gala that Ivan had been refusing to pay for months. She was reluctant to be drawn any further into the internecine war between the two of them. On top of that, she was in the middle of marking year twelve English essays, had to take Ollie to footy training (which hadn't been cancelled, despite an enormous storm heading their way), ring her father to check he was all right and decide what she was cooking for dinner. She asked if it could wait until tomorrow.

If only she could go back in time and listen. What if that was a moment that could have changed everything? She should have invited Vanessa to their place, persuaded her to stay the night with the Birnams rather than sitting out the storm alone at home. But it was too late, and now she would be doing a reading at Vanessa's funeral.

Looking in the mirror, she noticed the puckers around the corners of her mouth that seemed to have appeared overnight and the deep bags under her eyes. Sighing, she blotted her lipstick with a square of paper towel then threw it in the bin.

—

One bus was already leaving, manoeuvring around the circular drive – rosebushes on either side – before turning out onto the main road, but the minibus was still there, emblazoned with the St Brigid's Ladies College crest. Ivan stood beside it, clipboard under his arm. There had been an overzealous minor bureaucrat who was never seen without a clipboard in one of the skits in the gala. Everyone knew exactly who that was supposed to be.

Two year tens – Jasmine Langridge and Brianna Sharrah – stood behind him, also waiting to get on the bus. Something furtive about their body language caught Frankie's eye. Not exactly trouble, but certainly trouble adjacent. It was rumoured that Jasmine had been involved in the direct-action stunt protesting climate change at the school last year that had ended up with Nate Rivett in jail.

The girls knew her Danny and had in fact come around to Frankie's house one time looking for him. Danny claimed afterwards that he had barely talked to them before. Frankie wasn't sure about that. Both girls were part of the popular group in their year level. Jaz – not surprisingly, given her stepfather's status in the town – was one of the queen bees. Funny how every year had them, as synonymous with unhappiness as beauty, in Frankie's opinion. She wouldn't be a teenage girl again, not for all the money in the world. When she was their age it felt like she was missing a layer of skin; everything pierced so deeply. It was a time when the wrong kind of attention could end up being much more dangerous than no attention at all.

Jaz was talking quietly, her hands moving animatedly. Brianna lifted her head, her dark eyebrows heavy accents over brown eyes. She noticed Frankie looking at them and reached out to tug at Jaz's sleeve, muttering something under her breath. Jaz's head swung around to match Brianna's and the two girls stared at her, an unflinching blankness to their gaze.

Frankie had expected more tears and sadness from the pair of them; Jaz, in particular, had been close to Vanessa. But perhaps she could detect a kind of undercurrent of upset, grief mixed with fury.

'Already full,' Ivan said, holding out a hand to stop Frankie from getting on board. 'Junior Choir has gained some new members. Patrick needs them at church early for a practice.'

Frankie could see Patrick sitting in the driver's seat, lost in thought, oblivious to the hive of activity surrounding him.

'I'm sure we can squeeze on,' replied Frankie. 'There's only the three of us.

'Occupational health and safety, I'm afraid,' Ivan said officiously. 'Lovely day for a walk. Shouldn't take longer than twenty minutes.'

What about the OH&S implications of walking for twenty minutes in high heels? This was payback, pure and simple. Revenge for mutterings in the staffroom earlier and probably for Vanessa being hired in the first place. He was a bastard.

Still, she was surprised that Ivan was blocking Jasmine from getting on the bus too. Normally Ivan was obsequious towards anyone with the last name Langridge – he had headed up the fundraising efforts for some of Barton's political campaigns – but it seemed the forelock tugging did not apply to stepdaughters.

Jasmine didn't seem that concerned. 'Are you not coming to the funeral, Mr Roland?' she asked, managing to make the innocuous question sound insolent.

'Only if I can ensure the smooth running of the school day. My priority is, as always, our students' education.' He said this in a martyred tone, as if the rest of them were abandoning their posts to party.

'Didn't you like Vanessa?' Jaz asked.

Frankie's eyes opened wide at the bluntness of the question. Brianna shifted her weight from one leg to the other, but she kept her gaze laser-focused on the man, as if curious to hear how he answered.

Ivan spluttered, his face turning red, and decided to ignore the question. 'I trust that you'll be able to attend the funeral, Miss Langridge, without chaining yourself to the altar or throwing paint on the statue of the Virgin Mary.'

There was silence for what seemed like an age as Jaz stared at him. Eventually she said, 'The Bible claims Jesus fought injustice – in a church, what's more. Jesus definitely would be protesting climate change if he was here.'

'Then I'm sure Jesus would walk to the church rather than use fossil fuels,' Ivan said, a smug expression on his face, as though certain he had regained the upper hand.

Frankie decided this interaction had gone on long enough. She had also noticed that Jaz's hair had pink tips, which was contrary to school regulations, and her skirt was at least two inches above the knee, while Brianna was wearing the incorrect socks.

'It *is* a lovely day,' she said quickly. 'I think we can walk.'

'Sure,' said Jaz.

'Okay,' Brianna agreed.

Ivan looked suspicious.

Black smoke exploded from the exhaust of the minibus as Patrick crunched through the gears, driving past them. There was frantic waving from year sevens kneeling up on the back seat, which Frankie acknowledged and Brianna and Jaz studiously ignored.

Vanessa would have just waltzed onto that bus, regardless of what Roly said. Frankie had spent most of her life wishing she was more like Vanessa and today they were burying her. That thought was suddenly so shattering Frankie almost began to cry but Brianna and Jaz had already started walking so there was nothing else to do but keep on going.

CHAPTER 3

The supermarket always did pork roasts on Fridays. So when Mer Davis had asked to have Friday off to go to Vanessa Walton's funeral, her boss, Sue, was not impressed.

'Did you even know her?' Sue demanded.

Mer was short for Meredith but also Mermaid because a long time ago Mer had been a champion swimmer. It was one of the reasons she couldn't leave Welcome, because then she'd be surrounded by people who didn't know that about her.

'We were at school together.' Mer waited for the tirade because Sue had a tongue sharp enough to carve the ham.

They were sitting in the back office next to the loading bay, Sue's favourite spot to fire people. To be fair, plenty of people also quit the supermarket but not Mer. Seeing which Sue you got when you walked into the deli each morning kept life interesting. The one who called you 'pet' and let you take home day-old cakes for your kids or the one who tore strips off you because the salads hadn't been rotated. Sue could be so inventive with her criticisms there were times when Mer wanted to applaud. Besides, when Sue went completely off her rocker, her husband, Gino, currently sitting at his own desk in the office and pretending not to listen because the deli was Sue's domain, slipped everyone a few extra dollars to keep them sweet. Sometimes, when Mer was short on rent, she would set Sue off on purpose.

Gino looked up from his desk. 'Tell Sue about the time you snuck out of school together and got detention.'

It had been the only time Mer had anything to do with Vanessa at school. There had been a missing relief teacher, and instead of going to the library Vanessa, Mer and Frankie had stolen out of the school grounds and mucked around down at the river. Vanessa had danced one of the Baby Vee routines for them on the bridge and told them she had left the program the moment she got a manager so she didn't get typecast. 'Most of the people I work with will never get on TV again once they leave,' she told them. 'That's not going to happen to me.'

They had been caught on their return and given detention. Only Frankie and Mer sat in an empty classroom on a Saturday morning, though, because Vanessa had to be driven to the city for an important audition and ended up leaving the school the next term when she got a recurring role as a troubled teen in a soap opera. The injustice had infuriated Mer at the time and still stung now. She had told Gino the story when Vanessa turned up in town almost two years ago and everyone was going nuts over her.

She repeated the story for Sue now, trying to look a little upset.

'I'm very sorry for your loss, Mer,' Gino replied, attempting to steer his wife in the right direction.

Sue gave her husband a look that would shrivel concrete. Gino got the message and went back to his invoices.

'That leaves Chip to do the cooking,' Sue said sourly.

Chip's real name was Pete, but everyone called him Chip because he walked around with a massive one on his shoulder due to the fact that his former business, a roast chicken shop between the real estate agent and the butcher, had burnt down. Apparently, grease caught fire in the flue, travelled into the roof space and then back into the store and took out all three businesses. Chip claimed that it was arson. Normally, Mer wouldn't believe a word Chip said, but the truth was Barton Langridge owned that row of shops and not only got a large insurance payout but then the council let him replace the row with a five-storey monstrosity. Sue was more sceptical and kept her beady eye on Chip to ensure that every surface was kept spotless, especially the flue.

'Chip will cope fine,' Mer said.

Sue gave her a look of pure disgust. 'Why do I employ you then?'

Gino cleared his throat.

'Don't make a habit of it,' Sue said.

'Going to funerals?' Mer asked. 'Or schoolfriends dying?' The 'friends' was pushing it.

Sue opened her mouth. It was going to be really mean, Mer could tell, so she got in first. 'Appreciate it. I'll see you Monday then.'

She practically ran out the door before Sue could change her mind and almost walked in front of Lennox Rivett on his forklift.

'Look out,' he yelled. 'I've got enough to deal with already.' A truck had come in late and he was still unloading.

According to the rumours, Lennox was involved in dealing of an entirely different kind as well. Busy supermarkets were a convenient pickup point for more than groceries.

'Love you too,' Mer yelled back, because right now she loved the world. Vanessa Walton was dead and she had scored herself a three-day weekend.

Now, on the morning of the funeral, Mer sat at the kitchen table in an oversized t-shirt and undies, drinking a cup of coffee as she scrolled through her phone. Ky, her youngest child, stumbled past on his way to the fridge. A yawning, still growing, tousled boy-man, he had finished school last year and now worked at a call centre, listening to people complain about their internet connection all day.

'What are you still doing here?' he asked. 'Are you sick?'

'I'm going to Vanessa Walton's funeral.'

Ky pulled the orange juice out of the fridge, no doubt planning to drink straight from the bottle even though he'd been told not to a million times. 'I thought you hated her?'

Mer shrugged her shoulders. 'Do I? Can't remember.'

'You said it.' Ky never forgot a complaint. 'It was because she got out of some detention and then when she came back to town she blanked you in the deli and you said that the next time she came in for the Greek salad you were going to spit in it.'

Mer, prepared to set old grievances aside, had been about to say, 'Well, hello, stranger,' across the counter when Vanessa had started ordering her around like she was a nobody, insisting that her prosciutto be sliced thin and that she needed exactly two hundred grams of the Danish feta. And then at the gala, when Mer had been backstage helping Frankie with costumes, Vanessa had called her

Marilyn the whole night. Mer was certain that she did it on purpose because, in her opinion, Vanessa wasn't that good an actor.

'Don't speak ill of the dead,' Mer said to her son.

Ky took a swig of juice and then said, 'I didn't. You did.'

'She wasn't dead then.'

Ky frowned. 'Why shouldn't you speak ill of the dead? I mean, they don't care. You're only going to this funeral to see the celebrities. Admit it.' He dumped the juice container on the counter next to the fridge, where it would no doubt stay until Mer cracked and put it away. So close and yet so far.

Mer had spent most of the morning scrolling to see what people had been saying about Vanessa. There had been an article on the front page of the local paper: TOWN MOURNS FAVOURITE DAUGHTER. Like hell it did. A small obituary in *The Guardian* – not even in the main section but under 'Others': 'Former Australian actress who started her TV career as a child tap-dancing across a biscuit.' Vanessa would have been so furious at the word 'former' that it was almost a shame she wasn't alive to see it. But Mer's absolute favourite had been the Facebook page – the VeeBees, short for Vanessa's Babies. Some sucker had catalogued every single show Vanessa had ever been in, including as the director/performer of Welcome's gala three months ago, like it was a Broadway production.

The tributes on the page had been hilarious. There was a fuzzy still from the TV commercial Vanessa had done when she was seven, with the words underneath describing it as the moment when she'd 'danced out of the television and into a nation's heart'. Mer thought about creating a fake account and posting a comment saying that maybe everyone should put out their packs of Sugar Snap Biscuits as a sign of respect, but idiots would probably do it. Besides, digital was not her cup of tea.

'There aren't going to be any celebrities there,' she told her son.

'Vanessa was proper famous,' he insisted. 'When one of the customers on the phone yesterday found out I lived in Welcome, she almost started crying.'

She wasn't the only one. Some goose had done a TikTok of themselves bawling while doing a dance in their living room to the most popular Baby Vee single. It had almost half a million views. Nostalgia turned people into marshmallows, which meant that the narcissistic, talentless, two-faced and now dead Vanessa Walton was in the process of becoming perhaps more famous than the alive Vanessa Walton had been in years.

Karma was the biggest bitch of all.

'Why are you going then?' asked Ky.

'I'm going to support your godmother and my best friend, who is doing a reading,' Mer said, putting on a saintly expression. 'It's my good deed for the day.'

Her friendship with Frankie was the best thing to have come of that detention and puzzled the school, the town and especially Frankie's mother, Alice. There was nothing that Mer wouldn't do for Frankie Birnam.

Ky rolled his eyes and left the kitchen.

—

Mer, arms folded against the wind, stood on the steps of the cathedral next to Patrick Selwyn. Head and shoulders taller than those around her (mostly St B's students), she couldn't see Frankie anywhere – or any celebrities, for that matter.

The last time she had been here for a funeral was for Frankie's mother. Frankie had insisted that Mer, Joe and the boys keep their masks on and sit across the aisle from herself and Des. Restrictions had meant no one else could come. Alice Patchett, who had been Welcome's Volunteer of the Year twice, had six people at her funeral, seven including the priest, whereas Vanessa Walton, who never helped anyone in her life, had a full church.

'Ding-dong, the witch is dead,' she said to Patrick.

Patrick pulled his coat tighter, hunched his shoulders. 'Jesus, Mer, she wasn't that bad.' But he looked uncertain. 'I'm not saying that she didn't bring a certain chaotic energy to the school ...'

'Chaotic evil.'

Patrick ignored her. 'But she was the one person who told me my talents were wasted on teaching, that she could see me writing music for the stage.'

From the way he was ignoring the bunch of year sevens precariously balanced on the stone balustrade at the top of the steps right near him, Patrick was halfway to giving up on teaching already. Not that Vanessa would have cared. The only person she was interested in was herself.

Mer turned and waved as Frankie crossed the road, skirted around the hearse parked right out the front and came limping up the stairs.

'Nice walk?' Patrick asked.

Frankie gave a tight smile in reply and then, glancing over his shoulder, said, 'Perhaps it's time the girls went inside and warmed up.'

'We're not singing now,' Patrick said, looking delighted. 'Beth heard our practice and decided that perhaps she would sing "Ave Maria" instead.'

'Now I'm going to cry,' said Mer. 'I always cry when Beth sings.'

'I guarantee you would have cried if you heard the year sevens,' said Patrick.

'Better they head in all the same, Patrick,' said Frankie firmly. 'They're running amok.'

Patrick stood there, clearly waiting for Frankie to take the lead, but Frankie didn't move, because it was like a game of chicken and this was the teacher equivalent of you break it, you buy it. Patrick had brought them so he was in charge. Eventually, he sighed and began to wave his hands around, shooing the girls inside.

'I wasn't expecting to see you here,' Frankie said to Mer.

'Wanted to see if any actual celebrities showed up.' Shoot me, Mer thought. I'm only human.

The two of them scanned the faces in the crowd, all of them familiar, only a little tidier, hair neatly brushed, clothes more sombre. There were no glamorous strangers.

'Who's that over there?' Frankie asked. She nodded her head in the direction of Billy Wicks. A strong-looking woman, dark hair, mid-fifties, stood next to him. She had a shrewd face, rounded at the chin, and wore quite a smart houndstooth coat with a fuzzy fur trim.

'That's Billy's new boss, Carole,' said Mer. She had served her at the deli a couple of days ago. Mer had added a couple of small quiches when Sue wasn't looking, just to be friendly. Stay on the right side of the law. You never knew when it would come in handy.

'A woman?' Frankie replied in surprise. 'That makes a nice change. I should get her to—'

'—come out to the school and talk to the girls,' finished Mer.

Frankie's smile morphed into a surprised look as she took in Mer's outfit. 'That's a bit low-cut.'

Mer only had one black dress in her wardrobe and it had a plunging neckline. She hadn't bought it with a funeral in mind.

'You're lucky I didn't wear my red one.'

Frankie moved closer. 'But you did wear your scarlet push-up bra.'

'It's not that bad,' protested Mer, but then glanced down and saw exposed lace.

'You'd better watch out that Harvey doesn't slobber on your cleavage at the wake.' Harvey Fettling, Vanessa's uncle, was prone to planting lingering kisses on women's hands and paying extravagant compliments.

'Five bucks he mentions Shakespeare during the eulogy,' said Mer.

Harvey ran a side business of bringing Shakespeare to schools and liked to talk about the Bard as though they were intimate friends of equal genius.

There was a ripple of movement as people began to file into the church. Mer and Frankie walked through the nearest stone arch and into the side porch. Frankie dipped two fingers into the small stone basin inside the door and blessed herself.

'Superstition,' said Mer, not nearly quietly enough.

'It's good manners. Obeying house rules.'

'Like no singlet or thongs?' said Mer, but Frankie was already saying hello to people. Mer didn't bother. She'd see them all at work.

She caught sight of Miss Helen, Harvey and his wife, Dolly, in the first pew. The casket was directly in front of the altar, a large bouquet of white lilies sitting on top. Miss Helen stood beside it, her face old and crumpled with grief.

Frankie stopped halfway up the nave, next to an almost empty row. 'Let's sit here.'

Mer noticed that two St B's students, Brianna and Jasmine, were sitting opposite. 'Worried Jaz's going to make off with the collection plate and donate it to Greenpeace?'

Frankie made a face like she was trying not to laugh. 'Good turnout,' said Frankie.

Mer sniffed and looked around. 'Nothing special. Everyone dies famous in a place like this.' She noticed Joe and Danny coming up the aisle towards them and elbowed Frankie, who turned to see, and then wriggled over to make room.

'What are you doing here?' Mer asked Joe.

'Supporting our family's most valuable player,' said Joe smoothly.

Frankie reached out and gave his hand a squeeze.

'And in your good suit as well,' Mer said, only a little sarcastically.

'Bit tight around the middle,' Joe admitted. 'Must have shrunk in the wash.'

The floppy fringe and pretty-boy looks that had made Joe Birnam a local teenage heart-throb had disappeared. The slicked-back hair was shot through with grey, the face softer, and he could bore the socks off you when he got started on funding submissions and corporate governance, but the cheeky smile was the same. Everyone had been amazed when he had chosen Frankie. Everyone except Mer. In her opinion, he was the lucky one, and he needed to remember that.

'Good to see you, Dan,' she said.

Her godson was taller than his father now, thick eyebrows, square chin, arms and legs that were all elbows and knees. Not quite as good-looking as his father at the same age, but enough to get attention. Mer noticed that both Brianna and Jaz were craning their necks to catch a look at him. Jasmine Langridge was trouble,

Mer thought – trouble being something she knew a bit about. Jaz was always looking for attention, a born actress. A bit like Vanessa when you thought about it.

She nudged Frankie and dipped her head in their direction and then nodded towards Dan. 'Someone's popular.'

Brianna noticed them noticing her and quickly turned around to face the front.

—

Vanessa's uncle looked handsome as he stood at the lectern to deliver the eulogy. Harvey wore a deep blue, double-breasted jacket with gold buttons and had a mane of brilliant white hair that flowed over his collar. Always on the brink of delivering a monologue, here he had an audience who couldn't escape.

'Bet Vanessa always thought she'd be delivering his,' Mer whispered to Frankie.

Frankie nudged her to hush.

'Friends,' Harvey began, arms outstretched, 'as Shakespeare himself put it: *Out, out, brief candle . . .*'

Mer gave Frankie an I-told-you-so look.

Harvey didn't shut up for the next twenty minutes. Mer tuned out the words and watched the photos that were being projected on the screen to the side of him. The Baby Vee phase featured heavily but then moved on to the late-teenage Vanessa, now a soap opera starlet, wearing either a bikini or school uniform or, in one notorious episode, a bikini she had made out of her school uniform for a dare, which then fell apart in the surf.

Vanessa's style kept evolving. Mer openly sniggered at the ill-advised perm that made Vanessa's hair look like a fountain of fairy floss, even though she herself had a similar style at the time. Taffeta dresses with sweetheart necklines gave way to boxy suit jackets with aggressive shoulder pads and sleek bobs. That was Vanessa's look when she scored a guest role in an American legal drama that got cancelled after one season. Next were a series of photos involving mysterious severed arms around her shoulders, the men they belonged to having been cropped out of the pictures.

Finally, Harvey stopped reminiscing and said, 'Now, Frances Birnam and my daughter, Beth, shall read some of Vanessa's favourite poems.'

Beth was wearing a paisley-patterned turban that did not suit her at all. Mer had heard that the chemo was all done now. Beth had been travelling to the city for it, some fancy specialist that Vanessa had organised for her. There was still some radiation to go.

The poem Beth read was short – something about not having time to stop for death but death arriving all the same, which was depressing. Still, she had sung so beautifully earlier in the service that Mer forgave her the poem and the turban. The sound had filled the cathedral, rising up into the vaulted ceiling.

Then it was Frankie's turn. She cleared her throat, which reverberated through the microphone. Mer noticed that her hand shook slightly as she flattened out a piece of paper and placed it on the lectern. There was a slight delay in the various speakers attached to the sound system. Whenever Frankie paused after each punctuation point, another ghostly version of herself was still talking. After she finished, Beth patted her shoulder.

Mer glanced across at Brianna and Jaz as the two women walked back to their seats. Jaz, straight-backed, blank-faced, seemed almost contemptuous of her surroundings. Mer had noticed that she wasn't sitting near the front with her grandmother and father. Brianna was a different matter. She didn't look sad – or, rather, that was only a partial description of her expression, it seemed to Mer. It was only as Frankie squeezed past Danny's knees, his long legs out in the aisle to give her room, and settled herself down back between Joe and Mer that Mer deciphered the look in her own mind.

Brianna Sharrah was scared.

CHAPTER 4

Sitting on the hard pew, Brianna's leg began to jiggle and she pushed her foot into the floor to make it stop. Just a nervous twitch, that's all.

'Leave Town Slut or Die!' she thought as a weeping Mrs Birnam walked up the aisle to take her seat. It was Jaz's current catchphrase and other girls at school had started saying it in a faux-ironic way, having no idea that the phrase had originated from an anonymous note Brianna had found in Vanessa Walton's handbag a few months ago. The 'death threat' Jaz now called it.

Her leg started jiggling again.

'Do you think Vanessa is wearing a wig in the casket?' Jaz had asked when they entered the church before the funeral had started.

The fact that Vanessa wore wigs had been a matter of some discussion at the school. Some people said it was so she didn't have to dye her hair all the time or maybe she had alopecia.

Brianna thought it probably meant she was menopausal and had thinning hair, like Brianna's grandmother.

'They put on make-up, so maybe.'

'What's the point if it's not an open casket?'

There had been a storm of tears when the girls heard the news of Vanessa's death. Now their sorrow had been replaced by something more volatile.

Jaz had kept turning around to gaze at the crowd walking in. 'We should have sat up the back. Then we could see if stalker Roly turns up.'

With three different entrances to the cathedral, there was no guarantee that they would spot him.

'You shouldn't have said anything to him about Vanessa,' whispered Brianna out of the corner of her mouth. 'He'll guess we know something.'

'He doesn't have a clue,' scoffed Jaz. 'Making all those smart-arse remarks about climate change. He won't be laughing soon enough.' She craned her head to look over the crowd towards the main doors.

'Maybe he won't come.'

'Of course he will,' said Jaz. 'It would be too suspicious if he didn't. Besides, everyone knows that the killer always comes to the funeral.'

There was something contradictory about these two statements but Brianna didn't bother pointing it out.

At rehearsals for the gala, Vanessa had been a pale skinny woman with overplucked eyebrows who lost her temper pretty quickly and was always complaining about how exhausting everything was. She had actually thrown a drink bottle at one of the year nine dancers, hitting her on the arm. And then there was the glittering fabulous vision that you couldn't take your eyes off. She had been the star of the gala, tap-dancing and singing her way through the night, raising more money than Brianna believed possible in Welcome.

Maybe everybody had multiple people inside of them – but no matter how many you had, they all still ended up in the one casket.

That thought overwhelmed Brianna and she slid to her knees, propped her elbows up on the ledge, clasped her hands and prayed, until Jaz murmured in her ear, 'Look who's watching you.'

Hopefully not God was Brianna's first thought, but then she opened her eyes. Danny Birnam, the boy who had kissed her then ghosted her soon afterwards, was sitting directly across from them. Her heart froze mid-beat.

'It's lover boy,' Jaz said, smirking.

Brianna's mother, Amber, never understood why she was friends with Jaz and sometimes Brianna didn't either. She knew it was unlikely that they would be friends forever, but they were friends right now and that felt far more important.

'Maybe we should tell Mrs Birnam about the note,' she whispered back. Danny's mum had taught her English last year and everyone knew she was a good friend of Vanessa's. Amber would go off her rocker at Brianna if she found out – phone confiscated, grounded, chores, the 'I'm very disappointed in you' talk – but at least the dilemma about what to do would be resolved. It would all be someone else's responsibility.

But Jaz wasn't listening. She sat bolt upright, staring. 'What's the Real Estate Agent doing here?'

Jaz, who hated her stepfather, referred to him as the Real Estate Agent both to annoy him – he had actually failed his agent exam after school – and to remind everyone else that Barton Langridge only ever wanted to sell you something. Lots of people complained about him, but they would all still vote for him in the next election. It didn't make any sense to Brianna.

She turned and there he was, along with Jaz's step-grandmother. Lonnie Langridge was a tiny talon of a woman in her eighties, barely five feet tall and that was mostly gristle, according to Brianna's mother. She was wrapped in black and wearing a small hat and veil, holding her son's arm. Disappearing behind one of the enormous stone columns, they reappeared around the other side of it, walking parallel to the altar, until they stopped in front of the casket. Brianna wondered if they were going to say something to Miss Helen – offer condolences, perhaps – but instead they moved into the front pew across from her. For all Brianna knew, that might be a dedicated Langridge pew where they always sat when they came to the cathedral.

'Should you go sit with them?' she asked Jaz.

Jaz's head gave an impatient shake. As the organ music began, she leant over to Brianna and said, 'We'll talk about the note to Danny afterwards,' in the sort of voice that suggested Danny had no say in the matter.

The minute the service was over, Jaz jumped up like a rabbit and was out in the aisle so quickly that she nearly beat the casket out of the church. It was wheeled out rather than carried on the shoulders of relatives. The Waltons were a female-heavy family and Harvey Fettling, who was as close to a patriarch as they got, wasn't the type to bear other people's burdens.

Brianna found Jaz standing on the corner of the two streets that bordered the cathedral, keeping an eye on all three of the entrances.

Danny came out the side entrance and was standing next to his mother and Mer Davis. He looked in Brianna's direction and then quickly ducked his head, as if pretending he hadn't noticed her.

They had met at one of the rehearsals for the gala. Danny had been roped in by his mother to help out backstage, moving equipment and organising props. There had been some Snapchat flirting, and then before the following weekend's rehearsal he had knocked on her door and said he was in the neighbourhood and they had walked to the Palais together.

The weekend after the gala, there had been a thankyou gathering at Jaz's house, all her mother's idea. Brianna had stood next to Danny in the downstairs garage, so close that she could smell the minty-muskiness of him, which made her body warm. He had reached out and grabbed her hand, and she stood there delighted, except for the fact that her hand was sweaty.

That was the exact moment Jaz had dared her to take something out of the spare room where everyone's coats and bags were. A 'souvenir' Jaz called it. Jaz had been wearing a 'souvenir' at the time: a black skin-tight dress she had nicked from the local boutique when she had bought a top and earrings last week.

Brianna had stood there, unsure what to do, but Danny had laughed like it was a good idea. Afterwards, she thought she had probably got that wrong and maybe he was laughing like it was a ridiculous idea and you'd have to be an idiot to do it. Maybe she should have laughed like that, as if Jaz was joking, except she knew that Jaz wasn't. Jaz didn't joke very much these days, not since what had happened to Nate.

'Go on,' said Jaz. 'Everyone's busy and won't notice.'

Brianna looked at Danny and, in that moment, wanted to be the daring one, the activist who protested things, the risk taker, the person at the centre of attention. It was just mucking around, a prank, not proper stealing. Besides, she could just take something out of her own bag and make up a story about it.

She missed Danny's hand when she let go of it, hoped that he felt the same. Heading up the internal stairs, she manoeuvred around other guests, past the laundry and into the spacious open-plan kitchen, all stainless steel and marble.

Vanessa stood there, a water glass in her hand, as Jaz's mother, Sheridan, checked on something in the oven. Just two skinny uptight women. Mrs Birnam and a bored Mer Davis were sitting next to each other at the table.

'Thank god it's over,' Vanessa was saying. 'People who say not to work with children have never worked with teenagers. Absolute nightmare.'

Mrs Birnam's eyes opened wide at this and Sheridan interrupted quickly to say, 'Oh, Brianna, is everything all right downstairs?'

'I need to go to the bathroom.'

But Jaz's mum was already distracted by Vanessa, who had started talking again about her plans for Broadway as Mer muttered something at Mrs Birnam that sounded like, 'How much longer?' No one noticed when Brianna didn't turn towards the bathroom but moved instead through the double doors into the formal part of the house, with a reception area, lounge suite and a piano topped with framed photos of Jaz at different ages, leading on to the spare room.

Loud music came blaring up from the garage, making the windows vibrate.

She needed to be quick. Brianna opened the spare bedroom door and then shut it behind her. If anyone came in, she'd pretend she had a headache and was getting some aspirin from her backpack.

There was a mountain of coats draped on the bedspread. Most of the bags were on the floor but one sat proudly near the pillows. It was light blue, the colour of a bird's egg. The type you saw on reality TV shows and Instagram posts. A gorgeous treasure chest with handles that stood up to attention, just waiting for someone to slip their arm through and take it away.

Practically begging to be stolen, Brianna could almost hear Jaz saying. Imagine if she just tucked it under her arm and went out the front door, circled around to the back garden and casually walked past Jaz with it. That would show her.

The bag had to be Vanessa's. No one else in Welcome would own something like that. The temptation to look inside was too much.

Pulling her sleeve over her fingers so as not to leave telltale smears or fingerprints, Brianna fumbled with the brass clasp. The pleated sides opened out into a wide mouth. There were large internal pockets, but the main cavity was a jumble of small tins, an envelope, scribbled lists, old receipts, a wallet, sunglasses, pens, lipsticks and scrunched-up tissues. It was tempting to empty the whole thing out and carefully rearrange it. A bag like that deserved to be looked after.

She could just take something small, something Vanessa would never notice, and take it back to show Jaz that she could be daring too.

Suddenly, there were noises outside the room, the low hum of voices. Mer Davis's voice floated towards her. 'She called me Marilyn at the gala,' she was saying. 'Marilyn!'

Brianna reached into the bag and grabbed the first thing her fingers settled on.

It was the envelope.

Brianna followed Danny and Jaz across the road to the park. Danny walked, shoulders hunched, looking like he wanted to be anywhere but here. Jaz was already talking when Brianna walked up.

'—wasn't an accident.'

'Why not?' Danny asked. 'People fall down stairs all the time. In the US, twelve thousand people die from falls every year.'

Brianna had read the same statistic, which meant that he had googled it like she had.

'You saw the note,' said Jaz, for what felt like the millionth time. 'She was being threatened.'

'It was just a coincidence. That was months ago and even Vanessa didn't take it seriously.'

Jaz glared at Brianna, guessing rightly that she had told Danny. Brianna just shrugged. That had been one of a handful of texts that Danny hadn't responded to but clearly had read.

It was Jaz who had insisted on taking the note to their teacher. Not because she thought it was particularly serious but because anything dramatic drew her like a moth to a flame. Brianna had tried desperately to talk her out of it, scared that Vanessa might phone her mother, but still she found herself being dragged to Vanessa's office after school the next Monday.

Brianna's face had been scarlet as she stumbled over a made-up story about finding the note next to the bag at the party and how it must have fallen out.

Vanessa reached across the table and Jaz handed her the opened envelope with a flourish. The girls watched as she read it.

Leave Town Slut or Die!

Vanessa's face pinched momentarily, but then she looked at the girls and laughed. 'What a sad little person Ivan is,' she said.

Brianna gasped as Jaz crowed. 'I knew it was him. Didn't I say?' She nudged Brianna to have her confirm, but Brianna didn't remember her saying anything about Mr Roland, just that the note was ridiculous.

'Best ignored,' Vanessa said, folding the note. 'I can count on your discretion.'

'Of course,' mumbled Brianna, keen to leave.

'But shouldn't you tell someone?' Jaz asked. 'That's harassment.'

'I was a child actor on TV,' said Vanessa. 'This is nothing. Besides the Ivan Rolands of the world don't deserve any attention.'

'Vanessa was murdered,' said Jaz now, 'and we might be the only three people who know it, other than the killer.'

Brianna felt sick.

'Vanessa didn't believe she was being threatened and neither should you,' replied Danny. 'For all you know, Vanessa wrote that note herself and was going to put it in someone else's bag. I wouldn't put it past her. She wasn't a nice person.'

It was a stalemate, and the two of them turned to Brianna as if hers was the deciding vote. Brianna looked back across the road at the congregation. The cathedral had been full to bursting. A thousand people, maybe more, and none of them celebrities, which meant the only really famous person at the funeral was dead.

'I think we do need to tell someone about the note,' she said to Danny. 'Maybe the police?'

It was more question than answer, because even the thought of that made her queasy.

'No way,' said Danny.

'We can ring Crime Stoppers anonymously.'

'And tell them what, exactly? There was no murder and you don't even have the note anymore!' Danny threw his arms up in disgust. 'This is all in your heads.'

'How about we tell your mum then?' Brianna was getting increasingly desperate. 'She'd know what to do.'

'Absolutely no way.' He was angry now, face contorted. 'You leave my mother out of this.'

Brianna raised her hands in surrender.

'What do you think we should do?' Jaz asked him.

'Nothing,' Danny said. 'Go back to being a climate warrior, Jaz. This is just stupid.'

Brianna wanted to agree with him, wanted to feel the relief of knowing that they had got this wrong and it could go away, but she just didn't believe it. A small part of her thought Danny didn't really believe it either.

'Whatever, Dan,' replied Jaz.

Across the road, Mrs Birnam gestured for Danny to join her. The boy shoved his hands into his pockets and walked away.

'There's Roly now,' said Jaz, eyes narrowing. 'And look who he's talking to.'

Ivan Roland stood on the church steps in conversation with Jaz's stepfather, Barton Langridge. Their teacher kept looking around, as if he wanted to be sure they weren't overheard. It was clear that the Real Estate Agent wasn't too keen to be standing there either; he was shaking his head dismissively.

'Will we go to the police then?' Brianna asked.

'No point,' said Jaz. 'My stepfather has the local police in his pocket and Roly has been his chief fundraiser for years. They'll never take us seriously. Besides, like Danny said, where's our evidence? We haven't got the note anymore. Vanessa took it. And you didn't even get a photo of it.'

Brianna felt like pointing out that Jaz hadn't taken a picture either. 'So what do we do?'

Jaz smiled. 'Oh, I'll think of something.'

CHAPTER 5

Carole stood in front of the Palais. From a distance it was grand, with columns and a trio of long windows on the second floor leading out to an ornate balcony. At the front, an imposing red door was flung open, with an awning and stained-glass semicircle over-head. On closer inspection, the building was tired and shop-worn, damp spots in the plaster, paint peeling on the window frames, with rickety wooden external stairs on the side that screamed fire hazard. Like a beautiful woman with a dirty face, which wasn't original, but then the best lines rarely were.

There was a gleaming sign out the front for Walton's Academy of Dance, with a picture of a smiling Vanessa on it. In curly writing were the words *Home of Baby Vee*, and a helpful arrow pointing up the outside stairs. A mound of wilting flowers and wreaths slowly turning to compost lay underneath it.

Carole was beginning to find her feet, working out who was who in the zoo or, in her case, both the town and the station. She was in charge of eight constables, ranging in age from young, obnoxious Troy (she had overheard him discussing the fact that Vanessa Walton had definitely had a boob job) to Billy. She had talked to each of them individually, asked them what they liked best about the job, what they hated, while at the same time trying to assess their strengths and weaknesses. Billy was the one who worried her most. In cop terms he had put his pool cue back in the rack. He couldn't think of any goals or ambitions, but when she pressed him, he said it would be nice to be famous, which probably had to do with the outpouring of grief around Vanessa Walton's death. This was hardly something to build a career around, though, so she had designated him as her driver for the first couple of weeks to see if together they could work on more tangible goals.

Walking in the front door of the Palais for the wake, she was welcomed by Vanessa's aunt, Dolly Fettling, ballet-elegant in heels that took her from short to petite. Carole had already heard that you didn't want to get between Dolly and a five-cent piece, not unless you were prepared to put your body on the line.

'Drinks are in the cocktail lounge,' Dolly said curtly, looking as though she would have liked to charge a cover fee. 'Food will be circulating.'

Carole smiled and nodded at people as she made her way through the crowd. Funerals always made her hungry, so she grabbed an arancini ball from a passing tray. Hellishly hot molten cheese was at its centre. Covering her mouth with the serviette, she debated spitting it out, as she could feel the inside of her mouth beginning to smoke. Slowly chewing, letting in as much air as possible, Carole then swallowed, tears forming as the lump of lava made its scalding way down. She could almost feel internal blisters forming.

Looking around for some water, she noticed one of the waitresses standing there, staring at her. A young girl, blonde hair with pink ends, wearing a school uniform.

'You're that new policewoman,' the girl said.

Carole cleared her throat, felt like she could breathe fire. 'That's right. Carole Duffy. I've been here about a week.'

'Did you know Vanessa?'

'Never had the pleasure. I did see her in a play once. She was very talented.'

'Is that why you're here?'

Carole made a seesaw gesture with a hand. 'Probably more because I went to her house the morning she died. Coming along today seemed the respectful thing to do.' And there was also the fact she was curious, and it was a good opportunity to meet half the town at the same time, start putting faces to the names she had heard at work.

The girl's eyes lit up. 'How do you think Vanessa died?'

Carole wasn't surprised to be asked this. In her career she had discovered that if you scratch the surface, most people were conspiracy-theory-loving ghouls at heart.

'An accident,' she said firmly, 'which is what the coroner found as well. May she rest in peace.'

The girl frowned at this. 'What if it wasn't an accident? Would you open an investigation?'

'That's beyond my skill set,' said Carole. 'I'm just a humble sergeant. You'd need Homicide for that.' Trying to change the subject, she asked, 'And your name is?' She tried to smile but found it too painful.

'Jasmine Langridge,' said the girl grudgingly.

How many bloody Langridges were there in this town?

'I think I might have flown into Welcome on a helicopter with your father,' Carole guessed.

In an instant, she could see this was the wrong thing to say. Jasmine's face turned from sullen to a kind of fury.

'He's my *step*father.' She spat out the words, then turned on her heel and marched off, leaving Carole to deal with third-degree burns to her oesophagus.

The fact that Barton was a step-parent almost made Carole pity him. So easy to be cast as the villain and blamed for everything. It had been like that with Lexie at the start, but she had come around eventually. Jasmine seemed more inflexible.

Carole looked around the room, noticed that the woman who cried while reading out the poem at the church was sitting at the bar. She had the sort of kind, dimpled face that meant strangers would ask her for directions and lost children would approach her for help. Carole was about to introduce herself when she clocked the person standing beside her. The woman who had served her in the supermarket, wearing a low-cut dress with more than quiches on display, was monopolising Vanessa's uncle.

'Make it a whiskey, Harvey – a double.'

'How about a glass of house white?' Harvey suggested smoothly.

'A whiskey,' the woman demanded. 'I'm celebrating.'

'Mer!' said the kind-looking woman.

'Vanessa's life, of course, Frankie,' said the woman called Mer, perhaps realising that she had gone too far. Carole wondered if she already had a few celebratory drinks under her belt.

'Spirits are not on the tab,' Harvey said apologetically. 'Dolly's orders. White or red, pink if I mix them.'

Mer opened her mouth to protest, but Frankie got in first. 'We'll have two white wines, Harvey, thank you, and that was a lovely eulogy you gave.'

Carole could do with a white wine herself, if only to cool her mouth, but it was a bit early in the day and she was on night shift tonight, part of her way of getting to know the station properly. So she headed in the opposite direction, passing speckled gilt mirrors and scuffed tables. They were covered in flyers advertising next week's jazz night and free tryouts for junior ballet proclaiming dance to be the number one recreational activity in the nation – why not join today! The threadbare couches were calling to her but Carole feared they were the plush equivalent of quicksand, easy to sink into, impossible to get out of, so moved towards a display cabinet full of trophies and medals. There was Vanessa memorabilia on display, including a board game, collector cards and even a yoyo from the 'Baby Vee' and *Shining Stars* era.

Carole inspected an original Sugar Snap Biscuit poster. A seven-year-old version of Vanessa, the future Baby Vee, hair in sweet little bunches, wearing a pink leotard with a tulle skirt, caught in the act of tap-dancing her way across a giant biscuit while sprinkling sugar into the air. *Sugar Snap Biscuits – The Tasty Treat!*

'All Dolly's idea,' came a voice from near her elbow. 'She likes to remind people about it. That ad is the reason that Vanessa got asked to audition for *Shining Stars*.'

Janet Ross, swathed in an immense black curtain, was sitting next to the doorway. Carole was reminded of a spider, waiting patiently to see what would turn up in her web. No hat today, her straw-coloured hair neatly brushed.

'Did Beth do commercials as well?' asked Carole, looking back at the poster, taking in Vanessa's pert expression and fixed smile, while trying not to feel like a struggling fly.

'Completely different personality,' said Janet. 'Not fond of the limelight. She's the stage manager for the Welcome Players Dramatic Society and does a very good job. I used to think that the two of them together were like a penny-farthing bicycle: Vanessa all show up front, Beth providing the stability behind the scenes. They were more like sisters than cousins. We got lucky today as she rarely sings in public. Stage fright, I think you call it.'

'It's a shame she doesn't sing more often. She's very talented.'

'Her real talent is teaching people to dance. If this was a normal Friday afternoon, she'd be upstairs and all we'd be hearing would be a lot of little three-year-old rhinos thumping their way through a routine and the same piece of music being played over and over. Patience of a saint. Now, tell me: are you enjoying Welcome and the station?'

While Janet's description of the superintendent had been apt, Carole wasn't about to tell her that. 'Getting used to the cold spring mornings but it has been a pleasant change,' she answered. 'On the whole, people in the town have been very welcoming, just like it says on the tin.'

'You'll find some locals refer to Welcome as a regional centre rather than town,' Janet replied. 'Sounds more important. Some even claim "city", because of the cathedral, but that's pushing it, in my opinion. Named after a gold nugget. There's a replica of it in the local museum. And what did you think of the funeral?'

Her eyes fixed on Carole in a look of piercing concentration. Here was another ghoul.

Carole didn't really have a strong opinion on the funeral. 'Vanessa was obviously loved by many.'

'She'll be missed by her family, of course, having been their meal ticket for years, and Frances Birnam did seem genuinely sad, but many people hated her with a passion. I have at least ten people on my list – myself included, of course. I do try to play it fair.'

The world had gone mad in the last two years, giving Carole lots of practice at dealing with eccentrics, lunatics and general flat-earthers. She knew she was going to regret it but asked anyway. 'Your list?'

'Of suspects. I wrote it before she died. Just had a feeling. But, then, I do it for most people. If ever I'm murdered, check the inside pocket of my winter overcoat and you'll find an up-to-date list of suspects.'

The thought occurred to Carole that maybe it wouldn't be the most surprising thing if Janet Ross were found murdered. If Carole had to deal with her regularly, her own name might be found tucked into the overcoat. 'Who's at the top of your list?' she asked.

'Roger – that's my husband. Statistically most likely. Though I feel obliged to say that he is by nature quite a gentle personality. Still, people can snap after a long marriage.'

Sometimes not even a long one.

Carole tried to steer the conversation back to some sort of normal footing. 'The coroner found the death to be accidental.' Carole hadn't read the report herself, but the super had let them know the moment it had been received.

The older woman waved her hand in dismissal. 'They were at a disadvantage – as are you, having never met her. Vanessa Walton was to her core a dramatic person. It's what made her such a good actor. Now, anyone can be murdered, but she more likely than most, I would say.'

'Isn't that victim blaming?'

'I prefer victim understanding. You can hardly solve the crime if you don't know the first thing about the victim,' Janet said in a severe tone.

Carole was almost prepared to eat another arancini ball rather than get stuck talking to this peculiar woman for too much longer. 'So what didn't the coroner know?'

'For starters, that Barton Langridge was thumping angrily on Vanessa Walton's door at exactly ten minutes past six the evening she died. He didn't seem happy, but then he rarely does. I was in my garden across the way, moving my pot plants inside because of the storm that was coming, and I had the perfect view.'

That got Carole's attention. 'Anything else?'

'Vanessa didn't drink. When she came over to my house for the neighbourhood catch-up, she happily accepted glasses of wine all afternoon but left them untouched. I saw her empty a lovely pinot gris into my Monstera deliciosa. Ridiculous, really. The Singhs don't drink and no one makes a fuss.' Janet paused here and gave Carole a pert look.

'But there was a half-empty bottle of champagne on her kitchen table and alcohol found in her stomach,' Carole protested.

Janet smiled now, her top lip razor-thin. She had a sharp expression, much like her chin and pencilled eyebrows. 'You'll learn that it takes a town to solve something as complicated as a murder,' she said. 'Now, I think I'll get a nip of sherry from Harvey at the bar.'

—

Beth was bone-tired, hadn't slept well in days, but as people stopped to say how sorry they were she smiled politely and said thank you. The thing Vanessa hated most was to be pitied; Beth was far more accustomed to it. She had taken her turban off, displaying a thin layer of hair that looked soft and downy, like the fuzz on a mohair jumper.

Dolly, her mother, came past and hissed at her, the skin around her lips puckered in disapproval. 'You can't go round looking like that. You look like death warmed up.'

Beth wanted to say that if you couldn't look like death at a wake, when could you, but knew better than to start a fight with Dolly. Her mother was already furious at the expense of the funeral – the fancy casket, nice flowers, free wine and food for the wake – but Beth didn't care. In life, as in death, her cousin deserved the best and she was determined that Vanessa would get it.

They would have to get through this and the bills that followed like they got through everything else: with a bit of luck and a lot of hard work on her part. These last few years had been brutal. The pandemic had meant cancelled dance classes and no one coming to the Palais for a drink but then Vanessa had arrived back in town along with grand schemes and big plans, refusing to let a ridiculous cancer diagnosis get in the way of them, no matter how much Beth protested. Vanessa's attitude was that it was just an obstacle they would get over together. In a funny way her magical thinking had been contagious and Beth had dreamt along with her.

But that was all gone now and Beth was left alone to face reality. The only slight glimmer in what had been the worst week of her life was that instead of students leaving the academy in droves following Vanessa's death as she had feared, the reverse had occurred. Four new students had enrolled in the last two days alone. One woman explained that she had told her daughter all about how Baby Vee was discovered because of the Sugar Snap television commercial. Sugar Snap Biscuits had already announced a new competition to find the star of their next advertising campaign, supposedly in honour of Vanessa's memory, but really to ride the publicity and sell more products. Vanessa would have loved all the attention, if only she had been here to see it.

There was a photo of the two of them that Harvey had pinned up behind the bar. Vanessa must have been no more than four, Beth three. Both of them in matching handmade dance costumes, hair in tight buns, stage make-up, standing side by side in identical poses. Beth shorter and wider, as if she were the showground mirror version of her cousin. There had never been a time when they didn't know how to smile for the camera: lift your head, elongate your neck, think of the line you were making with your body.

Harvey had been a bit shaky this morning and Beth had caught him drinking before the service. Just one to settle the nerves before church, her father had assured her, but it must have been more judging by the way his hand trembled, and in the end she had put his tie on for him.

No one in the church would have guessed, but Beth heard it in his voice, a faint alcoholic slur. She didn't blame him. Standing at the grave, she couldn't comprehend that Vanessa was actually dead. It seemed like a bad dream. There had been the reading of the will at the solicitor's office. Dolly had taken it very badly that Helen was the only beneficiary and Beth had been named as executor. The only named asset had been this building, the Palais. It was Beth who had insisted Vanessa buy it, back in her heyday, when money flowed through her hands.

There had been such plans for it, a vision that could support the whole family: concerts in the ballroom, theatricals on stage, music residencies, a fine dining room and a private function area for parties. Upstairs would be artists' studios, as well as the premier dancing school in the region, discovering the stars of the future exactly as Vanessa had been discovered. It was up to Beth to make that happen now, in memory of her cousin.

'Can you believe Sandy Gunnison has turned up?' Dolly continued. 'The nerve of her to show her face.'

Sandy had taught at the academy before leaving three years ago to open her own school, Dance Daze. She had poached their entire senior competition team by offering three-for-the-price-of-two classes. Parents had been apologetic but left all the same.

'Probably wants her job back. Thinks we will be needing another teacher now,' her mother said. 'Apparently COVID hit her school hard.' It sounded as though Dolly would like to hit her harder.

'She's only here to pay her respects,' Beth soothed.

'Likely story. And how are you going? Not getting too tired?'

Beth smiled but could feel her mouth turning down at the edges of its own accord. This was as maternal as Dolly got. 'I'll survive.'

'Good, then you'd better go check on Helen. Ensure she's not making a spectacle of herself.' Dolly couldn't abide emotional displays of any kind.

Beth moved through the scrum of the crowd, smiling her hellos and nodding as people told her how sorry they were, carrying two stiff gin and tonics in water glasses so that no busybody could wonder aloud if someone suffering from cancer should be drinking alcohol.

Janet Ross clutched Beth's arm and said how surprised she was at Vanessa dying.

'A terrible shock,' Beth agreed, 'but excuse me, I really must . . .' and walked away without actually explaining what it was she needed to do. Janet had been bailing people up all over the room, including the new sergeant. She was such a busybody and Beth didn't have the energy to cope with her today.

Helen was tucked away in a dark corner of the lounge, sitting in one of the booths, the plush seats almost as bald as Beth. She sat down beside her weeping aunt, Helen's face a soggy mess. Beth had to press her lips together to stop herself from crying with her. Instead, she placed a gentle hand on Helen's back and put a gin in front of her.

Nearby, Jasmine Langridge pushed open the door from the kitchen with her backside; she was carrying a tray full of little sausage rolls. The smell of them travelled and Beth wondered if Helen should eat something.

'Did you talk to Lonnie Langridge at the funeral?' Beth asked. Lonnie was almost a recluse these days. Beth had been surprised to see her, though not her son. Barton would go to the opening of an envelope if he thought there were votes in it.

Helen sniffled, took a sip of the drink, coughed a little, but stopped crying. 'It was good of her to come. She loved having Vanessa next door.'

Maybe Barton was worried about Vanessa dying in a house the family owned, like they might sue him or something. It could be a scandal if the tabloids got hold of it. MP OWNS HOUSE OF DEATH.

Yes, that was probably why he'd come, even though suing him was the last thing Beth would do.

Frankie limped out of the women's toilets and, catching sight of them, came and sat down at their table.

'It's these shoes,' she apologised. 'I should never have worn them. How are you holding up, Beth?'

'I was dreading the funeral but it was good to be kept busy.'

'It was a lovely celebration of her life and you sang so well. Now why don't I sit with Miss Helen for a bit?' Frankie offered. 'You go take a moment for yourself.'

Beth stood up. 'Thanks Frankie, I appreciate that.'

—

Frankie watched as Beth walked away and then turned back to Helen. She had already extended her condolences at the grave site, hugging the old woman hard and they had both cried. Afterwards, she had spent some time at her mother's grave, binned the wilted flowers she had put there a fortnight ago, and tried to give it a quick clean.

Helen sat there looking bewildered. Perhaps she was on medication.

'I keep thinking' – Helen leant forward and Frankie could feel the woman's breath on her face – 'that I must ring her up and tell her everything that's happened, and then I remember. Stupid of me.'

'That's not stupid at all,' said Frankie, reaching out to hold the other woman's hand, age-spotted, all veins and knuckles, heavy with rings. She had lingered herself outside Vanessa's office door after school the day before, convinced that if she knocked, Vanessa would call out and tell her to come in.

'Would you like me to clean her office out at school?' she asked. 'I could box up whatever was personal and bring it over to you.'

Even as she was making the offer, Frankie felt a sudden pang of guilt. She still hadn't been through her mother's belongings, even though Des had talked about it several times. Months ago, out at the farm, she had flicked through old copies of the *Women's Weekly* kept for recipes and photos of Lady Di, whom Alice had had a bit of a thing for, but she couldn't bring herself to read the old letters that had been bundled together and tied with a ribbon or make a decision about Alice's clothes. Perhaps you never felt ready but had to force yourself to do it.

There were traces of Vanessa's glamour in the old woman's face, even though her eyeshadow was heavy in the creases of her lids and dark trails of mascara dripped down her face. The air of medicated dullness seemed to disappear, replaced by something tougher. 'There is an errand you can do for me,' Miss Helen said. 'Vee's jewellery box. Beth is so busy with everything that I don't want to bother her. Could you go to her house and get it for me?'

Frankie hesitated.

'I could give you the key,' Miss Helen added.

'We already have a set. Danny watered her plants when she was away on holidays.'

The key ring had a tiny disco ball on it. Even Vanessa's spare keys were glamorous.

'She keeps it next to her bed. There's one piece in particular, a family heirloom – my mother's emerald ring. Dolly was furious when Mum gave it to her.'

'Oh.' Frankie knew the ring, had admired it on Vanessa's hand, and could sense this had the potential to wander into family unpleasantness – but what else was there to say? 'Of course, Miss Helen.'

'You always were an obliging child.' Now it was Miss Helen's turn to pat her hand, and Frankie had the impression that she had been played.

In the distance there was piano music. Patrick, Frankie guessed, recognising the distinctive trill up and down the keys that marked the start of every school performance.

Helen straightened up and began to rummage in the handbag beside her on the seat. Pulling out a make-up pouch and hand mirror, she started repairing the damage. It was amazing what you could do with make-up if you knew how, Frankie thought, as an improved Helen quickly emerged.

People began to move from the lounge past the velvet curtain into the hall. Over the sound of footsteps and conversation, a woman's voice floated in. Dolly was beginning to sing. Miss Helen patted Frankie's arm and said she was fine now and would go out to listen to the music.

When Frankie entered the hall, she noticed Brianna standing on the opposite side of the room. She was still in full school uniform with her blazer on, but her abundance of hair had been released from its braid and was cascading down her back in tight dark curls. When Frankie had seen her with Danny and Jaz across the road from the church, it had been as if she were looking at strangers. They were no longer children but people with their own secrets and troubles.

She walked towards Brianna. The girl didn't recoil but she didn't look happy about it either.

'It was kind of you to help out with the waitressing,' Frankie said.

'I often help out when Mum does her catering.' The girl's dark eyes were enormous in her narrow face.

'You know,' Frankie went on, uncomfortable but feeling it needed to be said, 'you can pop into my office for a catch-up if you feel like it.'

There was a hesitation in Brianna's face, as if there were words on her tongue waiting to be spoken, but then her head drooped, her mouth shut tight like a door closing, and she walked away without saying a word.

Mer was sitting at the bar talking loudly to some poor woman.

Frankie excused her way into the conversation and explained she was about to head off. Joe was going to drive her back to the school to get her car.

'Meet Carole,' said Mer.

Frankie recognised her from outside the church.

'This is Frankie Birnam, best goddamn teacher at St Brigid's.' Mer's eyes were now operating independently of each other. One was wandering down the bar of its own accord as though trying to find more drinks.

Frankie winced internally, hoped Mer hadn't been telling tall tales to the new policewoman.

'I've already made an appointment to come for an official visit with your principal,' Carole exclaimed, like this was a stroke of luck. 'Maybe I can have five minutes with you afterwards to find out about what really goes on in Welcome.' She beamed up at Frankie.

'Oh, frigid Brigids are never in trouble,' Mer said, sarcastic now. 'All saints at that school.'

'They're pretty good,' said Frankie quickly.

'Don't want too many saints,' joked Carole, 'or I'll be out of a job. I'll just pop to the loo before I head off as well.'

Joe appeared in the entrance.

'Here's the loving husband,' proclaimed Mer, and it seemed to Frankie she was being snippy about that as well. Mer was between boyfriends at the moment, maybe that's why she had been threatening trouble all day.

'I think it's time to go home,' Frankie suggested hopefully.

Mer waved an empty glass in Harvey's direction. He had been standing at the far end of the bar, ignoring her. 'What sort of wake is this if you can't even get a drink?'

'Are you sure you're going to be okay?' Frankie asked.

Mer gave her the sort of sour look she usually saw on teenage faces. 'I'm a big girl, Captain Sensible. I'll be fine.'

'Fine,' repeated Frankie, a sudden heat behind it. It had been a long day, she was tired, and all she wanted to do was take her shoes off. She'd pour herself a glass of wine and start reading the hundred or so emails from the school and students' parents that would have accumulated over the day. Then, of course, there was marking and lesson preparation for next week, but she'd give herself tonight off from that at least.

Joe kissed her when she walked up to him. 'I'm so happy to see you,' she told him.

Janet Ross was sitting outside the door. The old woman's hair was sticking up in sweaty spikes, her face flushed. 'Too much activity for one day,' she said in explanation when Frankie stopped to ask if she was all right. Joe kept walking.

'Do you need a lift anywhere?' Frankie asked.

'My Roger should be coming along to pick me up any moment now. Is that your husband over there in the white car?'

Joe was making a hurry-up face at Frankie.

Frankie nodded, said goodbye and left. As she walked to the car, it felt as though she were being watched, but when she looked back, Janet Ross had her head down, busily writing something.

CHAPTER 6

There was an electric chirp which trilled, paused, and then did it again. Frankie opened one eye only to find it was too dark to be morning yet.

Joe submerged himself under his ocean of covers.

The key to a good relationship, Frankie liked to tell her year eleven wellbeing class, was open communication and separate doonas. The girls scoffed, but Frankie was confident that they would reconsider in time. Mer had snorted when she told her and said her life advice was to always wee after sex.

The noise sounded again with an accompanying grunt from Joe. The clock beside the bed said 5 am.

'Your phone,' he muttered.

Frankie rolled over to the edge of the bed, stretched out an arm to find her handbag, caught in a messy puddle of yesterday's clothes. The phone glowed inside it, like a phosphorescent creature deep in the sea. Blinking away sleep, she tapped the screen, held it to her ear and listened.

'I'm going out,' she said, swiping the phone off.

Joe turned and lifted his head to look at the clock before falling back onto the pillow. He was already snoring by the time she had quietly pulled on jeans, t-shirt and a jumper. Last night he had organised takeaway for dinner, though she always cooked during the week.

'What have you done?' Frankie had joked and Joe had hugged her and said she'd had a tough day.

She walked down the hallway, nearly tripping over an abandoned schoolbag. Low snuffles came from the laundry, but then the dogs must have heard her, because instantly there was scratching at the door. She carried on to the kitchen, where she poured food into their bowls and put them on their placemat. The moment she opened the laundry door, the spaniels trotted past, their furry tails polishing the floor.

They were getting old now, their brown patches flecked with white, both on three different types of pills for a range of health conditions. Frankie had long ago stopped tallying up the vet bills.

She waited until they'd finished their breakfast before letting them outside and heading to the car.

It was still dark by the time she pulled into the car park of the Welcome Olympic Pool. Now she was properly awake, Frankie could appreciate the newness of the morning, that gentle quietness before the rest of the world woke up. Balancing two coffees she had bought from an ex-student working the early shift at McDonald's, she locked the car door and stood by the wire fence.

The pool's floodlights were on, illuminating the water. Fifty metres by eight lanes, empty but for a single swimmer.

'Didn't take you long,' said Mr Poole, opening the metal grille to her knock. He had been manager long enough that his name no longer raised a smile in town. Frankie had watched his hair go from red to white to non-existent.

'Sorry Mer got you out of bed,' she said.

'Don't sleep much these days anyway. Got a phone call from a neighbour over the way there, saying Meredith Davis was jumping the fence and should she ring the police station. I arrived to find her wrestling with the pool cover.'

He led Frankie through the turnstile and into the indoor play area. It was the new part, replacing the outdoor baby pool where Frankie, Mer and everyone else who grew up in Welcome had learnt to swim. Frankie could remember standing there, hair dripping, shivering, while her bare feet almost blistered on the hot concrete. She had been all right at swimming: the second leg of the freestyle relay, the backup for the fifty metres breaststroke. Not like Mer, who had been one of the most talented swimmers the district had ever seen. There had been championships and trophies, talk of talent scouts and national teams, but then rivals grew and bodies changed. Mer suffered injuries to her shoulder and neck and everyone stopped saying those things, even her coach, and the dream had slowly deflated. It still accorded Mer certain privileges, though, like swimming in an empty pool when the sign said it was closed.

Outside, the reflections from the overhead lights danced across the water and Mer carved a perfect line through it.

'She's sitting a little low but her shoulder's holding up okay,' Mr Poole observed.

Frankie had learnt over the years that Mer only went swimming if something was wrong. She guessed that Mr Poole knew the same and that's why he had phoned. He disappeared back into his office as Frankie walked along the barrier, watching Mer tumble at the far end, feet whipping around as she changed direction, then rising to the surface to continue beating a white trail. Halfway up the pool, she stopped, hung on to the lane rope and pushed the goggles onto her forehead, glaring at the water like she had been caught doing the wrong thing.

'I brought coffee,' Frankie called. 'It's still hot.'

Mer slid over the lane rope, the movement eel-like, and then swam under the other ropes to the side of the pool. Using her arms, she pushed herself onto the ledge and then to standing, arms folded, dripping, next to Frankie. She pulled off her cap.

Frankie looked over at her best friend, took in the whole five foot eleven of her, the way her wet fringe clumped untidily together, how her coathanger shoulders gave way to a trim waist, neat hips and long legs. It was only in Mer's face that you could see the years that had passed, freckles making way for age spots, concertinaed skin around the eyes, how the line of her mouth was more severe, dragged down by time. They had been friends for more than thirty years. Mer was the first person who had thought Frankie was special. It had given her much-needed confidence at a time when she had little, and Frankie would never forget that, but sometimes Frankie worried that she might be Mer's enabler. Could Frankie's rule-following be the reason for Mer's rule-breaking? Did Mer only stand at the edge of tall buildings because she knew that Frankie would always be there to catch her? Her greatest fear was that one day Mer would go too far and Frankie wouldn't be able to drag her back.

'Hurry up and get changed,' was all she said. 'We can drink them in your car.'

Squad members were walking in as they headed out, mostly teenagers in hoodies and swim coats, looking half asleep. One of the coaches called out to Mer, a greeting with a question mark attached, but she walked on without acknowledging it.

Mer's car, a grimy metallic-blue Toyota Corolla, had a bumper sticker reading *Driven by a Hot Bitch* on the rear window and cosmetic panel damage on the side. It was parked across two bays. Des had helped her choose something reliable after she had kicked Matt, her kids' father, out of the house for the last time. Whenever the Corolla played up, which wasn't often, Mer would phone Des and say it was his fault she bought a lemon, and a patient Des would head over to fix it. Frankie loved her father for that.

Clambering into the driver's seat, Frankie saw mud and gravel in the footwell, crunched-up plastic bottles on the floor and old lolly packets shoved in the side pocket of the door. Mer always talked about giving it a good clean, or more likely telling her son, Ky, to do it.

'Everything all right?' Frankie asked. 'You got home okay yesterday?'

A fug of stale booze mixed with chlorine and coffee permeated the space. Frankie thought about winding her window down.

'It was a good night, a proper wake,' Mer protested. 'You should have stayed.'

Frankie sighed. Not this argument again. 'I was tired. It's been a tough week.'

'Not just this week. We never go out anymore.' Mer's voice had a petulant tone.

'Life's been busy, I guess.' She was trying to mollify.

Mer leant her head back on the headrest, large drops of water dripping down the seat. 'You mean Vanessa came back and had you running around after her, like you were—' She stopped, as if she couldn't think of a word bad enough.

'Like I was what?'

'Like you were Beth!' said Mer. '*Yes, Vanessa; no, Vanessa; three bags full, Vanessa.* It's as if she cast a magic spell over the entire town.'

Frankie gave a soft 'ha' of surprise.

'And you haven't been out to see Des in ages. When I was there last—'

'When were you out visiting Dad?'

Mer shrugged. 'He wanted help with Alice's stuff. You were busy so I offered.' She shot a sly look at her friend to gauge the reaction.

Frankie tried her best not to feel defensive. 'You started seeing Willis,' she reminded Mer.

Sue at the supermarket often referred to Mer's boyfriends as 'white stripes', married men missing their wedding rings. Secretly, Frankie thought this was pretty accurate but knew never to say as much to Mer.

'He was a mistake.' Mer picked up the takeaway coffee that sat between them and took a sip. 'Still doesn't change the fact that Vanessa wasn't a good person.'

'Is that why you climbed a fence to go swimming in the middle of the night? You didn't like Vanessa?'

She waited for Mer to answer because Frankie was keeper of all her secrets, but Mer shook her head.

'I might have been a little drunk,' was all she said.

'You would have lost your licence if you had been pulled over.'

Mer yawned as if it were too early for hypotheticals.

'Are you even sober now?' Frankie asked.

'Swimming always makes me feel better,' Mer said. 'And this delicious coffee you bought for me. How will I ever repay you?'

Frankie was caught between laughing and wanting to throttle her best friend. It wasn't an unusual sensation. What Mer needed to do was go home and sleep, but not yet.

'Actually, there is something you can do,' Frankie said. 'But I'm driving.'

CHAPTER 7

Getting out of the car, Carole slammed the door shut and regretted it. The noise echoed around the empty street and set off the birds in the nearby pin oak. The curtains twitched in the house opposite.

'I feel like someone's watching us,' she said. Clumps of sawdust were still scattered in the grass but the branch was gone.

'That'll be Janet,' Billy said. 'She has eyes in the back of her head.'

All eight of them, thought Carole.

She opened the small wrought-iron gate that led to the verandah and stood in front of the green wooden door.

It had been a pretty standard night shift, with two drunks and a ham-fisted punch-up in the park. Carole's favourite customer had been someone arriving at the station to report a missing Akubra, saying they were prepared to put up a slab of beer as a reward. She had wondered if it was the same hat Barton Langridge had worn at the airport the day she arrived or if everyone in this town had one in their wardrobe. She'd had a nice chat with one of her senior constables, Angie Rosso. In a former life Angie was a nurse but decided she needed more excitement so joined the force.

Then, just before they were about to knock off, someone called to report a prowler. It would have been fine to leave it for the day shift, but when she heard the address, Carole decided to check it out.

She put an ear to the door and was certain there was a hum of voices inside. Listening carefully, she heard the noise of water going through old pipes, a knocking sound.

'Could someone have moved in already?' she asked Billy.

He hung back at the car, reluctant to come closer. 'My wife was talking to Beth yesterday. They haven't even cleared it out yet.'

A place like this would be snapped up instantly. Renting in Welcome was far more expensive than Carole had anticipated. Going by the prices she'd seen while perusing the local paper during her meal break, she'd be lucky to get a depressing brick veneer on a treeless estate halfway to the next town with a bus going through once a day.

She knocked loudly on the door.

No noise inside now.

Barton Langridge had knocked on this door, Vanessa Walton's door, the night she died. Angrily was how Janet Ross described it. Barton's stepdaughter seemed to think that there might be more to the death. Did any of that matter when the coroner had ruled it to be an accident? Unlike public perception, most of the coroner's cases were accidents or natural causes. Suicides counted for roughly ten per cent and homicides only one per cent of deaths investigated. Carole had faith in the professionalism of those involved in making that assessment, like she had faith in the forensics process, but the whole system was under-resourced and overworked and mistakes could be made.

'Do you believe in ghosts?' she asked Billy.

He had made it to the footpath now and was looking anxious.

Billy hesitated before answering. 'I'm not sure, to be honest.'

'If Vanessa's ghost is here, I've got some questions,' said Carole. 'Better bring your torch in case the electricity's been turned off.'

They could go next door and ask Lonnie Langridge for a key, or perhaps it was too early and they should just check the perimeter. Carole had already met two Langridges and didn't really feel like adding to the list.

She turned the front doorhandle. It was unlocked and the door opened.

'Go round the back,' she ordered Billy.

Billy gave her an uncertain look but didn't volunteer to reverse positions. He began walking down the driveway.

Carole stepped inside and called, 'Police!' several times.

There was a faint industrial tang, as if someone had been busy with the disinfectant, and Carole's mind went to body fluids.

The house didn't look burgled. No graffiti tags on the nice clean walls. Nobody had taken a dump on the polished floorboards, which happened far more often than she would have thought possible before joining the police force.

'Police!' she called again.

She was standing in a small sitting room, with deep red walls, squishy armchairs and a fireplace with an empty grate. Framed pictures of theatre productions were everywhere, walls of fame dedicated to one person.

She walked down the hall and out into the combined kitchen/ living area. Even though nothing much had changed since she was last here, other than a body being removed, the house already had a neglected feel, as if it were a forlorn pet pining for its owner. Vanessa had been dead for little more than a week but standing here it felt much longer.

An enormous window on the back wall took in neighbouring tall trees, though probably a few were missing since the storm. There was a lovely view down the hill, across the river, into a patchwork of fields and then to the mountains in the distance.

A discordant scratching sound came from behind her and Carole whirled around, her hand automatically going for her gun.

It was a bird, a noisy miner, dark head, yellow splashed around the eyes, its feet scrabbling against the glass. It shot her a beady look and then kept pecking at the cobwebs, wings a controlled flutter.

Carole wanted to laugh but then she heard another sound, hesitant but unmistakable. Footsteps were coming up the stairs.

It was probably Billy, but she kept her hand on her holster all the same.

A face appeared around the corner, flushed, anxious.

It was the woman who'd given a reading at the church the day before. Carole went through the virtual Filofax in her head and came up with Frankie Birnam, teacher out at St Brigid's.

'Only me,' Frankie said, cheeks pink as though she'd run a marathon. She was carrying a handbag with a manila folder sticking out of it. 'You gave me such a fright that I almost called the police.'

'I identified myself several times,' Carole said.

'Sorry, had earbuds in. Always complaining about the kids doing it and then I'm as bad.' She talked so quickly that her words practically ran together and Carole was almost certain it was a lie. 'Miss Helen asked me to come and pick up a few things for her.'

'You have a key to the place?'

'Danny – that's my son – watered Vanessa's plants when she was away for a few weeks last year.' She gave a nervous laugh.

'You seem a bit flustered,' Carole said.

'Being here all alone, I got the jitters. I tell myself that I'm not a superstitious person and yet . . . it's just a bit creepy.'

There was a noise from downstairs which sounded like something falling over.

'All alone?'

'Other than Mer, of course . . .' Frankie amended. 'I asked her to come with me.' The pink on the woman's face deepened into red blotches.

Carole would have thought that dissembling was part of a teacher's skill set and yet this woman did it badly. Why pretend she was alone?

Frankie went to the stairs and called out, 'Mer, it's time to go.'

A second pair of footsteps now. Mer Davis appeared with wet hair and exuding a strong smell of chlorine.

'Oh, hi,' she said, seeming far more at ease than her friend, even though her hands were wedged into her tracksuit pockets as if someone had glued them there.

'Early start for you both,' Carole said. It wasn't a question but one lay beneath the surface of the statement.

'Morning swim,' Mer answered, sauntering into the middle of the room. 'Did wonders for my hangover.'

This one would have no problem with lying, Carole guessed; no doubt she was far more practised at it.

'But now I'm starving,' said Mer with a grin. 'We should get some Macca's on the way home, Frankie.'

'What did you come for?' Carole asked.

At this Frankie blushed so hard that Carole could almost feel the heat rising off her. The woman turned and gave Mer an exasperated look. Mer sighed and pulled out her hand.

There was a stunning square-cut emerald ring on her fourth finger. The stone was the size of Carole's thumbnail, sitting on a thin gold band, held in place by four little gold prongs.

'Vanessa's mother, Miss Helen, asked us to come and get it for her,' Frankie explained, as Mer said, 'I was only trying it on and then it got stuck.'

Mer's finger was looking as red as Frankie's concerned face.

'We've tried twisting it,' Frankie explained, 'but the setting feels loose and we didn't want to break it.'

'That looks very valuable,' Carole said. 'You shouldn't have tried it on.'

'Well, I know that now.'

'Run it under cold water,' Carole instructed. 'That should bring the swelling of your finger down enough.'

'I've already tried that,' protested Mer.

'Use dishwashing liquid and once it's off bring that ring straight back to me.'

'All right, all right.'

'I'm going to have to verify that you had permission to be here,' Carole told Frankie.

'What?' The woman looked horrified. 'You don't think we were stealing it?'

'There were reports of a prowler and a break-in.'

'But Helen's an old woman and sometimes gets confused,' Frankie said.

Carole was liking the sound of this less and less. 'Wait here.'

She walked down the stairs and opened the back door. Billy was over by the side fence, peering into Lonnie Langridge's backyard. His torch was sitting on the outside table, nowhere near him.

'Excellent backup, constable,' Carole said sarcastically.

'Saw Mer and Frankie through the window,' he told her. 'Knew it wasn't a problem.'

There was plenty Carole could say to this but now was not the time. 'I want you to call Beth Fettling and ask if she can come around straight away to clear something up.'

It was more than twenty minutes before Beth got there, looking gaunt in denim overalls and a faded bandana.

'Is everything all right?' she asked, looking at the three women sitting around the table, an emerald ring lying next to the fruit bowl.

'I believe your aunt asked these two women to pick up this ring for her,' Carole said, handing it to her.

'Not me,' said Mer. 'I was dragged here,' and at the same time Frankie said, 'Helen didn't want to bother you with it, Beth, so she asked me to fetch it for her.'

Beth looked at the ring then gave a tired smile. 'Was she trying to keep it a secret from Mum?'

Frankie looked uncomfortable but nodded.

'The ring's a fake,' Beth said. 'Original setting so it still looks good, but Vee hocked the stone years ago. Aunty Helen would be devastated if she knew, because that's one of the few pieces her mother had. When I think about how much money Vee made over the years, and how little she had to show for it . . .' She sighed. 'If it wasn't for the Palais, she would have been penniless.'

Carole noticed that the blotches on Frankie's neck pulsed red again as she gave a slight shake of her head in disagreement, but she didn't say anything.

'Well, that's sorted,' Carole said. To Beth she added, 'Sorry to call you out so early on a Saturday.'

'If that's all, I'll head off. Saturdays are busy at the academy.'

'That's fine,' answered Carole. 'I'll make sure the place is properly locked up and then drop the spare key back in Lonnie Langridge's letterbox.'

She held out her hand and Frankie reluctantly handed over a disco ball key ring. 'But you should arrange to have this place emptied soon. The whole town knows it's vacant, and it might prove too much of a temptation for some.'

'It is on my list,' said Beth.

Carole watched as the three women walked up the dark hall and out the front door. Frankie's handbag was jammed under her armpit, she noticed, as if she were worried that someone might try to snatch it from her. There was something about the woman that didn't quite make sense, a thread that needed to be pulled, but then Carole was getting that same sort of feeling about Vanessa's death in general.

She found Billy sitting outside in the sun, scrolling on his phone. 'False alarm,' she said.

'Knew it,' he replied, standing up.

'Seeing we're already here, let's have a bit of a look around.'

Billy checked the time on his phone, shrugged and followed Carole as she returned to the house, but then hung back at the door, as though reluctant to go further.

'Isn't a bedroom downstairs a bit unusual?' asked Carole, opening the door into the next room.

'It was originally a sitting room,' said Billy. 'Think Vanessa might have wanted the privacy, what with Janet across the road.'

'It does have a nice view of the back garden,' conceded Carole. She closed the door and then tried the switch over the stairs, but no light came on. 'Electricity still off?'

Billy took a few steps forward and flicked the switch in Vanessa's bedroom. 'This one's fine.'

Carole asked for his torch and directed it at the ceiling of the stairwell. She kept it trained there, looking hard before saying, 'There's no light bulb in the socket.'

'Didn't notice that the other day,' Billy admitted. 'Assumed it was because the tree had taken out the power lines.'

Carole continued to stare up at it.

'And this is where the body was.' A circle of light from her torch illuminated the tiles at the bottom of the stairs. There was a stain and the grout was discoloured. 'What were your first impressions when you found her?'

Billy swallowed hard. 'I guess that it all made sense. There was a bucket on the stairs, the spilt water and Vanessa's body at the bottom.'

'Telling you a story,' Carole said. She moved her torch up again, a faint wobbly circle climbing the wall until it reached the ceiling. 'Now what does a missing light bulb tell you?'

Billy moved to stand next to Carole.

'Come on,' she coaxed. 'Tell me what you think.' She'd put money on Billy being one of the kids in school who prayed not to be called on and then inevitably stumbled through the wrong answer if he was.

He stared up at the socket desperately as if trying to come up with something.

'Umm . . . firstly, they keep saying those LED lights last for years, so it's not good that it needs replacing.'

'Keep going,' she encouraged.

'I've got a couple of lights high up in the ceiling since we did our extension. That would be a tricky light to fix, especially when you live alone, because it's above the stairs. Maybe Vanessa had one of those stick things you can use to take out light bulbs. I've got one myself. Saw it advertised online. Got this suction thing on the end of them. Find it a bit fiddly, to be honest. I usually put it off until there's two or three that need doing. When one goes, another's not far behind, like they're going out in sympathy.'

'Do you ever take out a bulb and not replace it?'

Billy shook his head. 'Then you've got to get the stick out twice, and that's annoying because it's in pieces and you have to put it together.'

'Interesting,' said Carole, and she wasn't being sarcastic like she had been earlier. 'Are any of the other lights out?'

They spent the next few minutes turning on and off every other light in the house.

'So every other fancy LED light seems to be working,' said Carole. They were back at the bottom of the stairs, looking up at the empty light socket. 'Only the one over the stairs that Vanessa fell down is out.'

'Isn't that the point, though?' said Billy. 'She fell down the stairs because it was dark.'

'You've had a few drinks.' Carole had checked through the cupboards when they were waiting for Beth but hadn't found any alcohol at all; another strange fact to add to the rest of them. 'You've taken a sleeping pill, and you're woken by the storm.' She pointed to the bedroom. 'A little confused and groggy, but you hear something or remember you've left a window open, whatever, so you get up. You walk up the stairs, missing the bucket on the way. You go around the house and then head back down the stairs with no light, trip, fall and knock yourself out on the tiles. Just a terrible accident.'

'Like the coroner said,' Billy agreed.

But one of the reasons the coroner had said that was because there was no sign of forced entry – which wasn't that strong an indication if there were plenty of spare keys floating around.

'What if it wasn't Vanessa who took out the light bulb?' asked Carole. 'Let's assume for a moment that she was murdered and the murderer took it out. Why would they?'

'To explain why she tripped, why she didn't see the bucket.'

'Yes!' said Carole, and Billy beamed in relief. 'And also because there was something else they didn't want others to see, something else that was missing. It's rained on and off since Vanessa died. If there was a leak, by rights these stairs should be drowning in water, but there are no water stains on the floor and none on the ceiling.'

She shone the torch high over the stairs. There was no discolouration on the cream ceiling. 'Where's the leak?'

Billy swore. 'I should have spotted that. We've got stains in our bedroom from when the gutters overflowed during the storm and water came cascading down the walls. Tracey's been at me to take annual leave to paint over them.'

Carole hadn't met Tracey but had already heard a lot about her. She tried to direct the conversation away from Billy's bedroom. 'The killer wasn't to know that the electricity would go off, so they took out the light bulb, ensuring it would be dark, hoping no one would notice. Tells you a lot about the killer.'

'That they're handy with light bulbs,' said Billy, 'because those sticks are never as easy to use as it says on the YouTube clip.'

Carole made sure the doors and windows were locked securely and then she rang the doorbell at Lonnie's gate.

There was no answer.

'I'll drop off the key to Barton Langridge later on,' she said. She was beginning to appreciate how difficult it would be to reopen an investigation into Vanessa's death. To start telling people that they hadn't done their jobs properly, that the coroner had got it wrong, when she had only just arrived in town, wasn't the smartest thing to do. To accuse the local politician of murder on the strength of a missing light bulb and a bottle of wine would be career suicide. She needed much more before she even discussed it with anyone other than Billy. All she had was breadcrumbs, and who knew where they would lead next?

CHAPTER 8

Frankie gripped the steering wheel, taking a few deep breaths.

'That was so stressful,' she said. 'I can't believe that policewoman thought we were stealing from Vanessa's house.'

'*You* were stressed,' exclaimed Mer. 'I've got figs shoved in my bra and was petrified Carole was going to frisk us.'

Frankie turned to her, scandalised. 'You stole Vanessa's figs?'

'They're almost eight dollars a pop! Would you prefer they went all mouldy and Miss Helen had to deal with that?'

'When did you do it?'

'You popped to the loo and Carole was in the kitchen going through the cupboards. She was looking for something but she didn't seem to find it. There was barely anything worth taking. I'd already checked the fridge, too. No spare bottles of French champagne, no caviar.'

'Thank god for that or Joe would be having to bail us both out this morning for burglary.' She shook her head and then started the engine.

'You worry too much,' said Mer. 'Beth's got the ring and it was a fake anyway. Everything turned out all right in the end.'

Frankie wasn't so sure about that. Mer had been too busy checking out Vanessa's wardrobe and trying on her wigs to be much help looking for the ring. Frankie, diligently opening one drawer after another, had been confronted with a froth of lace and lingerie in one with a set of handcuffs, saucily fluffy, next to a half-used tube of lubricant and a vibrator. It had felt like she was a voyeur, pawing over someone else's secrets. Red-faced, she had slammed the drawer shut. Vanessa's sex life was absolutely none of her business.

But that hadn't been the worst of it. While Mer had been in the bathroom trying to get the ring off, she was replacing the contents of that final drawer, which included a buff-coloured manila folder with a piece of paper poking out. She had opened it up to put the paper back in place when she saw it was a letter from a solicitor in the next town. A typewritten *Dear Mrs Langridge* had been crossed out and replaced with a fountain pen slash in blue ink, *Dear Lonnie* scrawled beside it.

She hadn't meant to read it but words jumped out at her. Rifling through the other pages in the manila folder, she found the rest of the correspondence. That had been the moment when she heard someone call 'Police!' at the front door and Mer came rushing out of the bathroom, the ring still stuck, and a panicking Frankie had shoved the documents into her bag instead of back in the drawer. She had thought she'd get a chance to replace the folder, but then

Carole had confiscated her key and escorted her and Mer off the premises.

How she wished she had not seen those documents.

Still, she wasn't sure she should leave the folder for someone else to stumble across. It was a landmine. Vanessa had never said anything to her about it, which made it a secret, maybe even from her own family. People said you couldn't keep secrets in a place like Welcome, but Frankie knew that was rubbish. You might not be able to have a private life in Welcome, but you could still have secrets. She often had to handle sensitive information at work, things that were confidential about students, their families, sometimes even other teachers. Court orders. Medical diagnoses. Family disputes. At school there were clear procedures to follow. Chains of command. Times when you needed to disclose and times when you didn't. Frankie knew how to be discreet, understood the importance of it. She needed time to work out what, if anything, she should do, but she knew she couldn't breathe a word of it to Mer. If she told her best friend what she had found, the entire supermarket would know on Monday.

There was a ding on her phone. It was Ollie asking if today's soccer match was home or away.

White shorts, she texted back.

There was a dancing three dots in reply. *I can't find my socks.*

Ask Dad.

'I think I'll head out to the farm after I've checked in at home,' she said, deciding it right then. It had been ages since she had visited and she always did her best thinking out there.

Another ding. Now it was Joe. *Ollie can't find his socks.*

Laundry basket.

She checked the street, indicated and started to drive down the hill back towards Mer's car at the pool. Surely she'd be okay to drive by now.

'I always thought I'd love to live by myself,' said Mer. 'No one to please, organise things the way you want. But what if I collapse at the bottom of the stairs? Who would find me?'

'Your place doesn't have stairs,' said Frankie.

'Shannon says she wants to live in Sicily and Ky has started to spend nights with his girlfriend who hates me. He won't remember to check up on his mother.'

'You might meet the man of your dreams,' said Frankie, slowing at the give way sign before accelerating again.

'More like have a heart attack and die. No one will find my body for days. I'll be slowly rotting and decaying. You know if you leave a corpse long enough blood starts running out of the orifices.'

'That is not going to happen to you,' said Frankie.

'It could.' Mer flicked her head emphatically. 'And you should care, because you'll be the person who finds me, half-eaten by my cat.'

Mer was actually allergic to cats, which made this unlikely.

'If Shannon goes to Sicily and Ky moves out and you haven't found the man of your dreams, you can live with me. We will be decomposing ladies on the couch together.'

Mer brightened. 'What about Joe?'

'I'll sort out Joe,' Frankie assured her, knowing he'd have a heart attack at the thought of Mer living with them.

Mer gave a dazzling smile. 'How about I come out to the farm with you, show you how we've started organising Alice's stuff?'

Frankie had been putting off going through her mother's belongings for reasons she couldn't quite articulate. Grief, perhaps.

The finality of it. Not wanting her mother's life to be reduced to some old dresses and the entire back catalogue of *Women's Weekly*.

'No,' she said. 'You should get some sleep. I'll do it myself.'

'Sure,' said Mer, unconcerned. 'Give Des a big kiss from me and tell him my air conditioner is playing up again.'

No one answered Frankie when she 'helloed' as she hung her bag on the peg at the back door of her house. Joe and Ollie would have headed out to soccer and Danny was probably still asleep. There were breakfast dishes out on the table, a snail's trail of spilt milk leading to a clump of cereal next to Ollie's placemat. More plates piled up in the sink and a dishwasher to unpack. She'd leave that for Ollie when he got home.

Moving on autopilot, Frankie quickly cleared the table, picking up Ollie's schoolbag and putting it next to hers. Ollie's violin was on the floor, next to where Joe had left this week's newspapers. The papers went in the recycling. The violin was returned to its case and propped against the wall. Turning on the hot water tap in the kitchen to rinse the plates, she heard a shout of protest. Danny had made it to the shower.

'Sorry,' she called.

There was no reply.

Heading into the living room, Frankie found a load of clean laundry dumped on the couch, no doubt in the hunt for socks, and began to fold it, all the while thinking about those damn documents. Should she ring Beth about them?

Danny's school shirts were at the bottom of the pile. Pulling them out, Frankie assessed them critically. If they were hung up in his wardrobe now, she might get away without ironing. Grabbing them, some undies and a couple of t-shirts, she walked down the hall and past the bathroom, where Danny was still in the shower. He would stay there until the hot water ran out.

His bedroom was dark, blinds drawn, smelling of teenage boy with top notes of deodorant and a hint of sourness at its heart. There was the whiff of dog, too, because Danny let them sleep on his bed sometimes even though they weren't supposed to be allowed in bedrooms. The bed was unmade and clothes, dirty and clean, strewn over the floor. Occasionally, Frankie would relent and tidy up for him, but today was not that day.

She put the clothes on the bed and pulled back the curtains, light spilling in to highlight the mess. It took a few heaves to open the window for fresh air and it immediately threatened to shut again. The sash cords needed replacing. She'd ask her dad about it next time he was over for dinner.

There were a couple of milk-smeared glasses with Milo dregs at the bottom sitting on the wooden desk next to the old chest of drawers, a relic from her childhood. The middle drawer jutted out like a protruding lip. Frankie pushed but it wouldn't close. Something was jammed inside. Yanking it back open, she scrabbled through the tangle of t-shirts to find a jumper stuck up the back. Red-and-blue-striped, it was too small for Danny now but would be perfect for Ollie after a good wash.

The drawer required an expert wiggle to shut it, the runners having warped over the years. Frankie smoothed the rest of the contents to make sure nothing else was going to get jammed, and in the process found a box of condoms.

She had just picked it up when she heard Danny say, 'Mum! What are you doing in here?'

He was standing in the doorway, dripping wet, a towel around his waist.

Frankie stared at her sixteen-year-old son.

Danny went straight to shouting. 'Why are you going through my stuff?'

'I didn't mean to—'

'What's going on?'

Now Joe was standing behind Danny, and for good measure Ollie, in a pristine black-and-white football kit, also stuck his head around the door.

'Mum sneaked in here and—'

'I wasn't sneaking.' Frankie held up her hands, appealing to Joe, and then realised she was still holding the condoms, so quickly shoved them under Danny's school shirts.

Joe immediately turned to Ollie. 'Go find your mouthguard and wait for me in the car.'

'Can I play *Legend of Zelda*?' bargained Ollie.

'Go!' said Joe, placing his hands on Ollie's shoulders to guide him forcibly out the door.

'Danny . . .' Frankie began, not quite knowing what the rest of the sentence was going to be.

'Can I at least put some clothes on?' Danny walked past her, grabbing his dressing-gown off the floor.

'Why do you have condoms in your drawer?' she asked. She tried to keep any hint of judgement from her tone, make it more a casual enquiry. If she weren't so surprised, she might have managed it.

Danny glanced over at his father, eyebrows raised.

Joe came into the room, shutting the door behind him, and approached her with his palms raised, like he was negotiating a hostage situation, and Frankie realised he was not surprised.

'You knew?'

Danny stood there with a strange expression on his face, as though he was embarrassed for her.

'Joe, is that right?'

Her husband stood there saying nothing, which was as good as saying everything. Identical hangdog expressions on their faces. There was something secret between them that she had been excluded from.

'I bought them,' said Joe.

A hard lump settled in Frankie's throat. She was the stick-in-the-mud, the uncool parent, the one from whom things were kept. Never mind she was trained to deal with teenagers, spent her entire working life with them and had actually given birth to this particular teenager.

'You shouldn't have gone through my stuff.' Danny was still upset.

The situation was being recast as if she were in the wrong and something broke inside Frankie.

'I'm sorry,' she said, feeling that if this went on for much longer she might start crying, though she didn't really know why. She turned and walked out.

In the living room, Ollie had not found his mouthguard but was wholly absorbed in choosing armour. Frankie stood there staring at the back of his head. Four years. Four years before Oliver too became a stranger – unless he couldn't find his socks. She tried to remember the last time Danny had asked for help and couldn't.

Joe headed into Oliver's bedroom and noisily looked for a mouthguard. Frankie grabbed her bag and went outside to the car, only to find she was parked in.

She sat on the front verandah and waited, staring at the Japanese maple in the garden. It had been battered by the storm and lost the uppermost part of its crown. Des had warned her that the tree could have been fundamentally weakened, that more bits might fall down, and he'd warned the boys not to play under it for a while.

Was she overreacting? Mer would probably have given Ky a high five for being proactive about protection.

Frankie tried to remember what it was like when she was sixteen. For most of that summer, the one where Vanessa was off auditioning to be the nation's sweetheart, Frankie and Mer sunbathed at the pool. Mer was taking a temporary break from training because of the shoulder injury that would eventually stop her competing. Frankie was happy to keep her company, surreptitiously watching Joe Birnam, who had started working there as a lifeguard. It was a time of being self-conscious about sprouting breasts and ensuring legs were always shaved, life a strange mixture of boredom and longing, flaunting and awkwardness.

The front door banged and Joe came out holding a cup in his hand, tea bag still in, which was how she liked it. A peace offering.

They looked alike, Danny and Joe. Her son might have inherited her dark, unruly curls, but the rest came from his father. Joe was wearing his weekend uniform of sweatshirt, jeans and sneakers. This had been his weekend wear for as long as Frankie had known him. His hair was greyer now. It made him look distinguished.

'Were you going to tell me?' Did being excluded hurt more than the actual discovery of the condoms? Perhaps.

He at least had the decency to look sheepish. 'I thought it was the right time. That you'd prefer he had them.'

'Has he been having sex?'

'If you'd looked more closely, you would have seen the pack was unopened.'

There was a battle in Frankie's chest between upset and relief. She breathed deeply and the lump in her throat melted. 'We should both talk to him about respectful relationships and enthusiastic consent. There are pamphlets we could get him to read. I've done workshops on this exact subject.'

As a parent, she had always tried to be approachable, open to any questions her children might want to ask.

'Just what every teenage boy needs: a seminar on safe sex delivered by his mother. And I'd like to think that I'm capable of talking to my own son, even if I haven't earnt professional development points on the topic. It came up and I did what was appropriate. It really isn't that big a deal.'

Maybe Joe was just a better parent of teenage boys than she was.

She thought of Danny talking to Brianna and Jaz after the funeral. She couldn't imagine him being interested in Jaz, but Brianna was a possibility.

'Brianna Sharrah is my student,' she reminded him. 'That's who's involved, isn't it?'

Joe made a face like he wasn't sure. 'This is a teacher thing?'

'It complicates the situation.'

'Maybe that's why Danny asked me specifically not to talk to you about it.'

That stung.

Joe shrugged as though he didn't like telling her, but there it was. 'Did you talk to your mother about sex when you were Danny's age?'

'That's not fair.'

'I had the crudest of instructions handed down to me from my brothers and yet we managed to work it out.'

'We were older.'

Joe laughed, nudged her with his elbow. 'Not by much.'

The first time was in Mer's bedroom on a weekend that Mer's parents were away, a fact Frankie had kept from Alice and Des. Far more experienced than she was, Joe took it slowly. The exquisite shock of kissing with his body on top of her was so overwhelming that she barely noticed his gentle fumbling. His fingers and mouth seemed to be everywhere until she felt like her skin was on fire and she didn't want to be gentle anymore and it was up to Joe to be sensible and make sure they used a condom.

Unfortunately, someone had spotted Joe leaving Mer's in the middle of the night. Frankie knew she was in trouble when both parents picked her up the next morning, a time when Des would usually be out checking fences, dams and livestock. Alice's lips were pressed tight and yet she was the one who did all the talking on that awful trip home. Her main concern seemed to be what the neighbours would think, even though the Rivetts were two hills away and blissfully unaware that Frankie Patchett had lost her virginity.

Des drove them home, saying nothing as Alice delivered the sentence. Frankie was only allowed to leave the property to go to school, and she was not allowed to have Meredith Davis out to stay again. As far as Alice was concerned, Meredith was to blame for all of this; Joe was not mentioned by name.

It was only after Alice had left the car in a furious huff to go inside that Des had turned around and asked if Frankie was all right. She was crying by now.

'That boy didn't hurt you, did he, love? Didn't make you do something you didn't want to?'

Frankie just beamed at her father through her tears. Her heart was already dancing on the highwire of love.

It was so long ago and yet here they were, still together. Leaning sideways, she rested her head on Joe's shoulder. He put an arm around her waist, dropped a kiss on her hair. Danny was a good person and Joe was a good father. She could trust them both to do the right thing.

'You left so early. Where were you this morning?' Joe asked.

She considered telling him about all the crazy things that had happened, including her run-in with that new policewoman, but then thought better of it. Joe just about tolerated Mer for her sake, but he had never really liked Vanessa, making excuses to disappear whenever she came over.

If she told him what had happened that morning, then she'd also have to tell him about the documents currently sitting in her bag, and she just wasn't ready to do that. Those documents suggested that there was a lot Frankie hadn't known about Vanessa.

CHAPTER 9

T he gate was open when Frankie turned off the road. That was a punishable offence when she was a child, like for any farm kid. Not that there was much livestock to worry about. Without Nate to help anymore, Des had downsized. All he had now were fifty sheep and one prize ram, and they were safely up in the paddocks on the hill. There were still Alice's hens, of course, next to the house.

Frankie drove through the gate, then got out and closed it behind her. The engine muttered as the car lumbered up the hill. The rain had left even bigger potholes. Any more and you'd need a four-wheel drive to get through or have to leave the car at the gate and walk in. Wood ducks spread out along the track and she slowed to crawling pace. One darted out in front before changing its mind and retracing its steps. Frankie didn't drive on until it was safely back in the grass.

When she was growing up, this farm had run substantial cattle and sheep, and had the ability to do so again, but it was too much work for one person. Des had been approached to sell but he was holding on to the land in case one of his grandsons wanted to take it over. Ollie seemed the most likely prospect. The fact that Frankie had turned into a 'townie' and, even worse, married an indoor man, who only used his hands to type on a computer, had been an unspoken disappointment that weighed heavily. She had tried to explain what a communications consultant did to her father several times but it had never made sense to Des.

The road divided, the lower track leading through the bush to the river. The ground would be marshland after all the rain, perfect for getting your car bogged. Frankie turned instead towards the house that sat below the peak. The hill had been cleared more than a hundred years ago, exposing a rolling slope that saw plenty of sun. There was an orchard of fruit trees, twiggy knots standing ready for the next season like a row of soldiers.

A mob of kangaroos, not quite wild but definitely not tame, sat on the lawn. These would be mostly female. The males tended to wander, coming back to the group for breeding in summer. Sentinels stood on their hind legs, watching as her car trundled past, while others lounged. Any threat – the beep of a horn, the tractor starting or another loud noise – and they would be bounding over fences and off into the bush.

Ollie loved seeing the joeys in summer. Frankie couldn't bring herself to tell him that only half of them would survive the winter, fewer if it was a cold one. He had wanted to hand-rear one, but Des explained that those with no fear of humans could be the most dangerous of all. He knew of dogs that had been killed by alpha males, lured into dams to be drowned or disembowelled with a kick from their feet.

That was what you learnt growing up on a farm. Out here there was little room for sentimentality. Even her father, one of the kindest men she knew, was prepared to shoot anything that was a threat to his flock, whether it be wild dogs or pigs or snakes. He never liked doing it, but he didn't flinch from the task.

Frankie drove past the new tin shed, large and squat, and then the older one, wooden slats with so many gaps you could see clear through to the other side. She parked next to the trees near the back door, green grenades of lemons peeking out between the leaves.

Des appeared in the doorway of the house, mobile phone in hand.

'You've had a haircut,' Frankie said, getting out of the car, slinging her bag over her shoulder. 'It looks really good.'

Normally Des came back from the barber's looking like a shorn lamb. This was more than a pass with the clippers, though. Shaping was involved, graded from the sides to the top, as if someone had put real thought into it. It made him look different and, for a second, Frankie missed the old Des. Hugging him, she stood back to inspect it closely. Was that aftershave she could smell? 'Tony's upped his game.'

'Didn't go to Tony,' said Des, face colouring underneath the farmer's tan. 'Mer told me about this new fella in town, on Howick Street.' He ran a hand across his hair like he was still getting used to it.

It was all beard maintenance and pomades there. Danny had nearly talked her into taking him but then she'd seen the prices.

'Got a shave as well. Hot towels were involved.'

Her father was wearing the dark blue jumper Frankie had bought him for Christmas. His pants were ironed and good boots polished. Not the usual muddy work boots, faded collared shirt and old blue jeans that he'd wear for a morning of chipping weeds or jumping on the quad bike to check fences.

'Were you going somewhere?'

'Can't a man look smart for his own daughter?' Des asked.

'You didn't know I was coming.' Frankie was getting suspicious now.

'Might look in at the golf club later on. A couple of old-timers wanted to get together for some beers.'

This was unlike Des as well.

'Now is Mer not with you?' His face lit up with genuine pleasure when he said her name.

Frankie shook her head. 'I thought I'd come out to go through some of Mum's things,' she said. 'But there's something serious I wanted to talk to you about first.'

Her father's face, craggy and lined as a walnut shell, sagged with concern, and in that instant he was old again.

'Ollie and Danny are fine,' she assured him.

Des's shoulders relaxed.

'And Joe is as well, you'll be pleased to know.'

Des gave her an innocent look, like he had no idea what she was talking about. 'Let's put the kettle on.'

An eastern spinebill hovered around her mother's geraniums, darting back and forth. Nearby, Patch, the collie, lay untroubled, sprawled across the outside table next to his water bowl. Des had trained him to lie up high, safe from snakes, in the warmer months. The dog sat up in eager anticipation, but when Des walked inside he slumped back down. Patch was getting old, like her dogs, like her father.

Inside, Frankie noted that the linoleum floor had been swept, the breakfast dishes were washed and drying in the rack by the sink, and the tea towel was neatly folded, hanging off the oven rail.

There was no sign of the pieces of oily machinery that usually cluttered the kitchen table.

'You're just in time for morning tea,' said Des. 'I've got some lamingtons.'

A clear plastic container sat on the counter with a big 'reduced' sticker stuck to the side.

Frankie laughed. 'Stale lamingtons.' Her father never could resist a bargain.

'That's so Mer can get them past Sue.' There was admiration in his voice.

Frankie felt a pang. She had arrived empty-handed, unless you counted dilemmas, whereas Mer was bringing him cakes.

'I'll risk it,' she said, suddenly hungry.

'Take a seat,' Des replied. 'I'll get it sorted.'

The kitchen had always been her mother's domain, with Des busy working outside or tinkering in the shed. Sitting here, Frankie had the feeling that if she turned her head quickly enough, she would catch sight of her mother, arms in the sink washing the dishes, stirring dinner on the stove, but when she did, it was only Des, getting out the mugs, putting the lamingtons on a plate.

As he brought over the teas, steam rising off them, he started talking about Mer again. 'She's done good work, divided it into what can be donated and what to keep. Been out here so often I've half a mind to tell her to move in.'

The words hit Frankie awkwardly, and perhaps because she had just been confronted by her son's sexuality, her mind shifted a gear and she looked at her father in a different light. Here he was, almost eighty years old, with a fancy new haircut, in his good clothes, gate open, spring in his step, looking like he was anticipating an arrival or on his way to meet someone. You didn't need a new haircut for the bar flies at the golf club. Was the someone Mer?

No, that was impossible. His daughter's best friend! He had known her since she was in high school.

But, then, you did hear of widowers rebounding with much younger women. Des didn't really get the opportunity to meet new people, certainly not women of his own age, and there was Mer, who would flirt with a telegraph pole to pass the time.

'That's nice of her.' Frankie tried to keep her voice even. 'But I think Mum would prefer that a family member went through her things.'

Des gave her a questioning look as he sat down across from her, but then he said slowly, 'You're probably right.'

'There was a big turnout at Vanessa's funeral,' she told him, to change the subject.

'Did your reading go well?'

'Cried the whole way through it.'

Des gave her a shy smile. 'Always were soft-hearted.'

Her father wrapped his battered old hands around his mug. They were as gnarled as the trees outside. There was no wedding ring on his finger, Frankie noticed. Not that he wore it often around the farm, but he should have put it on with his good clothes.

'I couldn't help but think of Mum's funeral,' she said. 'How it was just us.'

Des nodded. 'But then Alice never expected a fuss, unlike—' Rather than finish his sentence, he sipped his tea.

'Actually,' said Frankie, 'I wanted to talk to you about Vanessa. I found something at her house this morning as I was tidying up.'

Des raised his eyebrows. He was never one to offer his opinion on people – his motto was to say nothing and live a peaceful life – but

Frankie had the impression that he wasn't a fan. He had come along to the gala only because Frankie had insisted.

She pulled the manila folder from her handbag, took the documents from it and laid them flat on the kitchen table in front of him. Des lifted the one nearest to him and brought it close to his nose. He had reading glasses but rarely used them.

He frowned. 'But this is addressed to Lonnie.'

Frankie nodded, gestured for him to read on.

She had googled the solicitor's name. It was a firm based in Barralier, over half an hour away, when everyone knew that the Langridges used McCartney Law & Conveyancing in town. Des began to read the letter aloud, skipping over what was unimportant and stumbling over 'pursuant'.

'*Pursuant to your instructions, we have prepared a Deed to immediately gift the real property, referred to as the Cottage, to Vanessa Walton . . . Please also find enclosed the draft of your new will, naming Vanessa Walton as a beneficiary to your estate, entitled to receive a payment of four hundred thousand dollars . . .*'

He raised his eyes to stare at his daughter before returning to the letter: '*Please ring to make an appointment to organise signatures.*' Des carried on nonetheless, and when he'd reached the end he started again at the beginning, as if wanting to make sure of what he had read.

'Vanessa owned the Cottage when she died,' Frankie said, explaining it to herself as much as to Des. 'That would be worth at least half a million.'

Des propped an elbow on the table, covering his mouth with his hand, which was something he often did in lieu of replying.

'And she was going to be a beneficiary in Lonnie's will.'

Frankie remembered how Lonnie had sat at the front of the church yesterday, without so much as a glance over to Miss Helen. 'What if Vanessa's family doesn't know any of this? Should I tell them?'

'What do you think?' Des asked.

'I don't know.'

'Where there's money, there's trouble.'

'But there's more,' Frankie said. On the way out in the car she debated if she should even show it to him. Her father was an old man, he didn't need more worries, but if she wasn't going to involve Joe or Mer, Des was the next person she would ask for advice.

She unfolded a creased piece of paper. There was a paperclip attached, which suggested that Vanessa had kept the two documents together. She passed it to Des and watched as his face turned from puzzled to concerned.

The letters were glued across an otherwise plain sheet of paper, a mixture of magazine and newspaper cut-outs, like an old-fashioned ransom note or, she couldn't help thinking, some sort of dumb school prank. The crookedness of the letters, higgledy-piggledy across the landscape-oriented page, somehow made the threat more menacing, and Frankie felt a creeping sense of dread just looking at it.

Leave Town Slut or Die!

Des read it and then carefully folded it up again and pushed it back across the table to her. 'Where did you find it?' he asked, and Frankie described how the day had unfolded, from Mr Poole's phone call to her sitting with her father now at the kitchen table. Des said nothing but just listened, sipping his tea.

'Why didn't Vanessa tell me about the threat?' Frankie asked, and then she was suddenly struck by a memory. 'You know, I think she might have wanted to.'

'What?' Des gave her a sharp look.

Vanessa had stood in the doorway to Frankie's office the afternoon she died, holding a piece of paper in her hand.

I need to talk to you about something delicate.

'I thought it was about the invoices and Ivan. I told her I was too busy. I asked her if we could we do it another time.'

'You don't know for sure it was about that note.'

'Well, I know about the note now,' Frankie replied. 'What do you think I should do?'

Des shook his head, and in that moment she realised that she hadn't come out to the farm for her father's advice; rather, it was her mother who she wanted. Alice Patchett always had plenty to say, whether you wanted to hear it or not.

'I miss Mum,' she said.

A quick nod of agreement from Des, and they sat there sipping their tea. Frankie finished her lamington in silence, showering the table with desiccated coconut. Des handed her his, said he wasn't that fond of shop-bought food really, found the cake a bit too sweet.

'I miss her at every meal,' he said.

The first time they had spoken to Alice on the iPad, she had been propped up in bed wheezing. The next time she was prone, lying on her stomach, her face losing shape and definition, the iPad beside the bed. Right before she was intubated they said goodbye, sitting in Frankie's living room. Ollie cried and Danny wore an expression that suggested he wanted to cry too but had forgotten how. Joe took them outside while Des and Frankie sat there, holding each other's hand tight. Frankie did most of the talking, even though the face no longer resembled her mother, the hair long and ragged and her eyes closed, so they weren't even sure she was listening.

Stumbling a little, Des told her about the sheep and her hens. How broccoli would be going into the garden soon. The word 'love' wasn't spoken but it was implied in every utterance. All three of them were scared, Alice most of all. She had barely seen the inside of a hospital since Frankie was born, had been as fit as a flea, except for her asthma, but none of that mattered in the end.

They had met with one of the nurses afterwards. Her name was Anne Costello and she had been with Alice when she died. Frankie hadn't wanted Des to go, afraid he might catch COVID again, but her father had stood firm. They were at a park near the hospital. Minus the gown, gloves, mask, shield and hairnet, the nurse was a different person. She had recognised them both because of the photos Frankie had sent in. Anne had wanted them to know that she had been their proxy, holding Alice's hand until the end, but she wasn't sure she was going to be a nurse for too much longer. She couldn't stand the protesters and all their freedoms; the way people wore masks on chins; talking to patients' relatives who refused to believe COVID even existed. Even her own mother was starting to spout nonsense, sending her ridiculous conspiracy videos.

'I'm boiling with rage all the time,' she said, and to Frankie's surprise Des had reached out and held Anne's hand as she told them more of what it had been like. She watched as two strangers in the park tried to find comfort in a world that seemed to have gone mad.

'Have you told anyone else about this letter?' Des asked Frankie now.

She shook her head.

'Don't. You know how this town gossips. Helen's lost her only child. There's nothing worse than that. To put doubts in her mind, to make her wonder if it wasn't an accident, would be cruel. Let that poor woman grieve in peace.'

'You think it was an accident?'

'I'm certain whoever wrote this note had nothing to do with Vanessa's death.' There was an assurance in his voice that was so familiar, and Frankie recalled sitting at this same table years ago and Des telling them it would be raining by morning or that there would be new lambs by the time she was home from school. He was always right.

'What about her owning the house and being in Lonnie's will? This morning Beth told me Vanessa was practically broke.'

'If she owns that house, it will be registered. The lawyers will tell the family. No need for you to get involved.'

Frankie sighed. 'That makes sense.'

Her father was silent on whether she should try to put the letter back where she found it, and Frankie didn't push.

'Have you heard how Nate is going in jail?' she asked instead.

Des stood up from the table, grabbed the plates and mugs, took them to the sink and began clattering about, washing them. There was no dishwasher here. Alice hadn't seen the point. 'Visits are still restricted,' he said. 'Mostly Gerri talks to him on the phone. Says he's struggling a bit.'

'How much longer has he got?'

'A few months.'

'He should have appealed,' Frankie said. 'We could have had a fundraiser for his legal fees. People might not have contributed like they did for the gala, but it would have been something.'

'It's the principle of it,' Des said. 'Apparently he thinks it will have a bigger impact if he serves the full sentence. Gerri's worried he might go on a hunger strike.'

Frankie shook her head. That fear completely dwarfed her worries of the morning, including whether her son was having sex.

She stood. 'All right then, show me what you've done with Mum's clothes.'

They spent the next hour going through Alice's belongings. By the end of it there were piles of clothes sitting on the bed. Frankie had to concede that mostly Mer had got it right; she only pulled out an additional cardigan and a scarf to keep. Des found cardboard boxes, filled them up and loaded it all into Frankie's car. The good stuff would go to Vinnie's, where Alice had volunteered, the not-as-good into the clothing bins in the supermarket car park.

Patch stood next to Des as she got into her car. Frankie felt a pang of guilt at leaving her father, asked what he was going to do with his day. Des was vague, talking instead about the sheep. He might take some to market this year because prices were good. Maybe he'd take Ollie with him, show him the ropes.

'How about if Ollie comes out and stays with you next weekend?' Frankie asked. He'd miss soccer but that was no loss to his team.

Des nodded and said he'd like that.

She tooted her horn and stuck an arm out of the window to wave goodbye, but as she caught sight of her father in the rear-view mirror, there was something preoccupied about his expression, shoulders hunched, and for the second time that day she wondered if he also had secrets she knew nothing about.

CHAPTER 10

Late on Monday afternoon, a white van braked violently in front of Jasmine Langridge. It was a dusty, dirty delivery workhorse. At first Jaz thought the driver might be looking for directions, asking where to leave a package or the way to reception.

Orchestra practice had run late as usual and it was almost 6 pm. Everyone else had gone home, so she stepped forward to tell him that this section of the school was already shut for the night. The cleaners, headphones on, music pumping, must have already come past, locked the back door and were now busy vacuuming the library.

Perhaps there was someone in the front office still, at the opposite side of the school. That was what she was going to say, but then the man exploded out of the van. It was the movement she saw, rather than the person making it, and her body registered trouble before her mind had snapped into gear.

He was wearing a balaclava.

Instinctively, she hooked her arm through the strap of her backpack, a muscle memory established over years of grabbing a schoolbag when heading out the door, getting in the car, sprinting for the bus.

It was a mistake.

He was closer to her now, and as she turned, already running, the bag was the first thing he grabbed, yanking her backwards.

She was pulled off balance, and scrambled to remain upright. Attempting to slip the bag off, she pushed it away, tried to do one of those magic tricks where the person is left holding the magician's cape with nothing inside it. If she had been thinking more clearly, she should have shoved it at him, surprised the man by going on the offensive. Instead, he was even closer now and, reaching out, he seized a thick fistful of her hair, pink and blonde combined, yanking it as he punched her in the stomach.

It was a shock, the brutality of hard knuckles on flesh, that brought her to her knees. She had never been punched before, never smacked, and her instinct was to cry out but she had no breath to do so.

She should have been screaming the whole time because she was infamous for never shutting up, a human loudhailer, but she didn't make a sound.

Her mouth was open, gasping for breath, but something was being pushed inside it. Material going in so far she almost gagged. More tears came to her eyes, blurring her vision, but then she realised that something had been put over her head.

She was moving now, not of her own accord. He had picked her up. By the time she thought to struggle she had already been thrown into the back of the van, hitting the metal with a terrible *thunk*.

Her forehead banged against the floor, hard enough to leave a bruise, possibly a cut.

He was beside her. She could smell him, a rank stale sweat. She kicked out, connected, heard a grunt, but he was kneeling on her back, squeezing the air out of her, and now she panicked, felt like she was choking, waiting for her dress to be pushed up, underwear yanked down.

Instead, her arms were pulled back so hard she could feel her shoulders strain and rough rope was twisted around her wrists and feet.

The door opened, slammed again, and the labouring engine was shoved into gear and they drove away.

It was too quick for anyone else to notice. She hadn't seen his face at all, hadn't heard his voice, and yet he was familiar. He might have been hanging around her stepfather's last campaign, one of those people who came in to put anonymous leaflets in letterboxes and rip down the opposition's posters in the middle of the night. Or maybe he was in construction, one of those guys who'd set fire to a shop for you.

Yes, thought Jaz, that was the story she was going to tell the police, and the consequences of what came after that burnt inside her.

CHAPTER 11

Brianna sat on the school bus on Tuesday morning, staring out the window as it wound its way through the west of the town. Kids were picked up from the new estates, then the established suburbs, before being dropping off at the primary schools and the high school, then out to St Brigid's last of all.

Brianna had complained about having to leave home before 8 am when other students, like Jaz, would still be in bed because their mothers drove them to school. Amber had pretended to get out the world's smallest violin, telling her to walk to school then, the exercise would do her good.

Brianna pulled out her phone and texted Jaz for the seventh time. The one-sided chat showed a sea of speech balloons. Was Jaz mad at her? At the wake, Jaz had come up with the idea of breaking into Roly's office to look for evidence, and Brianna had told her there was absolutely no way she was getting involved in that. Jaz hadn't seemed that bothered at the time, but then at school on Monday she had barely spoken to Brianna and had full-on ignored her at orchestra. The last time Jaz had been all secretive and scheming was about the protest at school, and that had ended up with Nate in jail. It seemed that it was always the people around Jaz who got punished, never Jaz herself.

Perhaps it wasn't anything mysterious; maybe it was just a simple ghosting. First Danny and now Jaz. At this rate Brianna wouldn't have any friends at all.

The only thing stopping Brianna from completely freaking out was that Jaz hadn't posted anything on any of the group chats last night – not that anyone else had noticed.

The bus stopped across from the park to let on a couple of year eights and Madie Fletcher, who came swaying down the bus towards her. Brianna slipped on headphones and pretended to be captivated by something out the window, so she wouldn't accidentally catch Madie's eye in a way that could be interpreted as an invitation to sit down.

'No Jaz today?' Madie asked.

Wordlessly, Brianna moved her schoolbag. Maybe she should be nicer; at least Madie wanted to talk to her.

'Perhaps Jaz's got gastro,' Madie said, answering her own question. She did that a lot, to the annoyance of those around her, including teachers. 'A kid puked in Junior Tap on Saturday.'

Madie had a part-time job at Walton's Academy and liked to talk about it as if she were teaching at Juilliard.

'Did you have to clean it up?' asked Brianna. There was not enough money in the world worth that.

'Only a little bit. Beth got her to the toilets pretty quickly.'

Brianna imagined what Jaz would say if she were sitting here and a smile flickered across her face.

'She's really grateful that I've been able to step up and take some classes myself,' Madie continued. 'It's been really busy. Mum thought they should have cancelled the classes out of respect, but I told her Vanessa would understand that the show must go on.'

Even when the show was chucking five-year-olds doing a soft-shoe shuffle to 'Uptown Funk'.

The bus went down the dip that took them under the railway tracks and they both did the customary bounce in their seats.

'Are they going to get a new teacher to replace Vanessa?'

Madie shook her head. 'She barely had anything to do with the place.'

'Her face is on the sign.'

'That doesn't mean anything. She was supposed to take my Senior Musical Theatre class but was never there. Beth's a much better teacher anyway. Everyone in the class thought so.'

Yeah, all three of them.

Madie went on talking but it was lost in the sound of brakes and girls standing up and moving forward as they arrived at school.

Brianna checked her phone one more time. Still nothing.

Jaz wasn't in maths, English or art. Brianna sat by herself for recess with a knot in her stomach. Normally, Jaz would let her know if she was sick, mostly to laugh about how she was lying on the couch binge-watching television while Brianna was stuck at school.

Geography was straight after lunch. It was the first time she had seen Mr Roland since the funeral. He strode into the room with his stupid clipboard under his arm, pre-emptively grumbling about students being late, wearing the usual uptight suit. He was the only teacher to wear a tie. It was an old-school Mickey Mouse one that was probably a Christmas present a million years ago, but Jaz always said he wore it to make up for not having a sense of humour.

Was it possible that he'd killed Vanessa?

Mr Roland called the roll, which all teachers were technically supposed to do after lunch, though no one ever bothered other than Ivan the Terrible. The automated system had been down all week, so he ticked off each girl's name on his clipboard. There was a hesitation when he got to Jaz's. Brianna expected him to look up and glare at them, demanding to be told where she was or tell them yet again that when he was a student he had a perfect attendance record, but instead he went on to the next name.

Did he know where Jaz was?

The low-level anxiety she had been experiencing all day began to swell and she could barely listen to Roly's monologue on the importance of water catchment areas. Instead, she thought about how Jaz had got in trouble yesterday at orchestra because her phone had gone off in the middle of the concerto they were rehearsing. A phone ringing was the only thing guaranteed to send Mr Selwyn psycho. He made Jaz put it in her locker where it was supposed to be. When she came back into the room, Brianna gave her a sympathetic smile which she was certain Jaz saw though she didn't respond.

Amber, Brianna's mother, was one of the last parents to arrive for pick-up from orchestra because Mr Selwyn was notorious for finishing late. 'I'm not going to sit out here waiting because that dickhead can't read a clock,' she had told Brianna on more than one occasion.

As Brianna put her trumpet in the boot of the car, she had been surprised to see Jaz standing by herself, leaning against the school wall, near where the driveway looped around, minus her flute, because Sheridan Langridge always got there early to pick up her daughter. Driving out of the car park, her mother glanced back in the rear-view mirror, saw Jaz standing alone and immediately did a U-turn. Her mother didn't like Jaz, but it went against some ingrained mothers' code not to check that kids had a way of getting home.

As they pulled up beside her, Jaz came over, stuck her head in and said something about her mother being on the way, giving Brianna a quick wink at the same time as if everything was under control. That made Brianna guess she was planning to catch up with Lennox, who must be finishing up his shift at the supermarket.

'Thanks for the offer,' Jaz said in a polite formal voice that wasn't like her at all. It might have fooled most adults, but not Brianna's mother, even if she had missed the wink.

'Have you two been fighting?' Amber asked before they even got out of the grounds.

Brianna shook her head.

'Something's up with that girl,' she said. 'I've never known her to be well-mannered.'

Now, a day later, sitting in geography, Brianna decided she agreed with her mother. Something about that interaction troubled her. What if that wink hadn't been about Lennox? What if it meant something completely different, like she was waiting around to break into Mr Roland's office? What if he had caught her doing it? She could be suspended or even expelled.

Brianna stared up at Roly and suddenly she couldn't just sit in his class anymore. She needed to check her phone to see if Jaz had texted her back yet. Putting her arm across her stomach and hunching slightly, she asked to be excused. Like every other male teacher, Ivan the Terrible never asked questions when it seemed like periods were the answer, even when girls appeared to be having periods every other week.

She checked her own locker first. There were messages on her phone but nothing from Jaz. If Jaz had been expelled, then her locker would have been cleared out. It was only three up from hers and Brianna knew the code. Checking that no one was around, she opened it.

It looked completely normal. There was the usual mess of folders, paper, a block of chocolate, a box of tampons . . . but then she noticed a familiar brand-new phone.

Jaz's mobile had not left the locker since yesterday.

Almost on autopilot, Brianna shut and locked the door and started walking without quite knowing where she was going. The only thing she was sure of was that she was not going back to any classroom with Ivan Roland in it.

By the time she was halfway down the corridor she was running, not even certain where to, but when she reached the end she realised there was only one person she could tell.

Mrs Birnam fussed around with the kettle, while Brianna sat and sniffled a little into a tissue. Stupid 'go girl' posters were stuck on the walls of her office. 'Impossible' spelt 'I'm possible' and 'Women belong in all the places where decisions are made'. Jaz would have a field day if she were here.

'Start at the beginning,' Mrs Birnam said, as she walked back behind her desk with two cups of herbal tea. Chamomile made Brianna want to throw up so she didn't touch it. Instead, she began with what happened the night of the party at Jaz's house and stopped when she got to the bit about what was in the envelope. Rubbing her knuckles against her mouth, she tried to choose her words carefully. It was hard looking at Mrs Birnam's concerned face.

'What did the note say?' Mrs Birnam asked, and there was a spikiness to her voice. 'Exact words if you can remember them.'

That bit was easy. When Brianna said them out loud, Mrs Birnam gasped, and then clamped her mouth shut. She reached across the desk, passing Brianna a tissue.

Brianna balled it in her hand, not even attempting to wipe the tears away.

'Jaz thinks Vanessa was murdered because of that note.'

She waited for Mrs Birnam to tell her that she was being ridiculous or melodramatic. That this was all in their heads.

'Did she have any thoughts on who might be responsible?'

Brianna bit the inside of her cheek, closed her eyes, took a breath. She really didn't want to answer that, but what if it turned out to be important?

'She thought . . .' She dropped her head and stared at her hands.

'What did she think?' Mrs Birnam's voice was sharp and insistent.

'Mr Roland,' Brianna whispered.

'*Ivan Roland?*'

Brianna nodded.

Mrs Birnam pushed her chair back. There were questions imprinted on her face and Brianna braced herself for them, but she was still surprised by what Mrs Birnam asked first.

'Was Danny involved in all of this?'

Brianna shook her head. It wouldn't be right to get Danny in trouble. He was probably already going to be angry with her for going to his mother. She didn't want to make it worse.

Mrs Birnam stood up. 'You head back to class while I check in with the counselling team and the office to see if there has been any contact with Jasmine or her family,' she said.

Brianna shook her head. 'I won't do that.'

Mrs Birnam became impatient. 'It's almost bell time. Your teacher will be wondering what happened to you.'

'It's Mr Roland,' Brianna answered. 'If he finds out what I've told you . . .'

Mrs Birnam seemed to sag, as if the consequences of what she had just learnt were too heavy to bear. She stared at Brianna as though she didn't know quite what to do and Brianna began to panic. Mrs Birnam was supposed to take charge and make everything okay.

'All right,' Mrs Birnam said. 'You stay here while I go.'

'Can't I come with you?' Brianna asked.

'No. Lock the door and don't open it to anyone other than me.'

Brianna nodded. It wasn't much but it was a plan.

Mrs Birnam rushed out the door, and Brianna quickly locked it behind her.

CHAPTER 12

The night had been freezing and the day was little better. Jaz had never been so cold. Her breath came out in cottony puffs as if her body warmth was slowly leaching away. She huddled on a thin mattress, curled up in a ball.

At least she wasn't tied up or blindfolded. When the tape had been ripped off she tried not to cry, even though it felt as if her mouth would come off as well.

Jaz analysed the parts of her that were sore: wrists raw and scratched from being tied; shoulders strained; one hip and elbow bruised from lying on the floor.

There was a window, a small one. A faded curtain over it that was half off the rails, letting in a grimy greyness – not sunlight exactly, just less dark.

Her leg cramped. She forced herself to straighten, pushing her legs out in front of her. Her feet were ice, barely capable of moving.

Wiggling her toes was slow and painful. How many more days would pass like this? How would it end? Questions hung in the air around her.

Time dripped slowly and yet it felt like no time at all since she was standing out the back of the school. How could both things be true?

Perhaps she should see this as penance for what happened to Nate. She had often tried to imagine what jail was like. Completely different from this, she guessed. Nate's life would be predictable by now, a monotonous routine of waking up, eating, exercising, sleeping. Right now she wouldn't mind it. She had written letters saying sorry but not spelling out exactly why in case someone else read them. He would understand what she meant.

She wondered if someone had told him Vanessa was dead or maybe he saw some of the reporting on TV. It had been Jaz's idea that Vanessa could stand as an independent candidate against her stepfather so she could go to Parliament and get these stupid protest laws reversed. Vanessa had laughed when Jaz told her, said teal wasn't her colour, but then she started to come around to the idea. Jaz had written about that to Nate as well.

Nate refused to put her on his visitor list. Lennox told her that only Nate's mother, Gerri, went each month. Gerri had been kind to her when Jaz had gone out to their farm. She had served apple cake and left them alone to organise their protest. Her mother would have hovered nervously like a moth around a light, offering cups of tea and drinks and annoying everyone.

Gerri had looked very different when Jaz saw her last. Her hair was limp, her face inscrutable. The only reason she agreed to see Jaz was because Lennox took her along. No tea or homemade cake this time. Jaz sat at the same kitchen table, now sticky with neglect, and told her about Vanessa and what they intended to do.

The woman had stared at a spot over her shoulder, and when Jaz turned around to see what she was looking at, a clock or a picture, there was nothing there. She wasn't even sure Gerri was listening to her, but when Jaz came to a spluttering halt, the woman told Jaz she could do whatever she wanted, it was nothing to do with her or Nate.

Jaz slunk out the door, ashamed.

In the corner a handful of plastic bottles of water had been left on the floor. She had greedily gulped one whole bottle down, trying to soothe her throat, but from now on she would need to be more careful and ration it. There was a bucket for peeing in. She squatted over it, felt the warm piss gush out of her and splash down on the metal. It was like she was an animal marking its territory. Disgusted, she stood up so abruptly she almost knocked the bucket over. It didn't smell too bad yet but that might change, depending on what else she needed to do in there.

Outside, the bush was far noisier than she had ever realised, full of creaks and rustling. A clattering over her head and her heart leapt. Feet scampered across the low roof. There was the scratch of claws. Perhaps a possum with a low dirty-old-man rasp – or worse: a rat.

She shouldn't have thought of rats, because now she could imagine them creeping out from the cupboards or under the floor, looking for food. There were some apples and muesli bars lying about. She had barely eaten anything.

Other animals and creepy-crawlies occurred to her. There were wild dogs and feral pigs around here. Lennox told stories about how Nate hated to kill any living thing but needed to protect his livestock. Lennox had no such qualms. He loved shooting.

It was a bit early in the year for snakes or mosquitoes, though there would be plagues of mozzies in summer. She had already seen spiders. Great hairy huntsmen the size of your palm, bigger if you measured from tip to tip, lurking in the corners, watching the newcomer who had invaded their space. Cockroaches might have scuttled over her in the night and instinctively she drew her legs to her chest again, curling up in the sleeping bag with the broken zipper.

Jaz was beginning to realise that her passion for the environment was mostly theoretical. Yes, she wanted to save the world, but not for spiders and rats, and it must be a world that still had electric blankets and central heating. Right now she'd happily burn all the coal in Australia to get warm. She tried to imagine that she was in her own bed, in her own house, that if she shouted out her mother would appear in an instant, but it was too hard.

When the police finally arrived, she planned to give them the name Ivan Roland first. Let them join the dots. The satisfaction of that almost warmed her.

Closing her eyes, she tried to doze.

The important thing was to have a plan and follow it.

Luckily, that was exactly what she was doing.

CHAPTER 13

Carole spent the shift doing welfare checks on farms with Angie Rosso, who was not in a good mood.

'I'm still having to rebuild trust,' Angie explained bluntly. 'Ever since that prosecution of Nate Rivett, doors slam in my face. No one thinks he should have ended up in jail, especially now his mum is alone on their farm.'

Carole had heard there'd been a kerfuffle in the courtroom with activists. One glued themselves to the magistrate's bench and the proceedings had to be halted and moved to another court. None of this had helped the defendant; a furious magistrate had ended up sentencing him to one year in prison and issued a large fine.

'Jail time does seem a bit rough,' Carole said.

'He had priors for a protest that shut down the bridge, and according to Troy he resisted arrest.' There was a sceptical undercurrent to her tone but Carole decided against pursuing the subject. Conversation in the car turned to livestock theft and risk mitigation as they drove along potholed and patched back roads. Angie gave the country hello, fingers raised off the steering wheel, to every ute, SUV and 4WD going past. She got acknowledgements back from most of them, which Carole took to be a promising sign that relationships could be rebuilt.

Angie dropped her back to the station before the end of shift. Billy was at his desk, looking serious. He'd spent the day chasing a kangaroo up the main street of the town, blocking off traffic for a bit. What had started as a joke turned into a farce as the poor bugger, spooked by the car horns and a couple of stray dogs, got banged about pretty badly. In the end they had it cornered, bleeding badly, out the back of a local accountancy firm. Billy couldn't bring himself to shoot it, even though it meant putting an end to the animal's pain, so Troy had to do it.

'He's as weak as piss, sarge,' Troy complained, not really caring if Billy heard or not, which made him a pillock in Carole's book. 'I don't like shooting things either.'

Carole suspected the grumbling was because of the extra paperwork that went with discharging a weapon. She looked at Billy, who was hunched over his desk, talking on the phone. Something about it felt a little off and she walked over to check on him.

'What's up, Skip?' she joked, but Billy didn't laugh.

'There's been a development,' he said.

Frankie Birnam started talking the moment Carole and Billy walked in her back door, making up for the fact that the girl sitting in the corner of the kitchen was completely silent, arms folded, doleful eyes larger than those of the spaniels who padded in, hopeful that someone might give them treats.

The girl was Brianna Sharrah, the other waiter from Vanessa Walton's wake. Her mother, Amber, sat across the table from her, shorter, wider, with the same dark hair and features, looking furious. It was clear that words had been said before they arrived and, if Carole guessed it right, would continue once they'd left.

Billy wrote as Brianna spoke. Amber punctuated her daughter's words with barely controlled sighs, glaring at the girl. The note was produced and then bagged as evidence. Frankie gave them Jaz's mobile phone, saying she had found it in Jaz's locker. She confirmed that Jaz had not been at school that day and said that she had rung and left messages on both Barton and Sheridan Langridge's phones, asking them to contact the school about her absence. As far as she knew, neither of them had called back yet.

Carole asked questions about Jaz's friends and who she might be likely to get help from if she were in trouble. Billy shifted unhappily in his seat when Lennox Rivett was mentioned but he wrote it down all the same. Carole recognised the last name.

Frankie hovered in the background like an overzealous dragonfly, as if not sure that she should be there but wanting to stay all the same. Carole watched her out of the corner of her eye, saw how she picked up her mug of tea, *World's Best Mum* emblazoned on it, cradling it between her hands like she was starved for warmth. The woman had behaved quite peculiarly at Vanessa's house and now she was so tense she practically vibrated like a tuning fork.

Carole told Brianna that she had done the right thing reporting the disappearance, that she was a good friend to Jaz; she was saying it as much for the mother as for the girl. Brianna kept rubbing her knuckles against her mouth, as if she was already regretting talking.

'Please call me if you remember anything else, and let us know if Jasmine contacts you,' Carole said, pushing her card across the table. 'She won't be in any trouble. We want to know that she's safe, that's all.'

Brianna nodded, not even catching Carole's eye.

Frankie walked them outside, her handbag over her shoulder like she was about to leave as well, but she stopped them in front of a row of hydrangea bushes. They could hear that inside Amber was giving Brianna a piece of her mind.

Frankie winced. 'I'll give them a moment to themselves before I go back in. Amber's got a good heart really.'

'I'm sure,' said Carole.

'Jaz will be okay, won't she?' Frankie asked, seeming to direct this more to Billy than to Carole.

'We don't even know she's missing yet,' said Carole calmly. 'What's the girl like?'

'She's not the type to get into a stranger's car or fall in love online, if that's what you're asking,' said Frankie. 'Sometimes she gets caught up in flights of fancy and drama, but no one would talk her into anything.' The woman's head darted around as if she heard a noise. One of the dogs appeared, stared at them and then mooched away. 'It's the fact that she doesn't have her phone that worries me,' she said. 'Most kids her age would need surgery to be separated from it, my own son Danny included.'

About that they could agree.

'Is Danny friends with Jaz?' Carole asked.

A look of regret crossed Frankie's face, as if she wished she hadn't mentioned her son.

'He knows her,' she said. 'But no more than any other kid in town.'

Carole noted her defensiveness and wondered at it.

'You had the threatening letter in your possession when I saw you on Saturday morning but you didn't think to tell me about it and instead removed it from the property.'

Frankie breathed out as if she had been expecting this. 'Just panicked, I guess,' she said. 'The coroner had said the death wasn't suspicious and Dad thought it would upset Miss Helen, so I thought it best just to leave well enough alone. But when Brianna came to me, I rang Billy straight away. Is it possible that Vanessa's death wasn't an accident?'

'Our priority is finding Jasmine,' Carole said firmly. There was no need for anyone's imagination to run away with them but it was interesting that Frankie's mind had jumped to that particular question.

'Technically I should have followed school processes when Brianna made her allegations, but given who Jaz thought might be involved, well . . . it made things difficult. I have informed our principal. She'll be getting in touch with Barton and Sherry to offer support.'

Carole nodded, but Frankie hadn't finished. Another big breath before a gush of words came tumbling out.

'I found something else at Vanessa's. There was a document attached to that letter. I didn't think it was appropriate to mention it in front of Brianna.' Frankie delved into her bag and brought out an envelope. 'Lonnie Langridge was changing her will to include Vanessa and had already given her the title to the Cottage. I wasn't intending to do anything with it, didn't think it was my business, but now . . .'

Carole gave her a hard stare as Billy produced another evidence bag, put the paper inside it.

'It's such a relief to give it to you, I've been so worried about what to do. Thanks so much for coming over so quickly to deal with this.'

Frankie deposited a quick kiss on Billy's cheek. He blushed deeply at this while Carole made a note to mention to her constable that kisses from potential witnesses were problematic. No, not a witness – Frankie Birnam's behaviour made her more a person of interest.

There was the sound of raised voices from inside.

'We'll be in touch,' she said briskly. 'Now, you'd better go back in there before we have to arrest Amber for assault.'

There was no one at Jaz's home, nor at Langridge House, which they tried for good measure. They stood at the gate, heavy wood with great iron hinges and thick bands so that it looked like a treasure chest, and pressed the button on the side of it.

'You ever been inside?' Carole asked.

Billy explained that hardly anyone ever went in, except for the housekeeper, the family and, possibly, Vanessa. Lonnie Langridge was famously reclusive, which was why it had caused a stir to see her at the funeral, and Carole remembered how people had hushed and stared when Lonnie had walked in with her son.

Enormous trees stood behind the gate, a creeper tangled in them. The whole thing felt like a Gothic fairy tale in which girls went missing.

'Looks like the entire Langridge family has disappeared.'

'Maybe Lonnie's in there and not answering,' said Billy. 'I could jump the side fence.'

The two of them walked down the driveway and looked at the broken palings. 'Before we go in all guns blazing and give the old woman a heart attack, we'll try the electoral office,' said Carole. 'Surely they know where Welcome's elected representative is supposed to be.'

Billy turned, stared at the Cottage. 'Do you think Vanessa could have been murdered?'

'How much is that house worth?'

'Half a mil easy,' said Billy. 'Maybe more in this market.'

'I've known kids to be stabbed for a pair of sneakers, but at this stage, we're keeping an open mind, constable.'

Walking back to the car, she glanced across to Janet Ross's house, half-expecting her to come barrelling out to talk to them, but there was no curtain twitching. It looked like she wasn't home either.

The electoral office was in the main shopping strip, a block south of the supermarket, sandwiched between a twenty-four-hour gym and an Indian restaurant. Carole knew they were in the right place because a giant faded Barton Langridge was in the window, or at least a large picture of him was, looking a good deal happier than Carole had ever seen the real one.

'They say he owns this entire building,' Billy said, turning off the engine. 'Or, rather, some Cayman Islands shell company does.'

'Taxpayers picking up the rent – no wonder he's smiling.'

'It's a wonder more people don't lob a brick through the window,' said Billy, looking half-tempted.

'We're still a democracy. You don't have to vote for him.' Carole pushed open the front door, which had another, smaller Barton on it with the word 'Welcome' beside him.

'I didn't,' muttered Billy, walking in behind her.

There were even more Barton Langridges inside the office, so many there should have been a collective noun for them. A carton of Bartons, a parliament of Langridges. Everywhere Carole looked there were dazzlingly white smiles and hard pebble eyes. It was a bit like a cult with one Glorious Leader.

A woman sitting behind the glass divider looked up at them.

'Sorry, we're actually shut for the day,' she began, but then stopped. 'Carole! I wondered when I'd catch up with you again. How have you settled in?'

It was the aide from the helicopter, looking far more comfortable on the ground than she had in the air. Carole searched for a name.

'Not bad, Yvette. Still looking for a house. Let me know if you hear of any.'

'Take a number and join the queue if you want to complain about the lack of rentals. If I had a dollar for every complaint I get about them, I'd own as many properties as the boss. You're lucky you caught me. Wouldn't normally be here this late but a constituent is using the photocopier for a newsletter.'

Yvette was more talkative than at their last encounter, so Carole cut in by pointing over to a life-size cardboard cut-out of Barton Langridge wearing a high-vis vest over his suit and tie. 'We'd like to talk to the original, if he's about.'

Yvette made a disappointed face. 'On personal leave. I don't think he's in town. You can leave a message unless it's something I can help with.'

'Actually,' said Carole, 'I think you can.'

She said no thanks to coffee or tea as she settled into a chair in Barton's office and Billy headed to the bathroom.

'So you haven't found a new job yet?' she asked.

Yvette laughed. 'I was finishing up an application while no one else was around. Interview next week for a comms job in the private sector.'

'I'll keep my fingers crossed for you.'

Carole looked around the room. There was only one Barton in here, this one a poster on the wall. He stood with a thin blonde woman whom Carole presumed was his wife, and a younger Jaz, probably around ten years old, with braces and freckles. The slogan read *Barton Langridge – Your Welcome*. Whoever came up with that slogan needed to be shot.

'That was from his first campaign,' Yvette explained.

'And that's his daughter?' asked Carole.

'Jasmine – stepdaughter,' corrected Yvette, as Carole had expected her to do. 'The only time she featured officially in his political campaign. Now we think of her as part of the opposition, specialising in not-so-friendly fire. I'm expecting for the next election there will be someone in head office working full-time at keeping her on a leash.'

'The Nate Rivett incident?'

Yvette nodded. 'He was the only one charged but I expect Jaz was in it up to her eyeballs. I wouldn't be surprised if she was the reason that Nate knew about Barton and the Premier doing the policy announcement about cyber education for kids out at St B's in the first place. It was supposed to reassure parents that someone was doing something about stuff no one over forty really understands.'

Carole, who was well beyond forty, could only agree. 'What actually happened?'

'The plan was to hide backstage in the school hall and burst out at the right time with a garbage bag full of seaweed to throw over him and the Premier. I think there was milk involved, too.'

'Seaweed? Milk?'

Billy opened the door and sat down beside Carole.

'Regenerative farming, climate emissions and targets for the farm sector, take your pick. Anyway, the seaweed stunk; a teacher found it and called the cops. Billy was one of the first responders.'

Something complicated slid across Billy's face but he didn't say anything.

'So,' said Carole, returning to the task at hand, 'we're here because of Jaz. She wasn't at school today and none of her friends have heard from her since late yesterday.'

'Police doing truancy checks?' asked Yvette, surprised.

'Checking she's okay,' said Carole. 'Messages have been left for her parents but we haven't heard back. Do you know if she's with them?'

Yvette looked from one to the other, shook her head. 'Barton's taken his mum off to some fancy health retreat. I think Sherry went as well. He didn't mention anything about Jaz going, but it's possible.'

'Lonnie hasn't left town for as long as I can remember,' Billy said.

'She's been very upset about Vanessa's death and Barton thought she needed a break,' Yvette said.

Or was it a convenient way to get a potential witness out of the town?

'You know, Vanessa came in here the afternoon she died,' Yvette continued. 'Of course, she was supposed to be public enemy number one, but Lina, that's Barton's PA, was thrilled. She took a selfie with her.'

'Enemy?' asked Carole.

Billy quietly pulled out his notebook.

'She'd been threatening to run against Barton as an independent next election. He was furious. With her profile she could be a real threat. But apparently she was raising the white flag, came in with a fancy bottle of French champagne as a peace offering. Barton wasn't here anyway – he was guest speaker at the Chamber of Commerce and Industry drinks – so she left a message saying she needed to talk, that she had some proposal to put to him.'

'Did Lina let him know?'

'Sent him a text straight away, but later he said he didn't see it because he left the drinks and drove straight to the city. By the time he got back to town, she was dead.'

Except he was seen hammering on Vanessa's front door.

'Was he always planning to head to the city that night? I mean, what with the storm coming . . .'

Yvette checked her phone. 'Nothing official in his calendar. Perhaps it was personal – though like I said to you at the time, I just presumed he did it in order to make a grand entrance.'

Billy's face looked like he had further questions but Carole wanted time to think. There was a lot here to unpack and their priority in the first instance was to find Jaz.

Yvette scribbled down a number and then pushed the piece of paper over to Carole. 'We call this the bat phone, only to be used in case of emergencies, but I suppose it's all right to give it to you in these circumstances.'

Carole and Billy stood to leave.

As Carole opened the office door, she saw a familiar-looking person, pear-shaped in a blue-patterned caftan, a battered felt hat on her head, standing at the photocopier.

Janet Ross turned and gave her a cheery wave.

'Hello, sergeant, had an interesting chat?'

'What exactly are you up to?' Carole wouldn't put it past her to have held a glass up to the door to eavesdrop.

Janet's light blue eyes opened wide, supposedly to give her an innocent look but instead she looked cunning. 'Printing off the Neighbourhood Watch newsletter for this month.'

'Well, I won't interrupt you,' said Carole. She thanked Yvette, told her they could find their own way out, walked through the office, opened the front door and headed out into the street, all the while counting in her head. She had reached sixteen and the car when she heard a 'Yoohoo!' coming from behind them.

Janet was hobbling down the stairs, cane in one hand, as fast as possible.

'You ring Langridge,' Carole said to Billy, passing him the piece of paper. 'I'll handle this.'

Billy nodded and got into the car.

She watched as the older woman came towards her, slowing down once she realised Carole was prepared to wait.

'Any developments?' Janet asked, slightly breathless.

'I'm here on an unrelated matter.'

'So you've done nothing about Vanessa.'

Carole bristled. 'I'm still working two hours after my shift was supposed to finish. I'm busy doing my job.'

'But Vanessa was here that very afternoon asking for Barton.'

'With the champagne bottle found later in her house with only her fingerprints on it. The one you thought was very suspicious given Vanessa was supposedly a teetotaller.' Carole had checked the brief sent to the coroner's office.

Janet fluttered her hand as though that was of no consequence. 'Now, what did she want to talk to Barton about? I quizzed Yvette and then I rang Lina, the usual receptionist – now she's a mad keen VeeBee.'

'A what?'

Janet shot her an impatient look of oh-do-keep-up. 'That's what her fans call themselves. Anyway, she said Vanessa was all smiles and charm, acting like she won the lottery.'

No wonder she was excited. She had been gifted a very expensive house and who knew what else from a vulnerable old woman. Was she rubbing Barton's nose in it?

'Now, Lonnie had given her the house, of course, so that might have been the reason.'

'How did you know about that?' demanded Carole.

'I happened to notice she was getting all these solicitor's letters in her letterbox when I was delivering Neighbourhood Watch pamphlets.'

'Did you go through Vanessa's mail? That's an offence.'

Janet drew herself up to her full not-very-considerable height and put her hand to her chest, a look of mock outrage on her face. 'What a terrible accusation, sergeant. What happened was that a few days before Vanessa died, one of her letters was mistakenly put in my box, and I opened it purely by accident. Luckily, I always steam my correspondence open, so I was able to glue it shut. It was a letter from McCartney Law & Conveyancing on behalf of Barton, threatening legal action over the transfer of title. A scandal, of course, but it did make sense of something.'

'What?'

'Well, a few months previous – it was the morning of my life drawing class, but that had been cancelled at the last minute because the water pipe burst –'

Carole suppressed the urge to yell at the old woman to get to the point.

'– I found my Roger in his best jacket and slacks, sucking in his stomach in front of the mirror. He quite jumped when he realised I was there and muttered something about golf and lunch. Golf in his good tweed, I ask you. Best nip problems in the bud discreetly, so I told him I'd put on my nicest frock and come along, just for fun. And who should be waiting for him in a private booth?'

'Vanessa.'

'All about money, of course, because why else would a famous actress be interested in a sixty-seven-year-old man with a dicky ticker and rising cholesterol? Please don't think too harshly of him. Roger's kind and easily flattered. Now, she was delighted that I had joined them, of course, didn't mention anything about her business proposal, but I found out all about it afterwards. Emails had been exchanged, and there were coffee dates at the Cottage that I had missed. All to discuss a wonderful opportunity to invest in a new one-woman show on Broadway, if you don't mind.'

'How much?'

'A mere thirty thousand dollars. Of course, I put her straight, explained that despite appearances to the contrary, our only asset was our house and Roger was on a part pension. Poor Roger was never invited for coffee again but Lonnie Langridge was often over there.'

'You should have told me this before,' Carole said.

Janet's eyes gleamed. 'So you are opening an investigation into Vanessa's death?'

'I'm making inquiries. You are to stop whatever amateur sleuthing activities you are undertaking and let me handle it.'

'I told you last time, sergeant, that it takes a town—'

Carole interrupted. 'I suspect there are a few more important things you could have told me last time. Anything else I should know now?'

The look she received in reply was somewhere between withering and pity. 'You open that investigation first and then I might have some information for you.'

Behind her, Billy opened the car door and called out, 'Sarge!'

'I'm sure our paths will cross again,' Carole said.

'I'll make sure they do,' Janet replied.

Billy stood next to the car. Carole could tell by his expression the news wasn't good.

'Got it confirmed,' he said. 'Jasmine's missing.'

CHAPTER 14

Mer always took her breaks in the nook out the back of the supermarket, next to a sickly looking tree, chain-link fence and the
van. It was the best place to hide from Sue and get a few minutes'
peace from all the bloody customers wanting to tell her how much
they loved Vanessa Walton and wasn't the funeral wonderful.

If that wasn't bad enough, she had such a pounding headache
from last night's drinking that all she wanted to do was say she was
sick, go home and crawl into bed, but Sue would never buy that.
The next best thing was to sit outside in the nook for a few minutes
and drink water until she was missed.

She'd been hitting the bottle hard for a few days now, ever since
Vanessa's funeral, and although she'd tell anyone who asked that the
two things were completely unrelated, that wasn't the truth. But Mer
didn't want to drop stones into that particular lake. Instead, she'd

keep on drinking herself to sleep each night until whatever it was that she was feeling reeled away of its own accord.

The bottle of water was three-quarters empty when Billy and that new cop, Carole, pulled into the car park. Billy was an occasional smoker, always claiming it was the last one. She thought about waving him over to complain about her sore head and bitch about work, but maybe that wasn't a good idea in front of his new boss, who might take a dim view of slicing salami while under the influence. Besides, both of them looked grim and they headed straight into Gino's office, which meant they weren't here to grab lunch from the deli.

Someone was in trouble. Mer hoped it wasn't her.

There were a couple of messages on her phone. Shannon was going out tonight and Ky was staying over at his girlfriend's. Another night of just her and the whiskey bottle. Perhaps she might nick something substantial food-wise from the cabinet when Sue wasn't looking; you shouldn't drink on an empty stomach.

Luckily only Chip was in the deli when she went back inside fifteen minutes after her break was supposed to finish. Chip and a tempting array of salmon quiches, but Sue arrived before she had the time to pinch one and pop it in her bag.

'Those dishes need washing now,' Sue snapped.

It was the usual pile of dirty white containers from the deli window. Washing them up was technically everyone's job, but was traditionally left, along with the worst chores, to the school-aged casuals who came in for the afternoon rush.

'And that bin's full,' Sue continued. It was clear she was in a vile mood.

Maybe she had a hangover as well.

Mer specialised in giving the bin a shake to settle the contents and then shoving more in, but there was no point arguing with Sue when she was like this. Bitches get stuff done, but at the end of the day they were still bitches.

'I'll take it out,' she said.

Mer grabbed the bin and dragged it down the length of the counter, out through the plastic see-through doors and into the back. There was no load boy to empty it into the industrial bins.

'Where's Lennox?' Mer asked Gino.

He was looking pretty miserable as well, climbing off a forklift as a truck left the loading bay.

'He's gone home.'

'Is he coming back?' she asked. 'Sue wanted this bin emptied.'

Gino sighed and picked up the bin himself.

Rita, who supervised the registers, provided the missing details. Standing next to Mer with a tea towel for camouflage, she explained that the police had come in wanting to talk to Lennox and told him to come to the station in the morning to 'assist' in their inquiries. Lennox went off sick after they left.

'Their inquiries about what?' Mer asked.

'Bet it's drugs,' said Rita.

But then Sue turned up again, saying there were customers waiting at the front, so why were people standing around gossiping to each other.

Rita disappeared and Mer kept on doing the dishes in between serving pensioners and mothers with screaming toddlers. She didn't mind Lennox. He had a cocky kind of strut that she appreciated and he was good for a laugh. As she had scored some dope off him a couple of times, it wouldn't be right for her to get all puritanical now if he'd got into trouble for selling, and luckily he was the type to keep his mouth shut. But she had been bothered by some of the people who came in asking after him. There had been a few with a real steroid bulk, an electric crackle of violence humming off them, which made her think that there might be a whole other side to Lennox and that it wasn't just dope he was supplying. She had asked him about it and he'd spun a yarn about growth opportunities and business expansion, saying he needed money to develop his empire. She told him to go watch *Breaking Bad* to see how that could turn out.

The story of what had happened got more complicated when the schoolkids came in to start their afternoon shifts. Apparently it wasn't drugs and had everything to do with the fact that Lennox had been seeing Jasmine Langridge.

'That's not a crime, surely,' said Mer. Still, local drug dealer and richest kid in town – it was a wonder the police weren't investigating Lennox's murder after Barton Langridge got his hands on him. But then the girls told her the important part: Jaz was missing.

Mer couldn't believe she was only hearing about it now. Billy's wife, Tracey Wicks, had been in this morning, and her nickname was the Great Australian Bite because of her big mouth. And why hadn't Frankie let her know? Surely she couldn't still be annoyed about the ring getting stuck on her finger or her early morning dip at the pool.

The rest of the shift was a blur of customers gossiping. At least they had a topic other than Vanessa now. Mer slowly pieced together the information. Barton and Sherry had been away but they raced back to Welcome when they heard the news. The doctor had been seen making a house call to Sherry.

'She was in hysterics,' Mer heard a customer say.

'Well I heard that Lonnie—' another began, as she put out her hand for the twelve slices of thinly cut grandmother ham that Mer had wrapped for her, but then she moved away from the counter so Mer never found out what she'd heard.

When Mer knocked off she found Sue near the roller doors, arms folded, huddled with several of the other permanents who were also finishing up for the day.

'What's going on?' Mer asked Chip.

'People moaning about how they don't want to work with Lennox anymore. They think Sue should sack him.'

Prior to this, most of them had thought Lennox was a good bloke and laughed at his jokes.

'Has he been charged?'

Chip shook his head. 'Not as far as I know. A man's going to lose his job because people are going crazy over a bloody Langridge. If it had been any other kid they wouldn't care. It's one rule for the rich in this town and crumbs for the rest of us.'

Was it crumbs that Chip meant or cinders? Mer remembered the nice insurance payout Barton got while Pete had been left with really charcoaled chicken. What was a disaster for one was a pot of gold for another.

Frankie was in the kitchen when Mer arrived at the back door with a bottle of wine in hand. It was intended as a checking-we-are-okay sort of present as well as an information-gathering exercise. Mer was still affronted that she was behind the news. She was also desperate for a glass of wine.

Ollie wandered in and out of the kitchen, claiming to be starving. The two women tried to catch up on the day's events without saying too much in front of him. Mer explained about Lennox but Frankie already knew, which was annoying.

'Patrick Selwyn is being interviewed at the station as well,' Frankie told Mer, 'because he was supposed to be supervising the girls until they were picked up from orchestra. He asked me if I thought he should call the union to get legal representation and I didn't know what to say.'

'Stove,' said Mer, pointing behind Frankie.

Frankie stopped chopping the zucchini and frantically stirred the pot with a wooden spoon. It was a meal Frankie could make with her eyes closed but Mer could see she was doing everything wrong. The temperature was too high and the curry paste kept catching on the bottom of the pan. The chilli-heat from the mixture caught in the back of Mer's throat and she started coughing.

'It's because he's gay,' Danny said, coming into the kitchen.

'There you are,' Frankie said over-brightly as she poured in the coconut milk.

'My gorgeous godson,' Mer said. She put down the knife next to the raw chicken breast on the cutting board in front of her.

Danny subjected himself to a hug.

'They're scapegoating Mr Selwyn,' he insisted, once the ordeal was over. 'The police are homophobic.'

'He hasn't been arrested,' Frankie said. 'It's because he was one of the last people to see Jaz. And while I'm sure there are problems with the police generally, this is Billy Wicks you're talking about. You know, the guy who coached Ollie in basketball. He's a very kind man.'

'Had a crush on your mum when we were at school,' piped up Mer. 'In fact, at one Blue Light Disco—'

Frankie shot her a look, all eyebrows and mouth, so Mer stopped her sentence there.

That was the thing about Frankie, always pretending to the boys that she'd never done anything silly in her entire life. What did she want on her gravestone: *Here lies Frances Birnam – she was sensible?* Why not tell them about the mad things they'd done when they were Danny's age, like the time Frankie sculled three West Coast Coolers and pashed Billy, who was crazy about her, to make Joe jealous. Let Danny see that his mum was once a teenager making dumb decisions and having a laugh with mates. Billy wasn't the smartest bloke in Welcome, but he was good and kind. He'd been devastated when he realised that Frankie was in love with Joe.

Mer glanced over at Danny, who had retreated out of the reach of hugs and was at the fridge, pulling out a tub of yoghurt.

'It's fifteen minutes till dinner,' said his mother.

'But I'm hungry now!'

'Eat at the table. I'm sick of your bedroom being a Petri dish for various experiments in mould.'

'Don't go in there then,' Danny said sulkily, but he sat at the kitchen table and made short work of the yoghurt.

Mer resumed cutting the chicken into bite-sized pieces. When she was done, Frankie picked up the chopping board, slid the chicken into the pot and stirred it into the red curry sauce.

'Kids at school talking about Jaz?' asked Mer.

'The visual?' he replied. 'Yeah, of course.'

'The visual?' Frankie echoed. Her voice sounded like she already knew she was not going to like it.

'K-pop reference,' said Mer, quite pleased with herself for knowing. 'Means best-looking person in the group. The one that gets all the attention.'

Frankie opened her mouth to protest, but Danny got in first. 'Don't blame me. She gets noticed because she's pretty, rich and her parents are important. It's how the world works, Mum.'

Were those the exact same reasons why she'd gone missing? wondered Mer.

Frankie told Danny to change out of his school uniform before dinner, and when he left the room she pulled out her phone to show Mer a photo.

'Vanessa received a threatening letter,' she said. 'Jaz and Brianna discovered it weeks ago and I found it in her house the other morning.'

'What?!' Mer stared at her friend. 'Why didn't you tell me?'

'Billy told me that there are some other aspects of Vanessa's death that they're looking into.'

Mer could only look in horror at the photo of the note.

Frankie sat down at the table. 'When I first saw it I guessed it was a prank by students, but now I'm not sure. Kids would go online these days. They're not going to bother with glue sticks and newspapers.'

'Where's the note now?' Mer demanded.

'With the police,' Frankie said. 'They're taking it seriously. I think they're wondering if it has something to do with Jaz's disappearance.'

Mer clicked off the photo, trying to work out the implications of what she had been told. She grabbed the wine bottle, opened it. Frankie passed her a glass and she splashed the wine in and then gulped it down.

Frankie's phone buzzed next to her on the table.

'Patrick's home,' she said, relieved. As she began typing a response there was the ping of another message. Frankie frowned at it, hesitated, but then she held the phone out so they could both see it. It was a video of black-and-white security footage.

'Sharon in our front office sent this to him and the police have it too,' Frankie said. 'It's from two days ago. That's out the back of school, near the staff car park.'

Mer found it hard to focus.

There was a shadowy pixelated figure standing beside the wall. Moving forward, a face became more distinct but then retreated into a grainy haze of dots.

'Is that Jaz?' asked Frankie.

It was too hard for Mer to tell. The face wasn't visible now, the head angled down, and the figure wore the same uniform as seven hundred other girls.

'That's definitely Patrick,' Mer said, pointing to another figure on the screen. Even though it was only the back of him, she recognised the way he loped, hands in pockets. There was a moment when he stopped next to the first figure, before heading away and disappearing out of shot.

A car came past. Someone stuck her head out of the passenger-side window, a glimpse of dark curly hair.

'Brianna and Amber,' Frankie said. 'They told me they stopped to ask if she wanted a lift, so it must be Jaz.'

The footage stopped then jumped forward. A second car drove past and then stopped so that the back of the car was in shot. The driver was not in the picture. The waiting figure looked up.

'Don't go, Jaz,' Mer found herself murmuring instinctively.

A man walked into the frame. They could see the back of his head.

'If only there was volume,' said Frankie.

Jaz folded her arms, changed her stance to a more defensive one.

The man had his arm outstretched, finger pointed, like he was telling her off.

'They're arguing,' said Mer, fascinated.

It ran for minutes. Jaz was giving as good as she got. The man half-turned and, for a moment, the camera captured a look of absolute fury distorting his face and then the footage ended.

'Jesus,' said Mer. 'The police need to work out who that is.'

'I know who it is,' said Frankie, her voice shaky.

Mer stared at her, wide-eyed.

'That's Ivan Roland.'

CHAPTER 15

Billy sat in the interview room, chewing mints. It helped when he was anxious. Smoking would help more, but Tracey would kill him if he started again. With the repayments for the new car, he couldn't afford it, even if he wanted to.

And he didn't.

Not really.

Lennox Rivett sat across from him. He was alone, which was a surprise. Billy had expected demands for lawyers; those were the sort of stunts Lennox usually pulled when he was brought in. This time he was quite happy to talk, sitting there with a silver stud in one ear, a thick chain around his neck and a chunky ring on his little finger. His mullet of peroxided hair was slicked back across his head and he had dark stubble across his face.

Lennox Rivett was a real effing catch.

Carole had been asking the questions and was getting exactly nowhere.

'So you were at work the afternoon Jasmine Langridge went missing,' she confirmed.

'Not just the afternoon,' said Lennox, leaning back in the seat. 'Didn't knock off until after nine that night. Gino had been at me to help reorganise the warehouse.'

'And after you finished?'

'Went home. Needed my beauty sleep after a twelve-hour day at work. I'm not a bludger, like some I could mention.'

He gave Billy a sly half-wink, as though the police kept office hours. Bastard. He didn't even seem that concerned about Jasmine being missing.

'You've been described to us as Jasmine's boyfriend.' It was Brianna who'd told them that.

A lazy grin. 'Going a bit far. I know her, that's all. She liked to come over sometimes. I'm a friendly guy. Everyone's welcome at my house.'

It would be her money that was welcome, and maybe other parts of her that Billy did not want to think about. He could feel his jaw starting to clench.

'I think she only wanted to hang out with me to wind up her old man, especially after you lot fitted up my cousin. Apparently our local member goes ape shit whenever he hears the name Rivett. I'm not expecting a dinner invite to the mansion any time soon.'

'Nate pleaded guilty to the charges,' Billy muttered.

'You probably beat the confession out of him.'

Billy, who was not a violent person by nature, felt like he wouldn't mind thumping Lennox.

'Don't know why you want to talk to me,' Lennox continued. 'The whole town's seen the footage of old Roly having a go at Jaz right before she went missing. He's the one you should be talking to – and not just about Jaz either. He's got a lot of questions to answer.'

Billy glanced over at Carole. She had been furious to discover this morning that the security footage had got out, gave them all a lecture about how to conduct investigations, but right now her face was serene. Her reading glasses had this kind of leopard print up the side. Billy wouldn't have picked that she'd wear something like that. Tracey was more a pastels-and-white-sneakers kind of person.

There was a real spark to Carole. She had a great laugh and didn't put up with crap, which was good because there was a lot of that in the job. She didn't let stress get to her, even though it had been nonstop since she arrived. First the flood, then Vanessa's death and now this. Yet looking at her now, you'd never know she was still stuck in a poky motel, living out of a suitcase.

'Do you know a young woman called Heidi Millet?' Carole asked.

Lennox, who had been swinging on two legs of his chair, jerked forward, landing with a thump.

Not so confident now.

Carole had told Billy to pull the files on girls who'd gone missing in the district recently, in case there was any link to Jaz. There had been six of them in the last five years. All but one had turned up, if not quite safe and sound, then alive at least. In Billy's experience, girls who ran away were usually escaping from something rather than heading somewhere. Heidi Millet was still missing.

'Yeah, I know Heidi,' he said. 'Know her old man, Brad, as well. The whole town does. What of it?'

Brad Millet was a drunk and a thug. Probably a client of Lennox's too.

'As you know, Heidi has been missing for six months. You were one of the last people to see her.'

'Because she came into the supermarket,' scoffed Lennox. 'Besides, she isn't missing, she's just pissed off to the city.'

'Her family hasn't heard from her in that time. Her grandmother was the one who made the report.'

'Don't try and pin that shit on me. Heidi doesn't want to be found, and if you were Brad Millet's daughter, you probably wouldn't either.'

But Lennox was rattled now; the smirk had been wiped right off his face.

'I'm not trying to pin anything on anyone,' said Carole. 'We just want to make sure that these girls are safe and well.'

What if they're not? thought Billy. Imagine if there was a serial killer on their patch and he worked on the investigation that uncovered them. That would be a hero cop move. But then he shut the thought down. Billy tried never to cross the bridge towards bad news unless he really had to. That was how he coped with the job: keeping difficult things safely tucked away in boxes.

'Thanks for coming in, Lennox,' said Carole, getting up from her chair. 'Please be in touch if you hear from Jasmine.'

Lennox stood up, swagger returning, but Billy could tell there was relief as well.

'Certainly, sergeant. Nothing I love more than talking to cops.'

Billy and Carole stood on the steps of the police station and watched Lennox get into his hotted-up Holden Kingswood, bright yellow with a thick black racing stripe and fat mag wheels. He sat there revving the engine for a bit before speeding away.

'Just the sort of fella any parent would be delighted to have their sixteen-year-old daughter involved with,' said Carole.

As a father of three girls, that got a hard agree from Billy. He snorted and felt a bit better.

'He's a walking time bomb,' said Carole. 'Even if he's not caught up in this, one day he's going to get himself into real trouble.'

If Billy was a better cop, he would have found a way to bust Lennox by now. Not so hero cop.

'So we leave him alone?' He tried not to sound too disappointed.

'An alibi that good from someone acting that bad makes me suspicious. Contact his boss and see whose idea it was for him to work back late.'

'Will do.'

'But first, go through Jasmine's phone thoroughly and see if there's anything there. Also, call the school again. I do want to talk to Ivan Roland. If he doesn't come in for an interview as soon as possible, then we'll head out there and pull him out of class. See if he likes that.'

It was a plan of attack.

Billy returned to his desk and tried Roland's mobile number. It was switched off. The school's phone just went to a message. Tracey had told him that St B's had been having tech troubles this week. He'd give it a few minutes then try again.

Welcome Council had spent over a million dollars upgrading and linking cameras in the CBD. There was even a live feed of images into the police station. When you added that to all the privately owned CCTV cameras in the town, there was probably over twenty-four hours' worth of footage to go through. He'd already scanned the train station, bus depot and school footage as well as the cameras in the soccer fields next door to St B's. If he had time later today, he would drop in to some of the places that had security cameras between the school and town, get them to sign release forms and upload what they had to the portal.

He pulled up the footage of Jasmine standing outside the school. It was low-quality vision because the school had gone for a cheap system after the seaweed incident. The footage was jumpy, occasionally blurry and pixelated, but there was something compelling about how the movement brought it all to life. Billy could play God, rewind, fast forward and pause. He watched Jasmine walk back to the school building. He guessed she'd realised she didn't have her phone, but the door was locked. There was Brianna and Amber asking her if she had a lift and, finally, Jasmine arguing with Roland. Billy tried to enhance the vision.

The interaction started mildly enough, a standard teacher telling-off, from what Billy could see, but then Jasmine started talking back. She had walked around so that she was facing the camera now. Billy slowed the footage. He mouthed the word 'Vanessa', breaking down the syllables, thinking of what shape his mouth made as he said the word. He was almost certain that Jasmine mentioned her, but whatever she had said sent Roly off his rocker. Was she accusing him of murdering Vanessa? There was finger pointing, arms thrown to the heavens and lots of shouting, but then he marched away, leaving Jasmine there. Jasmine waited a minute or so then, picking up her bag, she walked out of shot in the opposite direction. And then, as far as Billy could tell, she completely disappeared.

He scrolled through Jasmine's photos, methodically going through a million selfies. Lennox appeared in quite a few of them, which made him want to grind his teeth. Next were the messages and texts.

There was nothing on her phone to give any indication that she was planning on running away.

He tried the school again and this time Sharon in the office answered.

Afterwards, Billy immediately went to find his boss. Carole was in the meeting room on her mobile. As Billy knocked on the door and opened it, she held up a finger to stop him interrupting her from cajoling someone, calling in a favour perhaps.

Last week she had sat him down in this very same meeting room and asked if he was ambitious. What did he want from his career? No one had ever asked him that before, so he said he'd like to be famous. Carole didn't laugh at him but he felt like an idiot later on. If she asked him now, he would tell her all he wanted was Jasmine Langridge home safe, because if anything happened to Barton Langridge's stepdaughter then life for all of them would become very difficult indeed.

As she wrapped up the call, Carole gestured for him to close the door and sit down.

'Should get the analysis back on that note later today,' she said.

Billy was impressed. Normally it took weeks, and if you dared complain, you were given lectures about budgets or told scornfully that this wasn't an episode of *CSI*. If Billy had his way, that show would be cancelled.

'There's nothing of interest on her phone, sarge. The last photo on the roll was just some red Halloween costume.'

Carole nodded and then pulled off her reading glasses. 'And Roland?'

'He's on the year nine camp. They left yesterday to hike up in the mountains. Reception is poor. They're due back this afternoon.'

She shrugged. 'We still have to keep an open mind, I guess. I had plenty of teachers point a finger during my time at school and they didn't abduct anyone.'

'Sharon – she's my wife Tracey's cousin, who works in the office at St B's – told me that he insisted on going on the camp at the last moment when another teacher couldn't go, when usually he refuses to take any year nine classes and is well-known for getting out of excursions, camps and Saturday sport, even though every teacher is supposed to do their fair share. Sharon said she couldn't think of the last time he'd volunteered for anything.'

Tracey's cousin had whispered all of this to Billy from the stationery cupboard so she wasn't overheard.

'He's an awful bully, Bill,' she'd hissed. 'I've watched that footage of him with Jasmine. Ivan Roland's got something to do with the disappearance, I just know it.'

'He's trying to avoid talking to us?' Carole asked.

'Looks that way.'

Carole thought for a few minutes. 'Not sure we've got enough evidence to pull his phone records.'

'Sharon just happened to mention that his laptop was out at the school.'

'So that would be school property.'

Billy nodded.

'Tell Sharon to keep it safe and you go pick it up discreetly this afternoon.'

'I can go right now.'

Carole shook her head. 'We've been summoned to meet with the Honourable Barton Langridge to discuss the investigation. Apparently, he's not too pleased.'

Billy groaned. 'Not another dickhead.'

'How well do you know Barton?'

'We were at Welcome Primary together but then he was sent away to boarding school.' Barton was a few years older than him. At a swimming carnival, Billy had taken off his new digital watch he got for Christmas before his race and shoved it under his towel. It wasn't there when he came back. Other kids said Barton had taken it. When Billy asked, Barton pushed him over on the concrete and threatened to tell the teacher on him for making up lies.

'Old school friends then.'

'Last time I had any dealings with him was over the Nate Rivett incident.' That had been enough to last a lifetime.

'I wanted to talk to you about that,' said Carole. 'What happened with Nate's arrest?'

Billy froze. 'What do you mean?'

'Every time Nate's mentioned you clam right up.'

Billy exhaled audibly, felt a little sick. 'What happens if I tell you?'

'You should be more worried about what will happen if you don't, constable.'

Billy knew he was no match for Carole's interrogation skills and caved immediately.

'Troy and I went out to the school around half past seven in the morning. Roland was frothing at the mouth about sabotage because he'd found this garbage bag full of seaweed. The Premier was due that afternoon, so Troy and I separated to do a search of the school and I found them: Nate, Jasmine, and Vanessa Walton, all hiding in Vanessa's office with a bunch of banners. Nate fessed up right away. I knew Roly would want him charged with every possible offence under the sun and with those new protest laws he could get in real trouble.'

Billy stopped there, wondering how to say the next bit. Plenty of cops turned a blind eye when it suited them, but he suspected Carole wouldn't be at all impressed by that.

'I didn't see the harm in letting them go.' He couldn't meet her eye as he said it, turning instead to look at the first-aid poster stuck on the wall. 'Read them the riot act, of course, but then I told Jaz and Vanessa to stay where they were and come out when everyone arrived for school and blend in. Nate couldn't do that, so I looked out, saw the coast was clear, and told him to take the banners and leg it. Unfortunately, he ran into Troy, who saw things a little differently.'

He glanced over at Carole, waiting for her to say he was a bad cop. That it wasn't up to him to have an opinion on laws that were passed; he only needed to uphold them.

'And the resisting arrest?'

Billy shook his head. 'I didn't see it, but Nate's nothing like his cousin. He's a peaceful guy and sometimes Troy' – he swallowed, felt his throat tighten, but there was no going back now – 'Troy thinks climate change is a hoax. He gets quite heated about it. Says that all greenies should be thrown in jail.'

'And Nate didn't implicate the others?' she asked.

'Not a word. Didn't mention me either. He's a decent bloke, Nate, and I hear he's doing it tough at the moment.'

Carole didn't say anything for a few minutes, as if she were weighing matters carefully. 'Vanessa's dead and Jaz is missing. Nate might not be as unlucky as you think.'

CHAPTER 16

Carole looked out the car window as Billy drove through the town. He pointed out the Valhalla Bar, where things tended to get rowdy on a Saturday night, and the Chinese restaurant where they usually held their cop dinners.

'The combination Mongolian is top notch,' he told her.

Crossing the highway at the traffic lights, they drove up the hill.

'We're entering the part of town locals call "the Knot",' Billy said.

'As in "not Welcome"?' Carole guessed, beating him to the punchline.

Billy chuckled, even though he'd probably said it hundreds of times before.

Further up the hill he slowed down. 'And there it is.'

All Carole could see out her window was a tall brick wall with wrought iron. 'Better park around the corner,' she directed. 'The super made a particular point of telling me to be discreet.'

—

Standing in front of the house, Carole pressed the intercom button, leaning over to talk into the grille, but the front gate swung back noiselessly.

'Jesus,' she said, staring inside. 'It's Chateau Langridge.'

Behind the Versailles-like formal garden of tastefully manicured flowerbeds, dotted with lollipop-shaped hedges and tall cones of pruned trees, was a massive new house designed to look like it was a massive old house. There was an ornate front balcony stretching right across the first floor and more Grecian columns than was strictly necessary. Security cameras dimpled the facade.

'I'd hate to see their heating bill,' said Billy. 'Not that they need to worry about electricity prices.'

Barton Langridge stood at the front entrance (too grand to be described as a door), watching them. He was wearing shirt and trousers, a navy jumper over the top, the grown-up equivalent of a private-school uniform. His grey hair was cropped, trying to disguise the fact it was thinning. His eyebrows, dark and thick, looked as manicured as the garden. Carole suspected dye must be involved.

He reached out to shake Carole's hand, the pressure a little firmer than needed, as if to demonstrate who was really in charge here. He didn't shake Billy's.

'Come through,' he told them. 'My wife is in the sitting room.'

The hallway resembled a fancy hotel lobby, with artistically tortured flower arrangements in statement vases. Carole's footsteps rang out on the polished parquetry floor as they were ushered into a room where neutrals of every hue competed with each other to be the most tasteful. Outside the window was an enormous swimming pool, all white stone and clear water. Mosaic tiles on the wall made a kind of abstract outdoor artwork to be admired. But despite all the soft furnishings, the expensive materials, there was a sharpness to the atmosphere that couldn't be disguised.

Sheridan Langridge got up from the couch when they entered the room. She was long and elegant, from her limbs to her nose. A subtly good-looking woman, with the type of tawny blonde hair that would be almost a full-time job to maintain. Her make-up was immaculate, but behind the carefully applied mascara and perfect lipstick her eyes were hollow. Carole guessed at dark rings underneath the concealer.

Plenty of cops would judge Sheridan, finding it suspicious that someone could style their hair when their kid was missing. But Carole suspected it was her armour. That Sheridan was carrying on with the everyday rituals in the hope that the rest of her life would return to normal and her daughter would reappear. It seemed as if Sheridan Langridge was one eyeshadow palette away from a nervous breakdown and Carole felt a wave of sympathy for the woman.

'Can I offer you a drink?' asked Sheridan. 'Tea? Coffee?'

'Perhaps in a little while,' said Carole.

Cups of tea could help extend a visit if needed and it was amazing what you learnt about a person from spending time in their kitchen. Once Carole had attended a domestic violence complaint to find every cupboard in the kitchen padlocked by a psycho husband who only unlocked them when he was at home to supervise what was eaten. She couldn't imagine a clearer example of coercive control.

Choosing a chair from which she could see both Barton and Sheridan clearly, Carole started to explain what had been done so far in the search for Jasmine. As she emphasised the importance of reaching out to friends and family to see if Jaz had been in touch, she watched the parents, Barton in particular. His face was impassive.

'I know you have already been through this several times with various officers but I need to confirm you all had dinner together on Sunday night and then on Monday morning Jaz went to school as normal.'

'That's right.' Sheridan leant forward, her hands clasped in front of her as though she were praying. 'We told her we'd be away overnight. I asked if she wanted to stay at Brianna's but she refused.'

'But Jaz seemed fine, nothing out of the ordinary.'

Sheridan's eyes flickered towards her husband and he was the one who answered. 'Perfectly normal.'

'Anything missing? Clothes? Toiletries? Toothbrush? Money?'

Sheridan blinked as if she wasn't sure, but then shook her head. In her peripheral vision, Carole saw Barton was growing restless, trying to cover up the fact that he was getting annoyed. 'We've been through this already.'

'I'm afraid it will appear repetitive, but it is important we check and recheck to make sure. Now Jaz's biological father . . .'

'Is dead,' Sheridan said. 'Died in a car accident when she was a baby.'

Carole nodded. 'We've spoken to her friends – Brianna Sharrah, Lennox Rivett – but no one has heard from her.'

There was a quiet explosion from Barton at Lennox's name.

'Just so you know,' Carole went on smoothly, 'we are working to independently verify Lennox's whereabouts on the night in question, but so far there is no evidence to suggest he is involved. Can you think of any other boys, girls or significant others Jaz might have been involved with? Anyone online, perhaps?'

Carole always tried to be careful with her phrasing around gender. Her stepdaughter, Lexie, had been ferocious on the subject of pronouns, fluid identities and not misgendering people. From what she already knew about Jaz Langridge, she might enjoy a bit of experimentation, particularly if it had the added bonus of pissing off her stepfather.

Sheridan shook her head. 'Lennox was the only one she mentioned. Of course, there was Nate as well, but she hasn't talked about him for a while.'

There was a nostril flare from Barton.

'We will be putting out our standard Facebook alert today, and if Jaz remains missing, we will be talking to you about making a public appeal for information in the next couple of days.'

'No,' said Barton. 'That is not going to happen.'

'I know the thought of it may be uncomfortable, even intimidating, but we can give you support to do so and it's important that we—'

'I am not having this turn into a media circus. It's bad enough that the school security footage has found its way into circulation.'

Carole waited for Barton to blame her for this (there had already been an angry phone call to her boss), though there were plenty of ways that footage could have been leaked – Traccy's cousin, Sharon, for starters.

'I've already had poor Ivan on the phone assuring me that all he was doing was pointing out Jasmine was wearing incorrect uniform.'

Carole looked at him, trying to hide her amazement. If Lexie had been spoken to like that, Carole would have been up at the school in a shot demanding answers.

'When did you speak to him?' she asked.

'Earlier this morning.'

Carole nodded and took note of two things to ponder later. First, that Roland's phone was working at the camp and he knew very well what was going on back in town, and second, even in the best-case scenario that Roland's account of the exchange was accurate, for a grown man to throw a complete tantrum of more than five minutes' duration over a young woman's clothing didn't reflect well on him.

From the way Billy's eyes were bulging dangerously out of his head, he must be thinking something similar. She was going to have to talk to him about practising his poker face.

'Ivan shouldn't have shouted at her,' said Sheridan quietly.

It was the first tiny note of defiance and Barton was not well pleased. His face flushed an ugly red. Carole was determined to exploit it.

'Ivan Roland is back from camp this afternoon. We'll talk to him about that incident then.'

'I don't see why that's necessary,' Barton interjected.

Carole could feel her temper rising and did her best to keep it in check. 'You don't seem overly concerned that your stepdaughter is missing,' she observed.

'The whole thing is a bloody charade. Designed to get attention and inflict reputational damage. Jasmine has made it her life's focus to cause me political embarrassment. This little escapade falls squarely into that category.'

'She doesn't have her phone, her bank accounts remain untouched and you say she didn't take anything with her.'

All the time she kept glancing at Sheridan Langridge out of the corner of her eye. The woman sat there visibly upset, lips clamped together as if having to physically restrain herself from speaking.

'My stepdaughter enjoys nothing more than making a spectacle of herself and she has had ample practice. I presume you heard about the little stunt she masterminded at the school last year that resulted in criminal charges and jail time for that gullible fool. The whole thing was a debacle, including the policing. I can tell you, the Premier was not impressed at all.'

Carole couldn't even bring herself to dignify his assessment of the policing with so much as a nod.

'Jasmine is a human billboard craving publicity and I will not give it to her.' Barton was on a roll now.

Carole turned to Jaz's mother. 'Do you think the same?'

But the woman had retreated back into her shell, the rebellion extinguished. 'I don't know,' she murmured. 'I just want her to come home.' She was twisting a ring, studded with diamonds, around and around her finger, as though it were a mark she was trying to rub out.

'Have there been any threats made against you or your family?' Carole asked.

Sheridan looked up. 'You don't think—' she began.

'There's no evidence,' Carole assured her. 'We just need to cover all possibilities.'

'We do get the occasional deranged constituent. Some people are very exercised about so-called "climate change".' Barton's tone was dismissive. 'My chief of staff keeps any threatening letters we receive on file.'

Billy's eyes started to pop again at the mention of threatening letters, but mercifully he kept his mouth shut. Eyes in head, constable.

'I'll send someone to pick those up,' Carole told him.

Barton made a show of glancing at his expensive-looking watch. 'Well, if that's all . . .'

'One last question,' Carole said, 'then I'd love that cup of tea. Were you aware that Jasmine believed Vanessa Walton was murdered?'

Everything changed in an instant. Sheridan gasped, covering her mouth with both hands. 'Who did she say that to?'

'She spoke about it with friends.'

Barton had turned pale, worried for the first time, but he recovered.

'That's ridiculous,' he began. 'The coroner found—'

Carole talked over him. 'Were you aware that Ms Walton was receiving anonymous threats?'

'What?' A look of genuine confusion now. An entirely different expression from before, but it was quickly replaced by one of a man who would be calling his lawyer before answering more questions.

'Could I possibly use the bathroom?' asked Billy.

Barton turned to him in surprise, as if he had forgotten Billy was there. His eyes narrowed as if weighing up what to do. 'I'll show you where it is,' he said in the end, shepherding Billy out of the room.

Without her husband there, something broke in Sheridan and she started sobbing. 'I keep thinking she's going to walk through the door and ask what we were all worried about.'

'Let me make you a tea,' said Carole. 'Point me in the way of the kitchen.'

Sheridan shook her head. 'I mustn't keep you. Please, just tell me that you will find her.'

Carole had been a cop long enough to avoid making any promises. Instead, she knelt down beside Sheridan. 'Here's my card.' Pulling out a pen, she scribbled a number on the back. 'That's my personal mobile. You can ring that day or night.'

Over the years she had learnt to convey the impression of a spontaneous act of kindness rather than it being routine. She was convinced that Barton and Sheridan knew more than they were telling her and she needed to know what and why.

Sheridan held the card in her perfectly manicured hands and then looked directly at her for what felt like the first time. Her face aged, eyes ancient with tears silently spilling from them. Carole suspected this was a woman who'd had a good deal of practice in crying quietly to herself.

'When we first bought her the phone, I insisted she kept location tracking turned on so I could see where she was at all times. Jaz was furious, said I was just like the Stasi, because they'd been reading the Anna Funder book at school and I backed down.'

In a different context, this could be twisted into a darkly funny story about raising teenagers. Carole put a hand on Sheridan's arm and felt little more than bone. 'Jaz is just at the fuck-off-tuck-me-in stage of development, when they spend all day insisting they're a grown-up but still want you to hug and feed them.'

Sheridan gave a watery smile. 'But if I hadn't given in, then maybe . . .'

The question must be on repeat inside her head.

'She didn't have her phone with her,' Carole reminded her.

'But I would have known something was wrong earlier. The first twenty-four hours are the most important, aren't they?'

Carole didn't want to answer that. 'What was the fight about on the night before she went missing?'

It was a stab in the dark but an educated one. Chances were that any family with a mouthy teenager would be having a disagreement on any given day, but with a passionate climate activist and a stepfather who made speeches in Parliament about climate collusion and how he wouldn't mind warmer winters if it came to that, it seemed inevitable.

The woman glanced towards the door as if expecting her husband to burst through it.

'Anything you tell me will be kept between us.' It was like putting out a lure, seeing if she could get a nibble. 'What did they fight about?'

'Vanessa.' Sheridan's voice stumbled. 'Jaz found out from her grandmother that Barton had instructed his solicitors to evict Vanessa. He was convinced that Vanessa had been after Lonnie's money.'

Carole didn't react, willing the woman to keep talking.

'Did Jaz say anything about who she thought killed . . .' Sheridan trailed off as if reluctant to even say it aloud.

'Who killed Vanessa?'

The woman nodded.

'Apparently she alleged that Ivan Roland was involved.'

So many emotions swarmed over Sheridan's face that it was diffi-cult to identify them all, though Carole couldn't help but notice that not one of them was shock. It was as if her worst fears had been confirmed.

There were voices in the hallway, Billy talking particularly loudly about the weather, and by the time the two men returned to the room, Carole was standing well away from Sheridan, looking past the swimming pool and out at the tennis court. She needed Sheridan to feel confident that she could talk to the police without Barton finding out.

'Thanks for making time to see us,' she said. 'We'll be in touch the moment we hear anything. If Jaz should contact you, or you think of anything else helpful, please call me immediately.'

Sheridan stayed on the couch, but Barton escorted them from the premises, shutting the door swiftly behind them.

Neither of them spoke till they got back to the car.

'Told you he was a dickhead,' Billy said.

'That you did,' said Carole. 'Now, how far is Vanessa's place from here? There's something I want to have a look at.'

'Two-minute drive tops.'

'So a ten-minute walk?'

'I guess.'

'You head back to the station and keep going through the CCTV footage.'

Billy looked at her in amazement. 'I can drive you. It's a bloody steep hill.'

Carole had forgotten how people didn't like to walk in the country. 'I should be able to manage it.'

'Suit yourself.'

Billy got in the car, and as he drove past, he wound down the window.

'Didn't really need to go to the toilet. Thought you might do better alone with Sherry.'

The first signs of initiative. Constable Billy Wicks, take a bow.

CHAPTER 17

It took twelve minutes and thirty-five seconds to walk to Vanessa's cottage. It *was* a bloody steep hill. She hadn't seen a single pedestrian and only a handful of cars had gone past.

Puffing, she stared at the empty house and then turned to look at Lonnie Langridge's gate. No one home. Every instinct told her that Barton knew more about Vanessa's death than he was letting on. Sheridan too, for that matter. Here was the place where she might find answers.

Turning, she crossed the road to knock on the door of the house directly opposite Vanessa's.

Janet Ross wasn't home either.

It was like a ghost town.

Carole needed a moment to catch her breath, so she sat down on the stairs to work out her next move. It was a nice part of the world around here, lovely views of the mountains and deathly quiet neighbours. Pulling out her phone, Carole scrolled through to see if there were any rentals in the area. She was sick of staying in the motel.

There was a unit in the middle of town, a few blocks from where she was sitting. Perfect except for no backyard and 'strictly no pets'. The next was a villa in a development on the outskirts that was so close to the neighbours you would be able to hear them sneeze.

But then she saw an old-style brick house, two bedrooms, back garden, that had potential. She saved it to do a drive-by after her shift today.

A photo came up in her memories. It was of a much younger Lexie, smiling so broadly that you could see the full set of wonky teeth and gums, a pre-braces picture. Next to her was an empty milkshake glass. It would have been caramel, no doubt – her favourite.

Lexie and Jaz would have got on like a house on fire. She remembered when her stepdaughter sent through a link about the two young climate activists who had thrown soup at Andy Warhol's *Campbell's Soup Cans*.

Carole had replied with the only pertinent question: *What flavour?*

Surely it had to be tomato. It would be disappointing if it was pea and ham or cream of mushroom.

Would you charge them?

It was a game Lexie liked to play, sending Carole ethical dilemmas.

The truth was she would charge them in a heartbeat because a society without laws and consequences scared her as much as climate change did. Let them have their day in court. It was what they wanted, after all: attention for their cause. They could make a rousing speech from the dock and hopefully the judge would have enough of a sense of humour about it to sentence them to community service in a soup kitchen. But that was too long to put in a text, so she had sent back a thumbs-up.

Lexie must have anticipated her response because she had a meme ready. *Rise Up Before the Sea Does.* Carole still found it funny.

Jasmine Langridge was someone who enjoyed the limelight. It didn't make sense for a person like that to disappear willingly. The longer this went on, the more worried Carole was getting.

She had just decided to walk back to the police station, when a car pulled up and Janet got out. Today she was dressed in a purple smock and had a set of large rainbow beads around her neck. She didn't seem at all surprised to see Carole.

'It was the doctor,' the old woman said. 'He always runs half an hour late but insists you get there five minutes before schedule.'

Janet started walking up the steps to her front door. Her gait was uneven and she had to cling to the railing, breathing hard. Carole sensed that any offers of help would be rebuffed.

'Roger will be at golf for another hour, so we can talk without him coming in asking awkward questions.'

Carole followed her up the stairs and into the house.

She had expected a cluttered living room, full of knick-knacks and cushions. Instead, it was plain, almost austere, dominated by a front window framed by thick cream curtains with a subtle gold thread running through. Perfect for blocking out the light if someone was having a nap – unlike, say, a motel room the size of a shoebox with a broken blind and streetlights right outside. If Janet didn't offer her a coffee, Carole might have a quick snooze on the sofa.

There was a pretty watercolour of the mountains over the fireplace and a large bookshelf opposite, mostly stacked with thrillers, though Carole noticed a few forensic books and a well-thumbed copy of *Gray's Anatomy*. That suggested more than your usual online detective with their crackpot theories. She moved towards the leather lounge with two matching armchairs.

What was unusual was that there was no television in the room (perhaps she wasn't such a fan of murder mystery series after all) and the second of the armchairs was facing away from the room and towards the window. A nearby side table had binoculars on it. Carole noticed a pristine copy of a bird guide next to them, looking like it had never been opened. Camouflage for Janet's people watching.

The view stretched all the way from the majestic pin oak at the corner of the intersection, next to the Langridge House, down the block and partway into the next one. Vanessa's cottage was directly across the road. With binoculars you would even be able to see through her front windows, which was interesting. No wonder Vanessa moved her bedroom to the back of the house.

Janet came back into the room carrying a tray.

'I took the liberty of making you a black coffee. In my experience, police officers never trust the milk.'

Had Janet grown up in the age of pre-refrigeration? Carole was happiest with milk, two sugars and a dash of something stronger, if it was on offer.

'Should do nicely,' she said, trying not to sound disappointed that it didn't come with a couple of biscuits or a fat scone with cream and jam. Carole did some of her best thinking over a nice Devonshire tea.

'Roger likes to watch sport in the study, and I stay here and watch the world go by. The secret to a happy marriage is separate interests, don't you think?'

The secret to a happy marriage was probably not to get married in the first place.

Janet put the tray on a table and sat down opposite. 'Have you opened a homicide investigation into Vanessa Walton yet?'

Carole picked up the coffee, took a sip. 'That's not my decision. If there's enough evidence, we'll send a brief to Homicide and they'll work out how to proceed.'

'Well then, you might want to have a word with Tracey Wicks, who was shooting her mouth off at choir last night.'

Billy's wife! One step forward, two steps back for that officer. There was nothing Carole hated more than leaks. First the security footage and now this.

'And how long does it take for Homicide to make a decision?' Janet pursed her lips as if she knew she was not going to like the answer.

'Probably a couple of weeks once they've been sent the brief.' How long a brief might take to put together, to say nothing of convincing her own boss that one was warranted, was anyone's guess.

'Two weeks!' the old woman shrieked. 'Jasmine Langridge can't wait two weeks.'

'We still don't have any concrete evidence that Jasmine has been abducted,' said Carole. 'Or that her disappearance relates to Vanessa Walton or that Vanessa Walton was murdered.' Just a lot of coincidences that made her feel quite uneasy.

'But I haven't got two weeks,' said Janet. 'I'm back in hospital tomorrow.'

'Was that why you were at the doctor's?'

Janet gave a little shake of her head as if it wasn't important. 'What started as a nuisance many years ago has turned into a struggle. I should have spoken up much earlier but instead I endured it. Be stoic, society tells us, never complain. Well, I made a resolution to never be silent again.'

And you've certainly kept that, thought Carole.

'But I refuse to let it make my life miserable.'

'Very brave,' said Carole. Against her better judgement, she was becoming quite fond of Janet.

'More stubborn,' said Janet.

'That's as good a way to cope with it as any.'

'People don't appreciate how many ways there are to be chronically ill. All this rubbish about saints and angels, soldiers fighting battles, makes me want to scream. I mean, some people complain about their illness constantly or use it as a weapon to get what they want. Others refuse to acknowledge it at all, as if it might go away of its own accord. And there are those who deal with it in private, like swans in a pond, gliding beautifully across the surface while underneath their feet are in constant motion. My way of dealing with it is to distract myself by watching what's going on in the world.'

'Is that why you were interested in Vanessa?'

'Life is precious. Bad enough when your body decides to stop before your three score years and ten, but when another human being ends a life, that's plain wrong. Work out what happened to Vanessa and you'll learn what happened to Jasmine. I'm sure of it.'

Carole sighed, because in her view it was the wrong way around. Vanessa was dead, there wasn't anything she could do to change that, but hopefully Jaz was still alive. That needed to be her priority. It was hard to say that to someone about to go into hospital, though.

'It takes—' began Janet.

'No it doesn't,' interrupted Carole. 'What it takes is a town telling the police *all* they know, not scattering little crumbs of information whenever they feel like it.'

It was Janet's turn to sigh now. Then she stood up and hobbled over to a credenza, pulled open a drawer and got out an exercise book. 'It's only because I'm going into hospital,' she said with a severe expression, 'as you've not done enough to deserve it, in my opinion.'

She handed the exercise book to Carole.

'And what's this exactly?'

'A record of the comings and goings from Vanessa Walton's house for at least the last month. I'm not saying I got all of them – I do need to go out from time to time – but I'm confident that it's most of them. I had been at Roger to get a security camera pointed in that direction for months but he said I was being too nosy. Only because he didn't want me finding out about his visits there, I learnt afterwards. Anyway, there are numberplates, descriptions of cars, the lot. Quite a few repeat visitors. Male visitors. It makes for interesting reading.' Janet opened her eyes wide to give that fact special significance.

Carole opened the exercise book and flicked through the pages. Each one had been neatly ruled into columns headed *Time*, *Numberplate*, *Description*. There were constables who could take lessons in surveillance from Janet. She would be a deeply infuriating neighbour, but it was a truth rarely acknowledged that the most annoying people were often the best witnesses. One of the most successful drug busts Carole had ever been involved in started with a cantankerous grandfather across the road who had a bee in his bonnet about people parking directly in front of his house. He had written down the numberplate of every car that had done so for six months prior.

She gave Janet an appraising look. 'Anything else you want to tell me?'

'Follow the money, dear,' the older woman said. 'That often works, I find.'

The call came through from Angie late in the afternoon. She said it wasn't crucial to come out to the pine forest, but one of the farmers she had visited earlier that day thought they had seen Jaz hitchhiking just near it. Angie had done a quick search and thought she might have found something.

Carole, who had been watching the clock, waiting for Ivan Roland to return to the school, decided that they had time to go have a look before heading to St Brigid's. The ride out was quiet. Billy didn't bother pointing out local landmarks like the Big GoldPanner with the fake Welcome Nugget or the showgrounds, because he was still smarting from their 'discussion' about the importance of confidentiality. Tracey's name had been mentioned more than once.

Geo-targeted text messages had gone out to the district – *Have you seen this girl?* – because Barton Langridge didn't get to dictate how Carole Duffy conducted an investigation. More tips were coming in to Crime Stoppers.

If this was the breakthrough, then Carole would push to get drones into the air and call in the dogs. She loved the black labradors with their sleek panther coats and tails as thick as rope. Maybe she should get a dog, she found herself thinking, as they took the turn-off for the pine forest. It would be a good way to get to know people in town and force her to walk up some of Welcome's hills.

They parked at the edge of the car park and quickly headed into the gloomy twilight beneath the tall trees. Carole knew there were people who loved being out in nature, but she suspected that they weren't police. Places like this put her in mind of shallow graves and decomposing remains. Once, when she was a very young police officer, she had spent a spring night sneezing and wheezing in the middle of a forest not that different from this one, guarding the site of a plane crash. Forensics couldn't get there until the morning and the smell of cooked human flesh attracted every scavenger for miles. She was vegetarian for years after that. You could keep your creepy serial-killer forests. For relaxation, Carole Duffy would happily walk around a shopping centre full of people instead.

'Don't get your hopes up,' Angela said, when she met them. 'It's probably nothing.'

There was a piece of clothing lying in the gloom under a tree. It was a spray jacket, maroon with dark blue edging and stripes down the sleeves. Carole guessed it was part of St B's uniform.

'There's no name on the collar,' said Angela. 'Might be one inside.'

Carole crouched down beside it.

'That's part of their sports uniform,' Billy said. 'Jaz was wearing the standard school uniform the day she disappeared.'

The jacket's colour had faded and mud was soaked into the weave. At a guess it had been out here for a lot longer than Jaz had been missing.

A dead end, but Carole told Billy to photograph it and get it bagged for testing. No dog squad needed yet.

Walking out of the forest, she took a breath. It smelt like it was about to rain again and Carole looked up. Dark clouds, swollen pregnant, loomed overhead. Christ on a bike, could they not have a couple of sunny days in a row?

She made it back to the car as the first drops fell, sat checking her messages as she waited for Billy to catch up. Finally there was an email from forensics about the note. Wait until they caught a load of the jacket she was about to send. She was going to have to buy a case of something top-shelf for them after all this or she was never going to get anything tested in a timely fashion again.

The interim report was attached. She clicked on it, having to magnify so she could read by squinting because her glasses were back at the station. There had only been time to check for latent fingerprints. More complex testing for DNA would take longer and would be there only if the person had put saliva on the paper.

There were several sets of fingerprints on the note, but she had expected that, fingerprinting Brianna yesterday in order to rule her out. Then she sat up straight. Fingerprints had been found on the back of one of the glued letters. They had the author.

Carole exhaled. Was this the smoking gun they needed? If they were Ivan Roland's fingerprints, that could explain everything.

But it wasn't Ivan Roland.

Scrabbling through her bag, she pulled out Janet's exercise book. She hadn't had time to read it yet. She'd planned to go through it systematically tonight as she ate dinner, but now she wondered if there could be a connection between the numberplates Janet recorded and the fingerprints on the note. Running her finger down the page, she noticed one numberplate had appeared regularly, including on the night that Vanessa had died.

Radioing the station, she asked the constable on duty to look up the owner. The information came back in an instant.

Billy clambered into the driver's seat. He'd been caught in the rain and shook himself so hard that water flicked across Carole's face.

'You need to see this.' Carole handed him her phone.

His mouth moved as he read through the report, giving the words shape, but then there was the characteristic eye bulge and Carole knew he had come to the name attached to the second pair of prints. He read it through again as if wanting to check that he had got it right.

'That's impossible,' he said, turning towards her.

But it didn't matter whether he believed it or not because, unlike people, fingerprints didn't lie.

CHAPTER 18

Jaz had expected to feel many conflicting emotions when she was 'abducted', but what she hadn't realised was that boredom would be the most dominant. She lay there on the bed. Her phone, the burner one that Lennox had got her, sat on the drop-down Formica table. She only had one jetpack so couldn't check it too often, because she needed it to work for when Lennox rang. They agreed once a day at a time that suited him, unless there was an emergency. Any more might be suspicious.

It had been almost three days since she disappeared. No one seemed to notice for the first twenty-four hours, and she didn't know whether to be offended or happy that her plan was working. Brianna had come through, though, just as Jaz had predicted she would. Her stepfather always said that it was easy to manipulate good people and it turned out he was right.

The Real Estate Agent gave people advice whether they wanted it or not. One of his other favourite sayings was that politics was all about timing. That was why she had pushed Vanessa to announce she would run against Barton early. She knew it would take time to put together a campaign to unseat her stepfather. Jaz had even made buttons and posters to try to entice her. It didn't take a genius to see that Vanessa loved being in the spotlight, but she really only started to show an interest when Jaz had told her how much money politicians made and about their generous superannuation schemes.

Anyway, the first step had been achieved already. Lennox had told her that Brianna went straight to Mrs Birnam, who rang the police. In fact, it was even more than a first step, because Jaz had no idea that Mrs Birnam had already found the anonymous note. If Jaz had known that, maybe she wouldn't have had to go 'missing' at all.

Still, it was better this way. The one thing Jaz had learnt from all her campaigning, the rallies, the petitions, TikToks, fights for climate justice, demonstrations against native logging, support for refugees, was that adults don't ever listen to teenagers. Adults kept saying that young people would save the world, but all they really did was pat kids on the head, say, 'Aren't you cute?', and then go back to ruining everything. If she had been the one saying Vanessa had been murdered, the police wouldn't have listened. Not when they were all in the Real Estate Agent's pocket. Even that new cop who everyone was saying was so nice. How did she arrive in town? In Barton's fucking helicopter.

The local media was no better. There had been a junior journo at the local newspaper who interviewed Nate several times before his court case, but after Nate was sentenced she refused to run any more stories. In the end, Jaz actually phoned her, even though she hated talking on the phone. The woman set her straight. There wasn't anything new to report, and because her editor played golf with Barton she'd been told to give it a rest.

As far as Jaz could tell, the only time the media was interested in teenagers was when they were pretty, rich and missing. Not dead, missing, because missing meant there was still hope, and people would move mountains for hope. It was the only card Jaz had and she was going to play it for all it was worth.

So far the plan had gone even better than expected. She had made sure to be seen on the security camera, waiting to be picked up, and then pretended that she had left her phone inside the school so tried the back door, only to find it locked. It was all recorded.

The fact Roly got out of his car and came over to tell her off for her stupid non-regulation school socks was the icing on the cake. At the start, Jaz could barely keep a straight face she was that delighted, but then she decided to really set him off and said that she blamed him for Vanessa's death. He went completely off his head about it and for a moment Jaz had been worried he might actually hit her, but instead he just walked away.

It only made her more determined to go ahead with her original plan: hiding in the maintenance shed for hours, before cutting deep into the soccer fields (well away from the clubhouse's security cameras) to where Lennox was meeting her close to midnight. The idea was for Lennox to stay back at work, then drive home and act like he was going to sleep, before slipping out in his sister's Commodore to pick Jaz up and drive her out to the caravan.

The caravan belonged to Nate. He had towed it next to the gully on his property, near a narrow ribbon of bushland up from the creek that divided his property from Des Patchett's. It was private down here, out of sight of his mother's house, and most of the surrounding fields had been left fallow this year. Lennox said no one ever came down this way and everyone had probably forgotten there was a caravan here at all.

Even though her surrounds looked much better in the sunlight, there was nothing flash about the caravan. Lennox liked to joke that Nate would be a hermit or a monk if he could, wear a hairshirt, beat himself with a whip and live in a cave. This wasn't that much better. Stretching out her stiff legs, she stared up at the water stains on the roof. The whole place smelt of a damp kind of neglect. Maybe she should tidy it for when Nate was released, get it ready for him. Nothing too drastic – wash the windows, replace the broken pane, put clean sheets on the fold-out bed, buy new pillows, perhaps maybe even put some wildflowers in a jar. It would show she cared, especially if she dusted and swept up all the old flies on the surfaces. Lennox said Gerri barely left the house these days, and he had to bring groceries out to her once a week because she couldn't face going into town.

Jaz had spent yesterday cleaning out the cupboards. It helped pass the time. Next was cleaning the floors. There were still the bits of tape lying around. Vanessa had told her that for a performance to be convincing you had to believe in your head that the situation was real so they had acted it out in order for Jaz to describe it to the police more accurately. Lennox had got into playing the part of the abductor, making sure she was trussed up tight before roughly cutting her loose and ripping off the tape from her mouth. She decided against sweeping up the pieces. It was important to make this as authentic as possible. Maybe when she left here, Lennox should put her in the boot of the car before dumping her by the side of the road. If you were going to do something, you might as well do it properly.

The day was already dragging.

What did Nate do in jail to avoid going stir-crazy? Were there organised activities? Could you read? She couldn't believe she was actually thinking this, but perhaps she should have brought her homework.

They'd agreed that Lennox wouldn't come out to the caravan again until it was time to take her back. It was a pity, because she could do with extra blankets and insect spray, but it would be far too suspicious if he was seen out here, and the police would be watching him. He had been furious when they mentioned Heidi Millet in the interview that morning. Lennox had rung Jaz as soon as he could, telling her that they would stitch him up over this and it wouldn't affect her because Langridges always ended up on top. He had wanted her to go home right away.

'Not until the homicide investigation is announced,' she told him. 'That's the plan.'

Eventually he had calmed down.

She should get up and have something to eat. There were tins under the sink and there was a can opener in one of the drawers. Lennox had told her not to use the camp stove. Even with the wet weather, no farmer liked the look of smoke. If her mother saw her out here, eating spaghetti from a tin without complaining and wiping down surfaces without being told, she would never believe it. Jaz almost laughed at how surprised Sherry would be, but then she didn't want to think of her mother for too long. Sherry must be really worried and Jaz couldn't help feeling a bit guilty about that.

It was her mother's fault, though. If Sherry hadn't suggested that Jaz help out Amber and Brianna at Vanessa's wake, then she never would have heard Mr Singh tell everyone how he was the last person to see Vanessa alive. He talked on and on about it. Mr Singh was notorious for starting stories but never knowing how to finish them. Jaz was stuck there holding the tray of food, so she heard it all – more than once, in fact. On the night Vanessa died, Mr Singh had been worried about leaks at the pharmacy, so he'd headed out to make sure it was watertight. He was returning home around 10 pm when he saw her.

'Water was bucketing down then,' Mr Singh said, 'but the wind hadn't started yet. As I drove past the Cottage, I saw Ms Walton step outside. The visibility was so bad I wouldn't have recognised her if it wasn't for her hair and that red coat of hers. I would have stopped and asked if she wanted a lift, but she was walking in the opposite direction, up the hill. By the time I pulled into my driveway, I couldn't see her. Probably she had only been going over to Lonnie's house to check on her.'

That explanation didn't make sense to Jaz for two reasons. Vanessa hadn't gone to Lonnie's place, she knew, because Sherry was already there, trying to deal with the leaks, and would have seen her. On top of that, there had been storm warnings all afternoon. Why would anyone go walking in a storm?

Jaz got home from the wake in a bad mood, only to discover her vapes were missing from the top drawer of her dresser, which meant Sherry had been snooping through her room again. She had been doing it regularly ever since she found out about Lennox. Checking for drugs most likely. Jaz was incensed, especially when she had spent the whole afternoon being a good girl by serving stupid people canapés.

She didn't bother confronting her mother about it. That would have meant she'd get a lecture on how dangerous vapes were, how you couldn't possibly know what chemicals were in them and what they were doing to your body, and had she heard the story about how a kid lost their hand because it exploded. Instead, Sherry would pretend she hadn't taken the vape and Jaz would say nothing and get another vape from one of the year elevens at school who sold them, and it was only fair that she nicked her mother's money to do it.

Waiting until Sherry was busy downstairs making dinner, she headed into their bedroom. The Real Estate Agent wasn't home; he was probably at some meeting plotting how to ruin the environment faster or bulldoze some heritage-protected houses. Jaz knew that Sherry hid cash in a shoebox in the walk-in wardrobe to pay the cleaners and the gardener, but it wasn't in the normal spot when she checked. Pissed off now, she decided to check her stepfather's side of the wardrobe. There had to be some money among the neatly pressed suits, shiny shoes, striped ties and checked shirts – literally the most boring set of clothes in the world. Sure enough, in the inside pocket of a charcoal Hugo Boss jacket she found a money clip with fifty dollars. As she pulled it out, the jacket slipped from the hanger. Jaz reached down to pick it up and then noticed something at the back of the cupboard. A grubby supermarket plastic bag that seemed out of place in the wardrobe with the designer threads and bespoke dress shirts.

Looking inside that bag changed everything. That was the moment when she finally understood that it was all her fault that Vanessa was dead.

CHAPTER 19

It was the last period and normally Frankie would be teaching year nine English, but as they were being bussed back from camp, she decided to pack up Vanessa's office instead. The principal, Juliette, had been only too quick to agree when Frankie offered. There was a shortage of offices in the school, particularly single-person ones, and already the vultures were circling.

Awkwardly balancing empty cardboard boxes, Frankie unlocked the door to Vanessa's office. She had decided to make a handwritten inventory of each item for Beth and Miss Helen, so they didn't have to hunt through the boxes themselves to see what was inside. She would type the list up tonight before she took the boxes over, and if there was enough time, she might buy a curry as well to accompany them.

The scent of Vanessa's perfume in the room stopped Frankie in her tracks. Joe had asked her last night how she was going and she had said fine, but really she was a bit wobbly. Death was a hard thing to process any time but losing her mother and now Vanessa felt like a lot. Tears prickled in her eyes but there was no time for that.

The bell went and there was the immediate sound of hundreds of pairs of feet rampaging towards the exit. Parents would be doing laps of the car park or annoying neighbours by parking across driveways, waiting to pick up their children. The school buses were only half full since Jaz had disappeared.

It would be hard for a stranger to tell that the atmosphere at the school wasn't quite normal, but Frankie saw it in almost every lesson: students murmuring among themselves as they moved through the corridors in tight little bunches, lunchtimes far less boisterous than usual and teachers frowning at anyone laughing, without really knowing why. The more religious staff members had been conducting prayers in their lessons and the kids had gone along with chanting Hail Marys and Our Fathers far less mutinously than they ordinarily would as everyone waited for news. Frankie had decided that it was best to keep busy.

She started by pulling off the photos stuck to the walls. The first was of Vanessa at the gala, lifting an elegant hand to the air. Frankie picked up a pen and wrote a description of each photo on her list. She'd find an envelope to put them all in later.

A text from Joe came up on her phone. He had picked up both boys, 'as instructed'. It was accompanied by a picture of Ollie making a face and Danny looking thunderous. There had been a heated discussion the night before. None of them thought it was necessary for their father to pick them up from school, Joe included, but Frankie had insisted.

'Bad things don't only happen to girls,' she told them.

The looks on all three of their faces suggested that she was wrong.

The first desk drawer was full of stationery. Frankie decided against returning it to the stationery cupboard. A few pens and a stapler were the least the Department of Education could give to Vanessa's family, and Beth might find a use for them at the academy.

There was a knock on the door and a breathless Martha Reynolds popped her head around. 'The police have arrived. They're talking to Juliette now.'

'Any news about Jasmine?' Frankie put a hole punch into the box.

Martha shook her head. 'I've got a Google alert for St Brigid's and there's been no developments at all since that video footage. Do you think the police are waiting for Ivan? The year nines should be back from camp soon.'

Frankie didn't know what to think. While Ivan was an unpleasant colleague, he didn't seem like a murderer.

What did a murderer look like?

'I almost died with surprise when I heard Ivan was away on camp. That's suspicious behaviour in itself.'

'Juliette said she asked him to go when Katie pulled out sick.'

'Damage control,' said Martha. There was something about Martha's tone, almost gleeful, that Frankie couldn't bear.

'I won't keep you,' she said.

Martha's mouth became a thin line at the dismissal. 'I presumed that you would want to know, seeing as you were the person who reported the disappearance.' She gave a sniff of disapproval and then closed the door with a sharp little bang, no doubt off to find someone else to gossip with.

There was a button badge in Vanessa's second drawer. Frankie had to swallow hard when she saw it. Jasmine Langridge had got lots of girls to wear them until Ivan, predictably, banned them, saying they weren't part of the uniform.

VOTE 1 4 VEE – A WELCOME CHANGE.

Frankie cradled it in her hand. Would Vanessa really have run against Barton? She certainly talked about it and had got it into her head that Frankie could be her chief of staff. Frankie had dismissed this outright, saying Joe would be much better, but all the same the mere suggestion had sparked something inside Frankie. Maybe she was due a mid-life career change and teaching could be a stepping stone to something else. She didn't know what exactly, but it had been fun to dream all the same.

That was the beauty of Vanessa. She made the impossible seem just within reach and she believed that everyone deserved some excitement. Life was an adventure to be grabbed with both hands. It was what Frankie would miss the most about her.

Half an hour later, she had finished clearing out all the drawers. One and a half cardboard boxes were full and she was on to the next page of the inventory. It was time to tackle the filing cabinet. Frankie pulled out a bundle of paper to see what should be recycled but instead stared in horror.

Another anonymous note.

And another and another.

All like the one she had found at Vanessa's house, words and phrases stuck on white paper. Frankie forced herself to read them. There was a horrible sneering nastiness to them but also an awful familiarity because the words themselves came from magazine covers talking about stars' lives, diets and horoscopes.

Had Ivan done this? Perhaps she should go find the police right now, interrupt what they were doing, tell them there was something they needed to see.

She tried to straighten the notes into a neat bundle but the last one got caught and she pulled it out. One of the words, LIFE, had come half unstuck. Frankie carefully lifted up the paper fragment to read what was on the back of it. Something snagged at the back of her mind.

Another knock at the door. 'Frankie, are you still in there?'

It was Martha again, her voice almost suspicious.

Frankie hastily shoved the notes in her bag. Martha was the last person she would talk to about them.

Martha opened the door with a certain self-satisfied glint in her eye. 'Excuse me, but the police were wanting to talk to you!'

There was a peculiar emphasis on the end of the sentence that Frankie decided to ignore.

'If you have a moment,' Carole said, appearing behind Martha.

'Of course, of course,' Frankie answered.

Martha was still standing there, eyes and ears swivelling like satellite dishes.

'Thank you,' Billy said to Martha. She took the smallest step backwards and he closed the door practically in her face.

Both the police officers wore serious expressions. Billy had a laptop under his arm.

'Can I get you a coffee or tea?' Frankie asked. 'If I pop up to the staffroom, I might even be able to snaffle some gingernuts.'

Carole shook her head and pulled over a chair that had been next to the wall. Billy took up a position beside the filing cabinet and produced a notebook.

'Right there, Billy?' Carole said.

Billy nodded, didn't catch her eye. His body language was all wrong, shoulders up around his ears, back slightly hunched as though an invisible weight had settled on him.

'Now I was just . . .' Frankie began, but Carole talked over her.

'Normally we do this at the station,' the policewoman explained. 'I don't have time to do that today, but we still can if you don't cooperate. I need to be clear about that.'

Frankie's mind stumbled hard over this.

'We've got a dead body and a missing girl,' Carole continued. 'I've got to work out if those two things are connected and I don't have time to make a wrong call. With your permission I'm going to record our conversation.'

'All right.' Frankie was still waiting for this all to make sense, to understand how it related to her. Her mouth was stuck in a kind of rictus smile of confusion.

'When you rang the first time about Brianna and the note, you said that it could be some sort of school prank.'

'Did I?' Frankie couldn't quite remember what she had said to Billy.

'You did,' said Billy quietly.

'It's a possibility,' said Frankie, agreeing with her past self.

'Have you received death threats or something of a similar nature?' asked Carole. Her face was blank, hard to read.

Frankie shook her head. 'No.'

'Are you aware of any other teacher at this school receiving death threats?'

A lump in her throat appeared from nowhere. She swallowed hard. 'No.'

Billy wrote something in his notebook.

'How would you describe your relationship with Vanessa?'

'This is beginning to feel like an interrogation.'

Carole's face didn't change. 'We can do this at the station.'

Frankie didn't want that. 'Vanessa was a good friend. I've known her since school. We all go back a long way – don't we, Billy?'

Billy shifted his weight, leant against the wall, looking at his hands like he wasn't involved.

'That's why you read a poem at her funeral,' Carole commented.

'Her family asked me to.'

'And boxing up her office?'

'I offered to because she was a friend.'

Carole nodded as if this seemed a fair response. 'Was Vanessa seeing anyone at the time of her death?'

The question seemed completely out of left field. 'Not that I know of. Others might have a better idea. Patrick Selwyn or Beth, perhaps.'

Was it fair to bring Patrick into this? Frankie wasn't sure. All she knew was she didn't want to be the only one who was questioned.

'Your fingerprints are on the note,' Carole said. 'I got the job rushed through last night because of the possible connection to Jasmine's disappearance.' Her tone was mild, almost conspiratorial, as if they were all on the same side, but Frankie was beginning to realise that it was just an act.

There had been a break-in at the school and the science labs had been trashed. Billy had taken quite a few of the teachers' fingerprints to help with the investigation. Frankie had supervised a class in there the day before the whole kerfuffle. Stupidly, she had expected him to use an ink pad, like they did on TV when she was small. That's how little she had to do with the police. But Billy used a finger scanner. Everything was digital these days. Everything except that anonymous threat.

'You know I held it,' Frankie said. 'I gave it to you.' Why were they wasting time interrogating her when Jaz was still missing?

'Your fingerprints were on the *back* of the glued letters,' Carole said. 'Can you explain that to me?'

Frankie stared.

It was as though the three of them had been in a boat, sailing to an agreed destination, but with that one question they had capsized and now she was drowning.

Carole sat across the desk from her, unruffled, and even Billy had lost interest in his fingers and was looking at her.

'But that's impossible,' Frankie said at last. 'How would my fingerprints have got there?'

Carole gave her a measured look and waited, but all rational thought had momentarily leaked from Frankie's brain.

'Let me tell you what I think,' Carole said. 'I think you wrote that threat and then put it into Vanessa's handbag, possibly at the gala afterparty, where Brianna found it. The thing I need to know is why, and I need to know now.'

'But I would never do something like that.' Tears were welling up. Frankie's chin wobbled.

'I've been in the police force for almost thirty years. I'm guessing you've been a teacher almost that long.' Carole leant forward. 'Both of us have probably been underestimated our entire careers. I want you to know that I don't underestimate what someone like you might do if they felt their family was threatened. Good people can find themselves doing terrible things for love.'

None of this made sense. 'You can't think I've got anything to do with Vanessa's death.' Frankie was desperate now. She turned to Billy. 'Tell her I couldn't do something like that. I'm not capable of it.'

But Billy had gone back to staring at his hands and refused to look up.

'Did you write that threat?' Carole asked. 'Because a young woman is missing and I don't want to waste valuable time.'

'I've already answered your question,' said Frankie.

'You entered Vanessa Walton's house the day after the funeral,' Carole said. 'Were you attempting to retrieve this note or others?'

There were anonymous notes in her bag right now with her prints all over them.

'No comment,' she said.

'You know,' Carole mused, directing this more to Billy than to Frankie, 'people are usually reluctant to say no comment because they think it makes them sound guilty. Very well, you will present to the station tomorrow to be interviewed under caution. We will also require your husband, Joseph Birnam, and your son, Daniel Birnam, to attend for an interview.'

Joe! Danny! How could they be involved?

'You are to stop packing up this office. Any belongings must stay here and this office will be sealed for analysis.'

The notes. Should she tell them? If they found them in her handbag, that would only confirm to them she was the author. But if she handed them over they would probably think that anyway.

'There are two cardboard boxes,' Frankie said, her voice shaky. 'Here's a list of what's in them.'

Carole took the piece of paper as though this had all been a perfectly normal conversation and she hadn't turned Frankie's life completely upside down.

Frankie grabbed her handbag, holding on tight to the strap so they couldn't see her hands trembling.

Billy moved to the door, opened it for her, leaving Carole inside the room.

'You can't believe I'd do this,' she whispered to him, outside in the corridor.

'It's not just you. Barton Langridge will be interviewed as well. He was seen at Vanessa's place that night.'

Frankie wanted to wail. This was all too much.

'If I was you, I'd get a lawyer for tomorrow,' was the last thing Billy said to her.

CHAPTER 20

Mer's lower back ached and her feet hurt. Sue had been in a terrible mood and every second customer wanted to talk about Jasmine, and the ones who didn't were still bleating on about Vanessa.

People were trying their best to sound concerned about Jaz, but really they were angling for gossip. Maybe Chip actually had a point, that it was different because she was a Langridge. Girls had gone missing in Welcome before, Heidi Millet being one, and there hadn't been such a fuss over her.

'See you tomorrow,' she called out to Chip.

Out the back, Lennox Rivett was busy stacking pallets.

'Cops haven't come back for you?' she asked, only half-joking. 'I thought they'd lock you up and throw away the key.'

'They didn't have anything on me,' he said. 'It was all a complete beat-up.'

His words lacked their usual bravado.

'Sue didn't seem keen to have you back.'

Lennox gave her a quick grin. 'Don't believe everything you hear. Sue loves me so much she pays me extra.'

That got a belly laugh from Mer. Typical of Lennox: claim big and then hope that the truth catches up with his mouth.

'I'll get more money' – Lennox rubbed his fingers like he was already holding it – 'and when I do I'll piss off out of here. Sick of being everyone's whipping boy the minute there's any trouble. Now the cops are trying to fit me up for Heidi disappearing.'

That brought Mer up short. What had been meant as a joke twisted into something far more serious.

'Anyway,' he continued, 'someone's been asking for you. That teacher from St B's, Mrs Birnam.'

There was Frankie in her car.

'Don't call her Mrs Birnam,' said Mer. 'That's Frankie, my best mate.' She gave a wave.

Frankie didn't wave back.

'She's been sitting in her car for half an hour waiting for your shift to finish.'

'World's most patient person,' said Mer. 'Have to be to put up with me.' And in that moment she felt terribly sorry for Lennox. This was a week when he could have done with some decent friends and not only the local stoners and roid ragers. 'You need to find yourself some friends as good as her.'

Mer walked towards the car and Frankie gestured for her to get in.

'What's up?' Mer asked.

There was mottled red around Frankie's eyes.

'God, they've found Jaz, haven't they?' She looked back at Lennox, who was breaking down boxes and putting them in the recycling skip. He might be playing the big man as though he was totally unconcerned, but that didn't fool Mer.

Frankie shook her head.

Mer slumped back in her seat, relieved. 'Well, what? 'Cause I'm starving and we've been flat-out busy.'

'You really hated Vanessa,' Frankie said abruptly.

Mer stared at her friend, starting to get an inkling that Frankie wasn't upset generally but rather specifically upset with her. 'I wasn't her biggest fan.' She swallowed a confused snigger.

'I've been sitting here trying to work out why you sent her those threats and that's what I've come up with. You hated Vanessa Walton.'

'What?' The word came out of Mer's mouth all wobbly.

'And not just one, like I first thought, but many.'

Mer licked her lips. 'I don't know what you're talking about.'

Frankie reached into her handbag and brought them out, practically throwing them at Mer. 'The thing is, you used magazines that you got out at Dad's place, magazines that belonged to my mother and that I had flicked through.'

Mer had no idea how Frankie had worked all this out, but really, what was the big deal? If anyone had the right to complain it was Vanessa, but first, she was dead, and second, she completely deserved it. If Mer had known she was going to trip down the stairs, then she wouldn't have done it, but these things happen. No point going through life with regrets.

'Maybe it was stupid—' she began.

'*Maybe!*' There was a burst of white-hot heat in the word. 'Have you any idea what you've done? These things have consequences. Did you not think of that?'

But Mer had done a lot of thinking before she sent those notes. Thought about all the ways she could get Vanessa to leave town. And that was what she came up with.

The car park was filling up with people coming in to shop after work. Mer recognised regulars walking past with their shopping bags. Ray, who came in every day to buy his dinner from the deli, turned their way and gave a nod of recognition.

'Chill the fuck out,' Mer said. 'People will hear you.'

'My fingerprints are on that note. The police think I sent it.'

Mer opened her mouth to say maybe they shouldn't be discussing this in the middle of a public car park with half the town as spectators, but Frankie was already starting to cry in quiet raspy sobs. 'The look on Billy's face.'

'You're upset,' said Mer, reaching out to put an arm around Frankie's shoulders. 'Let's go back to my place, have a drink. We can work this out.'

Frankie pulled away violently. 'Don't you get it? They think Vanessa's been murdered and that's why Jaz has disappeared.'

'But it was an accident.'

'Well, they don't think that now. I've got to go to the police station to be questioned. They're even dragging Joe and Danny into this. Told me I should organise a lawyer.'

Aw, shit, thought Mer. Her stomach clenched.

'Why would you do something that awful? Was it because you were jealous of my friendship with her? Jealous that, for the first time in years, I was doing something that didn't include you?'

Mer blinked hard, looked out of the windscreen away from Frankie. Her heart began to beat as if she were running up a very steep hill. She needed to make up some excuse, plead temporary insanity.

Or she should agree: say yeah, she was jealous. It meant lying to Frankie but it was for the best.

'Yes,' she said in a quiet voice. 'That was it.'

'Juliette has suspended me. She hasn't suspended Ivan but she suspended me, saying that I wasn't to come back to school until this matter has been resolved. The year twelves are facing their final exams. They need their teacher. My career could be ruined.'

'I'll go to the police,' pleaded Mer. 'I'll go there now and tell them it was me, that you had nothing to do with it.'

'So many people over the years have asked why we're friends. Whenever you went on a bender or screwed someone's husband or fucked up in some way.'

Mer flinched at this. Frankie hardly ever swore. 'I've said I'll go to the police.' She was getting increasingly desperate. 'I'll ring Juliette and explain.'

'Get out of the car,' Frankie said.

Mer shook her head. 'I'm not sure you should be driving right now. You're really upset. I'll take us to the police station and we'll get this sorted out.'

There was silence, then Frankie looked at her and said, 'I can't do this.'

Thank Christ. Frankie would give her a chance to sort this mess out and Frankie would forgive her because Frankie always forgave her.

'I can't be friends with you anymore.'

There was a pain in Mer's chest. She wasn't sure she could breathe. She grabbed her bag but the strap got caught around the seat lever and she had to stoop to fiddle with it, all the while hoping that Frankie would relent, but there was an awful painful silence.

Mer fumbled with the doorhandle, now desperate to leave the car.

A couple of faces nearby turned in her direction like sunflowers looking for the sun. Their voices must have been louder than they realised. As she walked across the car park, Mer tried to smooth her face out and act like everything was normal. Inside she was bleeding.

Lennox was still flattening out the boxes. Mer was almost alongside him when Frankie drove past, braked hard and put her window down. Mer steeled herself, waiting for another barrage.

'Stay away from my father.' And then Frankie drove away.

Mer stood there, shell-shocked.

'Looks like I'm not the only one who needs to make some new friends,' said Lennox.

CHAPTER 21

Joe's car wasn't parked in their driveway, but when Frankie opened the door she could see Joe and Ollie sitting on the couch playing video games. The dogs lolled beside them, Ginger's snoring audible over the sound effects.

'Father–son bonding here,' said Joe, putting an arm around his youngest son. There was supposedly a strict rule about no games until after dinner. 'Ollie has promised to do his homework after this.'

'Shooting people is bonding?' Frankie asked. A sob was about to well up but she choked it down.

'There are way worse games than this, Mum.' Ollie kept his eyes fixed on the screen, fingers moving on the controls.

'It's educational,' Joe joked. 'War is bad, Ollie. Killing people is wrong.' He shot a sly grin at his wife.

Tears glistened in Frankie's eyes.

'How was your day?' Joe asked, concerned.

'We need to talk,' said Frankie.

'We're saving the world!' Ollie exclaimed.

Frankie shook her head at her husband.

Joe stood up, ruffled his son's hair. 'Leave some of the bad guys for me, buddy.'

'Put your headphones on, Ollie,' said Frankie. 'I can't be listening to machine guns.'

They went into the kitchen and Frankie stared at the breakfast dishes on the table, the milk out of the fridge, the floor sticky with crumbs, and then put on the kettle. Methodically, she got out the cups, the tea bags, and as the water boiled, she told Joe. The tears came when she explained that Juliette had put her on leave and how, as she drove out of the school car park, she had suddenly realised that Mer must be responsible for the notes.

Sitting at the kitchen table, Joe swore, pointing his finger at his wife like it was all her fault. 'You need to call that policewoman right away and tell her that Mer did it.'

Frankie, red-eyed, sniffling, explained that Mer had said she would do it herself.

'You can't trust her,' Joe said, furious now. 'Your reputation will be in tatters. You need to report it.'

The tea made, Frankie put the milk back in the fridge and went to sit across from him at the table, only to see that Danny was standing there, alert and anxious. He must have come in the back door and been listening to what she said.

'Oh, hello, love.' She stood back up again, quickly wiping her eyes with the back of her hands.

Joe turned around and saw Danny's agitation. 'Mum's a bit upset. Had a hard day at work.'

It was their regular double act, presenting a united front when it came to their kids, but how was she going to keep this from Danny when the police wanted to interview him as well?

Danny gave her a look of pity but there was something hard about it too. 'You didn't write that note?'

'How do you know about the notes?'

'Brianna showed one to me.'

'But you said . . .' Frankie began, but it didn't matter what he had said. 'Of course I didn't. Mer did, but there's been a mix-up and we're going to have to go to the police station tomorrow. They've asked us to come in: me, Dad and . . . you.'

'So incredibly stupid.' Joe's face was red. 'I don't know why we have to go just because Mer's gone mental again.'

'Mer isn't mental,' Danny said quietly, and while a small part of Frankie appreciated his loyalty to his godmother, the rest of her was inclined to agree with Joe's assessment. 'I think we know why she did it,' her son said, looking not at her but at his father.

'She said it was because she hated Vanessa,' said Frankie.

'Mer has always been batshit crazy,' said Joe, folding his arms but not quite meeting his son's gaze.

'Are you going to tell Mum or will I?' Danny's voice made it clear that this was an ultimatum.

'Tell me what?' Frankie interjected.

'There's a lawyer I know,' said Joe. 'He can handle the police for us.' He lifted his chin, angry now.

Frankie held up a hand to stop her husband. She stared at her son. 'What is it, Daniel?'

'No!' exclaimed Joe, rising from the table, as Danny said, 'Dad was having an affair with Vanessa.'

Frankie recoiled, put a hand to her chest as if she had been punched.

'It wasn't an affair,' Joe blustered.

'Stop lying to her,' Danny shouted.

Frankie had to sit down, her legs wobbly, luckily found the chair, otherwise she would have sunk to the floor.

'And when I asked him about it, he completely denied it. Lied to my face.' Danny was getting upset now. 'Afterwards, he told me not to tell you.'

'Enough!' shouted Joe.

The two of them stared at each other, like dogs about to fight, but then Danny turned to her. 'You have to believe me, Mum,' he pleaded.

'Go,' said his father. 'Your mother and I need to discuss this alone.'

Danny kept his gaze fixed on her and Frankie nodded slowly, covering her face with her hands.

Her son hugged her and she clutched at him, feeling shipwrecked. 'I'll be in the next room if you need me, Mum.' And then he was gone.

Joe started with an initial splutter of indignation, like an engine not quite catching, but when he started to speak, it began softly, slowly, as though Frankie were a confused child who had mis-understood the situation.

She had caught his words from earlier and they rang in her head because it seemed that there was a chasm between 'it' and 'there'. There wasn't an affair was what she had wanted to hear, but he had said 'it' wasn't an affair. What exactly was 'it'?

He stopped talking, stood up then crouched down beside her, putting a hand on each arm as he looked her in the eye and told her he loved her. It was just an infatuation, he was saying, a stupid crush. 'We never had sex,' he told her.

Frankie's mind rushed to what she had discovered in Vanessa's bedroom: the lingerie, handcuffs and lubricant. She felt sick.

'I swear to you,' Joe said.

It was the sort of thing you have to say if you are claiming that you are not having an affair. A kind of scientific equation. No sex. No affair.

'What did happen?' she asked. The words sounded so thin they seemed to dissolve in the air but Joe heard them.

It had started (still an 'it', she noticed) when Frankie suggested that Vanessa talk to Joe about her running for election, and there seemed to be an underlying implication that this somehow meant it was Frankie's fault that 'it' had happened, as if she were responsible for his desires and actions. Then he began to use words that were familiar to Frankie because he was describing feelings that Vanessa had evoked in her as well. Excitement. Passion. A life bigger than Welcome and working to pay a mortgage. They kissed and hugged, he told her, had slept in the same bed, but there was no sex. They agreed on that because that would be too great a betrayal. Frankie wanted to scream until every window in the house broke at the absurdity of that argument, but she said nothing.

Joe kept speaking, his words beginning to lose all meaning, just sounds, and Frankie drifted on them. It was as though she had left her body now and was watching two strangers on the edge of a broken marriage. Joe, as if realising this, began to argue that none of this mattered now because Vanessa was dead.

How blind she had been. Frankie prided herself on being a teacher who could spot trouble a mile away, and yet she hadn't seen what was going on right in front of her. What had been a tragedy happening to someone else now threatened to wash away her whole life as she knew it.

'The police must know about you and Vanessa,' she said eventually. 'That's why they've asked you to go to the station. That's why they could believe that I wrote the note.'

'I went to her house the night she died,' Joe said quietly. 'Vanessa didn't answer the door so I came home.'

He had been working in the city and had arrived unexpectedly. Frankie had been so happy to see him, touched that he had driven over the mountains through the storm to make sure his family was all right, when really he had wanted to be with Vanessa.

The feeling of betrayal was so immense she couldn't even look at it head on. If the police knew he'd been there that night, then he was a suspect, perhaps their chief suspect. If not him, then her. The question that had wandered into her head as she'd packed up Vanessa's room suddenly came back to her with force.

What does a murderer look like?

It had never occurred to her when she was talking to Mer, even though Mer had written those awful notes, but she was thinking about it now.

She lifted her head and looked at her husband.

He could never kill someone. But, then, until ten minutes ago she would have said with the same certainty that he would never cheat on her.

Joe had his head in his hands now and instinctively she felt like comforting him, could feel her treacherous body aching for him.

'I'll call that lawyer,' he said. 'Get them to liaise with the police. We will tell them it was a professional relationship, that we were strategising for her possible election campaign. That you knew all about it.'

The lie came to him so readily that Frankie wondered if he'd had it ready, just in case, as though he had been expecting trouble.

Joe looked over at Frankie to see if she was prepared to go along with this and she found, almost to her surprise, that she was. An echo of the words Carole had said to her only a couple of hours ago came rushing towards her. Never underestimate what a person would do if their family was threatened. Frankie realised that she would do almost anything to keep her family together, and that included lying not only to the police but to herself.

It didn't include killing anyone, though.

What would Joe do to keep his family together?

She thought back to the last time she saw Vanessa.

We need to talk about something delicate.

Had she mentioned this to Joe when they talked on the phone that afternoon? Was that the reason he had driven through a storm and gone straight to Vanessa's?

'You can do that?' asked Joe.

'Yes,' she said.

Dinner was quiet. The day's revelations felt like a corset of iron around Frankie's chest, making it almost impossible to breathe. Luckily, Ollie was happy to fill the holes in conversation. Des was picking him up tomorrow after school and he was going to spend the weekend out on the farm. He chattered on and on about their plans. The storm had cleared out the sediment in the creek, which could lead to more crayfish and shrimp. Danny barely looked up from his plate, wolfed down his food, and then left the table without asking to be excused. Joe opened his mouth to remonstrate, but a slam of the door told them that he had gone to his bedroom.

Frankie did the washing-up alone as Ollie performed his usual disappearing act and Joe muttered something about a missed call from the lawyer.

As she was heading to bed, Danny came out of his room.

'I'm going out for a bit,' he said.

Normally, she would have protested that it was late, tomorrow was a school day, where was he going at this hour, but she could feel the anger radiating off him and guessed that it was fuelled in part by the fact she hadn't acknowledged what it cost him to tell her, because the truth was she wished she didn't know and that she was still living in ignorance.

He turned and walked out of the door and she went to bed.

The light was off when Joe came into the room hours later. Frankie pretended to be asleep, and when he got into bed beside her, the space between them seemed an arid desert, impossible to cross.

Joe fell asleep quickly, as he always did, but she lay awake. It was after midnight when she realised that the pack of condoms were never Danny's, that they must have belonged to Joe and Danny had hidden them, trying to stop his father from betraying her. Her lovely boy had been withdrawing into himself in the last couple of months – the moods, the silences – and Joe kept assuring her that it was all a normal stage of growing up.

Her eyes squeezed shut to stop the tears but then stayed shut, her body too physically tired to take any more, and as she floated away into unconsciousness, her last thought was that she hadn't heard Danny come in yet.

CHAPTER 22

Brianna and her grandmother sat on the couch and watched the local news on television. Jaz was the third item, after a car crash that killed two people and a nurses' strike that was scheduled for the following week. Jaz's photograph was replaced by images of the police at the pine forest.

Brianna shivered.

'You cold there, love?' asked Gran, worried. Her grandmother was treating her as though she were ill, alternating between fussing and feeding. There was a fridge bursting with carbs of every type. 'Need me to get you a jumper?'

'I'm fine,' Brianna said.

Next was an image of Jaz's father and a voiceover saying there was no comment from the family at this time. And then back to Carole, saying if anyone had information to ring Crime Stoppers. Then, curiously, there was a picture of Vanessa on the screen and the journalist said something about how the community was already reeling from the shock of the death of a local celebrity.

'And what's that got to do with anything? Leave that poor woman to rest in peace.' Gran gave a snort of disgust about media sensationalism and switched off the television before Brianna had a chance to protest. She knew exactly what the connection was, had talked to that policewoman about it, but no one else was saying it yet, not publicly at least. Perhaps that was a hint at where the police might be heading, though.

Gran got up and stretched, telling Brianna it must be time for bed because she had school the next day. 'Think it's time for me to go to sleep as well.'

Brianna, who was planning on being sick in the morning, nodded. There was no way she was going back while Mr Roland was there. What if he had heard that she was the one who mentioned his name to the police?

Gran was staying at their house until Amber was comfortable leaving Brianna on her own. Amber probably wouldn't be comfortable till the end of the decade, judging by the way she was carrying on.

'I'm not taking any chances. End of,' Amber said, when Brianna argued that it wasn't necessary. Now Gran was in Amber's bed and Amber was on the couch. Brianna said Gran could have her room but Amber said no, that she needed the routine of sleeping in her own bed. It was something she had read about trauma. Then Gran said she would take the couch, but that was more of a gesture, because all three of them knew that she needed to lie on her back to hook up her sleep apnoea machine at night.

After Amber had left for work at the restaurant, Brianna and her grandmother had spent the evening looking for mentions of Jaz, even though Amber had strictly prohibited this because it was important that Brianna took psychological breaks from all that (another tip from the internet, apparently).

There was less online than Brianna had expected. Someone had started a Reddit list, which spelt Jaz's name wrong, linking to the first news report, but no one had commented on it yet. Brianna knew there would be plenty of speculation on private group chats from school but no one had included her in them. Maybe they were trying to be sensitive, but it felt like she was being excluded. Gran found some Facebook posts and said the local Christian group were talking about holding a vigil to pray for Jaz's safe return but hadn't been able to find a date that everyone agreed on.

The problem was Jaz needed to be richer, or American, or from a big city, or perhaps if there'd been a ransom note. Or maybe the truth was the internet was only interested in teenage girls when they were white and dead or alive and naked. Maybe Jaz needed to have had a sex tape leaked first to get noticed.

Gran had given up her weekly poker game to stay in with Brianna tonight. She said that was fine because she'd gone to her water aerobics at the pool and always needed an early night after that. Amber said that Gran had a better social life than the rest of the family combined.

'People were talking about Jasmine nonstop in the spa after class,' Gran assured her. 'Until we saw the look on Pam Millet's face. The police haven't found her granddaughter yet and it's been months.

That made us all shut up and then it was so awkward there was a stampede for the showers.'

Gran reached over to give her granddaughter a hug. Brianna was head and shoulders over her and could look down at her pink scalp and thinning hair.

'You're safe,' Gran said. 'Nothing for you to worry about, pet. I'm not going to lose you.'

And Brianna squeezed her grandmother tight until the old woman said her ribs might break.

Later, Brianna waited at her mother's bedroom door until she could hear Gran's Darth Vader machine start up. The doctor said if she didn't use it every night there was a chance she wouldn't wake up, and a world without her grandmother didn't bear thinking about. Then she went back downstairs and pulled the cookies 'n' cream ice cream out of the freezer.

Amber hated her eating straight from the container, thought it was disgusting and unhygienic, which was the main reason Brianna did it. She sat cross-legged on the bench, next to the sink, her favourite spot because it gave her a better view of the garden. The ice-cream container was cold in her lap as she buried the spoon into it in order to jemmy up frozen chunks.

Outside was inky black, as if everything familiar had disappeared. The window became a mirror, and Brianna saw her own face reflected back, ghostly pale.

She turned the light off in the kitchen to see better. It was a full moon tonight, searchlight bright, and no clouds for a change, turning the world more of a moody blue than proper black. It made her hope that, somewhere out there, Jaz might be staring up at the full moon as well.

Were they searching the pine forest again tomorrow? Or was that finished and nothing more had been discovered other than the St B's sports top? Amber had come home all excited about it as if in her mind the top was Jaz herself, but before she went to work, she received a text saying that Sherry had found Jaz's sports top in the laundry basket.

'Thought you should know,' Amber said, her mouth pinched and worried, 'but don't give up hoping. They'll find her.'

There were stories circulating around school that Sherry Langridge was beside herself and had demanded that Barton take fifty thousand dollars out of the bank in case they had to pay a ransom. Amber had heard about it at work and then told her daughter that she would call in sick tomorrow as well and all three of them could stay in their pyjamas and watch movies for the day. Brianna said no, because they both knew Amber's boss was a bastard and would leave her off the roster next week in retaliation. Still, she appreciated the gesture.

The cat from next door glided past the window, haughty and proud, flickering fur and glittering eyes. There was a rustling in the grass. A bird called. In the distance a dog howled as a baby wailed. Brianna was sucking on the spoon in her mouth, feeling the cold metal against her tongue, when she saw someone climb over the fence.

They were a patch of darkness, almost impossible to distinguish from the bushland at the back of the house. It was only the fact that the dark blob was moving that gave it away.

It must be Jaz, she thought, and her heart skipped a beat with joy. Wherever she had been, she was back and coming to explain what had happened.

But the shape was too tall, the shoulders too broad.

Brianna didn't move, didn't breathe.

Ivan Roland.

He crept slowly across the garden towards the house, skirted around the moonlight, kept to the shadows. His face was covered by a balaclava. No, there was a flash of pale skin; it must be a hoodie.

Brianna was stuck to the spot, unable to move.

A deep-throated howl from a dog, much closer than before, brought her back to reality. Dozer, the pit bull from next door, muscled, perpetually furious, all teeth and slobbering tongue, started throwing himself at the fence.

Roland froze.

A yell from the neighbour, telling the dog to shut up. Involuntarily, Brianna turned her head in the direction of the noise, and when she looked back the figure had vanished.

Maybe Dozer had scared him away.

There was another bark, quieter, more a growl, and then Dozer fell silent.

Brianna craned her neck, trying to see if the shadow was still there. Thoughts chased each other through her head.

Was the back door locked?

She couldn't remember.

Should she go to Gran? Should she call the police?

In her confusion, she let the spoon fall into the sink. The tinkle of metal on metal sounded as loud as a bell ringing. If Roland was still outside, he would know she was there. The horror of it forced her into action. Brianna jumped off the counter. She only had on a singlet top, no bra, and pyjama shorts – practically naked.

Gran's oversized cardigan was hanging off the back of a chair. She grabbed it, hands clumsy in the rush.

There was the knife block next to the fridge. She almost chose the scissors with their stabbing point, but picked the chef's knife, the biggest one, felt the weight of it in her hand, gripped it tight around the handle so that her knuckles turned white. She wasn't sure she would actually use it to damage someone but it looked convincing.

Running around the counter, she flicked on all the light switches, a set of four on the wall under the clock. Outside, the backyard looked ordinary, nothing there which shouldn't be. He must have gone.

Brianna felt overwhelmed with relief.

Dozer woke up again, started barking loud enough to wake the neighbourhood.

What next? She wouldn't disturb Gran. She was already freaked out about Jaz being missing and Brianna didn't want to worry her further. Maybe she should ring Amber, who would break the land speed record getting home and probably lose her job in the process.

Perhaps she'd imagined it? But Dozer knew someone had been there.

The neighbour was shouting at the dog again. The voice was louder. He must have come outside to see what was bothering Dozer. Brianna didn't know him well. They were a couple of twenty-something renters who had parties that drove Amber mad, but right now Brianna wasn't fussy. She could ask him to come over and look around for her.

She ran to the back door, opened it with a jerk, felt the night air rush in, goosebumps already on her skin. The knife, dangling at her side now, shiny in the moonlight, suddenly felt ridiculous and over the top. The neighbour would think she was a psycho.

Brianna dropped it onto the kitchen table then ran outside, heading down the patio steps to circle around towards the fence, desperate to get there before the neighbour went back inside.

She ran straight into him.

He must have heard the door open and hid around the corner, bursting out at the last minute to grab her as she ran past.

It was too quick for her even to cry out, as if he had snatched her voice as well as her body.

Rough hands turned her around until she was facing him.

'Keep quiet,' he hissed.

A different voice but one she recognised. Bewildered, she stared up at a face that looked every bit as scared as she felt.

It was Danny Birnam.

They sat across from each other at the kitchen table. Brianna watched as Danny gulped down an enormous slice of Gran's cheesecake. He had been coming to tap on her bedroom window, he explained between mouthfuls, had jumped the back fence from the park because he didn't want anyone to know he was here.

Brianna, still brittle and twitchy, heart not quite recovered, asked acidly what was wrong with a phone call or a text. 'You've got my number.'

The scraps of fear that still remained, melded with pride, fury and confusion. Here was the guy who had ghosted her now sitting in her kitchen.

'I had to see you tonight.'

And Brianna couldn't help thinking that if only he had said that to her months ago, life would have seemed wonderful, but instead the words filled her with dread.

She listened quietly as he told her what had happened. How he'd discovered the night of the party that his dad was having an affair with Vanessa. He'd been walking home after it ended, past Vanessa's house, and had seen his father's car tucked away down her driveway. He couldn't understand what it was doing there; his father wasn't due back in town until the next morning. He had confronted his dad about it, and Joe had begged Danny not to tell his mum, had promised that he'd break it off. Danny still wasn't sure whether Joe had done that or if it had been just another of his father's lies, because Danny had found condoms in his briefcase.

Then he told Brianna how the police thought his mother had written the threatening letter.

'But that's impossible,' she blurted out.

Danny looked daggers at her from across the table. 'I told you to leave the note alone. None of this would have happened if you had listened to me.'

'Your mum didn't write it,' she assured him. 'I can't imagine her threatening anyone.'

'Yeah, I know that now,' said Danny. 'Mum told me Mer did it.'

Brianna shook her head in disgust. 'And they keep telling *us* to grow up and act maturely.'

Danny nodded in agreement. 'Even if Mer goes to the cops and tells them, there still has to be a proper investigation into Vanessa's death. Mum and Dad might still be suspects. For all I know, *I* might be a suspect. Teenage boy trying to keep his family together.' He said this with a faux-American accent as if it was already a headline.

Brianna didn't know how any of this had happened. It was like the whole thing had careered across the rails, jumped tracks completely and started mowing down innocent bystanders.

'So what do you want me to do?'

'Isn't it obvious?' Danny replied. 'It's time for Jaz to come back from wherever the fuck she's been hiding so this whole circus can stop. Her missing is turbo-charging everything. It isn't a game anymore. People are getting hurt. My mum's walking around like a zombie.'

Brianna stared at him.

Danny stared back, desperation in his expression. 'You know where she is, don't you?'

She ran her finger across the knuckles of her hand, rubbed between the grooves. Part of her felt relief. Here was another person who thought Jaz had engineered all this somehow, when everyone else seemed certain that disaster had fallen.

She shook her head slowly. 'No, I don't.'

'But this is the plan the two of you dreamt up. She'd go missing, you'd raise the alarm, and the whole place goes nuts thinking that Jaz knows something about why Vanessa was killed.'

The way Danny put it made it sound much more certain than anything Jaz had said to her. All Brianna had to cling to was the look on Jaz's face when Amber had stopped and asked if she wanted a lift. The way her jaw had jutted out and the fact that she had left her phone inside her locker. Brianna felt certain that Jaz would never have done that by accident.

'But she isn't missing, not really?' Danny's hand, resting on the table, balled itself up into a tight fist.

The thing was Brianna didn't know. Sitting across from Danny made her feel that Jaz couldn't be missing, that she must be pulling everyone's strings to get what she wanted. But earlier, sitting next to Gran on the couch watching the search in the pine forest, Brianna had felt that bad things happened to girls all the time, a kind of awful game of musical chairs, and this time it might be Jaz's turn to lose.

Danny gave a kind of strangled gasp, a whimper, and put his head down on the table. To Brianna's shock, his breathing became hard and wet and she realised that he was crying. His face went all splotchy and there was snot involved, which he wiped on the sleeve of his hoodie. It was objectively revolting and yet Brianna knew that she still must like Danny a lot because it didn't bother her at all. In fact, it made her want to cry as well.

Danny lifted his head, pushed his fingers hard against his eyes, tried to stop.

Brianna wanted to help, to do something. Ever since she had spoken to the police she had felt helpless and now she felt worse. Danny was right: it was partly her fault that Mrs Birnam was in trouble.

And then an idea occurred to her. It was one of those ideas shaped like a hinge in that the consequences could go wildly one way or the other, and if Amber got even a sniff, it would be a disaster. She would have to be back by the time her mother knocked off or she might as well be dead.

'Can you drive?' she asked Danny.

'But I haven't got my licence yet,' he said, which meant that he could.

'We'll take my Gran's car,' she told him.

They kept to the back roads of Welcome, took the long way to get over the highway, heading out of town in the opposite direction from the pine forest. The car was a hatchback, small, and every so often Brianna glanced across at Danny, who was hunched over the steering wheel, all long arms and legs. Even though she was terrified beyond measure, in part because of what they were about to do and in part because Amber's rage would be ferocious if she ever found out, there was a small flame of excitement. The two of them were doing this together, which meant there was potential for them to do other stuff together as well.

They didn't talk at all. Brianna, now dressed in a t-shirt and jeans, couldn't think of anything to say, and she wondered if Danny was embarrassed about crying in front of her. She wanted to tell him that it wasn't a big deal but really it kind of was.

The heater started cranking and the windscreen fogged up. They couldn't find the demister and Brianna had to wind down the window. They went over the low-lying bridge which had reopened in the last few days. Brianna explained her idea to Danny on the way out, half-expecting him to talk her out of it, tell her that it was too dangerous, but all he did was give a hard nod of approval.

There was no turning back.

It was one of the new housing estates on the western edge of town, only half-finished. Locals called it the Wild West, half-joking, half not. The builder had gone broke a couple of years ago and there was some court case which meant everything had stopped. Families had moved in on one side of the street while across the way were vacant blocks, full of mud and weeds.

The roads were darker out here. Streetlights were spaced out, some broken. There were no footpaths and little landscaping, a place that had been bulldozed flat for the identical houses to spring up like mushrooms.

Brianna knew this was the right area but wasn't sure of the street name. Opening Google Maps, she zoomed in, reading each of them in turn but nothing rang a bell. Instead, she directed Danny to turn into Nicholson Drive. Last Christmas, half the road was shut to allow people to come and see the houses all lit up. The council had kicked in money to distract from the unfinished playground and non-existent community centre. Barton Langridge had declared the Christmas lights opened and Jaz had invited Brianna to come along for laughs (and to protest the waste of electricity).

Danny slowed down, let the car behind him pass, as Brianna tried to remember which side street they had walked up. They had to back-track once and then she found it. It was at the end of a cul-de-sac, Whiteman Place. Jaz had made a not-so-funny joke about privilege.

'Up the top on the right,' she said, feeling certain now.

They pulled up alongside an L-shaped brick house with a flimsy-looking carport, a roller door behind it. There were lights on, suggesting someone was home.

'There's his car.' Brianna pointed to the bright yellow Kingswood in the front garden. Suddenly, she felt a lot more nervous. She had only met him a couple of times. He might not even remember who she was. This had been a bad idea.

'Want me to come in with you?' Danny asked.

His face was in shadows, which made his expression hard to read.

Brianna would have loved to say yes, but she didn't think that would help. The fewer people who knew about this, the better.

'It's fine,' she said.

'Thanks for doing this.' In a quick movement, Danny put his hand out and rested it on her leg. It reminded her of how he'd held her hand that night at the party.

Brianna smiled back at him, trying to look confident, but was worried he would feel her tremble. What would he do if she didn't come back out? Should he call the police? Brianna's mind raced towards all sorts of possibilities.

'I won't be long,' she said.

Standing outside the car in the cold air, she looked up at the stars. The bright cold light was sharp enough to make her eyes water. She was going to have to bluff her way through this situation, pretending to know a lot more than she actually did.

Her footsteps sounded loud on the concrete as she walked up the path to the front door.

The world was quiet.

She rang the doorbell, heard the echo of it fade.

There was no noise from inside the house.

No one was home. This had all been for nothing. She felt almost weak with the relief of that realisation. Then she heard movement inside.

Brianna took a deep breath as the door opened to reveal Lennox Rivett. He had on a singlet, jeans, bare feet, hair messed up as though he had just got out of bed. A flicker of recognition crossed his face.

'What do you want?' he asked.

'I need to get a message to Jasmine,' Brianna said and walked inside.

CHAPTER 23

It was a little past dawn when Mer climbed the fence, wrestled with the cover and then dived into the pool. She loved that split second of being airborne followed by the plunge. The moment when the entire world turned wet.

This morning the water felt like splinters in her lungs, each breath out an icy gasp, but the memory of trainings long ago had prepared her for it, and she pushed through the first laps when the body feels leaden and has to force a rhythm.

The cold drove out all thought, emptying her mind until just the narrow world of her body and the water remained. Toes, legs, kicking from the glutes, stable core, high elbows, neck, head position, breathing every third stroke, head, shoulders, hips, rotating on the axis and then straight down, not looking forwards or backwards.

Life reduced to a black line bookended by walls.

Finding the path of least resistance, checking the way the water moved over her body, correcting her positioning, micro adjustments, aiming to be more efficient. She kept the pace at a constant, embraced the automatic flow of it and a body memory of what everything needed to do and when.

Her mind wandered now and kept circling back to Frankie.

I can't be friends with you anymore.

What was said yesterday was etched into her skin. All of it was her fault. Intentions were not enough. Those notes were a terrible idea. She had only wanted to protect Frankie and instead she'd made everything worse. Mer wasn't sure what she should be feeling, only knew what she felt, a mixture of anger, sadness and shame.

Months before, Mer had gone to the city to see a band from her childhood, one she had never got to see at the time. There was less hair and more chins, but they still knew their instruments and played their hits. It had been a real hoot. Heading out to a nightclub afterwards, thinking how much Frankie had loved the lead singer when they were young (Mer always went for the drummers), she saw Vanessa and Joe sitting outside at a restaurant. Plausibly two friends having dinner, but Mer knew beyond question they were having an affair. The way Vanessa leant towards him. How Joe only had eyes for her.

She told Des about it. He had been angrier than she'd ever seen him before, almost tempted to take his shotgun around to confront his son-in-law. But Mer had come up with another plan. It was Des who had given her the magazines and his tacit approval.

What would Frankie do about that if she found out? Disown her father as well?

Mer rang Des straight away when she got home from the super-market. He had been silent on the other end, listening as it all came out, and then he told her that he wouldn't disturb Frankie now, but he'd come into town and check up on her in the morning.

Wall. Black line. Wall.

Mr Poole turned up halfway through the next kilometre and waited down one end.

'Everything all right?' he asked her. 'You've been going for a while now.'

She nodded, breathless, not nearly fit enough. 'I'll finish soon.'

'Cup of tea waiting when you need it.'

By two kilometres her body was tired. Her left shoulder hurt. Every stroke felt the pull of something not quite right. She remembered the first time she felt that glitch, the grinding resistance that arrived unannounced one training and the immediate loss of power she felt in her stroke. She didn't tell anyone, not her coach, not her teammates, not anyone who might tell her to rest it, that perhaps she shouldn't swim in the next meet, and certainly not in all the events she was down for. It might have been different if there had been doctors and physios for her to see, but people like her didn't have access to that. All she knew to do was ignore it and keep pushing through, train even harder to keep winning, because that was the only option.

But the shoulder got worse, she started getting slower, rivals got faster, her father got angrier and in the end she gave up swimming, forgot her dreams, got a job to help out the family. Perhaps all of those things would have happened anyway.

It was Frankie who insisted that she stay at school, coached her through maths, forced her to learn the Shakespeare quotes for English, helped her limp through to finish year twelve.

Frankie had been the one constant.

What if yesterday was like hurting her shoulder? What if something had broken that could never be fixed?

She tumble-turned into the last lap and slowly made her way down the pool.

Mr Poole was waiting and after she'd wrapped a towel around herself he handed her a mug. Shivering now, she cradled it in her hands, put her face over it to feel the steam.

'You right to drive home?' he asked. 'Want me to call Frankie?'

He was assuming she was still drunk, like she had been every other time she'd climbed the fence. Mer was almost tempted to say yes, ask him to ring Frankie. Maybe she'd answer a call from Mr Poole.

'I'm stone-cold sober.' She had in fact poured an entire bottle of whiskey down the sink last night, determined to turn over a new leaf.

There was a slow smile, like the sun starting to rise. 'Beginning the day with no hangover and a swim. You're a reformed woman, Meredith Davis.'

That almost made her laugh. 'Still the same fuck-up I've always been, Mr Poole.'

CHAPTER 24

Beth arrived at the academy with a list of chores a mile long to get done before the first class at 10 am. She came up the external stairs, skipping the dodgy step halfway up like all the students knew to do, unlocked the door and walked down the hall to her office, only to find her mother was already there, putting a bundle of bills and invoices on Beth's desk to be dealt with.

'Lovely way to start the day,' Beth remarked, beginning to flick through them. Some days it felt as though the bills were spontaneously reproducing and if left unattended her entire office might soon be covered in notices and demands.

'I thought I'd wait until after the funeral,' said Dolly acidly. 'Didn't want to bring down the mood.'

Beth snorted, because otherwise she would have started crying, and it felt she had cried more in the last fortnight than in all the years before that. She didn't have the energy to cope with Dolly today. If some magic fairy appeared before her offering anything in the world, her first wish would be to sack her mother and appoint an admin manager who wasn't related to her. She'd have to sell a spare kidney to pay them, but it would be worth it.

The first thing to do was to divide the stack into two piles, those that had to be dealt with straight away and those that could wait a day, maybe even a week.

'We can handle all of these,' Beth reassured her mum. 'You go visit Aunty Helen. She'd love some company.'

'Perhaps I should,' said Dolly. 'I mean, now that she owns the entire building and half the business.'

'That's not what I meant.'

'She could close us down tomorrow if she wanted to. Throw us out of work.' Dolly threw her arms in the air dramatically. 'Sell the Palais to the highest bidder.'

Would Helen sell? The idea had crossed Beth's mind. If she could convince her aunt to sell this building, there would be money to have a purpose-built academy with its own car park, four or five studios with Tarkett flooring, walls of mirrors in every room, proper sound systems and dressing rooms. Beth dreamt about developing a proposal for the brand-new Vanessa Walton Dance Academy, one that her aunt couldn't possibly say no to, especially when she told her that it was Vanessa who had been thinking about selling the Palais in the first place.

But all she said to her mother was, 'It's not that simple. There's probate, for starters.'

That was one of the many things on her list, to call the lawyer back, along with invoicing new parents, organising the first-aid training for next week, trying to find a plumber to fix the upstairs bathroom sink before the afternoon classes and then working out how they would rearrange the end-of-year concert to include a tribute to Vanessa. Beth wanted everyone from the tots to the teachers doing an extended version of the steps from the original Sugar Snap commercial, but she still hadn't nailed the choreography in her head.

'Helen is quite the property mogul now,' said Dolly. 'Sole owner of the Palais and now that fancy cottage. Perhaps I should take some of these bills around for her to pay.' Her mother was working herself into a righteous fury born of envy.

'That's not fair.' Beth had left her aunt weeping this morning and still wasn't sure that Helen had eaten a proper meal since Vanessa died. The doctor had prescribed sleeping tablets but Helen refused to take them. 'It's likely that the Langridges will dispute that owner-ship was transferred. They say that Lonnie was not of sound mind. That there was coercion.'

'Lonnie Langridge is as sane as I am!' Dolly exclaimed. 'You can tell the vote-chasing weasel that from me.'

'I think it's best to wait until Jasmine has been found,' Beth answered, and any shred of happiness she had felt about new students or planning her dream studio withered. Jaz had helped at the funeral. Beth had actually walked in on her pashing that boy from the super-market and Beth had become quite flustered, retracing her steps to the sound of Jaz laughing. The thought that someone so alive could be missing or actually worse was too awful.

'Apparently they're interviewing Frances Birnam about that.' Dolly gave her daughter a sly look. 'At the station.'

'Frankie?' That sounded crazy to Beth. 'Because she's Jaz's teacher?'

'Word is she's been suspended from teaching. A fine one to pick for a reading at Vanessa's funeral. Certainly wasn't my suggestion.'

Goodness knows who Dolly would have preferred. Cate Blanchett? Nicole Kidman? Beth gave her mother an exasperated look.

Dolly, perhaps sensing she was teetering on thin ice in her customary sharp heels, decided to retreat. 'Now, don't tire yourself out,' said Dolly. 'Remember how the doctor told you to take it easy.'

'I'm fine,' said Beth. 'I'll just get on with these bills.'

There was the sound of her mother click-clacking down the hall and Beth exhaled, thought about putting the kettle on. She stretched an arm out and ran her fingers across her scalp. The hair was finally beginning to feel more substantial than fuzz.

But then there was the sound of her mother click-clacking back up the hall towards her and she almost had to stop herself from trying to grasp a meagre fistful of hair and pull it out in frustration.

Dolly appeared in the doorway. 'Do you know anything about the journalists hanging around out the front?' she asked.

'What?'

'Out the front,' she repeated. 'Next to the sign. That lass from the local paper. There's a photographer there as well.'

Beth followed her mother to the window in the front room, which was their biggest studio, where they held the Saturday morning ballet classes, as it had full mirrors and the best barre. Beth recognised the young journalist. She was the one who had come and interviewed students last year when the academy won 12 Years and Under Tap Troupe and Modern Expressive/Lyrical Improvisation in the same year at the Eisteddfod.

It was the same journalist who had been at the church reporting on Vanessa's funeral. Beth had read about it on the front page of the paper the next day. She had spoken to some onlookers and a group of the VeeBee fan club that had come to town especially but had mercifully left the family alone.

'Perhaps it's the Facebook post I put up about Jasmine being a former student,' said Dolly.

Beth thought it had looked ghoulish. Dolly wasn't bothered in the least. In her books there was no such thing as bad publicity and she had become a dab hand at getting it. She didn't just create content and post photos; she knew her way around bot accounts and fake positive reviews that were nevertheless quite revealing – if not about the academy, then certainly about Dolly. *Walton's Academy of Dance – not as expensive as you'd think*, or, *Stars aren't born, they're created at Walton's Academy of Dance*. Beth also worried that her mother anonymously commented on their rivals' sites, a charge Dolly always denied, but there was a surprising number of one-star ratings with reviews written in complete sentences and proper punctuation on the Dance Daze website.

'Well, get down there quick and see what she wants,' said Dolly.

'All right, I'm going.'

Dolly's gaze went north of Beth's eyes. The skin around her lips puckered in disapproval. 'Put a hat on – you can't go like that.'

'It's fine.'

Beth went back down the stairs. She had Tapping Tots in an hour and was getting nothing done. The wind had sharpened in the meantime, making her miss the beanie that was sitting in her handbag, but she refused to go back for it on principle.

The journalist clocked her approach, turning to meet her with a lipsticked smile plastered on. 'Beth Fettling, isn't it? We've met before—'

'Sorry, but I'm pretty busy this morning,' Beth interrupted. 'Can I ask why you're here?'

The journalist rearranged her face to look more serious. 'Jasmine Langridge, the girl that's missing, she was a student of yours.'

'When she was five.'

'It's that we need a different angle. We've done the forest, her school, and when I saw the post –'

Dolly was going to be delighted, stuffed full of I-told-you-sos.

'– and the connection to Vanessa, I thought it would be perfect.'

What connection?

'Could we do a short interview? It will only take a couple of minutes. We'll record it to put it up on our website and then perhaps take a photo of you in front of the sign.'

Beth wasn't sure about any of this but Dolly would have a fit if she missed the opportunity. No such thing as bad publicity.

'All right.'

The young woman hesitated. 'Do you want a minute to fix . . . um . . .?' She waved a hand in the direction of Beth's scalp.

'Not much to fix.'

'If you're sure.' The woman didn't seem chastened in the slightest. She nodded to the cameraman, who began recording. 'Now, you knew Jasmine well. What are your thoughts on her disappearance?'

Beth didn't really have many thoughts. 'We want to see her home safe and sound. We hope that will happen as soon as possible.' She probably spoke too quickly but the journalist didn't seem bothered.

'She was a student at your school,' the journalist prompted.

'That's right, Walton's Academy of Dance.' And then, because it felt crass to be spruiking the business, she added, 'But that was a long time ago.'

'And she was a student of your recently deceased cousin, the well-known actress Vanessa Walton.'

'Out at St Brigid's, not here,' Beth clarified.

'Are you aware that before she disappeared, Jasmine made shocking allegations about Vanessa's death, saying she believed it was suspicious?'

Beth blinked, bewildered, wondering if she had misheard.

'Are you calling on police to open a homicide investigation into your cousin's death? Do you believe that Jasmine Langridge's disappearance is connected to it?'

Beth stood there dumbstruck, unable to process the implications of what she had heard, and then she burst into tears.

—

At breakfast, Billy's youngest asked him if he was ever going to find Jasmine Langridge.

Not even eight years old and even she knew about the missing girl.

Before he could answer, Tracey got in first. 'Where's your lunchbox from yesterday?' she snapped. 'That's the only mystery that needs to be solved at breakfast.'

She was cross because Billy had refused to tell her why the police were out at St Brigid's yesterday.

Billy did want to ask Tracey if it was possible that Joe could have been having an affair with Vanessa, because Tracey didn't miss much when it came to gossip in Welcome, but Carole would be furious and throw him off the investigation if she found out he was revealing confidential information.

Maybe there was another reason why Joe's car was seen at Vanessa's house. Maybe Frankie didn't write those notes. Maybe it was a fuck-up in the lab. It was possible.

Angie was out at the front desk when he came in. No one else was around. It was still too early. 'Sarge is getting a bollocking from the super,' she told him. 'I'm staying out here until he's done.'

The new station's office walls weren't thick enough to drown out the superintendent's voice when he really got going.

'What's up?'

'That local journo from the paper has got wind of the fact that Jasmine Langridge was telling people Vanessa was murdered.'

'Who told her?' he asked, thinking, please don't let it be Tracey. He had already talked to his wife about needing to keep things confidential, like Carole had told him to do.

'It will be Troy,' Angie said dismissively. 'He's been trying to get into that journo's knickers for the past four months and she strings him along to get whatever tidbits she can. Won the lottery this time. Anyway, the super's furious.'

Wait until he heard who Jasmine was accusing.

Carole's face gave nothing away at the morning briefing. Billy liked the way she ran them, brief and to the point, everyone clear about what they were going to do that shift. Today included tours of the shopping district, keeping an eye out for amateur street artists and shoplifters, tracking down some hoons who had been disturbing the peace out at the Wild West and investigating a bad smell from one of the abandoned houses on Stanley Street.

Some other sergeants he had worked under liked to waffle on half the morning, getting distracted and playing favourites with the good jobs. He'd scored more security footage viewing today but at least it wasn't Stanley Street. He would put money on that being some kind of dead animal.

Before she dismissed them, Carole brought up the importance of confidentiality and gave the squad the exact same talk she had given him previously.

Billy glanced over at Troy to see if he looked even the slightest bit guilty, but Troy had on his poker face and even nodded his agreement with what Carole was saying. Crafty bugger.

CHAPTER 25

Showered, hair pulled back into a wet ponytail, Mer drove into the police station car park. She had already left a message for work, saying she wouldn't be in today, didn't give a reason. Sue would be apocalyptic, it was the second Friday in a row that she'd taken off, but Mer didn't care.

She hated police stations. Walking into them made her feel like she had done something wrong, even when she hadn't. Except this time she had done something very wrong. She could be charged and end up in court. The whole town would find out: her kids, people at work, those weirdo VeeBees – none of which she had thought of at the time. So many chickens were coming home to roost she was in danger of being flattened by feathers.

Clambering out of the car, bag over her shoulder, she saw Billy walking out of the station. He looked about as bad as she felt, eyes bloodshot, skin pale, like he hadn't slept much last night either.

'Are you on your way out?' she asked.

'Coffee machine's broken,' he explained. 'I'm walking down to McDonald's to get one. You want something?'

Mer shook her head.

'Everything all right?'

'I'm fine,' lied Mer. She couldn't bear to tell Billy what she'd done and see his puppy dog eyes get all disappointed – and then there was his wife with her big mouth. 'Need to see your boss about something. She in yet?'

He nodded, not even that curious. 'Ask for her at reception.'

Mer had to wait in the interview room for what felt like hours before Carole came in with that smart-arse Troy, who was actually looking a bit sorry for himself. Carole asked all the questions and he sat next to her not saying anything.

The interview was recorded. Mer put the magazines on the table, expecting a reaction. Troy's eyebrows rocketed upwards but Carole kept a steady gaze.

Mer explained how she'd made the notes, flicked through the pages to show where she had cut out words. She had put one in Vanessa's handbag while she was performing in the gala, another on her car and a couple through the letterbox. She had even snuck down the side of the house and pushed one under the back door to give the impression that she'd got into the house.

'I didn't want her dead,' Mer explained. 'Just wanted her to leave town.'

'Why was that?' Carole asked.

A shrug from Mer. 'I was drunk and it seemed like a good idea at the time.'

This got a sharp look from Carole, and Mer dropped her eyes and kept them fixed on the now-forgotten movie star on the front cover of the magazine on the table.

'You know, for someone who was universally loved, Vanessa Walton was sure hated by a lot of people,' said Carole.

'If you ever met her,' answered Mer, 'you'd understand why.'

'How did Joe Birnam get on with Vanessa? Were they close?'

There was no way she was going to confirm the affair. All she could hope was that Frankie didn't find out.

'No idea.'

'We have a witness who saw his car regularly parked in Vanessa's driveway overnight,' said Carole.

Mer shrugged and then leant back in her chair like she was bored.

Eventually the questions petered out and Troy switched off the tape.

'Am I going to be charged?' Mer asked.

'You certainly could be,' said Carole. Her voice sounded as if it could go one way or the other and she wasn't fussed which. 'We will assess all the evidence before making any decisions about that.'

A phone buzzed. Troy looked at his boss.

'You can take it,' said Carole. There was something icy in the words that Mer didn't quite understand but Troy shot out of the room without a word.

'For what it's worth,' said Mer. 'I think Vanessa died in an accident, like the coroner said. People fall and hurt themselves all the time.'

'That's not for you to determine,' Carole said. 'It's not even up to me. Any report will be sent to Homicide and they'll decide whether or not to open an investigation.'

'Frankie had nothing to do with any of it,' said Mer. 'You don't need to talk to her.'

'We'll take that on board.'

It wasn't a yes, but it wasn't a no either.

'Where were you on the night of the storm?' Carole asked.

'You can't seriously think that I killed Vanessa?'

'You threatened her.'

'I was at home,' Mer said. 'Want to talk to my kids or look at my phone?'

'Might take you up on that offer later, but you can go for now.'

The two women stood up.

'I am sorry,' said Mer.

Carole's face wore the sort of expression that said she heard people apologising all the time and didn't think much of it.

'I mean it,' said Mer, stung.

'Are you sorry for what you've done or sorry you've been found out?'

Mer hesitated. 'More the last, if I'm being honest.'

'It's not me you should be saying sorry to,' Carole said.

'I've already apologised to Frankie,' Mer said, angry now. 'I did that straight away.'

Carole shook her head. 'I live alone. Maybe you will one day. Receiving letters like this must have been unsettling, especially when there's no one else there. It just might be the reason you get up in the middle of the night to investigate some suspicious noise and end up falling down the stairs. Think about that.'

Mer already had.

—

Carole had already pegged Mer Davis as someone who would have no trouble telling lies, even more so if she was protecting someone she loved. Billy had told her on the way back from St B's that Mer had been Frankie Birnam's best friend for years.

Would Mer kill Vanessa to stop the affair?

Had Vanessa actually been murdered?

If Mer had told the truth, then the notes were a dead end, and without them there wasn't much left to say that Vanessa's death was suspicious – a light bulb that wasn't there, no water stains, the theories of one missing schoolgirl and one nosy neighbour who liked to give out cryptic clues like she was Welcome's equivalent of Deep Throat.

Barton Langridge might have been banging furiously on her door and Vanessa might have been fleecing her landlady for money, but Vanessa Walton was walking around Welcome alive after 10 pm, when Barton wasn't even in town.

All of this had been pointed out to her by the super this morning at a decibel range equivalent to a police siren. Finding Jasmine was the squad's clear priority.

Still, it would be worth talking to Joe Birnam, to 'shake the tree' as one of her old bosses used to call it. There had been a message from his lawyer saying that the Birnams wouldn't be able to come into the station today but would be in contact next week to negotiate a suitable time. The cheek of it.

Carole had to accept that it was possible Vanessa Walton accidentally fell down the stairs, but she couldn't help feeling that she was missing something obvious.

'Boss!' Billy stood there with a takeaway coffee in his hand and a big fat smile on his face.

'Goddammit, that better be for me,' Carole said. 'And I'm hoping you've spiked it with something hard.'

His smile changed to something more uncertain, which telegraphed that neither of those things were true, and because in this job there never was enough smiling, Carole felt bad when Billy held out the coffee he had clearly bought for himself, but she took it all the same. He needed to learn to anticipate better.

'What have you got?' she asked.

'I went back through all the security footage from the school and there was something we missed. Two things actually.'

One door closes, another opens.

'It's the footage of Jasmine,' he said. 'I'll bring it up.'

He moved to her computer, opened up the system and then clicked on the file. 'The first is when she tries to get back into the school because she'd realised that she forgot her phone.'

The black-and-white footage showed Jasmine going through her bag and then trying to open the back door to the school building, shaking it and then peering in to see if anyone could let her in.

'The school cleaner finally rang me back and I asked him about it. He says that door is never locked because he goes in and out of it to empty his bucket down the drain outside. He doesn't lock the back door until after nine pm, when he's finished cleaning the entire school.'

'He can remember that night in particular?'

Billy shook his head. 'Just swears blind he never locks it.'

'Someone else could have locked it.'

'But then there's the second thing. It's from the very start of the footage, before Brianna and Amber come past.'

He rewound the footage back until Jasmine was standing there, her schoolbag next to her.

'I've watched it several times,' Billy said. 'Look what she does.'

Carole watched as Jasmine reached into her bag and pulled something out. There was a micro glance down. The music teacher walked past her, along with other students and cars.

The camera was at a funny angle, only capturing the shape of Jasmine, head lowered, hand in front of her.

'What's she doing?' asked Carole. 'It looks like she's reading something.'

'She's looking at a phone,' Billy said. He pointed at the shadow in her hand. 'Watch.'

The movement is quick. One second she was reading something on it and then suddenly it was gone and she was looking straight ahead.

'She slipped it into the pocket of her school blazer.'

Carole let Billy have his moment of triumph uninterrupted. It was the least she could do.

'Jasmine Langridge had two phones,' he said.

'Which means that she probably left the other phone in her locker as a decoy.'

Billy nodded.

'So she has staged her own disappearance,' said Carole. 'Now why would she do that?'

CHAPTER 26

Lennox had told her not to go too far from the caravan in case someone saw her. For the first couple of days she did as he said, but Geraldine stayed up in the farmhouse, which was over the other side of the ridge anyway, and there was no one else around for miles.

The weather was getting hotter, too. The radio said it would be almost thirty degrees this afternoon, the hottest day of spring so far. The caravan would be like an oven. It had been Lennox's idea to bring out the radio and batteries for Jaz to keep track of the local news. It was odd hearing your own name with the word 'missing' attached to it. There'd been no mention of a homicide investigation into Vanessa's death, though, which meant it was still only the local cops looking into it – or, more likely, not doing a single thing about it.

It was her fault Vanessa had been murdered, so she had to do her best to bring the killer to justice. Jaz would stay missing until the police opened an investigation, and then she'd go back to town and tell the detectives what she knew and not pretend that she'd been abducted. She'd spent enough time sitting around thinking in the last few days to have seen all the holes in that story. If the police caught her lying, then that would undermine the evidence she actually had.

Barton was obsessed with power. How to get it. How to keep it. How to wield it. It was one of his favourite dinner table lectures, which Jaz had to listen to again and again. Not that he noticed, because he treated her as you might treat a pet dog: part of the family but incapable of rational conversation. She knew he preferred the smaller Jaz, cute and photogenic, able to be used in marketing to make him look more human. Her stepfather only wanted a two-dimensional family that could be displayed when required and then rolled up and forgotten about until the next campaign.

Barton could have disposed of the supermarket bag by now but it didn't matter because Jaz had taken pictures of the contents – Vanessa's black wig and long red coat, exactly as Mr Singh had seen her that night – and left them on her phone, including the location of where she found them. All she needed was for the police to notice.

But it wasn't just the wig and coat in the supermarket bag. There had also been the posters she had made for Vanessa's campaign all ripped up and the badges as well. It had been her idea for Vanessa to challenge Barton, and look how he'd responded. Well, not him exactly – Barton would never get his hands dirty like that – but he was the one responsible for giving orders.

Surely the homicide detectives would understand that as well as the other evidence she had found.

When she came down for dinner after finding the bag in the wardrobe, she discovered that Sherry and Barton were on their way out to the Welcome Warriors award night. The minute their car left the drive, she checked out the security footage for their house the night Vanessa died.

There it was. At 10.08 pm, a woman in a red coat and black wig appeared at the top of their driveway and walked around the side of the house, heading towards the back door, her head hunched over from all the rain, which was absolutely pelting down, so you barely make out her face.

Jaz had saved it all to a memory stick shaped like a creepy witch's finger with a long nail, which was currently in the front pocket of the schoolbag sitting on the caravan floor in front of her. What she wouldn't give to point that finger straight at Barton.

I accuse you.

Why had Vanessa come to their house? Who was she meeting?

Because at 10.08 pm Sherry had still been at Lonnie's checking on leaks. She had rung Jaz earlier that day to tell her to organise her own dinner because it was going to take a while. At 10.08 pm Barton would have been in the city.

The only person in their house at 10.08 pm was Jaz. She was up in her bedroom, watching YouTube clips, listening to Spotify and completely oblivious.

The guilt was almost overwhelming.

That's why she needed to do all this.

The only thing she wished she had checked before she left was the computer in Barton's home office, but she didn't want to tip him off that she was going through his stuff. She'd tell the police to do that straight away. It wouldn't take a master hacker to get access. Her stepfather, who made speeches to Parliament about protecting children from the evils of the internet and how the youth of today didn't understand that misbehaviour online lasts forever, was also the type of genius who put messages in the trash on his desktop but then forgot to actually empty the trash. Barton probably expected a digital servant or her mother to turn up and do it for him.

Jaz was prepared to spend quite a few days in a musty old caravan to avenge Vanessa, and when she reappeared she would contact that journalist from the local paper and give her an exclusive that would end up on every news bulletin in the country, claiming that she'd had to hide because she was afraid Barton would arrange to have one of his thugs kill her like he did with Vanessa.

But this afternoon she deserved a reward. She would go down to the creek for a swim. It had been days since she'd had a shower and she was beginning to stink of sweat and this caravan, and her hair was slick with grease. Lennox would flip his lid if he found out, but he wouldn't find out because there was no one out here to see.

CHAPTER 27

Frankie lay in her bed, not sleeping. She was vaguely aware of the sound of a car pulling up and the doorbell ringing but wasn't ready to engage with the outside world. Joe had left their bed wordlessly, slinking out of the room as though he didn't belong there. She had watched him go through half-closed eyes but couldn't bring herself to say anything.

Shame overwhelmed her. Part of her wanted to hold this new discovery, this hidden side of her husband, her own stupidity, tight to her chest, to trap and keep it there forever so that no one else would ever see, but she couldn't even do that. Everyone had worked it out before her, even their own son.

So many questions were in Frankie's head it felt like it could explode, but even so she deliberately avoided the biggest one – who might have killed Vanessa? – preferring to paddle in shallow waters instead.

Was it about sex? Because they had a sex life – a good one she had believed until yesterday, even if it tended to be more scheduled than spontaneous. But if it wasn't scheduled then it wouldn't happen at all, and surely that was worse. Mer had once been horrified to work out that if Frankie had sex once a week (feasible) then she would have had more sex over the years than Mer, with all her feasts and famines. Captain Sensible had been secretly delighted.

But Joe claimed he didn't have sex with Vanessa. Had he been in bed with Vanessa and then come home and had sex with her? Somehow that felt an even worse betrayal.

Was Vanessa the only one?

She lay there in the bed she had shared with him for years, thinking about his work trips. Frankie had never checked messages on his phone or entries on his bank statements. It had always felt to her an act of faith but perhaps Joe had interpreted it as permission. Mer had once quizzed her about what she would do if she found out Joe was unfaithful. Frankie had blathered on about true love and commitment in ways that now seemed equal parts smug and naive. If someone said those words to her right now she would want to punch them.

She knew why Mer had written those notes rather than tell her the truth, because although Mer would never choose a man over their friendship, the same couldn't be said of Frankie. Frankie would choose Joe over Mer in a heartbeat, was in fact doing that even now.

Frankie's high moral ground of yesterday now had more cracks than the San Andreas Fault, because if Vanessa were still alive, then Frankie would want to kill her. Mer would probably do it for her.

Not that she wasn't still furious at Mer. Her actions meant that the police were involved and she was suspended. In fact, now that was starting to sink in and the shock had worn off, she was even angrier with Mer than before, if that was possible.

There was a knock on the bedroom door.

Frankie closed her eyes and pretended she was asleep.

'Mum,' said Danny.

She opened one eye.

Danny stood in the doorway, hair standing on end, still in his pyjamas, looking uncertain. For a moment it could have been Joe, the teenage boy version with the lovely smile who had snatched her heart right out of her body and then broke it thirty years later.

'I've boiled the kettle,' her son said.

The alarm clock said ten minutes past nine. Danny and Ollie should be at school now and she was supposed to go to the police station.

She pushed herself up to sitting.

'Grandpa was here while you were asleep. He's taken Ollie out to the farm. He said to ring him if you need anything.'

'Does Ollie know?' she asked.

Danny shook his head. 'He thinks Dad's gone off for work today and he's getting the day off school. I told him you were sleeping in because you had a cold.'

She breathed out, relieved and sad at the same time. 'And Grandpa?'

'He didn't say but I think he knows something's up.'

That would be Mer interfering again. Frankie's jaw clenched.

Danny stayed at the door until he saw his mother getting out of bed.

The kitchen was too quiet. Danny had put her favourite cup on the table and made the tea the way she liked it, stewed with a splash of milk. There was toast on the plate, lots of butter and a scraping of Vegemite, the way she had it when she was poorly. Danny had watched her far more closely than she realised. Overnight their roles had reversed and he had grown up, was trying to be the family's encourager-in-chief, making sure she ate properly, that his brother was cared for.

Not overnight, she realised. He had been parenting his father for a lot longer. It was deeply unfair.

'I'll be all right, love,' she assured him. 'We all will be, you'll see.'

She sat down at the table and saw that next to the cup was a Mars Bar.

'Grandpa said that was for you.'

It was what they used to eat in the paddocks together, away from the eagle eye of her mother, who worried about appetites and children being spoilt. A Mars Bar was Des's answer to life's problems. He must know about Joe's infidelity.

Frankie ripped off the wrapper and took a bite.

Danny looked happy for the first time that morning.

'You've got messages on your phone,' he said.

She nodded, took another bite, tasting the sweetness but not enjoying it. She kept going through the motions of chewing and swallowing so that her son kept smiling.

'Dad's headed to the city to talk to the lawyer.' His voice sounded more uncertain now. 'He wanted you to know that the interviews at the police station have been postponed for the time being and he'll be back tonight.'

Joe wanted her to know that, did he? What about everything else that he had kept from her? All of a sudden she felt she might scream or do something other than dumbly listen to what exactly it was that her husband wanted her to know, but Danny was now looking worried, so instead she shoved the rest of the chocolate bar in her mouth and put the wrapper in the bin.

'I'm going to have a shower,' she mumbled. It was the only place she could think of where she could cry in peace.

Huddled in the bath, the water streamed over her, mixing in with the tears. She tried to make sense of her life. The last twenty-four hours felt like a horror movie in which someone was attacking her life with a rusty saw, hacking away bits of her identity. Wife. Best Friend. Teacher. Taking great lumps out of her so that she could bleed out entirely.

She stayed there so long that the hot water gave up, and Danny looked relieved when she walked through the living room, clutching her towel around her. Back in her bedroom, she stared at the laundry basket, full of Joe's dirty clothes, and a lava-hot rage overwhelmed her. All the meals, the clothes washing, the child rearing, the house-work, the prioritising of his career even though hers had always been the backbone of their finances, all of which she had accepted as being part of the deal. And his side of the bargain had been what? Don't fuck her friends?

How could Mer not have told her, she raged inwardly, while at the same time she still blamed Mer for having known. Even though this was unfair, she felt it deeply all the same.

Mid-afternoon, she was sitting on the couch, the dogs piled up next to her as if sensing she needed comfort, when there was a knock on the front door. Frankie ignored it. Danny was in his room, probably had his headphones on listening to music.

A few minutes later there was a banging on the back door, an impatient knock that sounded like Mer.

Danny appeared with a question on his face.

'I'll go,' Frankie said.

She marched to the kitchen, growing angrier with every step, and pulled open the door expecting to see Mer, ready in fact to slam the door in her face after saying a few choice words.

'Beth!' said Frankie.

For one moment she could see the resemblance to Vanessa, the same wide-spaced eyes and bone structure, but Beth was the more squashed version, with dark-rimmed eyes and skin a washed-out grey. She remembered how she had offered to pack up Vanessa's office. 'I completely forgot about bringing over the boxes,' she started, as Beth began talking at the same time.

'There are rumours about a homicide investigation into Vanessa's death but the police aren't telling us anything. Mum heard that you were at the station and I wondered if you knew what was happening.' She started shaking, a repressed sob in her voice.

They sat in the kitchen and Frankie told her the story as honestly as she could: the letters, her fingerprint and Mer.

Beth listened, sipping on the water that Frankie had poured for her. She didn't ask questions or interrupt with her own anecdote like Mer would. She didn't try to solve the problem halfway through as Joe was prone to do. Instead, she sat there, reaching out to hold Frankie's hand when Frankie began to cry while explaining how she'd found out about Joe and Vanessa.

'I thought she was my friend,' she told Beth. 'Did you know?'

Beth shook her head.

'Joe says they didn't have sex. He actually expects me to believe that.'

Beth looked pensive. 'I wouldn't discount it. I think for her the attraction was the attention, not necessarily the sex.'

What about the condoms or the contents of Vanessa's second drawer?

'I'm not saying this to excuse what happened,' Beth continued, 'but Vanessa never had to live by the rules that applied to the rest of us and that did have its downsides. Being famous so young warped her because nothing else in life could ever quite compete. It's a bit like an addiction, really.'

'It doesn't make it right.'

'Of course not, but don't be too hard on Joe. Vanessa has always had this ability to make people do crazy things they wouldn't have done on their own. She was kind of like an act of God, but we still loved her, right?'

Frankie couldn't answer that right now so changed the subject. 'Did she tell you about the threatening letters?'

Beth nodded. 'She made a kind of joke of them at the start. How they were tame compared to what was said online. I think she was just trying to ignore them, will them away, accept them as the price of doing business.'

Frankie shook her head in disbelief. 'That's insane.'

'Remember this is Vanessa we're talking about. Most of her life was insane.'

'How did you turn out to be so normal?'

Beth laughed, really laughed. 'You know, that's the first time anyone has said that and meant it as a compliment. Most of the time it's: "How can you be so ordinary when Vanessa is amazing?"'

'You're the amazing one,' said Frankie. 'I would have gone crazy.'

'Oh, I could go crazy between keeping the academy running and having to organise probate. How can I tell Aunty Helen there's going to be a police investigation? It's all just a hangover of Vanessa's fame, like her drama is contagious.'

'Maybe when Mer comes forward about the notes, it will all settle down,' Frankie said. 'But on the other hand, it is possible someone *was* responsible. I mean, Barton Langridge was seen at her house that night, for starters.'

Not just Barton. Joe had admitted being there as well.

'She was already dead when Barton was there,' Beth said. 'The coroner found she fell down the stairs. That's what happened, and I don't want any more journalists trying to get me to cry for clickbait.'

Frankie's phone rang. Beth stopped talking and looked in its direction.

'It's probably Mer or Joe, and I'm not ready to talk to either of them now.'

'What if it's the police?'

Frankie pushed back her chair and grabbed it. A missed call from Des. 'It's Dad,' she said. 'He's got Ollie. I'd better ring him back.'

Beth nodded as she picked up her water glass.

The phone rang again in Frankie's hand.

CHAPTER 28

Des pulled up outside the farmhouse and Ollie clambered out of the ute to find Patch. The dog had been lying on his table, next to the farmhouse, lapping water from his bowl.

'He's pleased to see you,' Des said.

Ollie scratched Patch's head with one hand as he took off his mask with the other. He had insisted on wearing it in the ute because Mum was sick and staying in her room, which meant she must have COVID. Des was more than happy to go along with that reasoning rather than explain why he had picked up Ollie first thing in the morning instead of after school. It had been an instinctive decision after he had gently knocked on Frankie's bedroom door and hadn't got any answer. Part of Des was relieved. He never would have been able to find the words to fix a situation like this. Alice wouldn't have been so reticent. His late wife would have marched into the bedroom, thrown back the curtains, and demanded to know what

Frankie was still doing in bed when there were chores to be done and meals to be made. Alice was never one to feel sorry for herself or have much sympathy for anyone else either. But if she had found out about Joe having an affair, she'd have confronted him directly. Des had always preferred action over words.

The boy crouched down and buried his face in Patch's fur.

'Not sure that's a good idea,' Des said. 'Been a while since Patch got a wash.'

'Mum takes our dogs to the groomers,' Ollie said, ruffling the dog's ears. 'They come back with bows and everything.'

Des couldn't imagine one of his dogs with bows in their fur. What a ridiculous thing to do – not that he would ever say that aloud. One of the reasons he liked being around animals was they never expected much conversation. Mer was a good one for speaking her mind. She had enough opinions for the two of them combined and then some left over.

When she had told him about Joe and Vanessa, Des had been overcome by a physical rage of a type he hadn't felt before. It shook him even now to remember it. He wasn't sure he would admit to his daughter that he'd played a part in the mess she was embroiled in. She might never forgive him for it.

Ollie turned, looked up, squinting in the sunlight. 'Let's go down to the creek.'

It was a lovely day, warm moving towards hot. There were dozens of things Des could be doing. That was the thing about a farm: it never stopped.

'Catch some fish, try for yabbies,' Des answered with approval. 'Let's get the rods out from the shed.'

The creek was technically the border between his property and the neighbours'. Des wanted to have a crack at reducing the invasive species and then get it restocked with perch and cod as a welcome home for Nate when he got out of jail. Maybe he should talk to Gerri about it, get her involved as well.

Des and Ollie walked along the dirt track, each with their own rod. Ollie had brought along his binoculars for birdwatching and Des had the esky. Patch mooched alongside them, showing some interest in the lounging kangaroos, but he knew better than to disturb them. Ollie chatted happily about how he could set up a tent and camp out here next school holidays but was less cheery when Des asked about school and then home. He complained about his brother's moodiness, how he had been bossed around this morning and was given Vegemite on toast for breakfast when he always had peanut butter. There was no mention of Joe, and Des wondered what this all meant for his daughter's marriage, didn't want to presume one way or another, but deep down he suspected that Frankie was too soft-hearted and would be inclined to forgive him. She would worry about the boys and money as well, though he could help with that.

What was it about kind people that they never valued their own happiness enough?

Words formed in his head that he'd like to say to her but never would, advice around knowing yourself, being brave and not to have regrets.

As he got the rods ready, Patch launched into the water, came out and shook himself dry as if he had listened to the talk of ribbons and dog grooming and that's what he thought of it. Ollie found a large rock, perched himself up high on it, asked if they could light a fire later on and cook their redfin outside.

Des was noncommittal. 'Got to catch it first,' he said.

Ollie decided to walk upstream, wanting to see the small rapids. Des told him to take Patch and not be too long, there was fishing to be done. Within a few minutes he had a nibble on the line but lost it and nothing happened for a while. He decided they would move to a different spot when Ollie came back.

His mind wandered to Vanessa. He had never warmed to her, even as a child, but she was talented, he couldn't deny that. Des had seen her backstage at the gala and she'd seemed small and depleted, a husk rather than the star she had been, and yet everyone was fussing around her. But then some people were the sun around which everyone else revolved. Joe had got caught in that orbit but Des couldn't forgive him for it.

It was at least half an hour before the boy returned but then he arrived in a rush. Des knew something was up the moment he caught sight of him, running along the bank, arms pumping, knees high, grimacing, as if he were being chased, Patch loping alongside, excited at the game.

Dropping his rod in the water, Des moved towards him.

'What is it?' he asked, chest tight. 'What's wrong?'

'The girl,' Ollie said, his breath catching on every word. 'The girl. The one who's missing. I've just seen her.'

CHAPTER 29

The water in the creek was colder than Jaz expected. It was tempting to dive straight in but she knew better than that and edged in gingerly from the side, careful not to cut her feet on sharp rocks or twigs. She had stripped down to her bra and undies, almost tempted to go completely nude, but the truth was they needed a wash as well.

It felt good to be wet, to sluice away the sweat, dust and dirt from the last few days. She took the plunge and submerged herself whole, keeping her eyes shut, before she came up gasping and wriggling, feeling new again.

There was a gritty, slimy feel underfoot and Jaz remembered stories of swimming snakes and bloodsucking leeches, but it was lovely to be out of the caravan. She lay on her back for a bit, floating further down the river until she got to a rocky area. Pulling herself out, she clambered up onto the bank. There was no breeze.

Shivering, she counted her mosquito bites. There were eighteen on one leg alone. Eventually, the sun began to warm her blood. She tried to remember songs about rivers, even sang a couple aloud, but there were too many words missing so in the end she la-la-laed for the most part.

It would have been nice to share this with someone else. She couldn't imagine it being Lennox, not after the way he talked to her on the phone, constantly complaining. Nate was different, though. Perhaps one day they could come out here together, stay in the caravan away from the rest of the world. She'd like that.

Jaz walked back upstream to where her clothes were and then headed back to the caravan. Maybe she could go home tomorrow or the next day, return to face whatever was waiting for her. It wouldn't be easy but she was at peace with what she had chosen to do and was prepared to live with the consequences of her decisions.

Lennox's sister's white Commodore was parked next to the caravan and Jaz quickened her pace when she saw it, calling out for him. He appeared from around the far side of the caravan, all muscle tee and ripped jeans.

She ran towards him. It felt good to see another human being, even this human being.

But Lennox stepped back, avoiding her outstretched arms. 'Where have you been?' he asked, impatient and borderline aggressive.

'At the river,' Jaz said, her good mood dissolving.

'We agreed that you'd stay in the caravan or near it,' said Lennox. He was talking to her like he was her teacher or parent. 'Otherwise you increase the risk of being seen.'

'You can't expect me to stay inside forever.'

'I've been waiting for you for over fifteen minutes. The longer I'm out here the more likely it is I'll be missed. You don't understand how hard this has been. I've been questioned by the police. People want me to be sacked from my job.'

It was the same complaints from before but Jaz wasn't going to put up with that now. 'I've been out here by myself for four days living on Barbecue Shapes and water. It's freezing at night, there are cockroaches in the caravan and it feels like something's crawling on my scalp.'

That shut Lennox up, but only momentarily. 'All right, it hasn't been easy for either of us, but I've got some good news.'

Jaz calmed down. 'Has something happened?'

Lennox grinned. 'You could say that. Let's have a drink and I'll tell you all about it.'

Jaz saw how his nose wrinkled when he walked into the caravan, but he didn't say anything, instead grabbing one of the bottled waters and sitting down at the fold-out table. She slid in opposite him.

'Your friend Brianna paid me a visit late last night. She was with that other boy, the one she fancied.'

'Danny? What did they want?' She couldn't imagine Brianna being brave enough to actually go to Lennox's house.

'Told me that they knew you hadn't been abducted, that you must be hiding somewhere and that it was time to come home. She says the police are interviewing people about Vanessa's death.'

Jaz felt like cheering. At last!

'But that's not all,' Lennox said. 'Rumours are your mum has got good old Barton to take fifty thousand dollars out of the bank in case there was a ransom demand.'

There was something almost lustful about the expression on Lennox's face. He'd had the same sort of greedy look in his eyes the first time she had undressed for him. 'And it got me thinking how, since we already planned to make this look like an abduction, why don't we take the money as well?'

'What?'

'Fifty thousand dollars. We send a text telling him where to leave it and then dump you on the road the next day. Easy. You're always saying how loaded he is. That money is nothing to him.'

Jaz knew straight away this was a stupid idea. It raised the stakes astronomically.

'No way,' she said. 'If the police found out it would ruin everything. We need to keep this simple, focused on Barton. I've decided not to tell them I was abducted. I'll just say I was too scared to come forward until I knew there was an official homicide investigation taking place because I didn't trust the local cops. If they find out we've taken money, they're never going to listen to me. We'll get charged with fraud.'

Lennox's brow furrowed. 'Don't you see? We could give some to Nate when he gets out.'

This was supposed to be the clincher, Jaz could tell. Lennox had probably spent the whole drive out in the car rehearsing it in order to convince her. But this was her plan, not his, and it was about doing the right thing, not getting money. Lennox Rivett was not going to stuff it up for her. In fact, she might as well wrap the whole thing up before he had another brainwave. Brianna had said the police were interviewing people about Vanessa's murder. Well, they should interview her.

'I'll come back into town with you now. We've achieved what we wanted. It's time for me to go talk to the police.'

He slammed his hands down on the table. 'You don't know what it's been like,' he snarled. 'People have been staring at me like I'm some sort of monster. The police are trying to fit me up.'

Jaz stood up. 'All the more reason to go back and let me tell my side of the story. I won't mention you. Give me two minutes and I'll pack up my gear.' She shuffled over to her schoolbag. Her uniform was in a crumpled heap on the bed. She'd used the blazer as another layer at night.

Lennox shot out a hand, grabbed her around the wrist, pulled her back towards him.

'It's karma. Nate gets out of jail with your stepdad's money in his pocket just as your stepdad heads in. Perfect. You asked Gerri if there was anything you could do for Nate, well do this.'

Jaz stared at him as she slowly and deliberately removed her hand from his grasp, made a point of rubbing where he had held her. Somehow she knew, without a shadow of a doubt, that Nate would never see a cent of the money.

'I said no.'

He went to reach for her again – and this time it was vicious, designed to win the argument by force – but she got in first with a slap across his face. It didn't land correctly, more on his jaw than cheek. The blow she got in reply was almost immediate, a more accurate aim which suggested he'd had more practice. The force of it flung her whole body backwards and she crashed against the wall, feeling the caravan shudder. There was a ringing in her ears. Pushing herself upright, she stood there dazed for a moment and he did too, fist still raised, but then he began to shake his hand, like it was an accident.

'Look what you made . . .' he began, as Jaz brought her hand to her face. He had connected with her nose and it was bleeding now, bright red blood on her fingers. She could feel the blood gush and drip onto the floor. The Jaz of four days ago would have cried or cowered but something had changed in her. She had spent so long thinking about abductions and how they would work and what she would do, that she knew her only option was to fight back, and hard. In an instant, she had grabbed the closest tin of beans and pegged it at him, hitting his shoulder. Lennox swore loudly, but she was already throwing the next one. This time she heard a crack as it hit his face and it was his turn to bleed. She was shouting now, screaming really, as loudly as she could, and he was yelling back. It was time for her to run, to head for the creek and then to the neighbour's house, but there was a moment's hesitation about the memory stick. What if Barton had wiped the footage? She scooped up her bag, fingers already fumbling with the zip and then the stick itself.

He grabbed her hair, pulled her back, and she could almost feel her feet lift off the ground as the world tilted.

'Get off me!'

There was an arm around her neck and then a violent push forward and she fell down the steps onto the dirt outside, slamming into the ground. Lennox sat on her back, as she thrashed around like a fish on the end of a hook, using his weight to pin her. He waited there, laughing, until she'd tired herself out, then he flipped her over.

There was blood on his face now. From his mouth, she guessed. He spat out something on the ground beside her. It might have been teeth.

'Stupid bitch,' he said. 'This could all have been so much simpler.'

The next punch had her doubled up in pain. She couldn't get enough air and had to gasp. Clutching her stomach with her hands she realised she was still holding the memory stick in them.

He stood up and walked away.

She tried to move but couldn't manage it, and then he was back again with the duct tape, taping her hands together first and then her feet.

As he dragged her to the boot and then hefted her in, she struggled, but it was more muted now. She had imagined all this before, but it had been play-acting, that they would be laughing as they did it. This might never have occurred to Lennox if she hadn't been so thorough. If she hadn't wanted to be authentic.

Breathing heavily, he stood there, looking at her lying in the boot before pulling out a phone to take a photo.

'Smile for the camera,' he said. 'Proof of life.'

As the boot slammed down and the engine started, Jaz lay there terrified because she already knew how this would end, how they always end. She was no good to Lennox alive. The minute he got the money, maybe even before he got the money, she would be dead.

CHAPTER 30

Beth accelerated along the road out of town so fast that Frankie almost told her to slow down.

Des said that Ollie had seen the missing girl. By the time he had got to the creek she had gone, but he had the idea that she might be staying in the old caravan that belonged to Nate.

'I don't want to call the police,' he said. 'Not if Gerri is involved. I don't want her in any trouble.'

'Don't call them,' agreed Frankie, decisive in that moment. 'Wait until I get there.'

It was only after she hung up that she remembered Joe had her car because his was at the mechanics, but luckily Beth had offered to drive.

Frankie opened the gates after they turned into the property and Beth managed to dodge all the potholes.

As the farmhouse came into sight, Frankie swore. There was a familiar-looking metallic blue hatchback parked near the water tank.

'Is Mer coming as well?' Beth asked.

'Not as far as I knew,' Frankie replied grimly.

Mer hovered behind Des in the doorway, dishevelled hair and a too-short denim skirt. Frankie felt a wave of emotions but settled on the simplest one: fury.

At that moment Ollie burst out of the house and ran over. 'I spotted her, Mum. I was looking for birds and that's when I saw her. Do you think there will be a reward?'

Frankie hugged him tight. 'You've done great, Ollie, but I need you to stay with Grandpa while I see if I can find her. Then we can organise for her to go home.'

'You're not going by yourself,' Mer said. 'I'm coming with you.'

'Why are you even here?'

'I came out to visit Des,' Mer said, a guilty look on her face. 'For a chat.'

At the same time, Des answered, 'I invited her,' and he looked shamefaced as well.

The only place Mer chatted was bars and Des didn't invite people over.

Frankie's former best friend was having sex with her father and they both seemed totally fine about it. If anything, Des was the happiest he had been since Alice died. Well, she was not okay. This was so overwhelming that she couldn't even verbalise how she felt about it. Words would come eventually, but she would wait until there was no Beth or Ollie there to witness them.

'And it was Jasmine?' It was a question directed to Des more than Ollie.

Her father nodded. 'We're pretty sure. Checked the photo that's been released.'

'And Jaz seemed all right, love?' she asked Ollie.

'She was singing,' Ollie said. 'Sitting on a rock and singing. Just past the bend in the creek.'

Frankie had woken up this morning having to face being suspended from her job and questioned by police in relation to the death of someone she thought of as her friend and the disappearance of a student, and now it was looking like Jasmine Langridge had never been missing. Instead, she was having her own version of a bush retreat while the whole town tore itself apart looking for her.

'Right,' she said. 'I'm going to talk to her.'

'I'm coming with you,' said Mer.

'No,' said Frankie. 'Jaz knows and trusts me.'

The trust was an exaggeration, but at least she did know her, had taught her *To Kill a Mockingbird* and *Romeo and Juliet*.

'I'm coming too,' said Ollie. 'I found her.'

'You are not,' snapped Frankie, looking at Des to help.

'Stay here with me, mate.' Des put a hand on his grandson's shoulder. 'Mum will be back soon. We can have our afternoon tea. Mer brought some cupcakes.'

Ollie sighed and then stomped off into the house.

'You can't send me into the house for a cake,' said Mer to Frankie.

'You shouldn't go alone, love,' said Des. 'Might be better with the two of you.'

'I'll go with her,' piped up Beth. 'If Jasmine is claiming to have information about Vanessa's death, then I want to hear it.'

'Good,' said Mer. 'All three of us can go.'

Frankie gave Mer the sort of look she normally reserved for misbehaving year nines but Mer was the patron saint of misbehaviour and didn't flinch.

'Fine,' Frankie said through gritted teeth.

The water was low enough to walk across the stepping stones to get to the other side of the creek. Frankie knew it was best to take them quickly in one fluid go.

This had been her backyard growing up, though she couldn't remember the last time she had come down here. It was like returning to your past and finding things had changed enough to throw you off balance. The flood damage was more obvious by the creek. There were reminders of the storm everywhere, unlike in town, where the damage had been cut, chipped, patched and swept away so that now there was only the odd missing tree or blue tarp on a roof to show what had happened.

But here there were great giants of trees down and the rest had mud on their trunks, marking how high the water had come. The world had been painted in clay, the green choked out by a chalky brown.

As Frankie made it to the other side, she turned to check on Beth. The woman moved with a dancer's poise, silent, face grim, and had no trouble making her way across.

Frankie didn't wait for Mer, could hardly bear to look at her right now. Besides, she would be fine with her long legs. Instead, Frankie began to scramble up the steep hill, clutching clumps of grass to pull herself up out of the creek bed to the bushland beyond, getting dirt on her hands and down the side of her jeans. She could make out the top of the caravan above the grass and wondered how on earth Nate had got it down here.

They walked in single file along the track, going up the hill. It was too early in spring for snakes but still she stomped her feet hard to be certain, as she thought about what to say to Jaz. There was a sense of profound relief that the girl was all right, that nothing terrible had happened to her, but also relief that this might put an end to the police investigation. People would stop being so ghoulishly interested in Vanessa's death, no one would care about the stupid notes, and finally the world outside would settle down and she could start picking up the pieces of her broken life.

Jaz had caused so much trouble and Frankie felt a strong temptation to let her know exactly that. She had to force herself to focus on the bigger picture of getting the girl home safely to her parents, while Mer complained loudly about how her shoes were getting all muddy.

Do you ever shut up? thought Frankie, knowing that Mer never did. Thank god Beth was here, because it meant that neither of them would talk about what happened yesterday. A small part of her felt guilty for what she had said to Mer, but a much larger part was angry, because it was much easier to blame Mer than Joe.

Behind her, she could hear Beth breathing hard and felt a pang as she recalled the state of the other woman's health. She hadn't even asked Beth how she was going, but instead had dragged her into this mess.

'You walk in front of me,' she said to Beth. It was flatter now and they could walk at a pace that suited her.

Beth nodded, head bowed. It seemed to Frankie as if Beth had been looking like this ever since Vanessa's death.

'Are we there yet?' asked Mer. She wasn't even trying to keep her voice low.

The caravan was old and shabby, rounded edges rather than just a rectangle, dusty as well, though you could see that someone had tried to clean it recently, leaving smears across the window. It was propped up on bricks at the front, but the grass had grown up and over the wheels.

There was no sound except the excitable trill of birds some distance away.

The caravan door was wide open, like a tooth missing.

'Jasmine,' Frankie called. Her voice broke a little.

It really was dilapidated, practically a wreck. One of the windows had cracked glass. Had she really been staying here?

'Jasmine!' Frankie's voice was louder now, waiting for the girl to appear and ask what on earth was she doing here.

She climbed the step, put her head inside. Frankie could see there was a school blazer and a schoolbag with the St Brigid's crest on it, but everything – blankets, dishes, a sleeping bag – was in disarray.

'There's blood on the ground,' said Mer, crouching down. 'It's fresh.'

Looking in the caravan again, Frankie could see there were dark spots of blood on the lino. Twisted bits of tape lay discarded under the table. A mobile phone was sitting next to the sink.

'Something has been dragged,' Mer said. 'Or someone.'

There were marks in the dirt, long lines with footprints nearby.

'JASMINE!' Frankie shouted now. Ollie must have misinterpreted what was going on. 'JASMINE!'

'We need to call the police,' Mer said.

'Are you sure?' asked Beth.

'Something's really wrong,' Frankie interrupted, looking across at Mer.

—

It was almost an hour before the sound of the siren wailed in the distance. Birds in nearby trees took flight or replied with all sorts of calls and caws.

'At last,' said Mer.

'I'll handle this,' said Frankie.

She walked out to greet them and could sense immediately Carole's disapproval. In fact, she felt it went further than that towards something like suspicion, and she wasn't surprised. If something had happened to Jaz because she had wanted to sort this out on her own, then she would never forgive herself.

'For someone who considers herself a law-abiding citizen, Mrs Birnam, I keep finding you in unusual situations,' Carole said, stopping at the blood spatter. 'Who else is out here with you?'

'Mer Davis.'

'Welcome's one and only letter writer,' Carole said. 'Of course. It must be at least four hours since I last spoke to her.'

The only positive Frankie could take out of this entire situation was that Mer had made good on her promise to go see the police.

'And Beth Fettling, Vanessa's cousin,' Frankie added.

That got a curt nod.

'Where's your son now?' Carole asked.

'Back at the farmhouse with my father.'

Carole was already shouting orders into the radio, talking about forensics, explaining where they were, telling a young policeman to go talk to Geraldine Rivett immediately.

'The three of you are to return to the farmhouse with Angie and stay there until I have a chance to talk to you properly. Do you understand?'

Frankie nodded.

Billy immediately walked off and began talking into his radio, stopping to pick something up off the ground. Perhaps it was a trick of the light, but for a second Frankie thought it was a human finger. As she turned to walk back towards the river, she could hear Billy getting an angry lecture from Carole about basic policing and the preservation of crime scenes.

CHAPTER 31

C arole rang Billy's doorbell after 9 pm, apologised to Tracey who answered the door and said hello to his daughters who all came running down the stairs though they should have been in bed. She had a quiet word with Billy out near her car.

'I thought you'd want to know what was on that memory stick you found,' she said. 'Among other things, there's security footage of Vanessa Walton walking down the driveway of the Barton's house the night she died.'

Billy shook his head in amazement. 'Christ, the town's going to go crazy when they hear that.'

'Super wants us to handle it with kid gloves. Their daughter is still missing after all. There were also some photos. What looks like Vanessa Walton's red coat bundled up in the back of a wardrobe, a black wig as well, right next to a briefcase with the initials B.M.L. that I saw Yvette carrying for him on my first day in Welcome.'

Billy frowned. 'A red coat?'

Carole nodded. She was biding her time, giving him a chance to put the pieces together.

'A red coat and black wig?'

'That's right.' Carole could see from his face that it was ringing a bell but apparently not quite loud enough for him to work it out. Oh, Billy.

'I went back to Jasmine's phone,' continued Carole, 'to see if there were similar photos on it to cross-reference, and lo and behold I found something. Not as much detail, more a close-up on the red coat.'

'I thought it was a costume for Halloween. I didn't connect it to Vanessa at all.'

'We've had that photo right from the start of the investigation and we missed it.'

Carole was saying 'we' but it was Billy who had fucked up.

'It's my fault, sarge,' he said. 'I'm sorry.'

'That's not all. Angie went through Ivan Roland's computer tonight and found incriminating emails between himself and Barton about Vanessa Walton.'

Billy closed his eyes. 'I forgot about that. You see, the thing with Frankie kind of knocked me for six . . .'

Carole sighed. 'I'm not saying you haven't been helpful. You went back through all the security footage and found that second phone, chased up the cleaner. But this is a stuff-up. You're going to have to learn to be a better policeman. Now I know there's never enough time and we're only human, but you need to show more initiative, stop telling your wife about everything you're doing and recognise what's staring you in the face. You've let personal feelings get in the way of this investigation.' Carole knew she was being harsh but she was already exhausted and they would be working through the night.

Billy didn't say a word.

'Angie's at the station organising a warrant to search the Langridges' property first thing in the morning. The brief to Homicide about Vanessa Walton goes off tomorrow. The super's agreed to that at least.'

Billy cleared his throat. 'Still no sign of Jasmine?'

'I reckon she must have realised she'd been spotted and moved on. Spiced up the scene with the tape and the blood to keep up the pretence it's an abduction. She loves her drama, I'll give her that.'

She was interrupted by her phone ringing. Her eyes opened wide as she answered. 'I'm five minutes away.'

She turned back to Billy. 'Barton Langridge has arrived at the police station wanting to give a statement.'

'Do you want me to come?'

It was more a plea than a request but Carole wasn't budging. 'Angie's already there and she can handle it going forward.'

As she drove away, she glanced in her rear-view mirror and saw Billy still standing by the kerb, looking completely alone. It's for his own good, she told herself.

'Langridge is here with his solicitor,' Angie told Carole. 'He said that a ransom demand came through about an hour ago.'

The two women were standing in Carole's office at the police station. Carole looked at the image of Jasmine tied up in the boot of a car. She squinted, glimpsed a white edge at the rim.

'Any ideas on the make or model?'

'Billy's our car guy.'

The person she had just kicked off the investigation.

'Send it through to him then.'

Carole sat down, trying to think through what she needed to do next.

'Was the ransom for fifty thousand dollars?' she asked Angie.

Angie's eyes opened wide in surprise. 'That's a lucky guess.'

'More an educated one.'

It had been Amber who had asked her about the rumour, said it was going like wildfire around the town. Carole had no idea if it was true. She had rung Amber on her way back into town, checking if Jasmine had got in touch with Brianna, because surely someone had helped her move quickly from the caravan. Amber said no, that Brianna had been under her eagle eye all day with her phone and computer confiscated.

'Last night she went to see Lennox Rivett, of all people, when I was at work. Her grandmother woke up and just about had a heart attack thinking she'd been kidnapped. Apparently she thought he could get a message to Jaz but he denied it, said he had nothing to do with any of it. Went out there with Danny Birnam, if you can believe it.'

Poor Brianna. She was going to be grounded until she was thirty the way things were going.

'So what do you think?' Angie asked.

'I think it's all a hoax. Chances are someone is trying to cash in and this is a completely faked picture, or Jasmine is a greedy little miss who, having staged the original disappearance, has somehow heard rumours about a ransom which hadn't occurred to her originally and is looking for a nice payout before she turns up alive and well. Either way it's not our problem. The super has already contacted the Missing Persons Unit, given the scene at the caravan. But I'm far more interested in talking to her stepfather about the contents of that memory stick. Seeing he's here already, with his solicitor, and Missing Persons are still at least a couple of hours away, we might as well spend the time productively.'

'Should we ring the boss? He said not to talk to Langridge without his express authority.'

Carole shook her head. 'Hate to ruin his night when Langridge came to us. Let's have the chat first. You got everything ready?'

Angie nodded, handing her a file.

Barton was standing up, leaning against the wall. The solicitor was already sitting at the table. The politician turned and frowned as Carole entered. There was a haunted expression in his eyes. Possibly it was the face of a man who would stop at nothing to protect his career, and yet, judging by what they had obtained from the memory stick, he may have acted in exactly the sort of way that guaranteed its ending.

But let's not get ahead of ourselves, Carole warned herself. One foot in front of the other.

'Good evening,' she said. 'I wanted to let you know that the Missing Persons Unit has been informed of all developments. Detectives are on their way from the city. They will be here within a couple of hours.'

'They should have been called days ago,' Barton blustered. 'This has been a stuff-up from the beginning.'

Carole put the file down on the table. Angie came in behind her and sat opposite the solicitor.

'I know this must be very upsetting for you, but up until recently you were not inclined to believe that Jasmine was missing,

Mr Langridge, and were most reluctant to make any formal report. You'll be pleased to know that considerable progress has in fact been made today, so perhaps I could bring you up to speed on what we've learnt so far and see if you're able to answer some questions. I can then feed that information back into the ongoing investigation.'

'You want *me* to answer questions? We came here to report a crime, sergeant. My stepdaughter has been kidnapped. You should be out there trying to find her. My wife didn't even want me to go to the police. I'm the one who insisted that we should. Perhaps I should have rung your boss directly?'

'Don't worry, I'll do that for you,' Carole said. 'You've done the right thing in involving us. Jasmine's safety is our number one priority.'

The solicitor gave his client a meaningful look, pulling out the chair for him. Barton threw his arms up but then sat down.

Angie switched on the tape and Carole ran through the formalities before pulling a few photos from her file and laying them on the table. 'These are some of the items we recovered today from a caravan on Geraldine Rivett's land. They have been taken away for forensic testing, but I was wondering if you could identify them for us.'

The photos were of the backpack, school uniform and other items of clothing.

'That's Jasmine's,' he said straight away, pointing at the photo of the bag. 'Her mother bought that surfboard pin for her on a trip to Honolulu.'

'And the clothes?'

He shrugged. 'They could be. Sherry would know better than me.'

Carole produced the next photo.

'This item was also recovered. Have you seen it before?'

It was the memory stick in the shape of a finger.

A complicated look crossed Barton's face.

'It's just a memory stick, not a severed finger, though I can tell you it did give the constable who found it a bit of a shock.'

'I don't know. It could be hers.' He didn't sound as confident now, yet Carole was certain he had seen it before.

'We found several images on the memory stick. Photographs and security footage.'

Barton shuffled in his seat. The solicitor next to him coughed and then turned to his client.

'But before we look at those,' Carole said smoothly, 'I'd like to show you some emails first. They appear to be a conversation between you and Mr Ivan Roland, the assistant principal of St Brigid's, concerning another teacher, Ms Vanessa Walton. Here's a copy of them.' She pushed the printouts across the table.

Barton swallowed hard but didn't pick up the pages. He didn't seem as surprised by this line of inquiry as she had expected.

'Are they your emails?'

Barton appeared to have frozen.

'You do know Ivan Roland?' Carole prompted.

After a pause, Barton stirred. 'Yes, I know him.'

'Would you like me to take you through the highlights of the conversation?' Carole asked. She deliberately kept her voice amiable, free of judgement.

Barton shook his head.

Not even a 'no comment'.

'The emails describe your need to "finish" her, stating that she, Vanessa Walton, "must go away". You use the phrase "rub her out" at one point. Could you explain to me what you meant by that?'

Barton cleared his throat. Carole could almost hear his mind ticking over, searching for words.

'It was not meant in any physical sense. Ivan believed she had submitted inflated invoices in relation to the gala. He was concerned that she might be embezzling school money. If this were true, I felt it was important to put it on the public record.'

'Before the next election perhaps?' Carole asked.

A small movement from the solicitor, a flinch almost, and Barton gave a half-nod. Reaching out, he picked up one of the pieces of paper and held it up to his mouth as if trying to put up a physical barrier to stop himself from talking.

The struggle for a politician to keep silent.

'We're trying to understand, Mr Langridge,' Carole pushed. 'Explaining them to us may assist with finding Jasmine.'

'My client has answered your question and has no further comment,' the solicitor chimed in, clearly desperate to shut up his client.

'Let's move on then. We also have security footage showing Vanessa Walton at your house the night she was murdered.'

Barton lifted his head, giving the impression of a rabbit in a spotlight.

'What time was that?'

'Just after ten.'

'But that's impossible.'

More photos out on the table. It was all like an elaborate card game.

'We need a couple of minutes,' said the solicitor.

'Of course,' said Carole.

Angie switched off the tape and then gathered up the photographs.

It was more than a few minutes. Carole rang the super and lived to tell the tale, but only just. If he'd had the ability to breathe fire through a phone it might have been a different matter. She had a cup of tea, watching the clock with one eye while she asked Angie about rentals and different parts of town. One of the night shift cops rang her back.

'Done what you asked, sarge. I'm at Lennox Rivett's place now. It's all quiet, lights on in the living room. That yellow car of his is out the front, engine's cold. Want me to knock?'

'Leave it,' she said. There wasn't the manpower on night shift to conduct a raid of the house to see if Jasmine was there. Besides, Missing Persons would want to handle it their way. 'But do me a favour. Drive past later on. Ring me if you think he might have a visitor or if there's any late-night activity.'

'Will do.'

She shut her phone.

'How much longer do you think they'll be?' Angie asked, yawning. 'I'm going to have to pull out my trick from night-time nursing of eating a Granny Smith and then brushing my teeth to wake me up.'

'Does that work?'

'Like a charm,' Angie said. 'Fools your body into thinking it's morning.'

Angie opened the file and went through the printouts again. 'So Jaz finds these emails, copies them, thinks her stepfather has killed Vanessa, then fakes her own disappearance. Why didn't she come to us in the first place, save us all this hassle?'

Because she didn't trust us, thought Carole. She had seen the police falsely charge her friend for resisting arrest and knew that the super was mates with her stepfather.

'Hopefully we will get the chance to ask her that. All we know is she disappeared into the bush, leaving a trail of breadcrumbs to follow, and the truth is we have done a pretty bad job of it. A ten-year-old kid found her before we did.'

'When will she turn up then? When Barton Langridge has been charged with murder?' Angie was incredulous. 'We won't even have a search warrant for his house until mid-morning.'

'She's upped the stakes with the ransom demand. That's fraud charges for a start. I hope she realises that she's getting herself into some real trouble now.'

Thirty minutes had passed by the time the solicitor came to find them.

'My client has prepared a statement,' he said.

'He's decided to give up Ivan Roland?' Carole guessed. 'Dob in the little guy to save his skin?'

The solicitor shook his head. 'It's about his wife.'

CHAPTER 32

Mer hated being in an empty house. God only knew where Ky was. Probably at his girlfriend's house, if she had to guess. Maybe she should text and ask if he would come home to keep her company. He could bring the girlfriend, even though whenever she opened her mouth it was mind-numbing. The world could be ending and Ky's girlfriend would be talking about her nail polish. Mer was happy enough to cook dinner for them both if that was what it took, but then she remembered that the girl had gone vegan, even though she didn't really eat vegetables, and decided that it was all too hard.

From the state of the fridge it looked like scrambled eggs again.

There had been a moment today, when they had agreed to call the police, that things with Frankie had seemed almost normal. But by the time they got back to the farmhouse, Mer was back in the deep freeze. Something about Mer and Des being in the same room seemed to tip Frankie completely over the edge; she went and sat outside with Patch, as if on the other side of a chasm, and Mer wondered if the bridge would ever be crossed again. Even Ollie, usually lost in a world of his own, asked what the problem was. No one had been game to say anything.

Mer didn't really have any other friends, not like Frankie. Plenty of drinking buddies and workmates, customers who always stopped for a gossip, exes who sometimes felt like a hook-up rather than a catch-up. But not friends who said you could come live with them when your kids left home. Not the type of person who checked up on you first thing in the morning because you were swimming laps. Mr Poole did that, but it was sort of his job. Des was her friend, but then Frankie had told her to stay away from him too, which didn't make any sense. She had asked Des about it but he didn't understand either.

Mer felt like crying and she felt like a drink at the same time. She wanted one so badly that she was considering getting the whiskey bottle out of the recycling in case there were still some drops down the bottom, but then she remembered there was some port in the top cupboard left over from Christmas and got that instead.

The bottle was only part full, but by the time she had made the scrambled eggs, then decided she wasn't actually that hungry and scraped the eggs in the bin, did the washing-up and tidied the kitchen, it was empty.

It was after 10 pm now, which meant all the shops were shut, but she needed something to get rid of the taste of the port. The Valhalla would still be open, as would several of the pubs, but Mer didn't feel like talking to anyone. There was no way of knowing if people had heard she'd written those notes to Vanessa (it was only a matter of time) but she sure didn't have it in her to pretend that life was hunky-dory. That just left 'borrowing' a bottle or two from work. She had done it before and usually paid the next day (it depended on whether it was a pay week or not). Gino knew, had watched security footage of her from his phone the first time she had done it, but turned a blind eye. He was prepared to overlook the occasional late-night 'purchase'. It wasn't a big deal, like her drinking wasn't a big deal. She could stop any time. She just didn't want to.

The night was cold when she went outside. *Go back inside*, said the voice in her head. *You've had enough for one night.* That voice sounded like Frankie, and tonight Mer certainly wasn't going to listen to her.

Be responsible, said the voice.

I am, she thought. I won't drive. She started walking down the street, found it a little hard to walk straight.

A couple of the streetlights weren't working and the world felt dark but the stars were out. Mer stopped to look at them at the top of the hill. She liked how they made her feel insignificant, as if her problems weren't worth worrying about. Perhaps she should tell Frankie the real reason why she wrote those notes, but then that might make everything much worse.

As she walked along, she jingled the keys in her pocket to hear the sound of something other than her own footfall. It was too quiet. Hardly anyone else was out. The town was hushed, more so than normal. Even the usual bored teenagers who just hung around were at home. Their parents were probably keeping them under lock and key, worried about Jasmine being missing. They would freak out more when they heard about the blood Mer had found near the caravan. Mind you, she had overheard Carole saying to Billy that there wasn't that much blood.

Surely any blood was bad enough.

Still, if it wasn't for bloody Jasmine (ha, that was actually funny when you thought about it), Mer wouldn't be in trouble. Carole said she could be charged. Surely the police had better things to do than waste time over that. She'd said she was sorry.

Turning onto the river path, it was even darker – no streetlights – and colder as well, but this was the most direct way into town. A dog howled in the last house she walked past, but luckily it was safely behind the fence.

The ground felt uneven; she almost tripped on a tree root but caught herself in time. Mer tried to remember when she had last eaten and couldn't. Probably should have had those eggs.

The path looped around to join up with the bridge.

Not far now to the supermarket. She had decided on a bottle of Wild Turkey, could almost taste it. There would be time for a couple of shots before she had to head home. That would make the trip feel shorter.

A car drove past her, lights on, music blaring, two young guys, all mullets and black t-shirts. The passenger put down his window and yelled something at her. She missed the specifics but got the meaning and flipped the bird in reply, hoping they wouldn't turn back for a second go, but they sped up and disappeared around the next corner.

Mer was sweating by the time she got to the supermarket. She walked through the car park, past the recycling bins to the loading bay. She entered Chip's access code into the system, which she knew from having to cover his early morning prep for him when he was sick.

There were enough lights on inside the store to find her way through the warehouse in the dark, then she pushed past the doors next to the deli, moved through the freezers and towards the alcohol department.

It was always strange being here when no one else was around. No chat, no music, just the hum of refrigeration. It took her less than five minutes to pick a couple of bottles. She grabbed a packet of salt and vinegar chips too, needing something to line the stomach. Decided against taking some bread. Too many carbs weren't good for you.

Maybe she was already a teensy bit drunk, she thought, almost colliding with a stand. Still, walking had been thirsty work and it was a long way home. A quick drink and then she'd head back. There were glasses in the kitchen but, checking under the counter, she found forgotten plastic tumblers from some promotion. A little dusty but they would do fine. Sitting on the floor, because why not, she poured herself such a generous double that it was more of a triple. Usually she had it with ice but neat would do in a pinch. She took a sip, felt it slide down her throat, warming her. That was better. Problems receded. Her feet felt less sore.

The day had been knackering. Leaning her head back, she yawned wide enough that it cracked her jaw. It was too far to walk home again. Maybe she could call Shannon, see if she'd come and pick up her mother. But then she'd have to listen to a lecture all the way home and probably for the rest of the week. Shannon considered alcohol to be a poison and never missed an opportunity to say so.

She could call Frankie. Oops. No, she couldn't do that. Maybe she should call her, though. Tell her that she didn't want to be friends with her either. She could stay at home by herself the rest of her life with that cheating husband of hers for company. See how she liked that.

Mer took another sip and then heard footsteps.

Surely she hadn't left the back door open?

If it was Sue then she was in big trouble. Gino she could manage.

There was the noise of someone walking through the aisles. Mer got to her feet very quietly and then peered around the corner to see if she could catch sight of them. There was a flash of movement in aisle six (cleaning products, laundry detergent, paper towels, garbage bags, toilet paper, pet food), a guy in a hoodie walking along it, grabbing stuff off the shelves.

Mer ducked back down. It was a looter. How had they got in? The alarm should have gone off. Someone needed to call the police. But if she did that then she could be in trouble as well. There had to be someone who would understand.

Billy Wicks.

Straining to hear if the looter was moving away or getting closer, she pulled out her phone and began texting. *Break-in at supermarket, robber still here.*

Luckily Billy responded almost straight away.

Where are you?

Hiding in liquor department!

Have you been drinking?

How was that relevant? She moved backwards and knocked the bottle of bourbon over. It made a muffled thump, a glug as the drink began to spill out onto the floor. Jesus. Mer scrambled to right the bottle and find the cap.

There was a shout. 'Who's there?'

Mer recognised the voice and instantly relaxed.

Don't worry, she texted back. *False alarm.*

No alarm, to be exact. Stupid security system never worked properly.

There was the bouncing three dots in reply but Mer dropped the phone back into her bag.

'You made me spill my drink!'

Mer stood up and walked out from behind the counter. The floor was a wet mess and somehow she'd managed to get some on her clothes as well. This would all need mopping up pronto or the place would stink of booze and someone might guess what she had been up to. Probably she should grab another bottle as well.

An only slightly out-of-focus Lennox Rivett stood at the entrance, hoodie over his head. There was something almost menacing about him but then she blinked and he turned back into normal Lennox.

'This is your fault.' Mer gestured at the floor. 'You need to help me clean it up. What are you doing here, anyway?'

He shrugged. 'Needed to grab some gear.'

Must be his second business.

'Impatient customer?' Mer laughed. Perhaps she might get a little pick-me-up as well. She certainly deserved it.

'They're gagging for it,' Lennox said and gave an odd laugh. He looked exhausted and Mer felt for him. These last few days had been hard on everyone.

'Don't you ever get worried that Sue's going to find out what you're up to?' Mer asked.

'You're assuming she doesn't know.'

Mer stopped in her tracks. The surprise of that sobered her up a touch. She forced herself to concentrate.

'Sue's a smart businesswoman. Can spot a good opportunity for easy cash. She knows that sometimes it's a good idea to turn off the security cameras.'

'And Gino?'

'He's got no idea. Don't go opening your big mouth.'

More secrets. Mer laughed. 'It's safe with me.' She mimicked zipping up her mouth. 'Now I better go find the goddamn mop.' She noticed that Lennox's backpack was bulging, but Mer wasn't in any position to be critical.

He headed off into the warehouse as Mer stumbled towards the cleaning supplies cupboard. It was darker here, without the illumination of the fluoros in the supermarket proper. Without thinking, she switched on the overhead light and earnt a sharp bark from a returning Lennox.

'Keep it off,' he said. 'We don't want everyone to know we're here.'

He had a point.

'See you,' he said, standing by the back door.

'Hang on,' said Mer, as she had a sudden brainwave. 'You can give me a lift home. I'll only be a couple of minutes.'

'I'm busy.' He started walking.

Mer followed him outside, dropped the mop in the doorway so that it didn't shut and lock her bag and keys inside. She was prepared to beg because it was a long walk home.

The moon was up now, yellow and full, and the sky seemed infinite. The cold air hit her in the face. She shivered, rubbing her arms with her hands.

There was one lonely car in the car park, a white sedan she didn't recognise.

'Where's your Kingswood?' she asked. If he was driving that she would insist on the scenic route, burn around the streets for a bit. Mer loved the smell of petrol.

Lennox turned back, pissed off now, gestured for her to go away, but Mer wasn't having that. She jogged to catch up to him.

'Is that your sister's car? How's Lindy enjoying Toowoomba?' If she kept him talking, then maybe he'd change his mind.

'Fuck off, Mer,' Lennox snarled.

But Mer was distracted by the sound of thumping, a kind of animal whimpering. A dog in pain? Following the sound, she moved closer to the car, dimly aware that Lennox was talking to her in an urgent hushed whisper, moving towards her, arms outstretched.

There was glass on the ground near the boot. She opened her mouth to say that his rear light was broken and bent down to inspect it, but when she saw the hand, fingers really, frantically waving at her through the light's cavity, the world that had seemed enormous seconds before suddenly shrank to the size of the boot and the girl inside desperate to get out.

An inhalation, not even knowing what she was going to say. Then the world telescoped again as there was a swish of movement behind her, the sound of metal meeting skull, and all was darkness.

CHAPTER 33

The moment Mer opened her eyes, her head throbbed so painfully that she thought she would be sick. In fact, she could already smell the vomit.

The world's worst hangover, she told herself, shutting her eyes again. Go back to sleep.

It was the cold that told her something was wrong, and then the stench, acidic and sweet. Turning to her side, she could see a face close by. Blinking hard, it took all her willpower to prise her eyes open. She moved and felt the sort of sharp pain that turned the world red.

She moaned.

'You're awake,' said a voice.

The sound came from a different direction. She moved her head, felt the pain again but was better prepared for it this time and refused to groan.

A white circle of torch light sliced across her face and she scrunched up her eyes in response.

'What happened?' she asked.

'Wouldn't move too much if I were you,' said the voice. It was male and familiar. 'Think that dodgy shoulder of yours has finally fallen apart.'

Her body responded as if on cue, the pain in her shoulder competing with the one in her head.

It was Jaz lying next to her. She was the one who had been sick. One arm was stretched over her head, dried blood on her face, and her skin was sweaty, like she had a fever. The girl's eyes were flickering half open but her gaze was vacant.

'You found Jaz.' Blinking, she looked again. 'I think she needs a doctor.' And Mer started to shiver – from cold, from fear, she barely knew.

'Jaz is in the Land of Nod,' said Lennox. Of course it was Lennox. 'Had to take her gag off because she keeps vomiting. Can't let her choke; not yet anyway.'

The girl gurgled and for a moment Mer envied her, wished she was the one floating away. The events of the night were coming back in sharp little splinters. Not all of it, but enough to know she was in deep trouble. Breathing out, she pulled herself up to sitting and nearly passed out at the same time, but she made it.

She tried to smile. They had done a course once on negotiation. It was supposed to help them deal with difficult customers. The main thing was to keep calm and use their name a lot.

Lennox moved the torch so it was no longer blinding her. She could see him now, sitting there, a gun in his hand.

Make them think you are on their side, build a rapport, don't take it personally. She had actually failed the course, but at least she didn't get into a stand-up barney with the instructor like Sue had.

'What's going to happen to Jasmine, Lennox?'

Maybe she shouldn't be asking questions. Maybe it was safer the less she knew. But it seemed to her that as long as he was talking, he wasn't doing anything else.

'She's going to get me an easy fifty thousand dollars. Just trying to work out where to pick it up from.'

Mer felt herself fading out, sleep beckoning as an escape from the throbbing in her head. She forced herself awake. Where were they? He couldn't have taken her far when she was unconscious. She felt the metal below her again. There was something familiar about it. It was like dragging her mind forward one inch at a time. And then she had it. The shipping container at the back of the supermarket. It wasn't cold enough to be the refrigerated one.

If she screamed would anyone hear? Hard to know. There were mostly shops around them; the nearest houses were in the next block. Besides, Lennox would find a way of stopping her from making noise pretty quickly. She couldn't outrun him, didn't even know if she could stand up, and he had a gun. A feeling of hopelessness washed over her.

'So what happens next?' she asked. It couldn't possibly be anything good but Mer was always someone who preferred to know, to rip the band-aid off.

If it were done, let it be done quickly.

Those weren't quite the right words but she knew where they came from. *Macbeth*. They'd studied it in year ten. Mer had tried hard that year, partly to show her new friend, Frances Patchett, that she wasn't an idiot and also because she had enjoyed it, though Lady Macbeth got a bad rap. There was no way she would have fallen apart at the first sign of blood. She was a woman, for god's sake. But then, it was a man who had written it.

'Oh, I've got plans for you,' said Lennox.

If neighbours couldn't hear a scream, would they hear a bullet?

He slowly, slowly put down the gun and picked up a bottle. It was bourbon.

Instantly, she wanted a drink more than she had ever wanted one in her life.

'This is your poison, isn't it?' he asked. 'I think you might drink yourself to death, maybe assisted by whatever else I can find. They'll find your body in the smoko area tomorrow and be shocked, until they see the footage of you breaking into the supermarket and stealing the booze. Then they'll just think you're sad.'

'People won't believe that.'

'You've been a fuck-up for years, going on benders, and now your best friend hates you. I think you give them too much credit.'

He came over to her, bottle in hand, grabbed her hair and wrenched her head back roughly. She screamed in pain but already the alcohol was pouring into her open mouth, choking her so she couldn't breathe. She clamped her mouth shut, tried to turn her head, but his hands were on the sides of her jaw, forcing it open.

The world turned liquid and it was everywhere, more going down her throat, until it stopped and she was pushed backwards, felt herself slump against the ground, coughing, eyes stinging.

'What was that?!'

Lennox's voice seemed further away. She wiped her eyes, tried hard to see.

There was a voice calling her name.

It was Billy.

She opened her mouth to scream, got a squeak out, but Lennox was back beside her in an instant, the cold steel of the gun on her temple.

'Make another noise and I'll go out and shoot him and then come back and shoot her and then you. You wouldn't want that now, would you? Not your old mate Billy.'

Mer knew that Lennox meant every word he said.

—

Billy had been bothered by those text messages from Mer. He texted her back a couple of times, tried phoning, but she didn't pick up. He let a bit of time pass and then tried again. Still nothing. He didn't ring Gino or Sue to check their security in case that got Mer into trouble.

All of this annoyed his wife, who wanted to watch the next episode in their current TV series. Tracey had picked a murder mystery, masquerading as a serious drama with fancy clothes and mansions. Billy preferred historical documentaries, to be honest.

'Mer might be a little drunk.' He'd had the feeling today that there was some sort of upset between her and Frankie. Maybe that had set her off.

'Mer Davis is perpetually drunk.' Tracey gave him a significant look as she reached under the couch to grope for the remote. 'If you're really worried, ring the station and get the night shift to handle it.'

Billy was tempted, but what if Mer had been stupid enough to drive to the supermarket? She could lose her licence.

'She said someone was breaking in at the supermarket.'

'What's she even doing at the supermarket at this time of night?'

Billy decided to keep the bit about her hiding in the liquor department to himself and stood up. 'I'll pop down there.' He might drive past the police station, see if Barton Langridge's car was still in the car park. If Angie was there he could try to enhance that photo she had sent through to him earlier, to check out the car detail rather than look at Jasmine's terrified face, mouth covered in tape. What must Sherry be going through? Carole thought it was a try-on, but she didn't know Jasmine that well, had only met her once. It seemed serious to him.

Tracey held her hand out triumphantly, remote clasped in it. 'I'm not waiting for you. I just know it's the husband who has done it. I never trusted him from the very first episode.'

'Yeah, me either,' Billy agreed, wondering which husband she meant. There were at least three of them on the show. 'Watch it without me and tell me what happened when I get back.' A win-win situation as far as he was concerned, but Tracey didn't hear as she was already switching on the television and settling in.

There was only one car in the supermarket car park and it wasn't Mer's. Hopefully that meant she had headed home and was sleeping off the booze safe and sound. He'd drive by her house next to check.

He parked and got out, torch in one hand. It all seemed quiet but he'd have a quick look around before heading off. Walking up the side of the building, past the industrial bins, he could see a kind of pale outline of light ahead. He switched on the torch. The back door was ajar.

Was the silly bugger still inside?

'Mer,' he called, walking towards it. 'Mer!'

Surely she wasn't so drunk that she'd left without locking up.

As he walked past the shipping container he heard a noise.

'Who's there?'

A human shape came out of it. He shone the light directly at them.

'Leave it out,' came a voice, Lennox Rivett putting an arm up to shield his face.

'What are you doing?' Billy shone the light past him but no one was there. 'Have you seen Meredith Davis?'

'She's left,' Lennox said. 'Think she said something about heading up to the Valhalla if you're looking for her.'

Billy shook his head. He'd done enough running around after her today. 'Why are you here so late?'

'Warehouse was a bit of a mess today. Gino got me to come back to get it straightened before deliveries tomorrow. Gave Mer a bit of a surprise when I turned up – spilt her drink and everything.'

It had been a long day and he was ready to throw in the towel. 'Mind how you go,' he said.

His phone dinged on the way back to his car. The photo had come through at last. Angie had tried to enhance it, focusing on a spot at the edge of the original. He'd have a better look when he got home.

'What's that?' asked Lennox, standing closer than Billy realised.

'The wife,' lied Billy. He wasn't about to divulge police business to a reprobate like Rivett. 'Wants me to grab some milk for the kids' breakfast.'

'I can get some for you inside,' Lennox said. 'No trouble.'

He was too eager. Billy gave him a cool stare. 'Don't worry. I'll stop at the petrol station.'

His antenna was up now. He was paying more attention. The other car in the car park was an old white Commodore with a broken tail-light, registration OPM 154.

'Where's the Kingswood?' he asked Lennox, glancing down at his phone. 'Not in the shop again, I hope.'

White car, said Angie's text. *Make/model?*

Billy sensed an alertness to Lennox, a kind of invisible charge, as if he were preparing to spring into action.

'Not my car,' said Lennox, a lazy smile at odds with the rest of him. 'Came on my pushie. Petrol prices are insane these days.'

There was no sign of a bike anywhere.

The two men stared at each other as the world stilled. Billy took in the fact that Lennox had one arm behind his back, appeared to be reaching for something. Billy pelted towards him, brandishing the torch, aiming at his eyes, but Lennox was already ducking away, moving backwards towards the container, pulling out something dark and metal.

By the time Billy reached him, bringing the metal torch down hard on Lennox's arm, his adrenaline-fuelled brain knew that Lennox had a pistol, most likely a semi-automatic, and he was at a complete disadvantage. Lennox turned, took the force of the blow on the other shoulder, which unbalanced him, but not enough to make him fall. He stumbled but righted himself, dancing backwards, swung the other arm around, the one with the gun in it, and pointed it at Billy.

'Don't come any closer,' he spat. 'Not another step.'

'You've got Jasmine,' Billy said, certain now.

Lennox didn't reply but Billy didn't need him to.

Billy had always prided himself on taking time to talk through situations, to try to de-escalate, but not this time. The smart thing to do would be to get around the corner and ring for backup, but he had heard that noise from the shipping container, was convinced it was Jasmine, and he couldn't leave her with Lennox fucking Rivett, a psychopath who liked locking teenage girls in the boot of his car and goodness knows what else.

This time he charged like a wounded bull, ready to tackle Lennox to the ground, sit on him, and then punch the snotty little bastard in the mouth until he was unconscious or subdued, whichever came first. Maybe he'd chuck him in the boot of his car and take pictures of him. Let him see what it felt like.

All these thoughts flashed before him in an instant but quicker yet was the bullet from the gun. As Billy took a couple of steps, still accelerating, it had left the barrel and entered Billy's abdomen. By the time he fell to the ground, blood was already filling his chest.

Billy made a guttural sound, dying but not dead yet.

Lennox staggered forward, lifted the pistol up, trained it on Billy's head. Billy lay there blinking, his breath in shallow pants, a pool of blood underneath him, life draining away.

'Fucking idiot,' Lennox muttered, and then Billy saw Mer behind him, slamming a bourbon bottle into Lennox's skull.

Mer had a long relationship with pain, had trained her body for years to ignore it, knew how to push through no matter what the cost. Plenty of practice at being drunk as well. Her left arm dangled puppet-like but her right arm made up for it, strong from swimming, lifting hams and carrying trays of chickens. The thump of the glass, the squish of flesh, crack of bone, and then the bottle smashed onto the ground with Lennox falling as well.

She staggered towards Billy, fell hard on her knees, crying now, and found his phone, slippery with blood. Blood was everywhere, on her hands, in his mouth, and as Billy's eyes shut, he could hear the operator ask what emergency service she wanted, and Mer screamed and screamed until it sounded like the wail of a siren in the distance.

CHAPTER 34

Carole sat in the corridor waiting. She had never liked hospitals but now she hated them. A nurse walking past told her if she fancied a coffee and a biscuit she could head to the breakout area around the corner. If she had offered an apple and some toothpaste, Carole might have taken her up on it, but instead she thanked her and kept waiting.

The bullet had entered Billy's abdomen, she knew that much. From there it could rip through his intestines, pancreas, spleen and stomach, or damage his diaphragm and lungs. So many options and none of them good, but at least he was alive and being operated on in the city right now.

There were no new messages on her phone. She could text Tracey to see if there was any word on Billy but decided against it. Tracey didn't need to hear from the person who had failed to keep her husband safe. Billy should have phoned in that call from Mer, but Carole couldn't help but feel that it was her fault that he didn't, because of the way she had treated him earlier in the night, telling him to show more initiative.

She stared at the door in front of her. Another officer probably would have gone into the room by now, but she preferred to give those inside a chance to start the slow process of trying to put the pieces back together as she contemplated what she could have done to prevent the disaster that had rained down on three people's lives that night – four, if you counted the damage inflicted on Lennox Rivett's head by Mer Davis.

Not the best day of policing.

Her phone dinged. It was Angie. She would stay at Tracey's house to mind the kids until Tracey's mother could get there. Troy was driving Tracey to the city right now. Hopefully, she would make it in time.

A young doctor came up the corridor, went into the room and reappeared a few minutes later, giving her the nod before walking away with the sense of purpose that came from many patients and limited time. Carole stood up, feeling almost light-headed with tiredness, and began to move, her ankles stiff at first.

A couple of nurses were talking as they watched television on their break. One of them directed her to the supplies. She made two cups of tea, black and sweet, and then walked back down the corridor, pushing open the door with her shoulder.

The room was dusky, with one small light on over a bedside table that had a water jug and a box of tissues on it. The woman sat huddled in the visitor's chair, eyes fixed on the person lying in the bed. She had one arm outstretched, gripping the hand of her daughter like a child might clutch a balloon, petrified it will float away and disappear.

'How is she?' asked Carole, handing over one of the cups.

'Sleeping,' Sheridan Langridge said. 'The doctor said that they would keep her in overnight for observation but that they'll probably be able to discharge her tomorrow. Physically she's okay, a few bumps and bruises but he didn't ...' Her voice dropped almost to a whisper. 'He didn't assault her sexually or anything like that.'

Trying to take comfort in how it could have been worse was the thinnest of gruels but you took what you could.

Carole came around the bed and looked down at Jasmine Langridge. She was so small lying there, so peaceful, that it was hard to square this person with the one who had caused such a fuss.

'She's tough, your daughter,' Carole said. 'She'll get through this and you will as well.'

Sherry looked up at her, eyes full of tears. 'I never meant for any of this to happen,' she said. 'I did what I thought was right.'

Carole pulled up a chair on the other side. 'You'll have to make a formal statement down at the station tomorrow.'

Sherry frowned, clutched her daughter's hand more firmly. 'I want to get it over and done with so I can concentrate on being with her.'

'You want to talk to me now?'

A quick nod of confirmation.

'I'll have to record it then.'

Carole sat down and sipped her tea, waiting for Sherry to begin speaking. When people asked her what was the most important skill for policing, she always said patience. It usually made the questioner laugh, but it was true.

'It was the night of the storm,' Sherry began. 'Barton was out at some drinks – I forget what, there's so many of them – but then he rang me and he was crying.' There was bewilderment and wonder on her face, as if she still didn't quite believe it. 'Eventually he calmed down enough to tell me that Vanessa had phoned him, wanting to sort out the legal dispute over the Cottage, and said that she had a business proposal to put to him.'

'Which was?'

'That she would sell him the Palais. She asked him to come over to her house to discuss terms. It must have been after six when he got there, a couple of hours before the rain started. He knocked for a while but she didn't answer and that infuriated him, thinking it was another of her stunts. So he went into his mother's place and got the key for the Cottage. Christ knows why, but I think he wanted to leave her a note saying he'd had enough of her games and that she would be hearing from his solicitor again. He used the back door, so the old busybody across the street wouldn't see him, and that's when he found Vanessa dead.

'He wanted to call the police but rang me first and I told him no, don't do it.' She shook her head, blinked away tears, but then looked across at Carole with a fierce expression. 'It would have been a disaster for him politically, after all we've worked for. The media would have had a field day once they heard about the dispute and what Lonnie had done. Ever since she'd said she'd run against him, Barton had been telling anyone who would listen that he hated Vanessa. He was evicting her from her home. If he was found anywhere near her body, his career would be over. People would say he killed her.'

She stopped there as if expecting Carole to argue the point with her but the policewoman didn't say anything. Never interrupt a suspect talking was her rule.

'I told him' – Sherry looked down again, kept her gaze on the white sheet in front of her – 'to close the door and leave the key in Lonnie's letterbox. Just get out of the house like everything was normal and he hadn't seen anything. "If that bloody nosy parker sees you on the way out, give her a big smile," I said, "and then drive straight to the city so that you're not in town when her body is discovered."

'I went round to Lonnie's to keep an eye on what was happening. You can see the Cottage quite well through the spare bedroom window upstairs. The weather was pretty bad and there was nobody around and no one came in or out. Barton rang me after he got over the mountains, worried. There had been Vanessa's political posters ripped up on the table, badges lying around. The police would automatically associate him with that. He insisted that I go back in and clean it up.'

Her mouth tightened as though she were still angry about this.

'So I went over after Lonnie went to bed. It was still a shock to see Vanessa lying there. The blood on her head. I've had nightmares about it. I thought about calling the police. I could pretend I'd popped over to check on her with the storm.' Sherry swayed a little in her seat. 'But I realised that still wouldn't work. I'd never be able to stick to the story, and politician's wife finds body of husband's enemy could still go viral. Then I saw her wig and coat lying on the armchair. She must have taken both off when she came in and we were roughly the same height and weight; I could put them on and leave the house, and chances were someone would see me and think it was her, walking around alive while Barton was hundreds of kilometres away.'

Her voice came out faster now, more adamant, as if this all made sense.

'So I waited and waited, peering out the window until I could see a car coming up the hill, and then I stepped through the front door out into the rain and headed up the hill and around the corner. It's only a ten-minute walk from our place. I was very careful when I came into our street that no one saw me duck down our drive, but the wind was up by then and all the neighbours were holed up indoors. I came around the back, went inside, took off the wig and coat and shoved them in the back of our wardrobe. That was supposed to be the end of it.'

She began to cry now, her face in her hands.

'And when I told you that Jasmine thought Vanessa had been killed?'

It took a while before Sherry could speak. 'I was petrified. We were sure it had been a horrible accident, but then Barton told me how agitated Ivan had been about Vanessa and he worried that maybe something had got out of hand. Really, I didn't know what to think.'

Carole sat there for a while, mulling it all over. 'Did Barton mention there being a bucket and spilt water on the stairs?'

'Yes,' Sherry said. 'A black plastic bucket, he said, that had been knocked over. There was water everywhere. I told him not to touch it, to leave it alone.'

Carole stayed to help Sherry make up the chair into a bed.

'They're not too bad,' Carole said. 'Quite comfortable, actually. It's more the hospital noise that makes it hard to sleep.'

She waited for the inevitable question but Sherry stayed silent, as if she had done enough talking for one night.

Carole headed to the lift, took it to the ground floor. It had been a long shift and tomorrow would probably be long as well. She hoped it would be a better day than this one.

It was still possible that Barton had murdered Vanessa. He was there, had motive enough, and he and his wife acted suspiciously afterwards, and yet she couldn't see it. Both Sherry's and Barton's statements would be included in the brief to Homicide. They would decide what happened next.

Outside the hospital the night was cold and the streets dark. Carole had sent the other officers home hours ago to get some sleep. She could call someone on night shift to pick her up and drop her home. She pulled out her phone and saw no new messages. Hopefully, Angie would be asleep now. On the spur of the moment, she decided to walk instead, to try to leave the worst of her self-recriminations behind her for at least a little while.

Walking around the block, she passed a building with a sign reading DAFFODIL HOUSE: CARE AND TREATMENT FACILITY lit up in front of it. An elderly gentleman was sitting by himself on a bench next to a flowerbed. He was breathing loudly, eyes shut tight.

'Are you all right, sir?' Carole called, walking closer.

As he turned in her direction, the man fumbled, pulling a perfectly ironed hanky from his pocket. 'Not really.' His eyes were red and streaming. 'Janet died about half an hour ago. Married for forty years we were.'

Carole stood in front of him now. 'Janet Ross?' Her mind suddenly went to the list in Janet's winter coat. 'What happened?' she demanded. 'How did she die?'

Tears continued to fall down his face. 'Initially the doctors thought the operation had gone quite well, but then she had a stroke and it was downhill fast.'

Carole stepped over a flowerbed and sat down next to him, her brain too tired to work out if she should feel relieved or just plain sad. 'I only saw her yesterday. She spent most of the time telling me how to do my job.'

'That sounds like Janet,' he told her. 'I always used to say that had things been different she would have made a very good judge. She had such an excellent brain.'

Carole found herself choking up, her own eyes starting to water. His name was Roger, she remembered that now: the first name on the list. 'Yes,' she whispered. 'Yes, she did.'

'I'm sitting here because she used to come to Daffodil House to volunteer' – Roger waved a hand at the building behind them – 'when she felt well enough and had the energy, because it was important to have people who really understood what a chronic illness was like. To not treat people as saints or sinners but as normal people to whom something terrible had happened.' He turned to her. 'She said you were like that.'

'How?'

'When she told you she was ill, you didn't try to cure her with some superstitious nonsense like drink lemon juice, or say you'd pray for her, or blame 5G or fluoride in the water or tell her that what she really needed to do was lose weight or have a more positive attitude or pity her or think that because she was ill her mind didn't work.' The old man sighed as he folded his hanky, placed it back into his pocket. 'She wondered if perhaps someone close to you might have gone through something similar.'

So Janet had seen that as well. 'Yes,' Carole said. 'My stepdaughter Lexie died last year. That's why I moved here, to be honest.'

Even saying the words aloud made something shift within her, as though she had been carrying the full weight of Lexie with her but never acknowledging it.

Roger nodded. 'That was Welcome's gain. Janet thought very highly of you, said you were a good policewoman.'

Not today, but perhaps there was a chance that she'd do a better job tomorrow. 'She told me to follow the money.'

'I loved her,' said Roger, 'but she could be infuriating with all her little clues. It was like living with a cryptic crossword sometimes.'

Carole laughed and it felt like the first time she had laughed in ages. Glancing behind Roger, she looked at the house again and something struck her.

Follow the money.

'You know, I think Janet might have been right in principle but we were both looking in the wrong direction. Perhaps there was another money trail I should have followed.'

'If Janet was here, she'd claim that was what she meant in the first place,' said Roger.

'Tell me, did Janet assist with the cancer fundraising gala that was held a little while back?' Carole asked.

Roger nodded. 'It was during one of her good spells. She helped out backstage, organising everything. It was such a wonderful event. You know, a funny thing happened that night. The sort of thing that only Janet would notice.'

'Tell me about it . . .'

CHAPTER 35

'm not dead, am I? Mer wondered, but she must have said it aloud because Frankie, who had been standing at the window, whipped around and gave a small cry, before recovering to say, 'No! Of course not.' She came over to sit beside the bed.

Mer wasn't quite sure, though. She certainly didn't feel like herself. Her head felt woolly, there was a drip in her hand and it hurt to talk. Something in the room was beeping all the time like a truck was backing up, which made her think of out the back of the supermarket, and then Lennox flashed into her mind.

'How are you feeling?' asked Frankie.

'Like a psychopath hit me over the head and then tried to poison me with cheap bourbon so everyone would think I drank myself to death.'

Frankie wiped away her tears. 'It wouldn't have fooled me. You'd have gone a bit more top shelf for something that serious.'

Mer tried chuckling but couldn't get far. 'Definitely martinis,' she whispered, and then, because she had to know, 'How bad is it?'

'You are going to have that shoulder operation you've been putting off for years, but I promise you'll be back swimming laps before you know it.'

It was hard to move her head, too heavy, too sleepy. Instead, Mer glanced around the room with her eyes. There were flowers everywhere, great big bunches of them, carnations, gerberas, dahlias, roses. Some she recognised from the supermarket and would put money on Gino having sent them.

'Like a bloody funeral home in here.'

'They've been coming all morning,' Frankie said. 'Not enough vases on the floor. I've already sent some bouquets home with Shannon.'

'Where is she?' Mer asked. 'Where's Ky?'

'They were here before when you were sleeping. Both of them went to work. They'll be back this afternoon.'

'I like that,' said Mer. 'Their mother nearly dies and they go to work like everything's fine.'

'They needed to be convinced,' Frankie assured her. 'I told them it was better not to use up their sick leave because they'll need it . . .'

She didn't finish the sentence and it took a moment before Mer understood what she meant. They'd need their sick leave to care for her, because she was broken.

'What else other than the shoulder?' she asked, urgent now.

'A few cuts and bruises,' said Frankie. 'Perhaps a concussion. You're going to have to take it very easy.' It was the teacher's tone now, giving instructions that must be followed.

One of the girls at work had a shoulder operation and couldn't dress herself for weeks.

'It could have been so much worse.' Frankie's voice wobbled. 'You're a hero, you know. You saved Jasmine. She's already been discharged this morning. Sherry came by earlier, wanting to thank you. She's very grateful.'

'It wasn't only me,' said Mer. She couldn't remember everything about last night. In fact, she didn't really want to try. Bits of it kept coming into her head unbidden. Suddenly she could taste bourbon in her mouth and felt bile rise and she had to swallow down hard. If it wasn't for Billy, she would be dead. She was just a drunken fool who'd blundered into a bad situation.

'How's Billy?' She turned her head, even though it complained, because she wanted to see Frankie's face clearly, to make sure she wasn't being lied to.

'They helicoptered him to the city last night and he's already been operated on. Tracey's with him now. Carole came past about an hour ago and said he was still unconscious, but they want him to stay that way for a bit. Let him do some healing before they try to wake him.'

Mer closed her eyes. Billy wouldn't have been there if not for her. 'And that bastard?' she asked.

'Carole didn't say,' Frankie replied. 'I would never have believed that he was capable of that . . .' Her voice trailed off. It could have been for minutes, it could have been hours, time was behaving differently in Mer's head, but then Frankie continued, 'I know about Joe and Vanessa. That they were having an affair and that's why you wrote those notes.'

Mer felt her eyes shutting of their own accord and had to blink hard to open them again. 'It doesn't change anything. It's over now.'

'It changes everything; I just don't know how yet.'

Mer felt real pain. She had failed. What she had wanted to do was fix it for Frankie, but instead she had made it much worse. The only thing that made her keep moving last night was the thought that Frankie might blame herself if Mer was found dead.

Frankie patted her arm and said it was time she got some rest. Mer drifted for a bit, felt the pressure of Frankie's hand on hers but didn't want her to lift it. She felt safer with Frankie being there.

When she woke again, Frankie said that she had to go see Beth but would be back later on. Mer told her to take the roses to her. Beth always bought roses when she got flowers at the supermarket.

It was when Frankie was at the door that she looked back and said, 'Dad's in love with you. I know it's not your fault, and you probably didn't mean to encourage him, or he misconstrued the situation. And I know you're both adults and that it isn't my business, but I don't want to see him hurt.'

Mer's eyes crinkled up and a small sob came out, followed by a bigger one. 'That's why you were pissed off with me?' And she started laughing, even though everything ached. 'Jesus, I can't be doing that right now. It hurts way too much.'

'I'm being serious.'

'Why on earth would you think he was in love with me?'

'The haircut and the shiny shoes. Why else would he be babbling nonstop about how wonderful you are?'

'That's because I *am* wonderful, but it's not me he's been screwing.'

Frankie's face showed relief and confusion in equal measure but then relief won. 'Who is it?'

'Promise not to be angry?' Mer winced in expectation.

'Literally anyone is better than you.'

'It's that nurse who looked after Alice at the end.'

Frankie was stunned into silence for a few minutes, then she said, 'She's a fair bit younger.'

'Our age,' Mer said, quickly adding at least five years, possibly more. Now wasn't the time to be too specific. 'Probably peter out of its own accord. I wouldn't make a big deal out of it.'

Frankie took a deep breath.

'You okay?' Mer was worried that this news was another piece of shit in an absolute storm of it, wanted to tell her that it didn't matter what all these stupid men did, where they put their dicks, because Mer loved her best friend and always would.

The rosebuds in Frankie's arms rustled as her head gave the smallest of inclines. 'It's always better to know the truth,' she said to Mer. 'I'll see you later on.'

—

Carole was across the road, standing next to a police car, a detective beside her, when Frankie walked out of the hospital. He had the sort of crinkled suit and face of a man who hadn't got much sleep last night. Carole, who Frankie knew for certain had got no sleep at all, was actually looking much better. She nodded to her but Frankie didn't stop. Instead, she drove straight to the Palais, parking right outside the sign with Vanessa Walton's picture on it.

She stopped in front of it as she got her phone out of her bag, pressed a button and then put the phone back in her bag. 'Bitch,' she muttered, and felt a little better.

Beth, in her usual uniform of beanie, black exercise tights and sloppy joe with *Walton's Academy of Dance* emblazoned across the front, was downstairs in the lounge, documents spread right across the bar. Above their heads, Frankie could hear music and the sound of multiple sets of feet dancing. Saturday was the busiest day of the week for a dance school.

'These are a present from Mer,' said Frankie, putting the flowers down on a nearby table.

'How is she?' asked Beth. 'It was such a shock to hear the news this morning.'

Mer had always reminded Frankie of a cartoon character, like Wile E. Coyote or Elmer Fudd. No matter what life dished out, she would always spring back up, ready for more, but this morning was different. Mer was fragile. Despite what Frankie had told her, the pieces might not be able to be put back together this time, but Beth didn't need to know any of that. Beth had enough to be going on with.

'Her shoulder will need surgery but it could have been so much worse.' She tried smiling, felt a pull downwards on her mouth that she had to push past in order to make it convincing.

'I'll wait until she's out of hospital before visiting,' said Beth. 'Make her a meal or something.'

'She'd appreciate that.' Frankie nodded, knowing that was unlikely to happen.

Beth picked up a handful of paper and tapped it on the wood until it made a neat pile. 'It's felt like the world has gone mad these last few weeks. Thank goodness it's all over now and we can start getting back to normal.'

IT TAKES A TOWN

Frankie tried again to smile, almost made it, but could feel tears prickling at her eyes and had to blink them away. 'What's all this then?' She gestured at the papers.

Beth stretched out her hands. 'Grand plans,' she said. 'The Palais is Aunty Helen's now – or it will be once probate is done. She has agreed that it's time to sell. We're waiting for the dust to settle and then I'll approach Barton, see if he wants to come in on it. Maybe develop it together. We supply the land, he supplies the rest, deals with the council, that sort of thing.'

'What about the dance academy? Harvey's bar?'

'It's about time Harvey and Mum retired, and there'll be enough money for an amazing purpose-built space, instead of having to make do all the time. It will be the premier dance studio for the district, a proper tribute to Vanessa rather than the rotting stairs and leaking pipes.' She hesitated, biting her lip. 'Sorry, we don't need to talk about Vanessa.'

We do, thought Frankie, but not yet. 'Can Barton get involved in something like that when he's a Member of Parliament? Isn't that a conflict of interest?'

Beth grinned. 'I expect it will be a shell company inside a blind trust, or something. You know how he operates. But you're prob-ably right. I don't know anything about big property deals. Forget I said anything.'

'Won't you be sad to sell?' Frankie pressed her hand down firmly on the bar, felt the wood, smooth against her palm and fingers. All that history gone. She'd had her first proper drink here. She and Mer dressed up to the nines, ordering cocktails. She had opted for a sedate Brandy Alexander and sipped it slowly for hours. Mer had chosen a Flaming Lamborghini and almost ended up with her hair on fire, thanks to the full tin of spray keeping her perm in place.

'Of course,' said Beth, 'but I think we all need to move on. Something good can come out of all of this mess.'

'Are you sure you're well enough for this? Shouldn't you be taking it easy, being in remission?'

'The doctors have given me a clean bill of health,' Beth said. 'I've even finished my radiotherapy.'

There was something about the way she said this, awkward, defensive, and for the first time unconvincing to Frankie's ears.

'I need to ask you something, and I need you to tell me the truth. You never had cancer, did you, Beth?'

It came out as a statement, an accusation, because how could something like that ever be a genuine question? The conversation teetered on the edge of becoming hostile. A couple of days ago Frankie couldn't imagine a world where she needed to say something like that, but now she could imagine so much more.

Beth stopped fussing with the pieces of paper, a flicker of horror on her face that was quickly smoothed out like a wrinkle in a bedsheet.

'What an awful thing to say.' Her voice wobbled momentarily as she made a disappointed, pitying sort of face.

Vanessa wasn't the only actress in the family, Frankie had to remind herself, merely the better one.

'I know you've been under a lot of pressure,' Beth continued, 'what with the police treating you as a suspect, but it's hardly fair to start throwing such terrible accusations around with absolutely no proof.'

It was Carole who had told Frankie this morning as they both sat by Mer's bedside. Janet Ross had come home from the gala talking about a curious thing. She had taken a cup of tea into Vanessa's dressing room and had spied Beth putting on make-up that made her look paler and more tired, while next to her Vanessa was adding colour to a whey-looking face. Afterwards, she had noticed how exhausted Vanessa was, while Beth, who had been running around after everyone, seemed energised by the event. 'If you didn't know what was going on, you'd think it was Vanessa who had the cancer and not Beth,' Janet had told her husband.

'Vanessa came back to Welcome because she had cancer,' Frankie continued. 'She was thinner and wearing wigs and we just thought that was what you did when you were a star. All you had to do was shave your hair and tell us you had cancer and we believed you, because why would someone so good and kind lie about something like that?'

She didn't look at the other woman's face now, almost didn't want to. It was Beth's hands she focused on, restless, agitated, pushing the paper around, lifting things up to only put them back down again.

'It wasn't my idea,' Beth said eventually. 'Vanessa made me do that.'

Frankie said nothing. Carole had told her to trust her teacher's instinct, reminding her that the weight of silence could push Beth to keep talking.

'Vee had triple-negative breast cancer. The prognosis was terrible and we couldn't tell anyone, not even Helen or Mum, she insisted. Because if people knew, her career would be over, and as far as she was concerned then her life might as well be over too. It's hard enough to get a job at her age when you're fit. The cover story would be that she was coming back to look after me. Always had to cast herself as the hero.' There was a harder edge to these words, a bitterness. 'She was broke, of course, except this time there was no family money to tide her over either. COVID had hit the academy hard. I didn't know how we could keep afloat, and that's when she came up with the idea for the fundraiser. She reasoned that it wasn't really a deception because the money really would be going to someone who had cancer, though the truth was that if people had known it was all for Vanessa, and not me, they probably would have donated twice as much. She actually said that to my face.'

Thousands and thousands were raised because people believed they were donating to charity, not an individual, but now wasn't the time to quibble. There should have been a paper trail, a novelty giant cheque, a photo with smiles in the newspaper, and instead the money had been quietly pocketed.

'What did you do with it all?'

'I didn't want to spend it but the bills keep mounting up. Once I'm back on top again, I'll put the money back and then we can donate it properly, if you'd like.' Beth was pleading now, desperate for Frankie to believe her. 'No one needs to know, do they?'

Too late for that. No matter how deep secrets are buried, they have a nasty habit of worming their way to the surface, gnawing holes in your life.

'Is that why you killed Vanessa?'

This conversation had been booby-trapped from the beginning, but now the moment had arrived it felt like a damp squib to Frankie. Instead of the explosion she had been expecting, the type to rattle windows and blow open doors, it was more like a plume of smoke floating upwards, curling around them, polluting the air.

'What?' Beth was staring at her now.

'Yesterday in my kitchen, I said that Barton Langridge could be responsible and you said, no, that it couldn't be him, because

Vanessa was already dead when he knocked on the door. Only one person could know that for sure.'

We reveal ourselves even when we don't intend to. Our secrets waiting to be exposed, chinks in the armour if only the other person notices. Frankie had missed her chance with Joe, could see now in retrospect how he had given himself away dozens of times, but she had been blind. She had learnt the lesson now, how important it was to pay attention.

Beth stood very still. The tip of her tongue poked out, touching her top lip before disappearing again. 'Someone must have told me that. Maybe the police. How could you think I would want Vanessa to be dead? I loved her.'

There was a slyness to her words, a denial that wasn't quite a denial, something technically true but designed to deceive.

'Someone said to me recently to never underestimate what we will do in the name of love,' was what Frankie said in reply. 'I know you loved her, Beth. Just tell me what happened.'

The woman melted in front of her, the facade made of wax not stone, and the truth that had always been there beneath the surface finally came into view.

'The cancer came back,' Beth said, an almost whisper, as though she still wanted to deny it. 'Quicker even than the doctors had predicted. Vee was adamant that there would be no treatments this time, no operations. She would sell the Palais to Barton, come to some arrangement about the Cottage, and throw all of the money at trying to have one more theatre run. To die in harness, she said – or, more likely, come back broke when it was time for palliative care.'

'Oh, Beth.' Frankie felt like her heart, already in pieces, was breaking again.

'It was crazy, an impossible dream. No one was ever going to let her put on a Broadway show in her condition. Who would back that? Vee still thought that she was on the way up, a star in the making, but she would humiliate herself in the process, ruin her reputation, be ridiculed or, even worse, pitied. I begged her to stay, to let me take care of her, and we could put the money towards ensuring her legacy. Perhaps have a scholarship in her name. Something that would honour her properly.'

'What did she say to that?'

'She didn't listen. She was prepared to take any offer from Barton, especially if he backed off about the Cottage, and if I tried to stop her, she'd tell everyone how I had lied about having cancer.' Beth was crying now. 'The academy would have to close because there was no money for relocation or paying rent at a new premises. Our family would lose everything. It would leave Aunty Helen penniless. I couldn't let that happen. There was no other choice.'

There were always choices; it was just that sometimes there were no good ones.

'I went to her house. She had got out all the posters and badges the students had made for her. Ripped them up as a lovely dramatic touch, so she could show Barton she was serious about not challenging him. I pretended to go along with it, told her we needed to celebrate with her champagne, just this once. That her doctor would understand. I didn't need to twist her arm, you know that Vanessa never had a problem with breaking rules when it suited her. While she was busy with the posters, I spiked her glass with vodka and a sleeping pill. It had been so long since she'd drunk alcohol, she didn't really notice any change in taste. Half a bottle in and she was plastered. I didn't even have to push her. We stood at the top of the stairs and . . .' Beth raised her hands like a puppet master and then dropped them. The invisible support that Vanessa had taken for granted, the satellite that had orbited her, dragged her off course and then let her fall.

'I knew it was going to rain that night, so I set up the scene. It was like dressing a set. It needed to tell the story that she had slipped on the wet stairs. I even took out the light bulb, to make it darker. I was putting on a production.'

Frankie propped her elbow on the bar, rubbed her face with her hands, worried about what would happen now.

'I gave her what she wanted, saved her from being ridiculed for desperately clinging on too long or pitied because of the cancer. And now, for the first time in her life, Helen can stop penny-pinching and relax, Mum and Dad can take a cruise and enjoy retirement, and Vanessa Walton's Dance and Drama Academy will grow and flourish. Vanessa's name will be up in lights. If you could only see all the emails I've been getting, how many views her funeral has online. There are kids in their bedrooms right now wanting to be the next Baby Vee. She will be remembered forever.'

Frankie had known Beth most of her life. She had been a year behind them at school. The not quite as talented, not quite as good-looking but actually a much kinder person than her famous cousin. Vanessa's relentless ambition had driven her to madness.

'Please don't tell anyone,' Beth pleaded.

But it was too late to ask that, because Frankie had already made the decision earlier that morning when Carole had come to check on Mer. Frankie mentioned that Beth had said something odd to her the day before and Carole had listened carefully before detailing her own concerns.

The crumpled, tired detective came into the bar, Carole and Angie with him. Beth didn't fight when they arrested her, just gave a sigh when they reminded her that she did not need to say anything, as though the warning had come too late.

Frankie got her phone out and turned off the record button, then stood shell-shocked until Carole came back in to find her.

'You look like I need a drink,' said Carole, and she moved behind the bar. 'How about you have one as well?'

'It's not even ten am,' began Frankie, but Carole was already setting two glasses out and was reaching for the bottle of Jameson Blended on the shelf.

'Did I do the right thing?' Frankie asked.

'Of course,' said Carole. 'A wise woman once told me that it takes a town to solve a murder. Turns out she was probably right.'

'But it was a mercy killing really. If I had known that Vanessa had terminal cancer, I might not have agreed . . .' Her voice trailed away, unsure about the rest of the sentence, let alone anything else.

Carole found a clean tea towel and started wiping the glasses.

Frankie tried again. 'Mer said that Vanessa was like a witch, casting magic spells over people. Making them do things that they'd never do otherwise.'

Like write threatening letters, having affairs and pushing people down the stairs.

'That's a very convenient way of looking at it,' said Carole. 'Absolves people of responsibility for their own actions.'

'I've known Beth all my life. She's a good person. She always put everyone else first. Half the town will be character references for her. Do you think a judge will take that into account?'

'Very early this morning I got in touch with the pathologist who conducted Vanessa's autopsy. She had noticed a collapsed vein in Vanessa's arm, which I had thought meant she was a junkie. But she had also seen that there were four blue radiation dots tattooed around her breast and a scar in her armpit because lymph nodes had been removed. So she got in touch with Vanessa's doctor, because having cancer can impede your balance, which might explain the fall. The doctor told her that when Vanessa Walton died, she was in remission.'

She poured the whiskey into the first glass and pushed it towards Frankie.

'She wasn't dying?'

Carole shook her head. 'No more than the rest of us. Apparently, if you're clear of that type of cancer for three to four years, then your odds of staying that way are good.'

Frankie stared at her. 'So that was all a lie too?'

It was a long while before Carole answered her. 'But which one of them was lying?' She took a sip from her own glass. 'In my job you have to learn to accept that sometimes you will never know all the answers or you'll go mad.'

CHAPTER 36

It was late on an autumn afternoon when Des rang to say he had made it to the winery. He had seen the weather warnings and was worried the gutters might be blocked. Anne's voice was reassuring in the background. Frankie told him to just enjoy the weekend and that she would get in touch with Nate. Des started talking about making sure he used the ladder stand-off but Frankie ended the conversation quickly before her father could think of another excuse to hop back in his ute and come home.

A proper storm was threatened for tonight with expectations of thunder rolling around the valley for minutes at a time as lightning sliced the sky open, but it promised to be useful rain this time, necessary and prayed for. There had been a bushfire little more than an hour away that had already burnt out thousands of hectares. An evacuee centre was set up by the council for those who decided to leave early. The fire was under control now but they still needed a lot of water to turn the flames to embers and then finally ash.

Frankie had been spending more and more time out on the farm. Supposedly it was to help her father, like this weekend when Des was actually taking Anne away for the first time, but the truth was it was easier being here than at home.

Was it possible to have suspected that your husband was capable of murder and still stay married?

It had been Joe's idea to try counselling. Frankie had done an individual session with the therapist, expecting the woman to sympathise with her about the affair, but instead she had been talked to gently about dependent behaviour.

She dragged the ladder out from the shed. The days were getting shorter and nights colder. Des had left a neatly stacked woodpile in case they wanted to light the fire. The school bus had deposited an excited Ollie at the end of the driveway. Frankie promised tinned spaghetti jaffles for dinner tonight if he spotted a rainbow bee-eater. Frankie had caught sight of some last visit, little masked bandits with their bronze-green flash of feathers, and now Ollie wanted to add them to his birdwatching list. He had taken Patch and promised to be back before sunset.

There had been a text from Danny saying he would stay in town. There was some excuse about Jaz being back from boarding school for the weekend and a party Brianna wanted to go to, but Frankie knew that her eldest wouldn't want Joe to be alone.

In half an hour or so it would be dark, and it didn't feel right to chase up Nate just to check the gutters when he would be busy getting his own property in order, having only been home a few weeks. One cousin out of jail while another had gone in, as though it was a trade in a footy team. Fodder crops were being sown now and bales of hay stored for winter. Des had spent time talking to Nate about running more sheep on the property, though he was worried about introducing foot rot and lice to his precious mob.

Jail had tempered Nate. There were more tattoos and an earring. He was even quieter now. Mer had taken quite a fancy to him, flirted outrageously whenever he was around, trying to make him blush, but Nate would just smile and say nothing.

Frankie googled to find out what a ladder stand-off looked like and then found that in the shed as well. Attaching it, she propped the ladder against the side of the house. Alice hated her going up on the roof when she was little, but once or twice Des had taken her up with him all the same. She had stared down the valley and up into the far hills and wondered about the people who lived over there. Could any of them see a small girl bursting with excitement, sitting on top of the roof with her father?

She gave the ladder a shake, making sure it was firmly in place. Taking risks and discovering new interests was something else the therapist had recommended.

Her hands tight on the rungs, she began to move slowly upwards. There were women who would have left their husband the moment they found out he'd had an affair. Frankie worried about what leaving would do to her boys, Ollie in particular. Martha had been talking in the staffroom the other morning about a couple who had separated recently. Women grieve and men replace, she said, before changing the subject to Soup Club in term two. Mer had laughed when Frankie asked her about the grieving and said that was what dating apps were for.

The gutters were fine. Frankie cleared out some gum leaves and twigs just to make the trip worthwhile. There were probably seedlings growing out of her own gutters in town. On the spur of the moment, she decided to climb up onto the roof and take in the view. There was a momentary wobble when transferring her weight from the ladder to the metal sheeting, but she got there. Sitting on the top of the farmhouse, feet propped against the now slightly cleaner gutter, Frankie watched as the sky became the same blushing reddish pink as the apples in the orchard. Ripe Williams pears were adorning the trees now, too, though the figs were late again this year. She had taken over the bottling and jam duties from Des, and was particularly proud of the relish she'd made, following her mother's recipe faithfully.

Her father would have her stay on the farm forever if it was up to him, the boys as well. It was tempting.

A SOLD sign had appeared on the Palais last week. Rumours floated around town that the money was needed to pay Beth's lawyers. But then there were rumours about a lot of things, including that Barton was unlikely to contest the next election. Mer had joked she might have to run, if only to beat Ivan Roland. Frankie prayed it wouldn't come to that.

Billy was going to receive the police medal for valour. He had been interviewed in the local paper, claiming to be the luckiest man in the world because the bullet had gone in low into his torso. Any higher and he would have certainly died. There was plenty of permanent damage, though. Carole was determined to get him back to work on modified duties. Frankie had run into her in the supermarket. She was living in the Cottage now. Lonnie had offered the place to her at a minuscule rent, simply to annoy her son.

'I don't believe in ghosts,' the policewoman told her.

Frankie wasn't so sure. She tried not to think about Vanessa too often, painfully aware that while she was barely a footnote in Vanessa's life, Vanessa could have chapters devoted to her in Frankie's. Still, it was impossible to avoid reminders of her completely. When she went to visit Alice's grave at the cemetery, she would have to walk past Vanessa's, full of fresh flowers and teddy bears and occasion- ally a weeping fan. When she did think of her, the feelings were complicated but there was little anger. The various Vanessas – her schoolfriend, the star, the woman her husband was having an affair with – were all dead now, while the only version of Frankie Birnam was alive. Knowing about the cancer diagnosis made a difference, but the truth was that Frankie's world was drabber without Vanessa in it.

It was much harder not to be angry with Joe. She had asked Mer if she should leave him, had expected Mer to tell her to pack her bags and walk away, just as she had done so many times. To her surprise, Mer told her to make up her own mind. 'It's not some test with right and wrong answers,' she had said. 'You've got the rest of your life to divorce Joe if you want to. There's no rush.' Then she sent her a podcast of a French therapist talking about how relationships can come out stronger after an affair.

The sun began to sink as shadows crept up the hill. If Ollie didn't come back soon, she'd have to climb down the ladder and get out an old frypan and bang it like a gong with a wooden spoon, just as Alice did when she was a child, the call that meant run home because dinner's getting cold.

A pair of lights shone over the rise as a car slowly made its way along the track, dodging potholes. A triumphant blast from the horn and birds cawed in response. It was Mer, coming to stay for the weekend to keep her company, just as she had when they were girls. Frankie watched as the car parked askew between the clothesline and the lemon tree. As Mer slammed the door shut her eyes travelled up the ladder to where Frankie was sitting.

'What are you doing up there?' Mer asked. She was still wearing the black apron and fleece jumper of her supermarket uniform.

'I wanted to see the sunset.'

Mer walked over to the ladder. 'If it's good enough for Captain Sensible,' she said, putting her foot on the lowest rung.

'Wait,' said Frankie, alarmed, 'what about your shoulder?'

'The other one works fine.'

'What if we both get stuck up here?'

Mer, who was about halfway up now, stopped and grinned up at her. 'We can call your handsome neighbour to rescue us.'

Frankie put out a hand to help Mer clamber off the ladder and sit down next to her. Together the two of them watched as the dying sun painted the low-lying sky the colour of fire. Frankie put an arm around her friend and held her tight. Vanessa may have demonstrated how to live a life unapologetically, but Mer had taught her so much more about loyalty. No matter what happened in her marriage, this friendship would last a lifetime.

'Come on,' she said. 'We'd better go back down before that storm comes.'

Mer went first and then Frankie climbed down carefully, one rung at a time, left foot, right foot. As she put the ladder away, an excited boy and dog came running out of the bush. Mer listened to Ollie's interesting facts about birds and burrows as she took the shopping out of the boot of her car. She handed him a giant pack of marshmallows for toasting later.

He ran into the house and Mer followed, while Frankie went out into the garden to lock up the hens. They needed no persuading tonight and were already inside their house clucking away to each other in a way that reminded her of Martha in the staffroom. Frankie walked back to the porch, pausing to watch the sun fall west, dark clouds chasing behind. The wind picked up, smelling of wet grass. As she turned to walk inside, the first raindrops began to fall.

ACKNOWLEDGEMENTS

When I was writing this book, my previous novel, *When We Fall*, was chosen as the Great Festival Read in Bathurst, the town I grew up in – a lovely and unexpected honour. Sadly due to COVID my appearance at the Festival was beamed in but I still enjoyed hearing how readers looked for (and found) familiar architecture and layout in the coastal town of Merritt, often to my surprise. For *It Takes a Town* I plundered freely parts of my hometown to build Welcome and I hope those readers have fun spotting their streets and buildings in these pages.

The generosity of strangers and friends, new and old alike, in spending time answering an author's sometimes ridiculous questions is one of the joys of book research. Ex-bookseller and champion of literature, Jenny Barry, generously sent me beautiful word pictures about her property, which made me feel like I was sharing a cuppa in her kitchen and gazing out the window. I sat next to

Ian Webster at a Hardie Grant gathering and he patiently answered questions about raising cattle and sheep. Emma Linke and Katie Bennett were the inspiration for my character Frankie's good heart and love of teaching, even if Frankie didn't inherit their wisdom and common sense. Lisa Archer took time from expertly teaching her dance students to discuss my theoretical (and not nearly as well run) dance school. Dr Serene Foo shared her expertise, and Liz Keith her experience, in dealing with cancer. Both perspectives were invaluable. Whenever my characters get in trouble, I always head to Michelle Gotting for legal advice. My sister, Aisling Clifford, is the family law expert for the imaginary people in my novels. Retired Police Assistant Commissioner Sandra Nicholson once again was on the end of the phone to let me tap her expertise. Car models that appeared in the story and other matters were informed by Paul Korganow and Meredith and Jim Trevillion.

All mistakes and twisted truths, deliberate or otherwise, are down to me.

Melissa Lowe and Tania Chandler were trusted early readers which means they see the manuscript equivalent of a half-built house. I thank them for their generous reading and brilliant brains (and discretion!). My mother-in-law, Glenys Harris, can be counted on to drop everything in her busy life to read my manuscript and will tell me it's great, no matter how many grammatical mistakes she has to point out.

It is a well-known rule of crime writing that it is fine to murder the humans but don't kill any animals. No fictional dogs died during the writing of this book, but sadly that's impossible to replicate in real life. Fred and Ginger would not have existed without knowing Prince and Lady. Also my nephews' puppy, Sox, will always be remembered for a loving nature and ability to gambol like a lamb.

A book that has at its heart a long-term friendship, made me reflect on my own luck in this regard. I benefit from the friendship of Kerry Ruiz on an almost daily basis and Leanne Hunter-Knight, who will always be my muse when it comes to great 80s hair and Flaming Lamborghinis. Writing pals Ruth Cooper and Carolyn Tetaz were there to nut out tricky plot problems and have enjoyable bookish chats.

My thanks as always to my fabulous agent, Clare Forster, and all at Curtis Brown. To my own personal A-Team at Ultimo Press, it is a privilege to be published by you again. My wonderful publisher, Alex Craig, combines a mind like a steel trap with a sense of humour and can always pick when I'm trying to fudge something. Appreciation also to Alisa Ahmed, Andrea Johnson and Zoë Victoria. This book benefited so much from the eagle eyes of Ali Lavau and proofreader Pam Dunne. Thanks again to Josh Durham for another fab cover. Anne Costello won a Better Reading competition to have her name in this book. I hope she enjoys reading about her fictional counterpart. Frank Ryan tried his best to win to the same competition but 'only' got the book prize. I gave my main character the name Frankie purely by coincidence!

I am lucky to work part-time at Fairfield Books and chat books to customers and fellow workers alike, in particular Heather who gets to hear my opinions more than anyone else. To my family, Cliffords big and small, Mars Bars all round. To my children Aidan, Genevieve and Evangeline, with love, always. Last, but never least, to Richard who is nothing like the husbands in this book (lucky for me!).

AOIFE CLIFFORD is the author of *All These Perfect Strangers,* which was longlisted for both the Australian Book Industry General Fiction Book of the Year and the Voss Literary Prize; *Second Sight,* a *Publishers Weekly* starred review and Book of the Week, and was Highly Commended at the Davitt Awards; and *When We Fall,* which was shortlisted for the Davitt Awards and the Ned Kelly Award for Best Crime Fiction. Aoife's short stories have been published in Australia, the United Kingdom and the United States, winning premier prizes such as the Scarlet Stiletto and the S.D. Harvey Short Crime Story Award.